Louise Penny is the Number One *New York Times* best-selling author of the Inspector Gamache series, including *Still Life*, which won the CWA John Creasey Dagger in 2006. Recipient of virtually every existing award for crime fiction, Louise was also granted The Order of Canada in 2014. She lives in a small village south of Montreal.

Also by Louise Penny

Still Life
Dead Cold
The Cruellest Month
The Murder Stone
The Brutal Telling
Bury Your Dead
Trick of the Light
The Beautiful Mystery
How the Light Gets In
The Long Way Home

LOUISE PENNY

THE NATURE OF THE BEAST

sphere

SPHERE

First published in the United States in 2015 by Minotaur, a division of St Martin's Press
First published in Great Britain in 2015 by Sphere
This paperback edition published in 2016 by Sphere

1 3 5 7 9 10 8 6 4 2

A CIP catalogue record for this book
is available from the British Library.

ISBN 978-0-7515-5268-3

Papers used by Sphere are from well-managed forests
and other responsible sources.

MIX
Paper from
responsible sources
FSC® C104740
www.fsc.org

Printed and bound in Great Britain by
Clays Ltd, St Ives plc

Sphere
An imprint of
Little, Brown Book Group
Carmelite House
50 Victoria Embankment
London EC4Y 0DZ

An Hachette UK Company
www.hachette.co.uk

www.littlebrown.co.uk

For our friends and neighbors –
our family of the heart

CHAPTER 1

———

Running, running, stumbling, running.

Arm up against the wiry branches whipping his face. He didn't see the root. He fell, hands splayed into the moss and mud. His assault rifle dropped and bounced and rolled from sight. Eyes wide, frantic now, Laurent Lepage scanned the forest floor and swept his hands through the dead and decaying leaves.

He could hear the footsteps behind him. Boots on the ground. Pounding. He could almost feel the earth heaving as they got closer, closer, while he, on all fours, plowed the leaves aside.

'Come on, come on,' he pleaded.

And then his bloodied and filthy hands clasped the barrel of the assault rifle and he was up and running. Bent over. Gasping for breath.

It felt as though he'd been on the run for weeks, months. A lifetime. And even as he sprinted through the forest, dodging the tree trunks, he knew the running would end soon.

But for now he ran, so great was his will to survive. So great was his need to hide what he'd found. If he couldn't get it back to safety, at least, maybe, he could make sure those in pursuit wouldn't find it.

He could hide it. Here, in this forest. And then the lion would sleep tonight. Finally.

Bang. Bangbangbang. The trees around him exploded, ripped apart by bullets.

He dove and rolled and came up behind a stump, his shoulder to the rotting wood. No protection at all.

His thoughts in these final moments did not go to his parents at home in the little Québec village. They didn't go to his puppy, no longer a puppy but a grown dog. He didn't think of his friends, or the games on the village green in summer, or tobogganing, giddy, down the hill while the mad old poet shook her fist at them in winter. He didn't think of the hot chocolate at the end of the day in front of the fire in the bistro.

He thought only of killing those in his sights. And buying time. So that maybe, maybe, he could hide the cassette.

And then maybe, maybe those in the village would be safe. And those in other villages would be safe. There was some comfort in knowing there would be purpose to this. His sacrifice would be for the greater good and for those he loved and the place he loved.

He raised his weapon, took aim, and squeezed the trigger.

'Bang,' he said, feeling the assault rifle thrust into his shoulder. 'Bangbangbangbangbang.'

The front line of his pursuers fell.

He leapt and rolled behind a sturdy tree, pressing so hard against it that the rough bark made a bruise on his back and he wondered if the tree might topple over. He hugged his rifle to his chest. His pulse pounding. He could feel his

2

own heart in his ears. It threatened to drown out all other sounds.

Like swiftly approaching feet.

Laurent tried to steady himself. His breathing. His trembling.

He'd been through this before, he reminded himself. And he'd always escaped. Always. He'd escape today. He'd get back home. And there he'd have a hot drink and a pastry. And a bath.

And he'd soak away all the terrible things he'd done, and was about to do.

His hand dropped to the pocket of his torn and muddy jacket. His fingers, knuckles scraped to the bone and bleeding, felt inside. And there it was. The cassette. Safe.

Or, at least, as safe as he was.

His senses, honed and heightened, instinctively took in the musky scent of the forest floor, took in the shafts of sunlight. He took in the frantic scramble of chipmunks in the branches above him.

What he no longer heard were footsteps.

Had he killed or wounded them all? Would he get home after all?

But then he heard it. The telltale snap of a twig. Close.

They'd stopped running and were now creeping up on his position. Surrounding him.

Laurent tried to count the feet, tried to estimate the number by the noise. But he couldn't. And he knew then it didn't matter anyway. There would be no escape this time.

And now he tasted something foreign. Something sour.

He had terror in his mouth.

He took a deep breath. In the moments he had left,

Laurent Lepage looked at his filthy fingers clasped around the assault rifle. And he saw them, pink and clean, holding burgers and poutine and corn on the cob and sweet, silly *pets de soeurs* at the county fair.

And holding the puppy. Harvest. Named for his father's favorite album.

And now, at the last, as he hugged the rifle, Laurent began to hum. A tune his father sang to him every night at bedtime.

'Old man look at my life,' he sang under his breath. *'Twenty-four and there's so much more.'*

Dropping the rifle, he brought out the cassette. He'd run out of time. He'd failed. And now he had to hide the cassette. Falling to his knees, he found a tangle of thick vines, old and woody. No longer caring about the noise approaching, approaching, Laurent Lepage parted the vines. They were thicker, heavier than he'd realized and he felt a spike of panic.

Had he left it too late?

He ripped and tore and clawed until a small opening appeared. Thrusting his hand in, he dropped the cassette.

It might never be found by those who needed it. But neither, he knew, would it be found by those about to kill for it.

'But I'm all alone at last,' he whispered. *'Rolling home to you.'*

Some glint inside the bramble caught his eye.

Something was in there. Something that hadn't grown, but had been placed there. Other hands had been here before him.

Laurent Lepage, his pursuers forgotten, knelt closer and bringing both hands up, he grasped the vines and yanked them apart. The creepers clung to each other, bound together. Years, decades, eons worth of growth. And concealment.

Laurent ripped, and ripped, and tore. Until a shaft of sunlight penetrated the overgrowth, the undergrowth, and he saw what was in there. What had been hiding in there longer than Laurent had been alive.

His eyes widened.

'Wow.'

CHAPTER 2

~

'So?'

Isabelle Lacoste put her glass of apple cider on the worn wooden table and stared at the man across from her.

'You know I'm not going to answer that,' said Armand Gamache, picking up his beer and smiling at her.

'Well, now that you're no longer my boss I can tell you what I really think.'

Gamache laughed. His wife, Reine-Marie, leaned toward Lacoste and whispered, 'What do you really think, Isabelle?'

'I think your husband, Madame Gamache, would make a great Superintendent at the Sûreté.'

Reine-Marie leaned back in her armchair. Through the mullioned windows of the bistro she saw a ragtag mix of kids and adults, including her daughter Annie and Annie's husband, Jean-Guy, playing soccer. It was mid-September. Summer was gone and autumn was on the doorstep. Leaves were just turning. Brilliant reds and yellows and amber maples dotted the gardens and forest. Some leaves had already fallen onto the grass of the village green. It was a perfect time of year, when late summer flowers were still blooming and the leaves were turning, and the grass was still green, but the nights were chilly and sweaters were out and fires were beginning to be lit. So that the hearths at night resembled the forests in the day, all giddy and bright and cheerful.

Soon everyone would head back to the city after the weekend, but for her and Armand there was no need to return. They were already there.

Reine-Marie nodded to Monsieur Béliveau, the grocer, who'd just taken a seat at a nearby table, then turned her attention back to the woman who had joined them for the weekend. Isabelle Lacoste. Chief Inspector Lacoste, acting head of homicide for the Sûreté du Québec. The job Reine-Marie's husband had held for more than twenty years.

Reine-Marie always thought of her as 'young Isabelle'. Not, she hoped, in a patronizing, or matronizing, way, but because she'd been so young when Armand had found and recruited and trained her.

But now there were lines in Isabelle's face, and gray just starting in her hair. It seemed to happen overnight. They'd met her fiancé, and been at her wedding, and attended the baptism of her two babies. She'd been young Agent Lacoste for so long, and now, suddenly it seemed, she was Chief Inspector Lacoste.

And Armand was retired. Early retirement, certainly, but retirement.

Reine-Marie glanced out the window again. They were in their amber years.

Or perhaps not.

Reine-Marie shifted her attention to Armand, sitting back in his wing chair in the bistro, sipping his microbrewery beer. Relaxed, comfortable, amused. His six-foot frame had filled out. He wasn't heavy, but he was solid. The pillar in the storm.

But there was no storm, Reine-Marie reminded herself. They could, finally, stop being pillars and just be people. Armand and Reine-Marie. Two more villagers. That was all. That was enough.

For her.

And for him?

Armand's hair was grayer than ever, and curling just around his ears and at his collar. It was longer, slightly, than when he was at the Sûreté. More from not noticing than not caring.

Here in Three Pines they noticed the migration of the geese, and the prickly chestnuts ripening on the trees, and the bobbing black-eyed Susans in bloom. They noticed the barrel of apples outside Monsieur Béliveau's general store, free for the taking. They noticed the fresh harvest at the farmers' market and the new arrivals at Myrna's New and Used Bookstore. They noticed Olivier's daily specials at the bistro.

Reine-Marie noticed that Armand was happy. And healthy.

And Armand noticed that Reine-Marie was happy and healthy too, here, in the little village in the valley. Three Pines couldn't hide them from the woes of the world, but it could help heal the wounds.

The scar at Armand's temple plowed across the other lines on his forehead. Some of the furrows were created by stress and worry and sadness. But most, like the ones showing now, were deep with amusement.

'I thought you were going to tell me what you really thought of him as a person,' said Reine-Marie. 'All those flaws you witnessed after years of working together.' Reine-Marie leaned closer, in conspiracy. 'Come on, Isabelle, tell me.'

Out on the green, Lacoste's two children were fighting with Jean-Guy Beauvoir for the ball. The grown man appeared to be sincerely, and increasingly desperately, trying to control the play. Lacoste smiled. Even against kids, Inspector Beauvoir did not like to lose.

'You mean all the cruelty?' she asked, bringing her attention back inside the comfortable room. 'The incompetence? We had to keep waking him up to tell him our solution to a case so he could take the credit.'

'Is that true, Armand?' Reine-Marie asked.

'*Pardon?* I was snoozing.'

Lacoste laughed. 'And now I get your office, and the sofa.' She turned serious. 'I know the Superintendent's job has been offered to you, *patron*. Chief Superintendent Brunel told me in confidence.'

'Some confidence,' said Gamache. But he didn't look put out.

Chief Superintendent Thérèse Brunel, appointed head of the Sûreté after the scandals and shake-up, had visited Three Pines a week earlier. It was, supposedly, a social visit. As they'd relaxed on the front porch one morning over coffee, she'd offered him the job.

'Superintendent, Armand. You'd head up the division that oversees Homicide and Serious Crimes and the annual Christmas party.'

He raised his brow.

'We're restructuring,' she explained. 'Gave the St-Jean-Baptiste Day picnic to Organized Crime.'

He smiled and so did she, before her eyes turned sharp again and she studied him.

'What would it take to get you back?'

It would be disingenuous for him to say he hadn't seen

this coming. He'd been expecting just such an overture since the leadership of the Sûreté had fallen into complete disarray, and the breadth and depth of the corruption he'd uncovered became clear.

They needed leadership and direction and they needed it fast.

'Let me think about it, Thérèse,' he'd said.

'I'd like an answer soon.'

'Of course.'

After Thérèse Brunel kissed Reine-Marie good-bye, she took Armand's arm and the two old friends and colleagues walked to her car.

'The rot in the Sûreté has been removed,' she said, lowering her voice. 'But now the force needs to be rebuilt. Properly this time. We both know rot can reappear. Don't you want to be part of making sure the Sûreté is strong and healthy and on the right path?'

She examined her friend. He'd recovered from the physical attacks, that was obvious. He exuded strength and well-being and a kind of calmly contained energy. But the physical wounds, as grave as they'd been, hadn't been the reason Armand Gamache had retired. He had finally staggered under the emotional burden. He'd had enough of corruption, of betrayal, of the back-stabbing and undermining and venal atmosphere. He'd had enough of death. Chief Inspector Gamache had exorcised the rot in the Sûreté, but the memories remained, embedded.

Would they disappear with time? Thérèse Brunel wondered. Would they disappear with distance? Would this pretty village wash them away, like a baptism?

Maybe.

'The worst is done, Armand,' she said, once they reached

her car. 'And now it's time for the best, the fun part. Rebuilding. Don't you want to be part of that? Or is this,' she looked around the village green, 'enough?'

She saw the old homes circling the green. She saw the bistro and bookstore and bakery and general store. She saw, Gamache knew, a pretty, but dull, backwater. While he saw a shore. A place where the shipwrecked could finally rest.

Armand had told Reine-Marie about the job offer, of course, and they'd discussed it.

'Do you want to do it, Armand?' she'd asked, trying to keep her voice neutral.

But he knew her too well for that.

'It's too soon, I think. For both of us. But Thérèse has raised an interesting question. What next?'

Next? Reine-Marie had thought when he'd said it a week ago. And she thought it again now, in the bistro, with the murmur of conversation, like a stream, flowing by her, around her. That one bedraggled word had washed up on her banks and set down roots, tendrils. A bindweed of a word.

Next.

When Armand had retired and they'd moved from Montréal to Three Pines, it had never occurred to her there'd be a next. She was still surprised and elated that there was a now.

But now had bled into next.

Armand wasn't yet sixty, and she herself had given up a hugely successful career at the Bibliothèque nationale.

Next.

She was, truth be told, still savoring here and still savoring now. But next was on the horizon, slouching toward them.

'Hello, you still here?'

Gabri, large and voluble, walked across the bistro he owned with his partner, Olivier. He hugged Isabelle Lacoste.

'I thought you'd be gone by now,' said Myrna, arriving with him and taking the slender woman in her ample arms.

'Soon. I was just at your bookstore,' Isabelle said to Myrna. 'You weren't there so I left the money by the cash register.'

'You found a book?' asked Myrna. 'Which one?'

They discussed books while Gabri got them a couple of beers and chatted with customers before returning to the table. In his late thirties, Gabri's dark hair was just beginning to gray, and his face was showing crinkles when he laughed, which was often.

'How was rehearsal?' Reine-Marie asked Gabri and Myrna. 'Is the play going well?'

'You'll have to ask Antoinette,' said Gabri, indicating with his beer a middle-aged woman at another table.

'Who is she?' asked Isabelle.

She looked to Lacoste like her daughter. Only her daughter was seven and this woman must've been forty-five. The woman wore clothes more suited to an infant. A bow was in her spiky purple hair. She wore a flowered skirt, short and tight around her ample bottom, and a tank top, tight around her ample top, under a bright pink sweater. If a candy store vomited, Antoinette would be the result.

'That's Antoinette Lemaitre and her partner, Brian Fitzpatrick,' said Reine-Marie. 'She's the artistic director of the Knowlton Playhouse. They're coming over for dinner tonight.'

'We'll be there too,' said Gabri. 'We're trying to get Armand and Reine-Marie to join us.'

'Join?' said Isabelle. 'Us?'

'The Estrie Players,' said Myrna. 'I've been trying to convince Clara to join too. Not to act, necessarily, but maybe to paint sets. Anything to get her out of that studio. She just stares at that half-finished portrait of Peter all day long. I don't think she's lifted her brush in weeks.'

'That painting gives me the creeps,' said Gabri.

'Isn't it a bit overkill, though?' said Reine-Marie. 'Getting one of the top painters in Canada to do sets for an amateur production?'

'Picasso painted sets,' said Myrna.

'For the Ballets Russes,' Reine-Marie pointed out.

'I bet if he lived here he'd do our sets,' said Gabri. 'If anyone could convince him, she could.'

He gestured toward Antoinette and Brian, who were approaching the table.

'How was rehearsal?' Reine-Marie asked, after introducing them to Isabelle Lacoste.

'It would be better if this one' – Antoinette jerked her head toward Gabri – 'listened to my direction.'

'I need to be free to make my own creative choices.'

'You're playing him gay,' said Antoinette.

'I am gay,' said Gabri.

'But the character is not. He's just coming out of a ruined marriage.'

'*Oui*. Coming out. Because he's . . . ?' said Gabri, leaning toward her.

'Gay?' asked Brian.

Antoinette laughed. It was full and hearty and unrestrained and Isabelle liked her.

'Okay, play him any way you like,' Antoinette said. 'It doesn't really matter. The play's going to be a hit. Even you can't mess it up.'

'That's on the poster,' Brian confided. 'Even Gabri Can't Mess This Up.'

He put his hands up in front of him to indicate a huge banner.

Reine-Marie laughed and knew it might actually be true, and a good selling point.

'What part do you play?' Isabelle asked Myrna.

'The owner of the boardinghouse. I was going to play it as a gay man, but since Gabri already claimed that territory I decided to go in a different direction.'

'She's playing her as a large black woman,' said Gabri. 'Inspired.'

'Thank you, darling,' said Myrna, and the two air-kissed.

'You should've seen their production of *The Glass Menagerie*,' said Armand. His eyes widened as though to say it was exactly what Isabelle imagined it would be.

'By the way, did you talk to Clara?' Antoinette asked Myrna. 'Will she do it?'

'I don't think so,' said Myrna. 'She needs more time.'

'She needs distraction,' said Gabri.

Isabelle looked at the script in Antoinette's hand.

'*She Sat Down and Wept*,' she read. 'A comedy?'

Antoinette laughed, handing her the script. 'It's not as dire as it sounds.'

'Actually, it's wonderful,' said Myrna. 'And very funny.'

'Some might even say gay,' said Gabri.

'Well, time to go.' Isabelle got up. 'I see the soccer game is over.'

On the village green the children and adults had stopped playing, and were all looking toward the stone bridge across the Rivière Bella Bella where a kid was shouting and running into the village.

'Oh no,' said Gabri as they watched through the bistro window. 'Not again.'

14

The boy paused at the edge of the green and gestured wildly with a stick. When no one reacted he looked around and his gaze stopped at the bistro.

'Hide,' said Myrna. 'Duck.'

'God, don't tell me Ruth's coming too,' said Gabri, looking around frantically.

But it was too late. The boy was through the door, scanning the crowd. And his bright eyes came to a halt. On Gamache.

'You're here, *patron*,' the boy said, running over to their table. 'You have to come quick.'

Grabbing Gamache's hand, he tried to pull the large man out of his chair.

'Wait a minute,' said Armand. 'Settle down. What is it?'

The boy was bedraggled, like something the woods had coughed up. There were moss and leaves and twigs in his hair, his clothes were torn and he clutched a stick the size of a cane in his scratched and filthy hands.

'You won't believe what I found in the woods. Come on. Hurry.'

'What is it this time?' Gabri asked. 'A unicorn? A spaceship?'

'No,' the boy said, looking annoyed. Then he turned back to Gamache. 'It was huge. Humongous.'

'What was?' Gamache asked.

'Oh, don't encourage him, Armand,' said Myrna.

'It was a gun,' said the boy, and saw a flicker of interest in Gamache. 'A giant gun, Chief. This big.' He waved his arms and the stick hit the table next to them, sweeping glasses to the floor.

'Okay,' said Gabri, getting up. 'That's enough. Give me that.'

'No, you can't have it,' said the boy, protecting the stick.

'Either you give it to me, or you leave. I'm sorry, but you don't see anyone else in here with tree branches.'

'It's not a tree branch,' said the boy. 'It's a gun that can change into a sword.'

He made to brandish it but Olivier had come over and caught it with his hand. With his other he held out a broom and a pan.

'Clean it up,' said Olivier, not unkindly, but firmly.

'Fine. Here.' The boy handed Gamache the stick. 'If anything bad happens to me, you'll know what to do.' He looked at Gamache with deadly earnest. 'I'm trusting you.'

'Understood,' said Gamache gravely.

The boy began to sweep while Armand leaned the stick against his chair, noticing that it was notched and etched and that the boy's name was carved into it.

'What did he want this time?' Jean-Guy asked, as he and Annie joined them and watched the annoyed sweeping. 'To warn you about an alien invasion?'

'That was last week.'

'*Oui.* I forgot. Are the Iroquois on the warpath?'

'Done that,' said Armand. 'Peace has been restored. We gave them back the land.'

He looked over at the boy, who'd stopped sweeping and was now riding the broom like a steed, using the pan as a shield.

'He's kind of sweet,' said Annie.

'Sweet? Godzilla is sweet. He's a menace,' said Olivier, after getting the boy off the steed and refocusing him on the broken glass.

'We thought he was fun at first too. A real little character, until he came running in here telling us his house was burning down,' said Gabri.

'It wasn't?' asked Annie.

'What do you think?' said Olivier. 'We got the whole volunteer fire department rushing over there, only to find Al and Evie working in their garden.'

'We've tried talking to them about him,' said Gabri. 'But Al just laughed and said he couldn't get Laurent to stop, even if he wanted to. It's in his nature.'

'Probably true,' said Myrna.

'Yeah, well, earthquakes and tornados are part of nature too,' said Gabri.

'So you really don't think Clara can be convinced to help us with the sets,' said Brian. 'We're just a few weeks from opening night and we can use the help. It really is a great play, even if no one knows who wrote it.'

'What?' said Isabelle Lacoste, looking down at the cover sheet of the script and noticing for the first time that there was no name below the title.

'No one knows?' she asked. 'Not even you?'

'Well, we know,' said Antoinette. 'We're just not saying.'

'Believe me,' said Gabri. 'We've asked. I think it was David Beckham.'

'But he's—' Jean-Guy started to say before Myrna cut him off.

'Don't bother. Last week he decided Mark Wahlberg wrote it. Leave him his fantasies. And mine. David Beckham.' Her voice became dreamy. 'He'd have to come to opening night. Alone. He and Victoria would've had a fight.'

'He'd stay in our B and B,' said Gabri. 'He'd smell like leather and Old Spice.'

'He'd need a book to read, at bedtime,' said Myrna. 'I'd bring some over—'

'Okay, enough,' said Jean-Guy.

'I want to hear more,' said Reine-Marie, and Armand looked at her with amusement.

'You'll never guess who wrote the play,' said Brian, laughing and tapping the place where the name had been whited out. 'You wouldn't know him. A fellow named John Fleming.'

'Brian,' snapped Antoinette.

'What?'

'We agreed not to tell anyone.'

'No one's ever heard of him,' said Brian.

'But that's the point,' Antoinette huffed. 'Acht.' She waved in his direction. 'You're a surveyor, what would you know about marketing. I wanted to build up mystery, suspense. Get people wondering. Maybe it was written by Michel Tremblay, or a lost classic by Tennessee Williams.'

'Or George Clooney,' said Gabri.

'Oooh, George Clooney,' said Myrna, and her eyes again became unfocused.

'John Fleming?' said Gamache. 'Do you mind?' He reached out and picked the play up from the table and stared at the title. *She Sat Down and Wept.*

'We got in touch with the copyright people to see who we had to pay for permission, but they had no record of it or of any playwright by that name,' said Brian, as though he had to explain to the cops.

The script in Armand's hand was dog-eared, stained with coffee, and covered in notes.

'It's old,' said Reine-Marie.

The typeface was ragged, not the clean look of a computer, but rather the chunky print of a typewriter.

Armand nodded.

'What is it?' she asked quietly.

'Nothing.' He smiled but no laugh lines radiated from the corners of his eyes.

'I'm in the play too,' said Brian, holding up his copy of the script.

'My gay roommate,' Gabri explained to them.

'He's not gay, and neither are you,' snapped Antoinette in exasperation.

'Don't tell Olivier,' said Myrna. 'He'll be a little disappointed.'

'And very surprised,' said Gabri.

Decaying leaves still sticking to his torn jacket and jeans, the boy swept up the last of the broken glass and trudged back to the table.

'Just so you know,' he said, handing the broom and pan to Olivier. 'I'm pretty sure there're some diamonds in there.'

'*Merci*,' said Olivier.

'Come on,' said Armand, getting up and giving the stick back to the boy. 'It's getting late. Grab your bike. I'll put it in my car and give you a lift home.'

'The gun was really, really big, *patron*,' said the boy, following Monsieur Gamache out of the bistro. 'As big as this building. And there was a monster on it. With wings.'

'Of course there was,' they heard Armand say. 'I'll make sure it doesn't hurt you.'

'And I'll protect you,' said the boy, swishing the stick so violently it struck Armand in the knee.

'I hope you have another husband waiting in the wings,' said Antoinette. 'I'm not sure this one will survive the walk to the car.'

They watched Armand put the bicycle in the back of the Volvo, then he put the stick in the backseat, but the boy took it out and stood firm. He was going nowhere without it in his hands. It was, after all, a dangerous world.

Armand admitted defeat and relented, though they could see him giving the boy ground rules.

'I'd go on match.com right now, if I were you,' said Myrna to Reine-Marie.

After a few kilometers the boy turned to Gamache.

'What're you humming?'

'Was I humming?' said Armand, surprised.

'*Oui.*' And the boy perfectly reproduced the tune.

'It's called "By the Waters of Babylon",' said Armand. 'A hymn.'

John Fleming. John Fleming. He associated the hymn with him, though Gamache could never figure out why.

It couldn't be the same man, he thought. It's a common name. He was seeing ghosts where none existed.

'We don't go to church,' said the boy.

'Neither do we,' said Armand. 'Not often anyway. Though sometimes I sit in the little one in Three Pines, when no one else's there.'

'Why?'

'Because it's peaceful.'

The boy nodded. 'Sometimes I sit in the woods because it's peaceful. But then the aliens arrive.'

The boy began humming again, in a high, thin voice, a tune Gamache recognized from long, long ago.

'How do you know that song?' Gamache asked. 'It's way before your time.'

'My dad sings it to me every night at bedtime. It's by Neil Young. Dad says he's a genius.'

Gamache nodded. 'I agree with your father.'

The boy clutched the stick.

'I hope the safety's on,' said Gamache.

'It is.' He turned to Armand. 'The gun's real, *patron*.'
'*Oui*,' said Gamache.

But he wasn't listening. He was watching the road, and thinking of the tune stuck in his head.

> *By the waters, the waters of Babylon,*
> *We sat down and wept.*

But the play wasn't called that. It was called *She Sat Down and Wept.*

The play could not possibly be by that John Fleming. He didn't write plays. And even if he did, no director in his right mind would produce it. It must be another man with the same name.

Beside him, the boy looked out the window at the early fall landscape and clutched the stick just below where his father had etched his name into the hilt.

Laurent. Laurent Lepage.

CHAPTER 3

~

Their dinner guests had already arrived and were sipping drinks and eating apple and avocado salsa with corn chips by the time Armand returned.

'Got Laurent home all right, I see,' said Reine-Marie, greeting him at the door. 'No alien invasions?'

'We nipped it in the bud.'

'Not quite,' said Gabri, standing at the door to their study. 'One got through Earth's defenses.'

Armand and Reine-Marie looked into the small room off the living room where an elderly, angular woman with ladders up her stockings and patches on her sweater sat in an armchair reading.

'It's the mother shit,' said Gabri.

A strong smell of gin met them. A duck sat on the old woman's lap and Henri, the Gamaches' German shepherd, was curled at her feet. Gazing up adoringly at the duck.

'Don't worry about greeting me at the door,' Armand said to Henri. 'It's fine. Really.'

He looked at the dog and shook his head. Love took all forms. This was, though, a step up from Henri's previous crush, which was the arm of the sofa.

'The first hint of infestation was the smell of gin,' said Gabri. 'Her race seems to run on it.'

'What's for dinner?' their neighbor Ruth Zardo demanded, struggling out of the armchair.

'How long have you been there?' Reine-Marie asked.

'What day is it?'

'I thought you were out clubbing baby seals,' said Gabri, taking Ruth's arm.

'That's next week. Don't you read my Facebook updates?'

'Hag.'

'Fag.'

Ruth limped into the living room. Rosa the duck goose-stepped behind her, followed by Henri.

'I was once head of homicide for the Sûreté du Québec,' said Gamache wistfully as they watched the parade.

'I don't believe it,' said Reine-Marie.

'*Bonjour*, Ruth,' said Antoinette.

Ruth, who hadn't noticed there was anyone else in the room, looked at Antoinette and Brian, then over to Myrna.

'What're they doing here?'

'We were invited, unlike you, you demented old drunk,' said Myrna. 'How can you be a poet and never notice anything and anyone around you?'

'Have we met?' Ruth asked, then turned to Reine-Marie.

'Where's numbnuts?' she asked.

'He and Annie left for the city, along with Isabelle and the kids,' said Reine-Marie.

She knew she should have chastised Ruth for calling their son-in-law numbnuts, but the truth was, the old poet had called Jean-Guy that for so long the Gamaches barely noticed anymore. Even Jean-Guy answered to numbnuts. But only from Ruth.

23

'I saw the Lepage boy come flying out of the woods again,' said Ruth. 'What was it this time? Zombies?'

'Actually, I believe he disturbed a nest of poets,' said Armand, taking the bottle of red wine around and refilling glasses, before helping himself to some of the salsa with honey-lime dressing. 'Terrified him.'

'Poetry scares most people,' said Ruth. 'I know mine does.'

'You scare them, Ruth, not your poems.'

'Oh, right. Even better. So what did the kid claim to see?'

'A giant gun with a monster on it.'

Ruth nodded, impressed.

'Imagination isn't such a bad thing,' she said. 'He reminds me of myself when I was that age and look how I turned out.'

'It's not imagination,' said Gabri. 'It's outright lying. I'm not sure the kid knows the difference anymore himself.' He turned to Myrna. 'What do you think? You're the shrink.'

'I'm not a shrink,' said Myrna.

'You're not kidding,' said Ruth with a snort.

'I'm a psychologist,' said Myrna.

'You're a librarian,' said Ruth.

'For the last time, it's not a library,' said Myrna. 'It's a bookstore. Stop just taking the books. Oh, never mind.' She waved at Ruth, who was smiling into her glass, and turned back to Gabri. 'What were we talking about?'

'Laurent. Is he crazy? Though I realize the bar for sanity is pretty low here.' He watched as Ruth and Rosa muttered to each other.

'Hard to say, really. In my practice I saw a lot of people whose grip on reality had slipped. But they were adults. The line between real and imagined is blurred for kids, but it gets clearer as we grow up.'

'For better or worse,' said Reine-Marie.

'Well, I saw the worse,' said Myrna. 'My clients' delusions were often paranoid. They heard voices, they saw horrible things. Did horrible things. Laurent seems a happy kid. Well adjusted even.'

'You can't be both happy and well adjusted,' said Ruth, laughing at the very thought.

'I don't think he's well adjusted,' said Antoinette. 'Look, I'm all for imagination. The theater's fueled by it. Depends on it. But I agree with Gabri. This is something else. Shouldn't he be growing out of it by now? What's the name for it when someone doesn't understand, or care about, consequences?'

'Ruth Zardo?' said Brian.

There was surprised silence, followed by laughter. Including Ruth's.

Brian Fitzpatrick didn't say a great deal, but when he did it was often worth the wait.

'I don't think Laurent's psychotic, if that's what you're asking,' said Myrna. 'No more than any kid. For some, their imagination's so strong it overpowers reality. But, like I say, they grow out of it.' She looked at Ruth, stroking and singing to her duck. 'Or at least, most do.'

'He once told us a classmate had been kidnapped,' said Brian. 'Remember that?'

'He did?' Armand asked.

'Yes. Took about a minute to realize it wasn't true, but what a long minute. The girl's parents were in the bistro when he came running in with that news. I don't think they'll ever recover, or forgive him. He's not the most popular kid in the area.'

'Why does he say things if they aren't true?' asked Reine-Marie.

'Your children must've made things up,' said Myrna.

'Well, yes, but not anything so dramatic—'

'And so vivid,' said Antoinette. 'He really sells it.'

'He probably just wants attention,' said Myrna.

'Oh God, don't you hate people like that,' said Gabri.

He put a carrot on his nose and tried to balance it there.

'There's a seal just asking to be clubbed,' said Myrna.

Ruth guffawed then looked at her. 'Shouldn't you be in the kitchen?'

'Shouldn't you be cutting the eyes out of a sheet?' asked Myrna.

'Look, I like the kid,' said Ruth, 'but let's face it. He was doomed from the moment of conception.'

'What do you mean?' asked Reine-Marie.

'Well, look at his parents.'

'Al and Evelyn?' asked Armand. 'I like them. That reminds me.' He walked to the door and picked up a canvas tote bag. 'Al gave me this.'

'Oh, God,' said Antoinette. 'Don't tell me it's—'

'Apples.' Armand held up the bag.

Gamache smiled. When he'd dropped off Laurent, his father Al had been on the porch, sorting beets for their organic produce baskets.

There was no mistaking Al Lepage. If a mountain came alive, it would look like Laurent's father. Solid, craggy. He wore his long gray hair in a ponytail that might not have been undone since the seventies.

His beard was also gray and bushy and covered most of his chest, so that the plaid flannel shirt underneath was barely visible. Sometimes the beard was loose, sometimes it was braided and sometimes, like that afternoon, it was in its own ponytail so that Al's head looked like something about to be tie-dyed.

Or, as Ruth once described him, a horse with two asses.

'Hi, cop,' Al had said when Armand parked and Laurent had jumped out of the car.

'Hello, hippie,' said Armand, going around to the back of the car.

'What's he done now, Armand?' Al asked as they yanked the bike out of the station wagon.

'Nothing. He was just slightly disruptive in the bistro.'

'Zombies? Vampires? Monsters?' suggested Laurent's father.

'Monster,' said Armand, closing the hatchback. 'Only one.'

'You're slipping,' Al said to his son.

'It was on a huge gun, Dad. Bigger than the house.'

'You need to clean up for dinner, you're a mess. Quick now before your mother sees you.'

'Too late,' said a woman's voice from the house.

Armand looked over and saw Evelyn standing on the porch, hands on her wide hips, shaking her head. She was much younger than Al. At least twenty years, which put her in her mid-forties. She too wore a plaid flannel shirt, and a full skirt that fell to her ankles. Her hair was also pulled back, though some wisps had broken free and were falling across her scrubbed face.

'What was it this time?' she asked Laurent with a mixture of amusement and weary tolerance.

'I found a gun in the woods.'

'You did?'

Evelyn looked alarmed and Gamache was once again amazed that this woman still believed her son. Was that love, he wondered, or the same form of delusion Laurent suffered from? A potent combination of wishful thinking and madness.

'It was just the other side of the bridge. In the woods.' Laurent pointed with his stick and almost hit Gamache in the face.

'Where is it now?' she asked. 'Al, should we go and see?'

'Wait for it, Evie,' her husband said in his deep, patient voice.

'It's huge, Mom. Bigger than the house. And there's a monster on it. With wings.'

'Ahhh,' said Evelyn. 'Thanks for bringing him back, Armand. Are you sure you don't want to keep him for a while?'

'Mom.'

'Go inside and wash up. We're having squirrel for dinner.'

'Again?'

Gamache smiled. He was never sure if what they claimed to eat was the truth. He actually thought they were vegetarians. He did know they were as self-sufficient as possible, selling their organic produce in *panniers* to subscribers. He and Reine-Marie among them.

In the winter they made ends meet by teaching courses on how to live a sustainable lifestyle. It was one of the great miracles that these two should find each other. Like Henri and Rosa. And then that Al and Evie should, later in life, have a child. One miracle begetting another. A wild child.

'Why's it always guns?' Al asked.

'Well, you're the one who gave him that stick for his birthday,' said Evie. 'Now all he does is dive behind furniture shooting at monsters. I can't tell you how often I've been mowed down,' she confided in Armand.

'It's meant to be a magic wand,' said Al. 'At most a sword. Not a gun. I'd never give him a gun. I hate them.'

'You gave him a stick and an imagination,' said Evie.

28

'What did you think a nine-year-old boy was going to do with it?'

'It's a wand,' said Al to Gamache.

Armand smiled. If he'd given his son, Daniel, a stick for his ninth birthday there'd still be tears twenty years later. What kid not only accepts the stick, but cherishes it?

'Say hi to Reine-Marie,' said Evie. 'The next *pannier*'s almost ready, we're just finishing the harvest. In the meantime, take this.'

She handed him the sack of McIntosh apples.

'*Merci*,' he'd said, trying to sound sincere, and surprised.

Evie went inside and Al followed her, turning to Gamache at the door. 'Thank you for bringing him home.'

'Always. He's a great kid.'

'He's crazy, but we love him.' Al shook his head. 'A gun.'

A monster, thought Armand as he got in the car and drove home.

But the monster he was thinking of wasn't from Laurent's imagination. This one was very real. And had a name and a pulse, though not, Gamache suspected, a heartbeat.

'Why don't you like Laurent's parents, Ruth?' Reine-Marie asked, putting the chicken stew with fresh herb dumplings on the table.

They'd moved into the large country kitchen and taken seats at the pine table. Antoinette cut the bread while Gabri tossed the salad.

'It's not her, it's him,' said Ruth, putting her glass on the table and looking at them. 'He's a coward.'

'Al Lepage?' asked Brian. 'I'd heard he was a draft dodger, but that doesn't make him a coward, does it?'

Both Ruth and Rosa glared at him but said nothing.

'They were kids themselves at the time, drafted into a war they didn't want to fight,' said Armand. 'They gave up home and family and friends to come here. Not exactly the easy option. They took a stand. I don't think they were cowards at all. I like Al.'

'They took a stand by running away?' said Ruth. 'Some other kid had to go in his place. Do you think he thinks of that?'

'This whole village was settled by people fleeing a war they didn't believe in,' Myrna pointed out. 'The three pines is an old code for sanctuary.'

'More like asylum,' said Gabri.

'I know the history of the village,' said Ruth.

'Let's change the subject,' said Brian. He turned to Reine-Marie. 'Are you going to join the Estrie Players?'

'Join?' asked Armand, looking at his wife.

'I was thinking it might be fun.'

'It is fun,' said Gabri. 'Drop by the rehearsal tomorrow night and see. I'll leave my script for you to read.'

'Great, I'll come by. What time?' said Reine-Marie.

'Seven,' said Brian. 'Wear something you don't mind throwing out. We'll be painting. How about you, Ruth?'

'Yes, you'd be good at it,' said Gabri. 'You've been pretending to be human for years.'

'Though not very convincingly,' said Myrna. 'I never believed it.'

But Ruth had fallen into a stupor, deep in thought.

'Let's go into the living room,' said Reine-Marie, once dinner was finished. 'Leave the dishes. Henri will lick them clean later.'

The guests looked at each other as they left the table, and saw Reine-Marie smiling. In the living room Armand tossed another log onto the fire, putting his hands, palms out, toward the flame.

'Are you cold?' Reine-Marie asked. 'Getting sick?'

She put her hand on his forehead.

'No, I just feel a chill,' he explained.

Antoinette came by and nodded toward the fire. 'They're nice in September, aren't they? Cheerful. In June they're just depressing.'

Reine-Marie laughed and walked over to join Ruth. Antoinette turned away but Armand called her back.

'The play,' he said quietly.

'Yes?'

'Brian said it was by John Fleming.'

She grew still, her clear eyes studying him. 'He shouldn't have said that.'

'But he did. Why do you want to keep it a secret?'

'Like I said, marketing. It's a new play, we need to do everything we can to pique interest.'

'A secret playwright is hardly going to get camera crews out.'

'Not at first, maybe. But the play's not your run-of-the-mill work by an unknown, Armand. It's brilliant. I've done professional and amateur theatrics for years and this is among the best.'

'For an amateur,' said Gamache.

'For anyone. Wait until you see it. I'd put it beside Miller and Stoppard and Tremblay. It's *Our Town* meets *The Crucible.*'

Gamache was used to hyperbole, especially from people in the theater, so this didn't surprise him.

'I'm not questioning the quality of the work,' he said, lowering his voice so that it was barely audible above the crackle of the fire as it caught the dry wood. 'I'm wondering about the playwright.'

'I can't tell you anything about him.'

'Have you met him?' Gamache asked.

Antoinette hesitated. 'No. Brian found the script among my uncle's papers after he died.'

'Why did you white out the playwright's name?'

'I told you. I wanted to create a buzz. Once the play opens everyone's going to want to know who wrote it.'

'And what'll you tell them?'

Now Antoinette looked decidedly tense.

'Who wrote *She Sat Down and Wept*?' Gamache asked, his voice low.

'Like Brian said, it's by some fellow named John Fleming.'

'I know a John Fleming,' he said. 'And so do you. And so does everyone.' He stared at her. 'Is it that John Fleming?'

'I don't know,' she said after a pause.

He continued to stare until she flushed. 'You know.'

'Know what?' asked Gabri, offering them coffees. Too late, he picked up on the tension between the two.

'Please tell me it's not the same man,' said Gamache, searching Antoinette's face. And then his went slack before he whispered, 'My God, it is, isn't it?'

'What is?' asked Gabri, wishing he could back away but knowing it was too late.

'Will you tell him?' Armand asked. 'Or shall I?'

'Tell him what?' asked Myrna, joining them.

Armand walked over to the table by the door where Gabri had left his script.

'Tell them who wrote this,' he said, holding it out to Antoinette. 'Tell them the real reason you didn't want anyone to know.'

32

Hearing the tone of his voice, Reine-Marie looked over. Armand was dangerously close to being rude to one of their guests, something he'd rarely been in all the years she'd known him. He hadn't liked all their guests, certainly hadn't agreed with all of them, but he'd always been courteous.

But now he toed the line. And then he crossed it, thrusting the play at Antoinette.

'Tell them,' he said.

She took it, then turned to the other dinner guests. 'It was John Fleming.'

'We already know that,' said Myrna. 'Brian told us this afternoon in the bistro, remember?'

'That's what's going to get people excited?' asked Gabri. 'Your brilliant marketing plan? He's hardly a household name.'

'But he is,' said Armand. 'Everyone in Canada knows him. In North America. He's famous. Infamous.'

They looked perplexed, genuinely baffled by Armand's behavior and insistence. But then Myrna sank down. Had the sofa not been there, she might have gone all the way to the floor. Brian took the cup and saucer from her just before it spilled.

'That John Fleming?' Myrna whispered.

Gabri, far from buckling, looked as though he'd been turned to granite as he stared at Antoinette. A Medusa in their midst.

'You didn't,' he said. 'Tell me you didn't.'

Once home, Ruth turned the key in the lock and leaned against the door, her heart pounding, her breathing rapid and shallow. She held Rosa to her chest and pressed against the thin wood of the door. All that stood between her and Rosa and an alien world that had produced a John Fleming.

Then she drew the curtains and pulled from her string bag the script she'd stolen.

Making herself a cup of tea, Ruth opened the play and started to read.

The party broke up and Armand went into the kitchen. Reine-Marie could hear the tap water and the clinking of dishes and cutlery.

Then the clinking stopped and she heard only the steady stream of water. Going into the kitchen, she stopped at the door. Armand was leaning over the sink, his large hands clutching the counter, as though he was about to be sick.

'Are you still going to rehearsal tomorrow?' Gabri asked, as he and Myrna walked home.

'I guess. I don't know. I ... I ...'

'I know, me too.'

Gabri kissed her good night on both cheeks, then went into the bistro to help Olivier with the last of the evening service. Myrna climbed the stairs to her loft apartment above the bookstore and got into her pajamas, then realized she was both tired and wide awake. Looking out the window, she saw a light at Clara's home.

It was eleven o'clock.

Putting a shawl around her shoulders, and slipping on rubber boots, she clumped around the edge of the village green and knocked on the door. Then she let herself in.

'Clara?'

'In here.'

Myrna found her in her studio, sitting in front of the unfinished canvas. Peter Morrow stared back, ghostly. Half-finished. A demi-man in an unfinished life.

Clara was wearing sweats and held a paintbrush in her mouth, like a female FDR. Her hair stuck out at odd angles from running her hands through it.

'Pizza for dinner?' asked Myrna, picking a mushroom out of Clara's hair.

'Yes. Reine-Marie invited me over but I wasn't really in the mood.'

Myrna looked at the easel and knew why. Clara had been obsessing over the portrait again. And Peter, now gone, was still managing to undermine his wife's art.

'Do you want to talk?' Myrna asked, drawing up a stool.

Clara put down the brush and ran her hands through her graying hair so vigorously that bits of pepperoni and crumbs fell out.

'I don't know what I'm doing anymore,' said Clara, waving at the portrait. 'It's as though I've never painted in my life. Oh, God, suppose I can't?'

She looked at Myrna in a panic.

'You will,' Myrna assured her. 'Maybe you're just doing the wrong portrait. Maybe it's too soon to paint Peter.'

Peter seemed to be watching them. A slight smile on his handsome face. Myrna wondered if Clara knew how very well she'd already captured the man. Myrna had cared for Peter very much, but she also knew he could be a real piece of work. This piece, in fact. And Myrna also wondered if Clara had been adding to the portrait, or taking away. Had she been making him less and less substantial?

She turned away and listened as Clara talked about what had happened. To Peter. It was a story Myrna knew well. She'd been there.

But still she listened, and she'd listen again. And again.

And with every telling Clara was letting go of a bit of the

unbearable pain. The guilt she felt. The sorrow. It was as though Clara was pulling herself out of the ocean, dripping in grief, but no longer drowning.

Clara blew her nose and wiped her eyes.

'Did you have fun at the Gamaches'?' she asked. 'What time is it anyway? Why're you in pajamas?'

'It's half past eleven,' said Myrna. 'Can we go into the kitchen?'

Away from the goddamned painting, thought Myrna.

'Tea?' Clara asked.

'Beer?' Myrna countered, and pulled a couple out of the fridge.

'What's wrong?' Clara asked.

'You know I joined the Estrie Players,' said Myrna.

'You're not going to ask me again to go and paint sets,' said Clara. When Myrna didn't answer, Clara put her beer down and reached out for her friend's hand.

'What is it?'

'The play we're doing. *She Sat Down and Wept*—'

'The musical?'

But Myrna didn't smile. 'Antoinette took the playwright's name off the script. She wanted to keep it a secret.'

Clara nodded. 'You and Gabri were all excited, thinking it must be by Michel Tremblay or Leonard Cohen maybe.'

'Gabri was hoping it was by Wayne Gretzky.'

'He's a hockey player,' said Clara.

'Well, you know Gabri,' said Myrna. 'Anyway, Antoinette said she did it to attract attention, interest. To get people talking.'

'Why did she really do it?' asked Clara, seeing where this was going.

'Turns out the playwright is famous,' said Myrna. 'But not in the way you'd hope. It's John Fleming.'

Clara shook her head. The name meant nothing. And yet, there was a small niggling, more a gnawing really.

Myrna waited.

Clara looked off, trying to place the name. The man. John Fleming.

'Is it someone we've met?' she asked, and Myrna shook her head. 'But we know him?'

Myrna nodded.

And then Clara had it. Headlines. Television images of jostling photographers, trying to get a picture of the little man in the neat suit, being led into court.

How different real monsters were from the film kind.

John Fleming was famous indeed.

Ruth closed the last page of the script and laid a blue-veined hand on the stack of paper.

Then, making up her mind, she lit the logs in the hearth and held the script over it until her thin skin sizzled. But she couldn't do it.

'Stay here,' she commanded Rosa, who watched from her flannel nest.

Finding a small shovel, Ruth went outside, and sinking to her knees she hacked at the earth. Cutting away at the grass. Digging deeper, fighting the ground for every inch, as though it knew her intention and was resisting. But Ruth didn't give up. If she could have dug down to the bed-rock, she would have. Finally she was deep enough for her purpose.

Picking up the script, Ruth placed it in the hole. Then she covered it up, shoving the dirt in with her hands. Sitting back on her heels, kneeling under the night sky, she wondered if she should say something. A thin prayer. A curse?

'*And now it is now,*' she whispered, quoting her own poem over the fresh-turned earth.

> *And the dark thing is here,*
> *and after all it is nothing new;*
> *it is only a memory, after all:*

She got to her feet and stared down and thought about what she'd done. And what he'd done.

> *A memory of a fear.*

Perhaps she should say something to Armand. But maybe it would be all right. Maybe it would stay buried.

Ruth went inside, locking the door behind her.

CHAPTER 4

~

'**I**'m thinking of quitting the play,' said Gabri. The breakfast rush at the bistro was over and his guests at the B and B had left after the weekend. Now he sat in a comfortable armchair in the bay window of Myrna's New and Used Bookstore. Myrna sat across from him in her own chair, unmistakable because it had taken on, over the years, her ample form. Beside her, on the floor, was a stack of books to be priced and put on shelves.

From the outside they might have looked like mannequins in a window display, except for their grim expressions.

'I've decided to quit,' said Myrna.

'Are we doing the right thing?' Gabri asked. 'It's so close to opening night, and if we pull out I don't know what Antoinette will do.'

'What she should have done all along,' came Clara's voice from the body of the store. She'd been browsing the 'New Arrivals' shelf. Though 'new' was a relative term. 'She'll pull the play.'

'That was banned, you know,' Myrna said to Clara when she saw what book Clara was holding. *Fahrenheit 451*.

'Was it also burned?' asked Clara, joining them. 'Maybe

that's what hellfire's made of. Burning books. I wonder if they'd appreciate the irony.'

'I doubt it,' said Myrna. 'But are we doing the same thing?'

'We're not burning the play,' said Gabri. 'We're just refusing to support it. Conscientious objectors.'

'Look, if we're going to do this, we have to face the truth of what we're doing and why,' said Myrna. 'We're demanding that a play not be produced not because it contains anything vile, but because we don't like the man who wrote it.'

'You make it sound like a personality conflict,' said Gabri. 'It's not that we don't like John Fleming, it's because of what he did.'

'Knock, knock,' came a familiar voice at the door to the bookstore.

They looked up to see Reine-Marie, Armand and Henri.

'We were out for a walk and saw you in the window,' said Armand.

'Are we interrupting?' Reine-Marie asked, looking at their faces.

'No,' said Clara. 'You can guess what we're talking about.'

Reine-Marie nodded. 'The same thing we were talking about. The play.'

'The goddamned play,' said Myrna. 'I'm going to quit and Antoinette's going to have a fit. I feel like such a shit.'

'Did you realize that all rhymed?' asked Gabri. 'Quit, fit, shit. Like a Shakespearean sonnet.'

'You feel you're letting down a friend,' said Reine-Marie.

'Partly, but I run a bookstore,' said Myrna, looking at the row upon row of books, lining the walls and creating corridors in the open space. 'So many of them were banned and burned. That one,' she pointed to the *Fahrenheit 451* Clara still had in her hands. *'To Kill a Mockingbird. The Adventures of Huck Finn.* Even *The Diary of Anne Frank.* All banned by people who believed they were in the right. Could we be wrong?'

'You're not banning it,' said Clara. 'He's allowed to write and you're allowed to pull your support.'

'But it comes to the same thing. If Gabri and I pull out and tell the others, it'll ruin the production. And you know what? I want it to. Once she knew who'd written the play, Antoinette should never have produced it. Right, Armand?'

'Right.'

If they were expecting a hesitation, some anguish over the answer, they were disappointed. His answer was quick and unequivocal.

Armand Gamache was in absolutely no doubt. This was a play that should never have seen the light of day. Just as its author should never again see the light of day.

'But other killers have written books, plays even,' said Myrna.

'John Fleming is different,' said Clara. 'We all know it.'

'You're an artist,' said Reine-Marie. 'Do you think a work should be judged by its creator? Or should it stand on its own?'

Clara gave a huge sigh. 'I know the right answer to that. And I know how I feel. Would I want a painting by Jeffrey Dahmer, or to serve a meal from the Stalin family cookbook? No.'

'That's not the issue,' said Gabri. 'It's about options, letting people make their own choices. Maybe Antoinette should produce it, and let people decide if they'll go or not.'

'Are you having second thoughts about quitting?' asked Myrna.

'Hell no,' he said. 'I'm not going anywhere near that play again. The play was written by a shit and there's shit all over it. Fair or not, that's just the way it is.'

'Look at Wagner,' said Reine-Marie. 'He's so associated with the Nazis and the Holocaust that his music, however brilliant, is spoiled for many.'

'It doesn't help that Wagner was also a raging anti-Semite,' said Gabri.

'But is that a reason not to perform music that is sublime?' asked Reine-Marie.

'Reason has very little to do with this,' said Myrna. 'I'm the first to admit I'd lose every debate over whether Fleming's play should be banned. Intellectually I know he has a right to write it, and any company has a right to produce it. I just don't want to be a part of it. I can't defend my feelings, they just are.'

'I go back to the question,' said Reine-Marie. 'Should the creation be judged by its creator? Does it matter?'

'It matters,' said Gamache. 'Sometimes censorship is justified.'

They looked at him, surprised by his certainty. Even Reine-Marie was taken aback.

'But, Armand, you've always championed free speech, even when it's used against you.'

'There're exceptions in a free society,' said Armand. 'There are always exceptions.' And John Fleming, he knew, was exceptional.

'Is the play about the murders?' Clara asked.

'No,' admitted Gabri. 'It's actually quite funny. It's about a guy who keeps winning the lottery and squandering the chances he's been given. He keeps ending up at the same rooming house, with the same people.'

'It's hilarious in places,' Myrna agreed. 'But then you find yourself incredibly moved. I don't know how he did it.'

'So it has nothing to do with Fleming and his crimes?' asked Reine-Marie. 'Nothing to do with him as a man?'

'It has everything to do with him,' said Armand, his voice clipped, strained. They looked at him. Never had they heard him come even close to being upset with his wife. 'If John Fleming created it, it's grotesque. It can't help but be. Maybe not obviously so, but he's in every word, every action of the characters. The creator and the created are one.' He laced his fingers together. 'This is how he escapes. Through the written word, and the decency of others. This is how John Fleming gets into your head. And you don't want him there. Believe me.'

For a moment he looked like a man possessed. And then it passed, and faded, until Armand Gamache looked simply haunted. Silence settled over the bookstore, except for the jingle of Henri's collar as he stepped beside Armand, and leaned against his leg.

'I'm sorry,' said Armand, rubbing his forehead and giving them a feeble smile. 'Forgive me.' He took Reine-Marie's hand and squeezed it.

'I understand,' she said, though she knew she didn't really. The Fleming case was the only one Armand never talked to her about, though she'd followed it in the media.

'The sooner we tell Antoinette we're out, the better,' said Gabri. 'I have some cleaning up to do at the bistro. Why don't I come by in about an hour and pick you up, Myrna? We can drive over together.'

Myrna agreed. Gabri left, followed by Clara, waving good-bye with her book.

'I'm heading over to the general store,' said Reine-Marie, leaving Armand and Henri in the bookstore.

Myrna settled into her chair and looked at Armand, who'd taken the armchair vacated by Gabri.

'Do you want to talk some more about the play?' she asked.

'God no,' he said.

She was about to ask why he was there, but stopped herself. Instead she asked, 'What do you know that we don't?'

It was a while before he answered.

'You have experience with the criminally insane,' he said, kneading Henri's enormous ears and looking at the groaning shepherd as he spoke. But then he looked up and Myrna saw sorrow in Armand's deep brown eyes. Genuine pain.

He held on to the dog as though to a life raft after the ship had sunk.

Myrna nodded. 'I had my own private practice but I also worked part-time at the penitentiary, as you know.'

'Did you ever work at the Special Handling Unit?' he asked.

'The SHU? For the worst offenders?' asked Myrna. 'I was asked to take on some cases there. I went there once, but didn't get out of my car.'

'Why not?'

She opened her mouth, then shut it again, gathering her thoughts. Trying to find words to express what was not, in fact, a thought at all.

'You know the term "godforsaken"?'

He nodded.

'That's why. I sat in the parking lot of the SHU, staring at those walls.' She shook her head. 'I couldn't go inside that godforsaken place.'

Both of them could see that building, a terrible monolith rising out of the ground.

'You continued counseling prisoners at the other penitentiaries,' he said. 'Murderers, rapists. But you stopped eventually and came here. Why?'

'Because it was too much. It wasn't their failure, it was mine. They were too damaged. I couldn't help them.'

'Maybe some can't be repaired because they were never damaged,' he suggested.

Through the window he could see splashes of astonishing color in the forest that covered the mountains. The maple and oak and apple trees turning. Preparing. That was where the fall began. High up. And then it descended, until it reached them in the valley. The fall was, of course, inevitable. He could see it coming.

'Coffee?' he said, hauling himself out of the chair and stepping over Henri.

'Please.'

As he poured he spoke. 'John Fleming was arrested and tried eighteen years ago.'

'Crimes like those don't fade, do they?' said Myrna, taking the mug and finishing his thought. 'Do you know him?'

'I followed the case,' said Gamache, retaking his seat. 'He committed his crimes in New Brunswick, but he was tried here because it was felt he couldn't get a fair trial there.'

'I remember. Is he still here?'

Gamache nodded. 'At the Special Handling Unit.'

'That's why you asked me about the SHU?'

Gamache nodded.

'Is he getting help?' Myrna asked.

'He's beyond help.'

'Believe me, I'm not saying he'd ever be a model citizen,' said Myrna. 'I'm not saying I'd ever trust him with a child of mine—'

It was subtle, but Myrna, who knew every line of Armand's face, was sure she saw a movement. A flinch.

'—but he's a human being and he must be in torment, to have done those things. It's possible, with time and therapy, he can be helped. Not released. But helped to release some of his demons.'

'John Fleming will never get better,' Gamache said, his voice low. 'And believe me, we don't want his demons released.'

She was about to argue with him, but stopped. If anyone believed in second chances, it was the man who sat before her. She'd been his friend and his unofficial therapist. She'd heard his deepest secrets, and she'd heard his most profound beliefs, and his greatest fears. But now she wondered if she'd really heard them all. And she wondered what demons might be nesting deep inside this man, who specialized in murder.

'What do you know, Armand, that we don't?'

'I can't say.'

'I also followed the court case—' She stopped, and regarded him.

Then it dawned on her. What he was really saying by not saying anything.

'We didn't hear everything, did we, Armand? There was another trial, a private one, for Fleming.'

A trial within a trial.

Myrna knew, from her association with the law, that the system allowed for such things, but she'd never ever heard of one actually being held.

There would be the public trial for public consumption, but behind closed and locked and bolted doors, there would be another. Where evidence, deemed too horrific for the community, would be revealed.

How bad, Myrna wondered, would something have to be to go against the fundamental beliefs of their society? How horrific would that truth have to be, to hide it from the public? Only the accused, the judge, the prosecutor, the defense attorney, a guard, a court reporter would be present. And one other.

One person, not associated with the case, would be chosen to represent all Canadians. They would absorb the horror. They would hear and see things that could never be forgotten. And then, when the trial was over, they would carry it to their grave, so that the rest of the population didn't have to. One person sacrificed for the greater good.

'You more than read his file, didn't you?' said Myrna. 'There was a closed-door trial, wasn't there?'

Armand stared at her, his lips compressed slightly.

Gamache and Henri left the bookstore and walked around the village green, feeling the fresh, cool autumn air on their faces. Breathing in the scent of overripe apples and fresh-cut grass, their feet shuffling through newly fallen leaves.

He didn't tell Myrna, of course. He couldn't. It was confidential. And even if he was allowed to tell Myrna what he knew about the crimes committed by John Fleming, he wouldn't do it.

He wished he himself didn't know.

Each day, when the door had been unlocked and he'd been allowed out, Armand had returned to his office at Sûreté headquarters in Montréal and stared out the window at the people below. Waiting for lights to change. Going for drinks, or to the dentist. Thinking about groceries, and bills, and the boss.

They didn't know. They read the newspapers and saw the

television reports on the trial and thought Fleming a monster. But they didn't know the half of it.

Armand Gamache was eternally grateful to the judge who'd had the courage to enact that most extreme of clauses. And he wondered if the courtroom had been scrubbed down when it was over. Disinfected. Burned to the ground.

Or had they simply closed the doors and gone back to their lives and, in the nighttime, in the darkness, had they prayed to a God they hoped was powerful, to forget? Prayed for dreamless sleep. Prayed to turn back the clocks to a time when they did not know.

Knowledge wasn't always power. Sometimes it was crippling.

Myrna had suggested therapy could, over time, rid Fleming of his demons. But Armand Gamache knew that wasn't true. Because John Fleming was the demon.

And now, from that prison cell, he'd managed to escape. He'd slid out between the bars. In the form of words.

John Fleming was out in the world again.

He'd come to play.

CHAPTER 5

'What do you want?' Antoinette called into the darkness.

She stood on the brightly lit stage, her hand to her forehead, peering like a mariner looking for land.

'To talk to you,' came Armand's voice from the theater.

'I think you've done enough, don't you?'

Brian came out of the wings carrying a prop lamp. 'Who're you talking to?'

Armand climbed the steps onto the stage. 'Me. *Salut*, Brian.'

'Are you happy?' Antoinette demanded, walking over to him. 'Myrna and Gabri have quit. Brian here has to take over Gabri's lead role—'

'I do?'

'A play's hard enough to put on without actors dropping out,' she said.

'You're going on with the production then?' Gamache asked.

'Of course,' she said. 'Despite all your efforts. The other actors are going to be here in a few minutes. I'd like you to leave before you do more damage.'

'Are you going to tell them who wrote the play?'

'Because if I don't you will? Is that why you're here? To make sure you well and truly destroy the production? Christ, you're a fascist after all.'

'I don't want to debate with you,' said Gamache.

'Of course not, because that would be more free speech,' said Antoinette. For his part, Brian stood by the sofa, still holding the lamp. Like a failed Diogenes.

'Gabri and Myrna made up their own minds,' said Gamache. 'But I didn't try to dissuade them. I think doing the play is wrong.'

'Yes, I got that. But we're doing it anyway. And you know why? Because while the man might be horrible, his play is extraordinary. If you have your way, no one will ever read it or see it performed. What a champion of the free society.'

'A free society comes at a cost,' he snapped, then reined himself in.

Antoinette smiled. 'Hit a nerve, did I? What're you so afraid of, Armand? The man's in prison, has been for years. He'll never get out.'

'I'm not afraid.'

'You're terrified,' said Antoinette. 'If I was casting a man driven by fear, I'd beg you to do the role.'

'I'd like to talk,' said Gamache, ignoring what she just said. 'Can we sit down?'

'Fine, but make it quick before the others arrive.'

'Can I join you?' Brian asked, putting the lamp down. 'Or is this private?'

'Yes,' said Armand. 'This involves you too.'

He sat on a threadbare armchair, part of the stage set. The few times he'd actually been on a stage, it had surprised him how very shabby everything was. From a distance, from the audience, the actors could look like kings and queens, titans of business. But close up? The costumes were cheap, worn, often smelly. Their castles were falling apart.

The illusion shattered. That was the price of looking at things too closely.

As an investigator he'd spent his career examining things, examining people. Looking behind the façade, at what was really there. The worn and shabby and thread-bare interiors.

But sometimes, sometimes, when he pulled back the illusion, what he found was something shiny, bright, far better than the stage set.

He looked at Antoinette. Middle-aged, clinging on perhaps a little too tightly to the illusion of youth. Her hair was dyed purple, her clothes could have been considered bohemian, had they not been so studied.

He genuinely liked Antoinette and admired her. Admired her even now, for standing up for what she believed in. And, after all, she didn't know the full truth about Fleming.

'I'm here because we're friends,' he said. 'I don't want this disagreement to come between us.'

'You didn't even read the play, Armand,' Antoinette said, the anger draining from her voice. 'How can you condemn it?'

'Perhaps the life of the writer shouldn't matter,' he said, his own voice soft now. 'But it does to me. In this case.'

'I'm not going to pull the play,' she said. 'It might be crap now, with Brian in the lead—'

'Hey,' said Brian.

'I'm sorry, you'll be fine, but you don't have much time to rehearse, and when you came in late for rehearsal today I thought you'd also—'

'I'd never quit,' said Brian, looking shocked and upset. 'How could you even think such a thing?'

Gamache wondered if Antoinette knew how lucky she was to have such a loyal partner. He also wondered about Brian, who could be so morally blinded by love.

'Honestly, Armand,' she said. 'You're behaving as though our very survival is at stake. It's just a play.'

'If it's just a play, then cancel it,' he said, and they were back where they'd started.

She stared at him. He stared at her. And Brian just looked unhappy.

'How did you come to have the Fleming play?' Gamache asked.

'I told you, Brian found it among my uncle's papers,' she said.

'What was your uncle's name?'

'Guillaume Couture.'

'Was he a theater director? An actor?' Armand asked.

'Not at all. As far as I know he never went to the theater. He built bridges. Little ones. Overpasses really. He was a quiet, gentle man.'

'Then why did he have the play? Did he know Fleming?'

'Of course not,' she said. 'He barely left Three Pines his whole life. He probably picked it up at a yard sale. We don't owe you an explanation. We've committed no crime, and you're no cop.' She got up. 'Now please leave. We have work to do.'

She turned her back on him and so did Brian, but not before giving Armand a slightly apologetic grimace.

As he drove down the dirt road toward Three Pines, feeling the familiar and almost comforting washboard bumps, Armand Gamache came to a realization. One he'd probably known since he'd discovered who'd written *She Sat Down and Wept*.

He would have to read the play.

Armand walked up the path and onto the rickety front stoop. And then he knocked.

'What do you want?' Ruth demanded through the closed door.

'To read the play.'

'What play?'

'For God's sake, Ruth, just open the door.'

Something in his tone, perhaps the weariness, must have gotten through to her. A bolt slid back and the door opened a crack.

'Since when have you locked your door?' he asked, squeezing in.

She shut it so quickly behind him the corner of his jacket caught in the doorjamb and he had to yank it free.

'Since when have you cared?' she asked. 'What makes you think I have the play?'

'I saw you take it when you left last night.'

'Why do you want to read it?'

'I might ask you the same thing.'

'It's none of your business,' she snapped.

'And I might say the same thing.'

He saw the briefest flicker of a smile. 'All right, Clouseau. If you can find it, you can have the goddamned play.'

He shook his head and sighed. 'Just give it to me.'

'It's not here.'

'Then where is it?'

Ruth and Rosa limped to the kitchen door and pointed to her back garden. The flower beds held late-blooming roses and creamy, pink-tinged hydrangeas, and trellises on which grew bindweed.

'Blows over from your garden,' she complained. 'It's a weed, you know.'

'Invasive, rude, demanding. Soaks up all the nutrients.' He looked down at the old poet. 'Yes, we know. But we like it anyway.'

And again the smile flickered, but didn't catch. Her eyes had dropped to a large planter in the middle of the lawn.

Gamache followed her gaze, then he stepped off the porch and walked over to the planter. It was empty. Without a word, he dragged it a few paces away, then looked down at the square of fresh-turned earth. Rich and dark.

'Here.' Ruth handed him the spade.

Sinking to his knees, he dug.

Ruth and Rosa watched from their back porch.

It was a deeper hole than Gamache had expected. He turned to look at Ruth, thin and frail. And yet, she'd dug, and dug. Deep. As deep as she could. He put the shovelful of dirt on the pile behind him, and jabbed it back in.

Eventually it hit something. Brushing away the dirt, he leaned in and saw the dark printing on the bone-white page.

She Sat Down and Wept.

He stared and from the ground came the audio recording played at the trial. Screams for help. Begging. Pleading with him to stop.

'Armand?'

Reine-Marie's voice cut through the sounds, but even before he turned he knew something had happened. Something was wrong.

Holding the filthy script in one hand and the spade in the

other, he stood up and saw Reine-Marie outlined in the light of Ruth's back door.

'What is it?' he asked.

'It's Laurent. He didn't come home for dinner tonight. Evie just called to ask if he was with us.'

Gamache felt the weight of the play in his hand, drawn back to the ground. Dirt to dirt.

Laurent didn't come home.

He dropped the play.

CHAPTER 6

A fter a night of searching, his mother and father found Laurent early the next morning. In a gully. Where he'd been thrown, his bicycle nearby. The polished handlebars had caught the morning sun and the glint guided his parents to him.

The other searchers, from villages all over the Townships, were alerted by the wail.

Armand, Reine-Marie, and Henri stopped their search. Stopped calling Laurent's name. Stopped struggling through the thick brush on the side of the roads. Stopped urging Henri even deeper, ever deeper, through the brambles and burrs.

Reine-Marie turned to Armand, stricken, as though a fist had formed out of the cries. She walked into Armand's arms and held on to him, burying her face in his body. His clothing, his shoulder, his arms almost muffled her sobs.

She smelled his scent of sandalwood, mixed with a hint of rosewater. And for the first time, it didn't comfort her. So overwhelming was the sorrow. So shattering was the wail.

Henri, covered in burrs and upset by the sounds, paced the dirt road, whining and looking up at them.

Reine-Marie pulled back and wiped her face with a handkerchief. Then, on seeing the gleam in Armand's eyes, she grabbed him again. This time holding him, as he'd held her.

'I need to—' he said.

'Go,' she said. 'I'm right behind you.'

She took Henri's leash and started to run. Armand was already halfway to the corner. Sprinting, following the grief.

And then the wailing stopped.

As Armand rounded the corner, he saw Al Lepage at the bottom of the hill standing in the middle of the dirt road, staring into space.

Armand ran down the steep hill, skidding a little on the loose gravel. In the distance he saw Gabri and Olivier arriving from the opposite direction. Converging on the man.

From the underbrush he heard moaning and rhythmic rustling.

'Al?' Armand said, slowing down to stop a few paces from the large, immobile man.

Lepage gestured behind him but kept his face turned away.

Even before he looked, Gamache knew what he'd see.

Behind him he heard Reine-Marie's footsteps slow to a stop. And then he heard her moan. As one mother looked at another's nightmare. At every mother's nightmare.

And Armand looked at Al. Every father's nightmare.

In a swift, practiced glance, Armand took in the position of the bike, the ruts in the road, the broken bushes and bent grass. The placement of rocks. The stark detail imprinted itself forever in his mind.

Then Armand slid down the ditch, through the long

grass and bushes that had hidden Laurent and his bike. Behind him he could hear Olivier and Gabri speaking to Al. Offering comfort.

But Laurent's father was beyond comfort. Beyond hearing or seeing. He was senseless in a senseless world.

Evie was clinging to Laurent, her body enfolding his. Rocking him. Her mousy brown hair had escaped the elastic and fell in strands in front of her face, forming a veil. Hiding her face. Hiding his.

'Evie?' Armand whispered, kneeling beside her. 'Evelyn?' He gently, slowly, pulled back the curtain.

Gamache had been at the scene of enough accidents to know when someone was beyond help. But still he reached out and felt the boy's cold neck.

Evie's keening turned into a hum, and for a moment he thought it was Laurent. It was the same tune the boy had hummed two days earlier when Armand had driven him home.

Old man look at my life, twenty-four and there's so much more.

From behind them, up the embankment and on the road, came a gasp so loud it drowned out the humming.

One gasp, then a heave. And another heave. As Al Lepage fought for breath through a throat clogged with grief.

Under the wretched sounds, Armand heard Olivier calling for an ambulance. Others had arrived, forming a semicircle around Al. Unsure what to do with such overwhelming grief.

And then Al dropped to his knees and slowly lowered his forehead to the dirt. He brought his thick arms up over his gray head and locked his hands together until he looked like a stone, a boulder in the road.

Armand turned back to Evie. The rocking had stopped. She too had petrified. She looked like one of the bodies

58

excavated from the ruins of Pompeii, trapped forever in the moment of horror.

There was nothing Armand could do for either of them. So he did something for himself. He reached out and took Laurent's hand, holding it in both of his, unconsciously trying to warm it. He stayed with them until the ambulance came. It arrived with haste and a siren. And drove off slowly. Silently.

A little while later Reine-Marie and Armand drew the curtains of their home, to keep out the sunshine. They unplugged the phone. They carefully took the burrs off a patient Henri. Then in the dark and quiet of their living room they sat down and wept.

'I'm sorry, *patron*,' said Jean-Guy. 'I know how much you cared for him.'

'You didn't have to come down,' said Gamache, turning from the front door to walk back into their home. 'We could've spoken on the phone.'

'I wanted to bring you this personally, rather than email it.'

Gamache looked at what Jean-Guy held in his hand.

'*Merci.*'

Jean-Guy placed the manila file on the coffee table in front of the sofa.

'According to the local Sûreté, it was an accident. Laurent was riding his bike home, down the hill, and he hit a rut. You know what that road's like. They figure he was going at a good clip and the impact must've thrown him over his handlebars and into the ditch. I'm not sure if you saw the rocks nearby.'

Gamache nodded and rubbed his large hand over his face,

trying to wipe away the weariness. He and Reine-Marie had caught a few hours' sleep then gotten up to the sound of rain pelting against the windowpanes.

It was now late afternoon and Jean-Guy had driven down from Montréal with the preliminary report on Laurent's death.

'I did see them. This's fast work,' said Gamache, putting on his reading glasses and opening the file.

'Preliminary,' Jean-Guy said, joining him on the sofa.

It was pouring outside now. A chilly rain that got into the bones. A fire was lit in the hearth and embers popped and burst from the logs. But the men, heads together, were oblivious to the cheerfulness nearby.

'If you look here.' Beauvoir leaned in and pointed to a line in the police report. 'The coroner says he was gone as soon as he hit the ground. He didn't . . .'

He didn't lie there, in pain. As it got darker. And colder.

Laurent, all of nine years of age, didn't die frightened, wondering where they were.

Jean-Guy saw Gamache give one curt nod, his lips tightening. There wasn't much comfort to be found in what had happened. He'd take what he could get. As would Evie and Al, eventually. The only thing worse than losing a child was thinking that child had suffered.

'His injuries are consistent with what the police found,' said Jean-Guy. He sat back on the sofa and looked at his father-in-law. 'Why do you think it might be more than that?'

Gamache continued to read, then he looked up and over his half-moon glasses.

'Why do you think I do?'

Jean-Guy gave a thin smile and nodded toward the report. 'Your face as you read the report. You're scanning for evidence. I spent twenty years across from you, *patron*. I know that look. Why do you think I wanted to be here when you read it?' He tapped the report. 'I cared for him too, you know. Funny little guy.'

He saw Gamache smile, and nod.

'You're right,' Gamache admitted. 'I thought something was wrong from the moment we found him. All sorts of small things. And one big thing. Kids fall off bikes all the time. I can't tell you how often Annie landed headfirst. Only repeated blows to the head could explain her attraction to you.'

'*Merci.*'

'But surprisingly few die. Laurent also wore a helmet most of the time. Why not yesterday? He had it with him. It was tied to the handlebars of his bike.'

'Laurent probably wore the helmet when he left home and when he arrived where he was going. But he took it off in between, when no one was looking. Like most kids. I used to take off my tuque in the middle of winter, as soon as my mother couldn't see me. I'd rather freeze my head than look stupid. Don't say it,' Jean-Guy warned, seeing the obvious comment coming.

Gamache shook his head. 'It just wasn't right, Jean-Guy. There was something off. The trajectory, the distance he traveled. The distance his bike traveled—'

'—is all explained here.'

'In a report slapped together quickly. And then there was the position of the bike, and Laurent's body.'

Jean-Guy picked up the photographs from the police report and studied them, then handed them to Armand, who placed the pictures back in the file.

He saw that face, that body, all day long. It was burned into his memory. No need to look at it again.

'They look like they were thrown there,' said Gamache.

'*Oui*. When he hit that rut,' said Jean-Guy, trying to be patient.

'I've investigated enough accidents, Jean-Guy, to know that this does not look like one.'

'But it does, *patron*, to everyone but you.'

It was said gently, but firmly. Gamache took off his glasses and looked at Beauvoir.

'Do you think I want it to be more than an accident?' he asked.

'No. But I think sometimes our imaginations can run away with us. A combination of grief and exhaustion and guilt.'

'Guilt?'

'Okay, maybe not guilt, but I think you felt a responsibility toward the boy. You liked him and he looked up to you. And then this happens.'

Beauvoir gestured toward the photographs. 'I understand, *patron*. You want to do something and can't.'

'So I make it murder?'

'So you question,' said Jean-Guy, trying now to defuse an unexpectedly tense situation. 'That's all. But the findings are pretty clear.'

'This is too preliminary.' Gamache closed the file and pushed it away. 'They've jumped to an obvious conclusion because it's easy. They need to investigate further.'

'Why?' asked Jean-Guy.

'Because I need to be sure. They need to be sure.'

'No, I mean, let's assume for a moment this wasn't an accident. He was a kid. He wasn't violated. He wasn't tortured. Thank God. Why would someone kill him?'

'I don't know.'

Gamache did not look at the pile of dirty pages on the table by the back door where they'd sat since he'd dug them up. But he felt them there. Felt John Fleming squatting there, listening, watching.

'Sometimes there's a clear motive, sometimes it's just bad luck,' he said. 'The murderer has a plan of his own and the victim is chosen at random.'

'You think a serial killer murdered Laurent?' asked Jean-Guy, incredulous now. 'A regular murderer isn't enough?'

'Enough?' Gamache glared at the younger man. 'What do you mean by that?'

His voice, explosive at first, had dropped to a dangerous whisper, and then he recovered himself.

'I'm sorry, Jean-Guy. I know you're trying to help. I'm not making this up. I have no idea why anyone would murder Laurent. All I'm saying is that I'm not sure it was simply an accident. It might have been a hit-and-run. But there's something off.'

Gamache reopened the dossier. At the list of items found in Laurent's pocket. A small stone with a line of pyrite through it. Fool's gold. A chocolate bar. Broken. There were pine cone shards and dirt and a dog biscuit.

Then Gamache looked at the report on the boy's hands. They were scratched, dirty. The coroner found pine resin and bits of plant matter under his nails. No flesh. No blood.

No fight. If Laurent was murdered, he didn't have a chance to defend himself. Gamache was relieved by this at least. It spoke of a boy doing boy things in the last hours, minutes, of his life. Not fighting for that life, but apparently enjoying it. Right up until the end.

Gamache raised his brown eyes to Jean-Guy.

'Would you look into it?'

'Of course, *patron*. I'll come back down for the funeral and try to have some definite answers by then.'

Beauvoir thought about where to start. But there wasn't much to think about. When a child dies, where do you look first?

'You said his father wouldn't look at the boy, at his body. Is it possible . . . ?'

Gamache considered for a moment. Remembering the weathered, beaten face of Al Lepage. His back turned to his dead son and wailing wife. 'It's possible.'

'But?'

'If he killed Laurent in a fit of rage he might try to hide it, but it would be simpler, I think. He'd bury the boy somewhere. Or take the body into the woods and leave it there. Let nature do the rest. If it was murder, then someone put some thought and effort into making it look like an accident.'

'People do, of course,' said Jean-Guy. 'The best way to get away with murder is to make sure no one knows it's murder.'

They'd wandered into the kitchen and were pouring coffees. They sat at the pine table, hands cupped around the mugs.

Beauvoir missed this. The hours and hours with Chief Inspector Gamache. Poring over evidence, talking with suspects. Talking about suspects. Comparing notes. Sitting across from each other in diners and cars and crappy hotel rooms. Picking apart a case.

And now, sitting at the kitchen table in Three Pines, Inspector Beauvoir wondered if he was humoring the Chief by agreeing to investigate a case that almost certainly only existed in Gamache's imagination. Or maybe he was humoring himself.

'If it was murder, why not just bury him in the forest?' asked Jean-Guy. 'It would be almost impossible to find him. And as you said, the wolves and bears ...'

Gamache nodded.

He looked across at Jean-Guy, the younger man's brows furrowed, thinking. Following a line of reason. How often, Gamache wondered, in small fishing villages, in farmers' fields, in snowed-in cabins in the wilderness, had the two of them struggled through the intricacies of a case? Trying to find a murderer, who was desperately trying to hide?

He missed this.

Was that why he was doing it? Had he turned a little boy's tragic death into murder, for his own selfish reasons? Had he bullied Jean-Guy into seeing what didn't exist? Because he was bored? Because he missed being the great Chief Inspector Gamache?

Because he missed the applause?

Still, Jean-Guy had asked a good question. If someone had in fact murdered Laurent, why not just hide the body in the deep, dark forest? Why go through the 'accident' charade?

There was only one answer to that.

'Because he wanted Laurent to be found,' said Jean-Guy, before Gamache could say it. 'If Laurent remained missing we'd keep looking for him. We'd turn the area upside-down.'

'And we might find something the murderer didn't want us to find,' said Gamache.

'But what?' Jean-Guy asked.

'What?' Gamache repeated.

An hour later Reine-Marie returned from visiting Clara to find the two of them in the kitchen, staring into space.

She knew what that meant.

*

65

Laurent Lepage's funeral was held two days later.

The rain had stopped, the skies had cleared and the day shone bright and unexpectedly warm for September.

The minister, who did not appear to know the Lepages, did his best. He spoke of Laurent's kindness, his gentleness, his innocence.

'Who exactly are we burying?' Gabri whispered, as they got down once again to pray.

Laurent's father was invited to the front by the minister. Al walked up, dressed in an ill-fitting black suit, his hair pulled back tightly, his beard combed. He held a guitar and sat on a chair set out for him.

The guitar rested on his lap, ready. But Al just sat there, staring at the mourners. Unable to move. And then, helped by Evie, he returned to his seat in the front pew.

The interment, in the cemetery above Three Pines, was private. Just Evelyn and Alan Lepage, the minister and the people from the funeral home.

In the church basement, Laurent's teachers, classmates, neighborhood children picked at food brought by the villagers.

'Can I speak with you, *patron*?' asked Jean-Guy.

'What is it?' asked Armand when he and Jean-Guy had stepped a few paces from the group.

'We've gone over it and over it. There's no evidence it was anything other than an accident.'

Beauvoir studied the large man in front of him, trying to read his face. Was there relief there? Yes. But there was also something else.

'You're still troubled,' said Jean-Guy. 'I can show you our findings.'

'No need,' said Gamache. '*Merci.* I appreciate it.'

'But do you believe it?'

Gamache nodded slowly. 'I do.' Then he did something Beauvoir did not expect. He smiled. 'Seems Laurent wasn't the only one with a vivid imagination. Seeing things that aren't there.'

'You're not going to report an alien invasion now, are you?'

'Well, now that you mention it . . .'

Gamache tilted his head toward the buffet and Beauvoir smiled.

Ruth was pouring something from a flask into her waxed cup of punch.

'*Merci*, Jean-Guy. I appreciate what you've done.'

'Thank Lacoste. She approved it and even put a team on it. The boy died in an accident, *patron*. He fell off his bike.'

Once again Gamache nodded. They walked back to the others, passing Antoinette and Brian on the way.

Brian said hello, but Antoinette turned away.

'Still mad, I see,' said Jean-Guy.

'And it's only getting worse.'

'What're you two talking about?' asked Reine-Marie, as Armand and Jean-Guy rejoined her.

'Antoinette,' said Jean-Guy.

'She looked at me with loathing,' said Myrna.

'Me too,' said Gabri, walking over with a plate filled with apple pie while Olivier's was stacked with quinoa, cilantro, and apple salad.

'Play not going well?' asked Jean-Guy.

'Once they found out who wrote it, most of the other actors also quit,' said Gabri. 'I think Antoinette was genuinely surprised.'

Myrna was looking at Antoinette and shaking her head. 'She really doesn't seem to understand why anyone would be upset.'

'So the play's canceled?' asked Jean-Guy.

'No,' said Clara. 'That's the weird thing. She refuses to cancel it. I think Brian is now playing all the parts. She just can't accept reality.'

'Seems to be going around,' said Armand.

'You mean Laurent?' asked Olivier. 'Now there was someone whose understanding of reality was fluid.'

'Remember when he claimed there was a dinosaur in the pond?' said Gabri, laughing.

'He almost had you convinced,' said Olivier.

'Or the time he saw the three pines walking around?' asked Myrna.

'They walk all the time,' said Ruth, shoving in between Gabri and Olivier.

'Fueled by gin,' said Clara. 'Funny how that works.'

'Speaking of which, there's no gin. Someone must've drunk it all. Get some more,' she said to Myrna.

'Get your own—'

'Church,' Clara interrupted Myrna.

'We're at a child's funeral,' Olivier said to Ruth. 'There is no alcohol.'

'If there ever was an occasion to drink, this is it,' said Ruth.

She was holding Rosa in much the same way Evelyn Lepage had held Laurent. To her chest. Protectively.

'He was a strange little kid,' said Ruth. 'I liked him.'

And there was Laurent Lepage's real eulogy. Stories of his stories. Of the funny little kid with the stick, causing havoc. Creating chaos and monsters and aliens and guns and bombs and walking trees.

That was the boy they were burying.

'How many times did we look out at the village green and

see Laurent hiding behind the bench, firing his "rifle" at invaders,' asked Clara as they left the church and wandered down the dirt road into the village.

'Lobbing pine cones like they were grenades,' said Gabri.

'Bambambam.' Olivier held an imaginary machine gun and made the sounds they'd heard as Laurent engaged the enemy.

Clara tossed an imaginary grenade. 'Brrrrccch.' As it exploded.

'He was always prepared to defend the village,' said Reine-Marie.

'He was,' said Olivier.

Gamache remembered the pine cone seeds found in Laurent's pocket. He'd been on a mission to save the world. Armed to the teeth. When he died.

'I actually thought his death was no accident,' Armand confided to Myrna as the others walked ahead, across the village green. 'I thought it might be murder.'

Myrna stopped and looked at him.

'Really? Why?'

They sat on the bench in the afternoon sun.

'I'm wondering the same thing. Is it possible I've been around murder so long I see it when it doesn't exist?'

'Creating monsters,' said Myrna. 'Like Laurent.'

'Yes. Jean-Guy thinks part of me wanted it to be murder. To amuse myself.'

'I'm sure he didn't put it that way.'

'No. It's how I'm putting it.'

'And how are you answering that question?'

'I suppose there might be some truth in it. Not that I'm bored, and certainly not that homicide amuses me. It revolts me. But ...'

'Go on.'

'Thérèse Brunel was down last week and offered me the job of Superintendent overseeing the Serious Crimes and Homicide divisions.'

Myrna raised her brows. 'And?'

'The truth is, I've never felt so at peace, so at home as I do here. I don't feel any need to go back. But I feel as though I should.'

Myrna laughed. 'I know what you mean. When I quit my job as a psychologist, I felt guilty. This isn't our parents' generation, Armand. Now people have many chapters to their lives. When I stopped being a therapist I asked myself one question. What do I really want to do? Not for my friends, not for my family. Not for perfect strangers. But for me. Finally. It was my turn, my time. And this is yours, Armand. Yours and Reine-Marie's. What do you really want?'

He heard the thump of pine cones falling and stopped himself from turning to look for the funny little kid who'd thrown the 'grenades'. Kaaa-pruuuchh.

Then another one fell. And another. It was as though the three huge pines were tapping the earth. Asking it to admit Laurent. The magical kid who'd made them walk.

Armand closed his eyes and smelled fresh-cut grass and felt the sun on his upturned face.

What do I want? Gamache asked himself.

He heard, on the breeze, the first thin notes. From Neil Young's *Harvest*. Armand looked up to the small cemetery on the crest of the hill. Outlined against the clear blue afternoon sky was a large man with a guitar in his arms.

And down the hill the words drifted . . . *and there's so much more.*

CHAPTER 7

'There you are,' said Olivier, as he and Gabri sat down at the Gamaches' table in the bistro. 'We've been looking for you.'

'You can't have been looking hard,' said Reine-Marie. 'Where else would we be?'

'Home?' said Gabri.

'This isn't our home?' Gamache whispered to Reine-Marie.

'Yes it is, *mon beau*.' She patted her husband's leg reassuringly.

They were still in their clothes from the funeral, Reine-Marie in a navy blue dress and Armand in a dark gray suit, white shirt and tie. Tailored and classic.

They were not yet ready to remove the clothes, as though to do that was to remove their grief and leave Laurent behind.

Olivier and Gabri must have felt the same way. They too were still in their dark suits and ties.

Olivier waved to one of his servers and a couple of beers and a bowl of mixed nuts appeared.

Gabri and Olivier sipped their beers and stared at each other, goading each other on.

'Was there a reason you were looking for us?' Armand finally asked.

'You go,' said Gabri.

'No, you go,' said Olivier.

'It was your idea,' said Gabri.

'Please, one of you tell us,' said Armand, looking from one to the other. He was not really in the mood for twenty questions.

'It's a small thing,' said Olivier.

'Hardly worth mentioning,' said Gabri. 'We were just wondering.'

Gamache opened his eyes wide, inviting something more precise.

'It's the stick,' said Olivier at last.

'Laurent's stick,' said Gabri.

They stared at Gamache, but when he stared back blankly, Olivier took the plunge.

'At the reception when we were talking about Laurent we all remembered him with that stick of his.'

'His rifle,' said Reine-Marie.

'His rifle, his sword, his wand,' said Olivier. 'How many times did we see him roaring down the hill on his bike into Three Pines holding that stick out in front of him like a knight in battle?'

'He was a menace,' said Gabri with a smile, remembering the fearless, fearsome boy tilting at God knew what, determined to save the village and the villagers.

The Gamaches stared at Olivier and Gabri, expecting more.

'He never went anywhere without it,' said Gabri. 'We just thought maybe Al and Evie would want it back.'

'Oh, right,' said Armand. 'That's probably true.'

He wished he'd thought of that but was glad the guys had.

'The police must've picked it up,' said Olivier. 'Do you know when they'll release it? Can we get it back now?'

Armand opened his mouth to say that he imagined all of Laurent's possessions would have been returned already. But then he stopped himself. And thought, searching his memory of the Sûreté report. It said nothing about a stick, but then even had the investigators seen it on the ground they probably wouldn't have picked it up. It would look like any other tree limb.

But he also searched his own memory of the scene.

The hill, the gravel, the long grass, the bike with the helmet still tied to the handlebars. He scanned his memory but there was no stick. No limb. Just a gully and grass and a keening mother and cold child.

He got up. 'The police didn't find it. We need to go back there and look. Why don't we all change and meet back here?'

Twenty minutes later they got out of the Gamaches' car wearing slacks, sweaters, jackets and rubber boots. The four of them slid down the small embankment and started looking.

But Laurent's stick wasn't there.

Not in the gully. Not on the verge of the dirt road. It wasn't in the tall grass, or the circle of flattened grass, or along the edge of the forest.

Armand walked up to the top of the hill and stood there, imagining Laurent hurtling down it on his bike. He retraced Laurent's final moments.

Down, down, down. Laurent would have gained speed, his legs pumping, the stick almost certainly out in front. A lance in a heroic charge.

And then something happened. He'd hit a rut or a hole or a heave. What old townshippers called a cahoo.

Armand stood at a likely spot, a pothole. Had Laurent been frightened as he took flight? Gamache suspected not. The boy had probably been giddy with excitement. Maybe even shouting, 'Caaaaah-hoooo.'

He was airborne. And then he wasn't.

Blunt force trauma, it was called in the report. What the autopsy couldn't show was the ongoing trauma to everyone who loved the child.

Armand stood on the pothole and lifted his body up on tiptoes, stretching his arms out in front of him. Mimicking taking off. He imagined sailing through the air. Up, up, and then down. Into the gully.

And where would the stick have landed? Perhaps quite a distance from Laurent, released from the little hand like a javelin slicing through the air.

Reine-Marie, Olivier and Gabri followed his actions and searched in the likeliest places. And then the least likely places.

'Nothing so far,' Reine-Marie said, then looking around she noticed her husband wasn't with her. He was standing at the spot where Laurent had landed, looking at the ground. Then he turned and looked back up the hill.

'Find anything?' asked Olivier.

'No,' said Gabri, getting closer to the woods. 'Just grass and mud.' He lifted his boots and there was a sucking sound as the ground reluctantly released him.

Armand had returned to the road and walked in the opposite direction of the hill. Reine-Marie, along with Gabri and Olivier, joined him.

'No stick?' Gamache asked.

They shook their heads.

'Maybe Al and Evie picked it up,' said Olivier.

But they doubted it. It was all Laurent's parents could do to pick themselves up.

'Maybe he lost it,' said Gabri.

But they knew the only way Laurent would lose it was if he lost his hand. It was more than just a stick to Laurent.

Al Lepage came out of the barn when he heard their car drive up. He was back in his work clothes and was wiping his large hands.

'Armand.'

'Al.' The men shook hands and Reine-Marie gave him a quick embrace.

'Is Evie at home? I have a casserole.'

Al pointed to the house, and when Reine-Marie left he turned to Gamache.

'Is this a social call?'

'No, not really.'

They'd dropped Gabri and Olivier back in Three Pines and then driven to the farm. And now Armand contemplated the older man in front of him. Al Lepage looked like a paper bag that had been crumpled up before being thrown away. But for the first time, Armand really studied his face and noted not the beard or the leathered skin, but the blue, blue eyes, shaped like almonds. Laurent's eyes. And his nose. Thin and slightly too long for the face. Laurent's nose.

'I have a question for you.'

Al indicated a trough. The two men sat side by side.

'Do you have Laurent's stick?'

Al looked at him as though he'd lost his mind. 'His stick?'

'He always had it with him but we couldn't find it. We just wondered if you might have it.'

It seemed an eternity before Al answered. Armand quietly prayed that he'd say, *Yes, yes I do*. And then Armand and Reine-Marie could go home, and start the long process of remembering the boy alive and letting go of the boy dead.

'No.'

The large man didn't meet Armand's eyes, couldn't. He stared straight ahead, his almond eyes hard with the effort of not going soft. But his lips trembled and his chin dimpled.

'It would be nice to have it back,' he managed to say.

'We'll try to get it for you.'

'I made it for his birthday.'

'*Oui*.'

'Worked on it every night after he went to bed. He wanted an iPhone.'

'No he didn't,' said Armand.

'He's nine.'

Gamache nodded.

'Nine,' whispered Al Lepage.

And both men stared off, in opposite directions. Laurent's father viewing a world where nine-year-old boys died in accidents. Gamache seeing a world where even worse things happened.

'It must be there,' Al said at last. 'Where we found him. Or the cops picked it up.'

'No. We looked. And the police didn't find it either. If it isn't here at home, and it isn't where Laurent was found, then we have to find it.'

'Why?'

Gamache didn't hesitate. He knew there was never a good time for this.

76

'It could mean that Laurent might've been killed some-where else, and put in that ditch.'

Al's mouth formed the beginning of a word. *Why*, perhaps. Or, *what*. But it died there. And Gamache saw Laurent's father pack up his home, take all his possessions, and move. To that other world. Where nine-year-old boys were killed. A world where nine-year-old boys were murdered.

Armand Gamache was the moving man, the ferryman, who took him there.

And once across there was no going back.

'A stick, *patron*?' Jean-Guy Beauvoir's voice had grown shrill on the phone.

'*Oui*,' said Gamache. He stood in his living room and looked out the window, past their front porch to the village green.

He could see Clara and Myrna sitting on the bench chat-ting with Monsieur Béliveau.

'You want me to go to Chief Inspector Lacoste and say we have to reopen the investigation into Laurent Lepage's death – an investigation we only did as a personal favor to you – because a stick is missing?'

'*Oui.*'

Armand Gamache understood how Laurent must have felt when trying to convince people he'd seen a monster. Gamache hadn't yet seen the monster, but he knew it was out there. He just had to convince others.

'I know how ridiculous it sounds, Jean-Guy.'

'I don't think you do, *patron*, or you'd never have said it.'

'Please, just do it.'

'But what are we supposed to do? We've already done a thorough investigation. It was an accident.'

'It was not,' said Gamache, his voice gruff. 'And it's not just the stick. We went to the site yesterday afternoon and searched, but something else struck me. How his body was lying. If you assume, as we have, that he was riding his bike down the hill and hit a bump, he'd have flown headfirst, right?'

'Which he did. Hit his head. I'm sorry, Chief, but where's this going?'

'He was pointed in the wrong direction, Jean-Guy. Your own photos confirm it.'

'What?'

Gamache could hear Jean-Guy scrambling, and tapping on his computer to bring up the file and the photos.

Then there was silence.

'Christ,' he finally said, exhaling the word like a sigh. 'Are you sure?'

'If you go to the site you'll see immediately. Laurent could not have been heading down the hill when he fell.'

'And the other direction?'

'Is flat. He might've hit his wheel against a rock or a pot-hole and fallen, but at worst he'd have skinned a knee, maybe broken an arm. He could never have flown that far.'

'Jeez, you might be on to something. But now what?'

'If he was killed, the murderer made a huge mistake. He moved the body but left the stick. If we can find the stick, we might know where Laurent was killed.'

'And who did it,' said Beauvoir. 'But even if all this is true, how in the world are you going to find a stick in the forest?'

Gamache looked out the window and raised his eyes past the village green, past the old homes. To the woods. The forest. Hundreds of square miles radiated out from the village. With millions of sticks on the ground.

But Laurent was nine years old, and nine-year-olds, even

with bicycles, didn't travel hundreds of square miles. And they sure didn't go all that far into the forest.

If he was murdered, it was close by.

'You were playing soccer on the village green when Laurent came running into the village a few days ago.'

'Right,' said Jean-Guy.

'Which direction did he come from?'

'He came past the old train station,' said Beauvoir.

'Over the bridge,' said Gamache. 'Yes, I remember him saying that. We'll start there.'

'Why there?'

'You asked me the other day why anyone would kill a nine-year-old boy,' said Armand. 'And there're only two things I can think of. It was either for no reason except the pleasure of the killer. A psychopath. Or there was a reason.'

'But again,' said Jean-Guy. 'Why?'

'Look at Laurent,' said Armand. 'What did he do? He made up stories. All sorts of stories. All of which were in his imagination. Myrna thinks he wanted attention. The boy who cried wolf. But even he was finally telling the truth. Suppose Laurent was too.'

'About the alien invasion?'

'About the gun.'

'And the monster riding it?' asked Jean-Guy.

Armand sighed. 'He was given to exaggeration,' he admitted. 'And that's where he lost us. Had Laurent stuck to just the gun story—'

'—the gun that was bigger than any house?'

'—then we might've believed him. As it was no one even listened. We just tuned him out. He begged me to go with him and I never even considered it,' said Gamache. 'Had I gone with him . . .'

His voice trailed off. It was a realization that had been creeping up on him most of the day, but this was the first time he'd voiced it.

'I'm coming down,' said Jean-Guy.

'It's all right, I've lined up some people to search,' said Armand. 'It could take a while. We might never find it.'

'Well, what can I do?'

'Ask the coroner to reexamine the medical evidence. Ask her if it's possible the injuries were inflicted by something other than an accident.'

'*D'accord*. I'll also go over the photographs and other evidence.' Jean-Guy paused. 'You really think someone killed the kid? You know what that means?'

Armand Gamache knew exactly what it meant.

It took a certain kind of person to kill a child. Chief Inspector Gamache had tracked a few of them down in his long career. Fighting to find the murderer, but also fighting to keep his own repugnance, his own rage, at bay. Fighting to keep the thought of his own children out of an already complex and volatile mix.

That was the problem. They were the most difficult murderers to find, not simply because if they were willing to kill a child, they were willing to do anything, but also because the emotions of the family, the witnesses, the friends, the public and the investigators were heightened. Volcanic. It could obscure the truth, warp perceptions.

And that gave the murderer a huge advantage.

It was also the kind of murder that could pull a community apart. Even he, looking out the window at the villagers going about their lives, was thinking only one thing.

Was it one of them?

*

People from miles around volunteered to help scour the woods for the little boy's stick. Armand hadn't explained why they were looking, not the truth anyway. Instead he'd told people it would mean a great deal to Al and Evie to have Laurent's prized possession.

It would take two days of searching the forest before they found it. And what they found wasn't the stick. Not at first. The first thing they found was the monster.

CHAPTER 8

~

Jean-Guy Beauvoir had come down to Three Pines to help on the second day of the search.

It was mind-numbing, back-breaking, frigid work in the dark, dank forest. But none of the villagers had dropped out. They took it in rotations, two hours at a time, and just about everyone had volunteered for a stint.

'The coroner agreed it was possible Laurent's injuries were caused by being hit, rather than hitting the ground,' said Jean-Guy. 'He was a little kid, even for a nine-year-old. It wouldn't take much. It's a terrible thing, to take the life of a child.'

'Yes it is.'

'I also looked again at the photos from the scene and stopped there on my way out. You could be right.'

'*Merci*,' said Gamache, picking up a stick, examining it and tossing it behind him.

'And since you begged for my help, it was the least I could do.'

Armand smiled. 'I'm lost without you.'

Jean-Guy looked around. They could hear the shuffling of the other searchers, but couldn't see them.

'You might be lost with me.'

Decades', centuries' worth of fallen leaves had dried and decayed on the forest floor, so that as they walked it gave off a musky, woody scent that was not unpleasant.

The leaves overhead were changing, and with the bright sun on them it felt like they were walking under a massive stained-glass dome.

'Over here,' came a yell.

Gamache and Beauvoir stopped and turned in the direction of the voice.

'I've found something.'

It was Monsieur Béliveau, the grocer. He stood, tall and thin, in the middle of the woods, waving. Gamache and Beauvoir began to walk quickly, then broke into a jog.

Others, hearing the shout, also began to head over.

'Stop,' shouted Gamache, picking up speed, running between the trees, trying to get ahead of the stampede. '*Arrêtez*. Right now. Stop.'

And they did. Not all at once, but the authority in his voice eventually registered and everyone ground to a halt, scattered through the woods.

'Did you find Laurent's stick?' Beauvoir asked as he approached the grocer.

'*Non*,' said Monsieur Béliveau. 'I found that.'

'What?' demanded Antoinette. She stood deeper in the woods, Brian by her side. She was unmistakable and unmissable in a bright pink woolly sweater that was covered in dried leaves and bark. She looked like an escapee from a Dr Seuss book. On the lam from green eggs and ham.

Monsieur Béliveau was pointing at something but they couldn't see what.

'What is it?' Gamache asked quietly as he got closer.

'Can't you see it?' Monsieur Béliveau whispered. He moved his hand in a circle, but all Gamache could see was a particularly thick section of forest.

'Holy shit,' Gamache heard someone say behind him. He thought it might be Clara, but he didn't turn around. Instead Armand Gamache stopped. Then stepped back. And back again.

And tilted his head up.

'*Merde*,' he heard Jean-Guy whisper.

Then he peered at where Monsieur Béliveau was pointing. It was a small tear in the vines. And beyond that it was black.

'Do you have your flashlight?' he asked Jean-Guy, holding out his hand.

'I do, but I'm going first, *patron*.'

Beauvoir put on gloves, knelt on the ground, turned on the light, and stuck his head through the hole. Jean-Guy looked, though Gamache would never say it to his face, a bit like Winnie-the-Pooh stuck in the honey jar.

But when he came back out there was nothing childish about his expression.

'What is it?' Gamache asked.

'I'm not sure. You need to see.'

This time Beauvoir crawled all the way through the hole and disappeared. Armand followed, first telling everyone else to stay where they were. It did not seem a hard sell. As he squeezed through the opening, Gamache noticed bits of torn camouflage netting.

And then he was through into a world where there was no sun. It was dark and silent. Not even the scampering of rodents. Nothing. Except the beam from Beauvoir's flashlight.

He felt the younger man's strong grip on his arm, helping him to his feet.

Neither spoke.

Gamache stepped forward and felt a cobweb cling to his face. He brushed it aside and moved another cautious step forward.

'What is this place?' Jean-Guy asked.

'I don't know.'

Both men whispered, not wishing to disturb whatever else might be in there. But Gamache's instincts told him there was nothing else. At least, nothing living.

Jean-Guy moved the flashlight around quickly at first trying to assess their situation. Then the rapid, sweeping movements of the circle of light slowed.

It fell here and there. And then it stopped and Beauvoir leapt back, pushing into Gamache and dropping the flashlight.

'What is that?' Armand asked.

Jean-Guy stooped quickly to pick up the light. 'I don't know.'

But he did know there was something else in there with them.

Beauvoir tilted the beam up. Up. Straight up. And Armand felt his jaw go slack.

'Oh my God,' he whispered.

What he saw was unbelievable. Inconceivable.

The camouflage netting and old vines concealed a vast space. It was hollow. But not empty. Inside it was a gun. A massive artillery piece. Ten times, a hundred times bigger than anything Gamache had ever seen. Or heard of. Or thought possible.

And stretching up from the base, apparently out of the ground, was a figure.

A winged monster. Writhing.

Gamache stepped forward, then stopped as his boot fell on something.

'Jean-Guy,' he said, and motioned to the ground.

Beauvoir pointed the flashlight and there, in the circle of light, was a stick.

Word spread fast. Within minutes everyone in the village knew that something had been found.

Al and Evie Lepage had been on every shift, searching the forest for their son's stick, only taking breaks when the damp and cold got into their bones and they couldn't take it anymore.

They were in the bistro taking a rare break to warm up when Jean-Guy Beauvoir strode past on his way to the Gamache home. They followed him and were standing in the doorway when they heard his phone call to the local Sûreté detachment.

And the next call. To his own office in Montréal. Telling them to send a forensics team.

'What did you find?' Evie asked from the doorway to the study.

Al stood behind her, not allowing Beauvoir past until he told them.

'We found Laurent's stick,' said Jean-Guy. He spoke softly, gently, clearly. Confirming the worst fear. That there was a ghost in the attic, a monster under the bed, a vampire in the basement after all.

Monsters existed. Their son had been murdered by one.

'I want to see,' said Al.

He and Evie had followed Beauvoir back into the forest and now confronted Gamache. Beauvoir had gone back through the hole, to start the preliminary investigation, leaving Armand outside to make sure no one else entered.

Gabri and Olivier returned to the village, to guide the police through the woods.

'I can't let you in,' Armand said to Al and Evie. 'I'm sorry. Not yet.'

Al Lepage, always large, had grown immense with anger. His chest was out, his broad shoulders back, even his beard seemed wilder than normal.

If Armand had expected Evelyn to be the voice of reason, he'd miscalculated. While smaller than her husband, her rage was no less immense.

'Get out of my way,' she snapped, barreling into him, trying to shoulder him aside. But Armand hooked his arm around her waist and held her in place, leaning over her, whispering into her long, loose hair.

'No, Evie, please. Please. Stop.'

It was no use, he knew, trying to reason with her. Warning her she might destroy evidence. Telling her the forensics team needed to get there first.

This was not about reason but raw instinct. Something primal. She needed to stand on the spot, not where her son had died, but where he'd last lived.

And Armand needed to stop her. Stop them.

'What else is in there, Armand?' Al demanded, taking his wife's hand. 'What aren't you telling us?'

Gamache didn't answer.

'We heard Jean-Guy on the phone, calling for help,' said Al. 'He told them to bring strong flashlights and floodlights. And ladders.'

Al Lepage lifted his eyes from Armand to the wall of woody vines, intertwined, creeping into and over and through each other, creating an almost impenetrable barrier. It also created a *trompe l'oeil*, the illusion that it was simply thick brush. It looked, to anyone walking by, like more forest.

But no one simply walked by here. They were half a kilometer into the woods behind Three Pines. Only an overgrown old path was visible from the Three Pines road, and even that disappeared after a hundred meters or so.

'What's in there?' Al repeated.

Gamache looked at Laurent's parents, and at the other searchers, including Reine-Marie, all of whom had the same question.

'I can't tell you yet,' said Armand.

He saw Reine-Marie's face grow anxious.

'You don't have to tell us everything,' said Antoinette. 'Just tell us if we should be worried.'

It was a reasonable question, but he didn't have the answer. Not yet.

They heard footfalls on the dry leaves, and three men appeared between the trees. Gabri and two Sûreté officers.

'We'll take it from here,' said one of the young agents, dismissing Gabri. Then he turned to look at the villagers, who were obviously relieved to see them.

'Why are we here?' he asked. He looked around. 'Is this a joke?'

'Not at all,' said Gamache. He stepped forward and put out his hand. 'My name is Armand—'

'Did I ask your name? *Non*. I asked why my partner and I are standing in the middle of these woods.'

The young man's olive-green uniform was stiff and fresh. Not from laundering, but from lack of wear.

It might be, Gamache realized, his first day on the job. Almost certainly his first month. It was more than an hour since Beauvoir had called. They clearly had not hurried over.

The agent looked annoyed and unimpressed as he rested his hand on the hilt of his gun and had his first taste of real authority.

Gamache saw the name band on the upper left of his uniform.

Favreau.

It was familiar and then he remembered. It was the name on the report into Laurent's death. The one that concluded it had been an accident.

'We were told to come here to look into something strange.'

He looked at Gamache.

'Would that be you, *mon vieux*?' he asked, and got a snort of amusement from his partner.

'Do you have any idea—' Gabri began, but Armand waved him quiet.

'Any idea what?' asked the Sûreté agent.

'I think it's best if you all go back home,' said Armand to the other searchers. 'I take it Olivier's waiting for Chief Inspector Lacoste?'

Gabri nodded. '*Oui*. He'll show them in.'

Gamache turned to Monsieur Béliveau. 'Chief Inspector Lacoste might bring ladders, but I expect you have some too.'

'Ladders?' the grocer asked. 'Yes. My own personal one, but I can find more.'

'Ladders, Armand?' asked Reine-Marie, searching her husband's face then looking behind him.

'*Oui*. Oh, and Monsieur Béliveau, can you make them big ladders?'

'Of course,' said the grocer. An unflappable man, he now seemed slightly flapped.

'Wait a minute,' said Agent Favreau. 'What's all this about? No one leaves until we get an explanation.'

Gamache stepped closer to him. The agent backed up and put his hand on his billy club.

Gamache cocked his head to one side, taking in the movement. Then he turned away from the agents, toward the villagers who were watching with unease.

'Go on,' he said.

'Armand?' asked Reine-Marie.

'I'll be home soon.' He smiled reassuringly.

And they left, glancing back now and then to the large man and two young men, squaring off in the old-growth forest. It was hard not to get the impression of lithe young wolves closing in on a stag. Having no idea just how very dangerous a stag could be.

Laurent's parents hadn't budged and Gamache hadn't expected them to. They were now the exceptions.

Gamache returned his attention to the young men.

'You see them?' When the agents didn't respond, he continued. 'That's Evelyn and Al Lepage. They lost their son, Laurent, a few days ago. I believe you wrote up the report.'

'Yes,' said Agent Favreau. 'An accident. Ran his bike off the road. What does that have to do with this?'

'His death was no accident.' Gamache lowered his voice so that the Lepages didn't hear, yet again, what they already knew. 'He was killed here, and his body taken to that ditch. The evidence is over there.'

Gamache looked behind him.

'Where?' Agent Favreau demanded.

'It's hard to see. It's hidden under netting.'

'Show me,' said the agent, walking toward Gamache, who stepped in front of him.

'Please don't go any further,' he said, locking eyes with the young cop. 'You're in danger of destroying evidence.'

'And you're in danger of obstructing our investigation.'

'I asked you here to guard the scene until the homicide team arrives from Montréal,' said Gamache.

'You asked us here?' the agent laughed. 'We're not guests at your party. Step aside.'

'I will not,' said Gamache. 'You're not trained for this. I was with the Sûreté too. Let the experts in homicide do their jobs and you do yours.'

'Step aside or I'll knock you aside.'

He brought out his club.

Gamache's eyes widened in shock. A look the agent mistook for fear. He grinned.

'Go on, old man. Give me a reason.' He glared at Gamache.

'My God, were you trained at the academy?' Gamache demanded.

'Don't use that tone with me or you'll see how the academy taught us to deal with people who harass an officer in the course of his duty.'

'Favreau,' Agent Brassard whispered, but his colleague refused to acknowledge him.

'You'll be my first arrest. One I suspect you'll resist.'

Gamache was looking at him with such alarm that the man laughed.

'Pissing your pants, *mon vieux*? Now get out of our way.'

The agent went to walk past Gamache.

'Stop,' said Gamache, stepping in his path. 'Step back.'

And the agent, surprised by the note of authority, did.

'You're new to the job,' said Gamache. 'Am I right?'

Brassard nodded but Favreau remained still.

'I know you want to make your mark, but your job is not to bully citizens. Nor is it to collect evidence, but to guard it. You're lucky. You'll get to see how a homicide is investigated in the real world. Most agents wait years before they get that chance.' He lowered his voice. 'But to Evelyn and Alan Lepage, this isn't a case. It's their son. Their child. Never forget that.'

'Don't tell me my job,' said Favreau.

'Someone has to. Did you hear me say the boy was murdered? And your name is on the report stating it was an accident. You messed up. Your first case and you failed to investigate properly. You failed to notice the body was in the wrong position.'

He stared into the young man's eyes. Eyes that now held more than a hint of aggression.

'You're young, new to the job. Mistakes happen. And when they do, you need to learn from them. You're going to go over to that boy's parents and you're going to admit your mistake and say you're sorry. Not because I'm telling you to, but because it's the right thing to do.' His voice softened slightly and he looked at Agent Favreau with genuine concern. 'Surely someone in your life has taught you that.'

Agent Brassard, who'd been listening, made a move toward the Lepages, but Agent Favreau stopped him.

'We don't need some broken-down old cop telling us our jobs,' he said.

'I'm glad you're here, officers,' said Beauvoir, coming out from the opening in the vines. He took out his ID and showed them. 'Inspector Beauvoir, with homicide. I see you've met Monsieur Gamache.'

'We have, sir,' said Favreau. 'I was just explaining to him

the chain of command. I understand he was once with the Sûreté, so he should know better than to interfere.'

Beauvoir raised his brows. 'He was interfering?' He turned to Gamache. 'And they had to explain things to you. I suspect the process of an investigation is much the same as when you were with the Sûreté.'

'With a few fairly noticeable differences,' said Armand.

'Really? And yet it wasn't all that long ago you were the head of homicide.'

Beauvoir turned to the agents and saw Brassard's eyes widen.

'Yes,' said Beauvoir, leaning close to them. 'Ohhhh shit.'

Gamache and Beauvoir walked a few paces away from the two agents, putting their heads together to discuss what was found.

'You asshole, do you know who that is?' Agent Brassard hissed into Favreau's ear. 'That's Chief Inspector Gamache. The one who found all that corruption. Didn't you see him on the news, at the trials? At the inquiry?'

He looked over at Gamache and Beauvoir, standing side by side, heads bowed. Inspector Beauvoir was talking and the former Chief Inspector was listening, nodding.

'The former head of homicide. Former,' Favreau stressed. 'Yes, I saw him on the news. But he quit the force. He's a burnt-out case, a pathetic old man who couldn't take the pressure and retired to this shithole.'

A few paces away, Gamache heard the words, as did Beauvoir.

'Do you want me to . . . ?' Jean-Guy asked, but Gamache smiled and shook his head.

'Ignore it. Did you find something?'

Beauvoir glanced quickly over to the Lepages, who were

watching them closely. 'It was shoved into the side of the opening. I left it there for forensics.'

'What is it?'

'I think you need to see.'

Gamache followed Beauvoir back through the tear and saw what Jean-Guy had found. There, half buried under rotting leaves, was a cassette tape. Armand leaned in to read the words.

'Pete Seeger,' he said, straightening up. 'It's an old recording, obviously.' He found his glasses in his breast pocket and looked closer. 'But I don't think it's been here very long. There's some dirt, but no moss or mold.'

'My thinking too,' said Beauvoir. 'How did it get here? And who in the world still listens to cassettes? And who's Pete Seeger?'

Gamache sat back on his haunches and stared at the tape, illuminated by the flashlight. He was aware of the darkness all around, and keenly aware of what loomed behind them.

'He was a folk singer. American. Very influential in the civil rights and peace movements.'

'Ahhh,' said Jean-Guy.

Ahhh, thought Gamache.

From outside they heard familiar voices, and both men crawled out of the opening to find Chief Inspector Lacoste talking to the Lepages, offering her condolences. Behind her Olivier was just lowering a ladder to the ground, and the forensics team was organizing floodlights and ladders and unrolling thick cable for power.

Isabelle Lacoste turned to Beauvoir and Gamache, who'd magically appeared.

'Where did you two come from?' Lacoste asked.

'From there.' Beauvoir waved behind him.

'Where?'

Lacoste peered, and then her eyes widened and her face went smooth with wonder.

'What is it?' she asked.

'It's camouflage netting, overgrown.'

'What's it camouflaging?'

'I think you need to see,' said Beauvoir.

Chief Inspector Lacoste turned to Gamache. 'Would you . . . ?'

She indicated the opening, but he shook his head and smiled slightly.

'*Non, merci.* Your case. I'll head back home, if it's all right with you.'

'*Oui.* Oh, and *patron.*' Gamache paused a few paces away. Lacoste walked back to him. 'I'm sorry. I was wrong about Laurent. I should have looked more closely.'

'I know you'll find out who did this to him. That's all that matters.'

Gamache waited until she'd disappeared inside, then walked over to the two young agents.

'I know you think this is beneath you,' he said. 'And that I'm some feeble old man, but I'm begging you. Stay alert. Keep your eyes open. This is no joke. Do you understand?'

'Yessir,' said Agent Brassard.

'Agent Favreau?'

'You're not with the force anymore. You have no authority over me.'

Gamache stared into the defiant eyes. 'We'll see.'

Lacoste looked around, acclimating to the strange new environment. Inspector Beauvoir was directing the Scene of Crime and forensics teams, and once he'd set them in motion he joined her.

Together they walked over to the spot where agents were setting up a cordon of yellow police tape. Beauvoir's flighty beam played on the ground then came to rest on the stick. It was about ten feet from the entrance.

'He was killed here?' Lacoste asked.

'I think so,' said Beauvoir.

He saw her nod, then her own beam swept the ground, making larger and larger arcs, working its way outward. But Inspector Beauvoir saved her time.

The industrial lights they'd brought were just hooked up and he turned one on now, directing it straight ahead.

Isabelle Lacoste instinctively leaned away and even Beauvoir, who knew what was there, felt his heart stutter. Around them the well-choreographed activity of the Scene of Crime team stopped while the hardened agents stared.

Mon Dieu, they heard whispered, the words disappearing into the deadened space.

The gun was even more massive in this huge beam than it had appeared in the smaller light. Now they began to get the scale of the thing.

Agents pointed flashlights at it, like weapons. More floodlights were turned on. Playing over it, but not altogether capturing the enormity of it.

'He was telling the truth,' said Lacoste beneath her breath. 'My God, Laurent wasn't lying after all.'

Before them was a massive gun, a cannon, its long barrel stretching beyond the reach of their lights to disappear into the darkness.

Jean-Guy Beauvoir lowered his light until it hit the base. And there they saw a monster etched onto the metal, twisting, writhing out of the ground. Its wings were extended. Its many serpent heads coiling, entwining like the vines that had hidden it for decades.

'We're going to need more light,' said Isabelle Lacoste. 'And longer ladders.'

CHAPTER 9

—

The Lepages had parked their truck on the road by the bistro and Gamache walked them back to it.

'I'll make sure you're told everything,' he said, leaning into the window as Al started it up.

'So far we haven't been told anything,' said Evie. 'Except that they found Laurent's stick inside that thing. What was it doing there?'

'We know what it was doing there, Evie,' said Al. 'Laurent was killed there, and moved, wasn't he?'

Gamache nodded. 'Chief Inspector Lacoste and her team will know more in a few hours, but it looks that way.'

'But what was Laurent doing there?' asked Evie. 'Did he surprise someone? What's in there? Is that a meth lab or a grow op? Did he stumble into some drug operation? Why did they kill him, Armand?'

'I don't know.'

'But you do know what's in there,' said Al. 'What Laurent found.'

'I can't tell you anything more right now,' said Armand.

'You can,' said Al. 'You just choose not to. You know you're making it worse by not telling us.'

'I'm sorry,' said Armand, stepping back as Al hit the gas.

He watched the battered pickup drive around the village green, then up the road out of the village. Then he walked back home, deep in thought.

He did know all those things. But he also knew something else.

As he'd leaned into the open window of the Lepages' truck he'd seen, scattered on the console between the seats, a pile of cassette tapes.

'Where's Ruth?' Myrna never thought she'd hear herself asking that question.

'Don't know,' said Clara, looking around the crowded bistro. 'She's normally here by now.'

It was five thirty, and every chair in the place was taken. They could barely hear themselves think for the hubbub.

Clara saw Monsieur Béliveau at the door connecting Sarah's boulangerie with the bistro. He was scanning the room.

'I'll ask him if he's seen her,' said Clara, getting up and weaving her way gracefully through the room.

As she passed the tables, she caught snippets of conversation. The words were slightly different, the language changing depending on the grouping. But the sense was the same.

'*Meurtre*,' she heard in hushed tones. 'Murder.'

And then, even lower, '*Mais qui?*'

'But who?'

And then the look, the furtive scan. Taking in friends,

acquaintances, neighbors, strangers. Who would suspicion, like an ax, fall on?

Clara had always found comfort in the bistro, never more so than after losing Peter. But while still soothing, the atmosphere was closing in on her. Words she'd worked hard to exorcise from her mind appeared again. Fresh and new and powerful. 'Murder', 'blame', 'killing' crowded out the comfort.

Laurent was dead, and there was a good chance one of them did it.

'Have you seen Ruth?' Clara asked the grocer.

'*Non*, not yet. She isn't here?'

'No.'

'I have some groceries for her. I'll take them over and check on her.'

On her way back to the table Clara caught more bits of conversation.

' . . . drugs. A cartel . . . '

' . . . booze, left from Prohibition . . . '

One table was listening as a passionate man told them about Area 51, and the irrefutable evidence that aliens had landed decades ago in New Mexico. And, according to him, Québec.

'Mark my words, it's an alien spacecraft in there,' he said. 'Wasn't the kid always warning us about an invasion?'

Incredibly, the others at the table, whom Clara knew to be sensible and thoughtful people, were nodding. It seemed a more comforting explanation than that one of them had suddenly become alien, and killed a little boy.

Clara sat down next to Myrna, grim-faced.

'Have you been listening to what people are saying?' Clara asked.

'Yes. It's getting ugly. That table is ordering more and more drinks and talking about going into the woods and forcing their way into that thing we found.'

Myrna pushed her glass of red wine away. Nature, she knew, abhorred a vacuum, and these people, faced with an information vacuum, had filled it with their fears.

The line between fact and fiction, between real and imagined, was blurring. The tether holding people to civil behavior was fraying. They could see it, and hear it, and feel it coming apart.

Most of these people knew Laurent. Had children of their own. Were tired, and cold, and filled with fear and booze and not enough facts. These were good people, frightened people. Justifiably so.

Olivier bent down and placed a bowl of mixed nuts on the table. He whispered to them, 'I'm going to start cutting people off.'

'I think that's a good idea,' said Myrna.

Clara got up. 'I think Armand needs to come over. I think he's stayed away because he doesn't want to create a difficult situation, but it's beyond that now.'

Voices were raised at a table in the corner, where Gabri was explaining that they could not have more drinks.

Clara went to the bar and called the Gamache home.

'Is it true what I'm hearing, Clément?' Ruth asked, as the old grocer took a seat in her living room.

'What are you hearing?' he asked.

'That the child was murdered.'

She said the word as though it had no emotional load, contained nothing more than any other word. But her thin hands trembled and she made small, powerful fists.

'Yes.'

'And that they found something in the woods, where Laurent was killed.'

'Yes. I showed them the way in,' he said. 'The path. No one else could see it, of course. It was overgrown.'

Ruth nodded. She'd thought the memories had also been obscured, hidden under so many other events. Poems written, books published, awards won. Dinners and discussions. New neighbors. New friends. Rosa.

Years and years of rich and fertile topsoil.

But now it was back, clawing its way to the surface. The dark thing.

'What's in there, Clément? What did they do?'

The moment Armand and Reine-Marie stepped into the bistro, the turmoil died out.

A hush fell over the cheerful room, with its beamed ceiling and fieldstone fireplaces lit and welcoming, so at odds with the angry faces.

'Is there a problem?' Armand asked, his steady gaze going from familiar face to familiar face.

'Yes,' said a man standing at the back. 'We want to know what you found in the woods.'

Gabri, Olivier and their servers took advantage of the distraction to clear away drinks from the tables and put out boards of bread and cheese.

'We have a right to know,' said another patron. 'This's our home. We have kids. We need to know.'

'You're right,' said Gamache. 'You do have a right to know. You need to know. You have children and grandchildren who need protecting. One child has already been killed, we need to make sure this doesn't happen again.'

Anger dissipated as they realized he agreed with them.

'The problem is, you see,' said Armand, stepping further into the room, his voice calm and reasonable, 'it's possible one of you killed Laurent.'

Beside him, Reine-Marie whispered, 'Armand?'

But she saw his face in profile, determined. His eyes unwavering, as he looked out at the faces of his neighbors. He radiated certainty and calm.

Her gaze shifted to the patrons of the bistro. They were sober now. Quiet. His words had slammed into them, knocking the booze, knocking the anger, knocking the stuffing out of them.

A few sat down. Then more. Until they were all sitting.

Gamache took a long, deep breath. 'I'm not saying anything you haven't already figured out for yourselves. That you haven't already said to each other. You've almost certainly looked around and wondered who did it. Which of you killed a nine-year-old boy.'

And now they looked around again, lowering their eyes as they met a friend, a neighbor staring back at them.

'I know what's in those woods,' he said. 'And I could tell you, but I won't. Not because I want to hide it from you. I don't. But because it would compromise the hunt for the killer. Laurent's murderer is counting on your help. He's sitting, perhaps among us now, hoping you'll storm into the woods. He's praying you trample evidence and disrupt the investigation. A killer hides in chaos. You need to not give him that.'

'Then what should we do?' a woman asked.

'You should stay out of the woods. You should keep your children out of the woods. You should be absolutely open and honest when the investigators ask you questions. The more light thrown onto an investigation, the fewer places he can hide. Laurent was not killed by some serial killer, or some errant madman. There was purpose to this. You need to make sure you and your children don't get in his way, or in the investigators' way.'

He let that sink in, making eye contact with many of the people there.

'Reine-Marie and I are proud to be your neighbors. And your friends. We could've lived anywhere, but we chose here. Because of you.'

He took her hand and together they walked further into the silent bistro.

'May we?' he asked Clara and Myrna.

'Please,' said Clara, indicating the empty seats.

Slowly a murmur of conversation grew around them, the voices a moderate level as reason was restored. For now.

Across from her, Clara saw Armand close his eyes briefly, and take a deep breath.

'Bet you thought you left all the talk of murder behind when Armand retired from the Sûreté,' said Myrna.

'Well, we did move to Three Pines,' said Reine-Marie. 'We had our doubts.'

'*Patron*,' said Olivier, bending down to speak into Gamache's ear. 'Isabelle called from the old railway station. She'd like to speak to you.'

'Do you mind?' he asked Reine-Marie.

As he left, he heard Clara ask his wife, 'So, did he tell you what they found?'

Ruth opened her worn and dog-eared notebook to the page she'd been reading before Monsieur Béliveau arrived.

He'd gone now, back to the bistro. She'd promised to join

him there later. To put on a show of normalcy, if such a thing existed for Ruth. For Three Pines. For anyone.

She smoothed the page, thought for a moment, then read.

Well, all children are sad
but some get over it.
Count your blessings. Better than that,
buy a hat. Buy a coat or pet.

Ruth looked over at Rosa, snoring in her flannel nest. It sounded like *merdemerdemerde*. Ruth smiled.

Take up dancing to forget.

CHAPTER 10

⁓

The Sûreté Incident Room had once again been set up in what had been the railway station, before it was abandoned and put to other use. The long, low brick building across the Rivière Bella Bella from the village was the home of the Three Pines Volunteer Fire Brigade, of which Ruth Zardo was the chief, being familiar, everyone figured, with hellfire.

And now it was being put to an even more dire use.

The old railway station was alive with activity as technicians and agents set up the equipment necessary to investigate a modern murder. Desks, computers, printers, scanners. Telephone lines. Lots of those. Since the village was so deep in the valley, no high-speed internet, or even satellite signal, reached it. They had to resort to dial-up.

It was infuriating, frustrating, grindingly slow. But it was better than nothing.

Armand Gamache had just arrived and was standing in the disarray. In his late fifties now, he'd started at the Sûreté when there weren't even faxes, just teletype machines.

Isabelle Lacoste watched him and remembered being with Gamache on one of her first murder investigations.

They found themselves in a hunting camp, with a body and fingerprints, and no way to transmit the information.

Chief Inspector Gamache had taken the old telephone receiver off its cradle, unscrewed the lower section, removed the voice disc, and hooked directly into the line.

'You hot-wired the phone?' she'd asked.

'Kind of,' he'd said. And then he'd taught her how to do it.

'It must've been tough back then,' she'd said. 'When this was all you had.'

'It gave us more time to think,' he'd explained.

And then they'd sat by the woodstove, and they'd thought. And by the time the information had chugged its way back down the phone line, they'd all but solved the case.

And now she was the Chief Inspector. And she looked at all the technology being installed, in the absolute certainty it was crucial to solving the case.

But she knew differently. And Jean-Guy Beauvoir knew differently.

And the man who'd just arrived knew differently.

'Thank you for coming, sir,' she said, walking with them through the boxes and wires.

'Anytime,' said Gamache. 'How can I help?'

She indicated the conference table, set up at the far end of the old railway station.

'It's time for a think,' she said, and saw him smile.

She hesitated by the chair at the head of the conference table. This was awkward. Every other time they'd sat there, Chief Inspector Gamache had assumed that seat.

This time, though, he walked right by it and sat to her left. Leaving Inspector Beauvoir to sit on her right-hand side.

Armand Gamache knew his place. Had, in fact, chosen it.

'So, this is what we know,' said Lacoste. 'We have a massive gun hidden in the forest and a boy who was killed there and then his body moved. You knew Laurent better than we did,' Lacoste said to Gamache. 'What do you think happened?'

'Well, he obviously found the gun,' said Gamache. 'It looks like someone wanted to stop him from telling anyone about it.'

'But he'd already told lots of people,' said Jean-Guy. 'All of us, for a start. Everyone in the bistro that afternoon heard him.'

'Maybe the murderer didn't realize that,' said Gamache. 'Maybe he wasn't in the bistro when Laurent came running in.'

'So you think after he left us, he told someone else?' asked Lacoste. 'Someone who killed him to keep him quiet.'

Gamache nodded. 'It's also possible he went back there on his own and interrupted someone. Though the site seems abandoned.'

'We'll know more when forensics is done,' said Lacoste. 'But that was my impression too.'

'So where does that leave us?' asked Beauvoir.

'I think whoever killed Laurent didn't know him well,' said Gamache.

'Why do you say that?' asked Jean-Guy.

'Well, for one thing, he believed Laurent. He was a great boy but he was a fantasist. Everyone knew he made up stories, and this one was as far-fetched as all the rest. A giant gun in the woods, bigger than any house.'

'With a monster on it,' said Lacoste.

The boy, like a specter, appeared. Skinny. Covered in mud and leaves and urgency. Eyes bright. His arms stretched as wide as he could make them. Reciting his tall tale. Too tall for any of them to climb.

But someone had heard the story. And believed it.

'The killer must've known Laurent was finally telling the truth,' said Beauvoir.

'*Exactement*,' said Gamache, nodding.

'You think someone knew about the gun and kept it secret for years? Decades?' asked Lacoste.

'Might've even been guarding it,' said Beauvoir, warming to the theory. 'And then Laurent finds it. Disaster. He had to silence the boy and the only way to do that was to kill him.'

'So who knew it was there?' asked Lacoste.

'Whoever put it there in the first place,' said Gamache.

'You think whoever built that gun is still around?' asked Lacoste.

'Maybe,' said Gamache, leaning forward in his chair.

'So who else did Laurent tell?' asked Lacoste. 'Where did he go after he left us?'

'Home,' said Beauvoir, looking at Gamache. 'You drove him home.'

'I did. May I?'

Gamache indicated the evidence they'd collected. It was bagged and sitting on the table.

'*Oui*,' said Lacoste. 'It's been swabbed and fingerprinted.'

Gamache picked up the cassette tape. *The Very Best of Pete Seeger*.

Gamache read the song list. 'Where Have All the Flowers Gone?' 'Michael Row the Boat Ashore'. 'Wimoweh'. He smiled. That had been Annie's favorite song as a baby. He too was a Pete Seeger fan. Or had been until he'd spent the first year of her life listening to '*the lion sleeps tonight*'. All day and all night.

He scanned the rest of the songs. All classic folk tunes, including 'Turn! Turn! Turn!' Gamache had forgotten Seeger had written that song, based on Ecclesiastes.

'*To everything there is a season*,' he said.

'*Pardon?*' said Lacoste. 'What did you say?'

'Al Lepage has cassette tapes in his pickup truck.'

He handed her the cassette and wondered if, in driving Laurent home, he'd delivered the boy into the hands of his murderer.

'General Langelier? This is Chief Inspector Lacoste, with the Sûreté du Québec.'

'Good evening, Chief Inspector.'

There was slight censure in his voice. Clearly a late call to the armed forces base was not to his liking. She could almost see him looking at his watch and thinking that the United States had better be invading, or this call was not warranted.

It was past eight in the evening and she was alone in the Incident Room. They'd had sandwiches and drinks brought over from the bistro, and worked through dinner.

She'd sent Jean-Guy off to organize their rooms at the B and B, and was just getting the paperwork done. How often had she left Chief Inspector Gamache alone in some far-flung incident room, in a shed, a barn, an abandoned factory? A single light burning late into the night.

And now it was night. And it was her light.

Sitting back in her chair, she'd stared at the photos on her computer. Then she'd looked up a number and made the call to Canadian Forces Base Valcartier.

It was only by some bullying and veiled threats that she got through to the base commander at his home.

'How can I help you, Chief Inspector?'

'I'm investigating a homicide and need your help.'

There was a pause before the clipped voice returned.

'Is there a link to the base here in Valcartier? Is one of my soldiers involved?'

'No, sir, not that we know of. It happened in the Eastern Townships, not far from the Vermont border.'

'Then why are you calling me? I'm sure you know we're a long way from there.'

'Yes, sir. Your base is just outside Quebec City, but we've found something you might be interested in.'

'What?'

She could hear his anxiety lower and his curiosity rise.

'A huge missile launcher. I've done some research and I can't find anything even remotely like it.'

'A missile launcher? In the Townships?' General Langelier was clearly perplexed. 'We don't have an armed forces base there. Never have. What's it doing there?'

She almost laughed, but didn't. 'That's why I'm calling you. We don't know. And this is no ordinary missile launcher. As I said, it's massive.'

'Well, yes, they are,' he said. 'Are you sure that's what it is? Maybe it's some farm tool, or logging equipment.'

'I can send you a few pictures of it.'

'If you'd like.' His interest was waning.

He gave her his secure email and she knew when they'd arrived by the whispered '*Merde*' down the phone line.

There was silence as he examined them.

'Is that a person standing next to it?' Langelier asked, when he'd regained polite speech.

'*Oui.*'

'*Tabernac*,' he swore. 'Are you sure?'

111

'I took the photograph myself this afternoon. It is a missile launcher, *non*? Not a milking machine?'

'*Oui*.' He sounded distracted, lost in thought. 'I don't know what to tell you, Chief Inspector. It's not like anything I've seen before. Frankly, while it's huge, it looks like an antique, something that might've been used in the Second World War.'

'Could it be from then? Maybe something put there for defense and abandoned?'

'We don't just leave weapons scattered about in the woods,' he said. 'And the defenses were out to sea, not pointing inland. Does it work?'

'We don't know that either. That's why I'm calling you. We need help assessing this.'

'Are there missiles with it?' he asked. 'Is the weapon armed?'

'We haven't found anything, but we're looking. So far it seems to be just the launcher itself. Do you have someone you can send?'

There was a sigh down the line and she could almost imagine him scratching his head.

'Honestly, our current ballistics and heavy weaponry specialists all deal with modern weapons. ICBMs. Sophisticated systems. This looks like a dinosaur.'

Lacoste looked at the photograph on her screen. He was right. It was the literal truth. It looked like they'd unearthed some behemoth.

But why was it hidden? And who in the world had built it? What was it for?

And why was Laurent murdered to keep it secret?

'Let me think about it and I'll get back to you,' he said.

'This is, of course, confidential,' she said.

'I understand. I'll do what I can.'

She thanked him and hung up. She hadn't told him about the other thing. The etching on the base.

She steadied herself, wishing it wasn't quite so dark and quiet and solitary in the old railway station, then she put up another photo and looked at the winged monster. Even in a picture, even at a distance, it was striking. And what it struck was terror.

She stared at it and wondered why she hadn't told the commander of CFB Valcartier about the monster with the seven serpent heads. Perhaps because she remembered the boy running into the bistro. With the tale of the huge gun.

As Gamache had said, had Laurent left it at that, they might, just might, have believed him. But then he took it that next, impossible, step too far. Into the unbelievable.

Lacoste knew that General Langelier almost certainly did not fully appreciate the size of the weapon. No picture could capture it, even with the agent there for scale. She suspected he thought she was exaggerating. And she suspected the winged monster would not have helped her credibility.

Isabelle Lacoste stared at the etching. It was, she had to admit, unbelievable.

Jean-Guy Beauvoir finished unpacking his satchel, hanging shirts and slacks in the closet of the B and B, folding garments in the pine dresser, and putting toiletries in the spacious en suite.

He'd made arrangements with Gabri for Lacoste and him to stay at the B and B for as long as necessary. Gabri had put him in the room he normally had with the large bed and crisp linens and warm duvet. The wide-plank pine floors and oriental throw rugs.

He pulled the curtain back and saw the light in the window of the old train station.

The Incident Room had been sorted out. The evidence sent to the lab in Montréal. The local Sûreté detachment had agreed to provide protection for the huge gun, though no one had been very taken with the quality of agent they'd sent.

'Fresh out of the academy,' Isabelle Lacoste had remarked. 'They'll learn.'

'Perhaps.'

'We were like that once.'

'We were never like that,' Beauvoir had said. 'It's not hard to do the math, Isabelle. The Sûreté Academy has them for three years. That means these two, and everyone in their class, were recruited at the height of the corruption.'

'You think they're corrupt?'

'I think they were looking for different qualities in recruits at that time,' he'd said.

And now there's a whole class of them, he thought, opening the window and feeling the cool breeze. Several classes of them. Scattered throughout the Sûreté. Scattered through the forest.

That monstrosity was being guarded by, at best, incompetents and, at worst, agents chosen because they could be easily corrupted.

He picked up the Bible he'd found in the bookcase of his room, and flipping through it he found Ecclesiastes. He was curious about the lyrics of that Pete Seeger song.

Out the window he saw lights on at the Gamache home and imagined them sitting by the fireplace, reading.

To everything there is a season, he read.

And across the village green, at Clara's place, there was a single light.

A time to mourn, and a time to dance.

He saw the three tall spires of the pines swaying slightly in the autumn breeze. He saw two dark figures leave the bistro.

One was tall, stooped. The other had a cane and was cradling something to her chest.

The two walked slowly across the village green, past the bench, past the pond, past the trees.

As he watched, Jean-Guy saw Monsieur Béliveau accompany Ruth up to her front door. But then the grocer did something almost unheard of. He went inside.

It was getting late, but Beauvoir wasn't tired.

A time to keep silence, and a time to speak.

He called home and spoke to Annie. They discussed buying a home, someplace with a backyard, close to schools and a park. And then they just chatted about their day. He lay on the familiar bed in the B and B and knew she was lying on their bed, her feet up.

He could hear sleep in her voice and, reluctantly, he wished her *bonne nuit*, and hung up.

A time to be born, and a time to die.

His hand lingered on the receiver, and he thought about Laurent. And the Lepages. And what it must be like to have a child and then lose that child.

Putting on his dressing gown, he went downstairs and plugged his laptop into the phone lines.

He was still there when the lights went out at the bistro. He was still there when Olivier and Gabri arrived back. He was still there when every other home in Three Pines went dark, and every other person was asleep.

Jean-Guy Beauvoir was there, his face bathed in the light from his laptop, until he found what he was looking for.

Only then did he lean back, stiff and weary, to stare at the name his search had run to ground.

He placed a phone call, left a message, and then climbed the stairs and crawled under the eiderdown. And slept. Curled around the little stuffed lion he took with him whenever he knew he'd be away from home.

A time of war, and a time of peace.

'Bed and Breakfast,' the singsong voice answered the phone.

'Bonjour. My name's Rosenblatt. Michael Rosenblatt.'

'Is it about a reservation?'

'No, you called me. Something about missiles.'

Rosenblatt heard laughter down the line.

'I'm sorry,' said the man. 'You must have the wrong number. This is a bed and breakfast. No missiles here. Not even a missus.'

That much Michael Rosenblatt had figured out.

'Désolé,' he said. 'I must've taken the number down wrong.'

He hung up and checked the number, shook his head and went back to preparing his breakfast. The call that morning from his former department at McGill University had been garbled. Something about a message left at the department the night before, and old missiles.

When the phone rang half an hour later, he picked it up and heard an unfamiliar voice.

'Is this Professor Rosenblatt?' the man asked in English with a Québécois accent.

'Yes.'

'My name's Jean-Guy Beauvoir. I'm an inspector with the Sûreté du Québec. McGill University gave me your home number. I hope you don't mind.'

'The Sûreté?' he asked.

'Yes.' Beauvoir decided not to tell him he was with homicide. The professor already sounded rattled. And elderly. He didn't want another death on his hands.

'Are you the one who left the message at McGill?' Rosenblatt asked. 'I tried to call you back but the man who answered said it was a bed and breakfast.'

Beauvoir apologized.

He sounds nice, Rosenblatt thought. *Disarming.*

But the professor emeritus knew what that meant. The most dangerous people he knew were disarming. He immediately put up his defenses.

'My cell phone won't work where I am,' Inspector Beauvoir said. 'So I had to leave the main number. I'm at a B and B, investigating a crime. We've come across something in the woods. Something we can't explain.'

'Really?' Rosenblatt felt his curiosity swarming over his defenses. 'What?'

'It seems to be a big gun.'

His curiosity skidded to a halt.

'I don't deal with guns,' said Rosenblatt. 'My field is, was, physics.'

'Yes, I know. I read your paper on climate change and trajectory.'

The professor leaned forward at his kitchen table.

'Really.'

Beauvoir chose not to tell him that 'stared at' might have been a better description than 'read'. Still, his internet search the night before had yielded Rosenblatt's name, and this article, and Beauvoir had understood enough to know that this was a man who specialized in great big guns.

And he had one.

'I doubt I can help you,' said Professor Rosenblatt. 'That

paper was written twenty years ago. I'm retired. If it's a gun you've found, you might want to get in touch with a gun club.'

He heard soft laughter down the line.

'I'm afraid I haven't described it well,' Beauvoir said. 'I don't have the vocabulary, especially in English. Or in French, for that matter. I'm not talking about a shotgun or a handgun. This seems like a sort of missile launcher, but of a design I've never seen before. It's in the middle of the forest, in the Eastern Townships.'

Professor Rosenblatt leaned back, as though shoved. 'In the Townships?'

'*Oui*. It was hidden under camouflage netting and overgrown. It seems to be old,' Beauvoir went on. 'Probably been there for decades. Professor?'

The silence down the line made Jean-Guy Beauvoir wonder if it had gone dead. Or Rosenblatt had.

'I'm still here. Go on.'

Beauvoir took a deep breath, then plunged ahead. 'It's huge. Bigger than any weapon I've ever seen. Ten times, a hundred times bigger. We needed ladders to get onto it, and even they aren't long enough.'

And again, the line appeared to go dead.

'Professor?'

Beauvoir did not expect an answer. What he did expect to hear was a dial tone.

'I'm here,' said Rosenblatt. 'Is there anything on it at all that might identify it?'

'Not a serial number or a name,' Beauvoir said. 'Though it's possible we missed something. It'll take a while to go over every inch.'

Rosenblatt made a humming sound, like his brain was whirring.

'There is one thing,' Jean-Guy said.

'Yes?'

'It's not exactly an identifying mark, but it is unusual. It's a design.'

Michael Rosenblatt stood up at his kitchen table, spilling his coffee over that morning's Montréal *Gazette*.

'An etching?' he asked.

'*Oui*,' said Beauvoir, standing up slowly at his desk in the Incident Room.

'At the base?'

'*Oui*,' said Beauvoir, caution creeping into his voice.

'Is it a beast?' Rosenblatt asked, finding it difficult to breathe.

'A beast?'

'*Un monstre*.' His French wasn't very good, but it was good enough for that.

'*Oui*. A monster.'

'With seven heads.'

'*Oui*,' said Inspector Beauvoir. He sat back down at his desk in the Incident Room.

Professor Rosenblatt sat back down at his kitchen table.

'How did you know?' Beauvoir asked.

'It's a myth,' said Rosenblatt. 'At least, that's what we thought.'

'We need your help,' said Inspector Beauvoir.

'Yes, you do.'

CHAPTER 11

—

'Hello?'

Michael Rosenblatt opened the wooden door and stuck his head in, without great optimism.

This must be a mistake, he thought.

The place looked abandoned, like most of the old train stations in Québec. But the guy at the bistro had pointed him in this direction.

'*Bonjour?*' he called, louder this time.

As his eyes adjusted, he saw the outline of something large and it stopped him from going further into the gloomy building.

He peered at it. His eyes must've been playing tricks on him because it appeared to be a fire truck. Parked in the middle of an old train station. Which he'd been told was the Sûreté office. Nothing was making sense.

He turned around, unsure what to do next.

'That was fast,' said a man's voice.

From behind the fire truck came a man with his arm extended.

'Professor Rosenblatt? I'm Jean-Guy Beauvoir,' he said. 'We spoke on the phone.'

'How do you do?' said Rosenblatt, taking the strong hand.

Before him was a Sûreté officer in his late thirties. Attractive and well groomed. Slender but not thin, he gave the impression of immense suppressed energy. A slingshot about to be released.

Jean-Guy Beauvoir saw a short elderly man in a tweed jacket and bow tie. His white hair was wispy on top and his midsection was comfortably rounded.

With one soft hand, Professor Rosenblatt pushed his glasses up the bridge of his nose. With the other he clutched a battered leather satchel.

But the eyes were bright. Sharp. Assessing. Despite his appearance, there was nothing muddled, nothing befuddled about this man.

'Thank you for coming. I didn't expect you so quickly,' Beauvoir said, and turned to walk back into the old railway station.

'I don't live all that far from here.'

'Really?'

'Yes, I retired down here, though I have to say this village comes as a bit of a surprise. I've never heard of it.'

'It's difficult to find,' said Beauvoir. 'Hope you didn't have trouble.'

'I'm afraid I have no sense of direction,' said Rosenblatt, following Beauvoir. 'It's a source of some embarrassment. I suspect it undermines my credibility as a specialist in guided missiles.'

He described how he'd wandered the back roads, pulling over now and then to consult maps and his GPS. But no village called Three Pines seemed to exist. He grew more and more anxious, turning, turning, turning at random, trying this road, that dead end.

'Three Pines,' said Rosenblatt. 'Even the name sounds slightly ridiculous in an area thick with pines.'

But then, just as he was about to give up, he crested a hill, along a rutted dirt road, and put on the brakes.

There appeared below him, like an apparition, a small village. And in the very center were three tall pine trees. Waving.

He looked at his GPS. It showed him in the middle of nowhere. Literally. No where. No roads. No community. Not even a forest. Just blank. As though he'd driven off the face of the earth.

Professor Rosenblatt got out of his car. He needed to gather his thoughts, his wits, before meeting that disarming Sûreté officer. He walked over to a bench on the brow of the hill and was about to sit down when he noticed two phrases, one above the other, carved into the wood on the back.

A Brave Man in a Brave Country
Surprised by Joy

Professor Rosenblatt turned and looked at the village and noticed the people in their gardens, on their porches, walking their dogs. Stopping to chat with each other. It seemed both languid and purposeful.

He wondered who they were, that they should choose to live in the middle of nowhere. And that those phrases should mean so much to them that they were carved at the entrance to the village.

Now Michael Rosenblatt followed the Sûreté officer into the main body of the old train station, where men and women were on phones, at computers, conferring over documents. Chalkboards and corkboards were filling up with photographs and schematics. A huge map of the immediate area had been pinned to a wall.

Inspector Beauvoir walked over to a young woman at a desk.

'Chief Inspector Lacoste, this is the man I was telling you about. Professor Rosenblatt is a physicist. He specializes in ballistics and high altitude.'

'Professor Rosenblatt,' said Lacoste, getting up to greet the older man. 'High altitude? An astrophysicist?'

'Well, not quite that high,' said Rosenblatt, shaking her hand. 'Just a plain garden-variety physicist. And I'm afraid your colleague should have used the past tense. I'm an old academic.'

'Well, we have an old gun,' said Lacoste with a smile. But he could feel her assessing him. Wondering if he'd gone gaga yet. 'Inspector, would you call the Chief Inspector and see if he'd like to join us?'

'I thought you were the Chief Inspector,' said Rosenblatt. He stood gripping his briefcase and willed himself to relax.

'I am. He's the man I replaced. He retired down here.'

'So did I,' said Rosenblatt. 'A peaceful place.'

'I guess it depends where you live,' said Lacoste, taking a seat and indicating one across from her. 'There's something you need to know before we head into the woods. The site of the gun is also a crime scene. A boy was murdered there. We think he was killed because he found the gun. Someone wanted to keep its location a secret.'

'I'm sorry to hear that,' he said, sitting down. Reluctantly. He was anxious to get going.

'But you don't seem surprised,' she said, watching him closely.

'If this gun is what I think it is, it would not be the first death associated with it.'

'You're not going to tell me it's cursed,' said Isabelle Lacoste.

'No more than any gun.'

Well, he thought. Perhaps a little more. For a gun that had never been fired, it had caused a shocking number of deaths. Of which the boy was just the latest, but not, perhaps, the last.

'And what have we found?' she asked.

'I need to see it first,' he said. 'To confirm.'

'What do you suspect it is?' she pressed.

Through the mullioned windows, Professor Rosenblatt saw a man in his fifties walking over the stone bridge, toward the old train station. He was tall and more sturdy than heavy. He wore a cap and slacks and rubber boots and a warm waxed coat against the chilly September morning.

And he looked familiar.

Isabelle Lacoste turned to see who the professor was staring at with such intensity.

'That's Monsieur Gamache,' she said.

Gamache, thought Rosenblatt. Chief Inspector Gamache. Of the Sûreté.

Yes, now he placed him. From news reports.

Watching the man approach with a strong, determined step, Rosenblatt suspected Gamache was no more retired than he himself was.

They walked through the woods, following bright yellow ribbons tied to the trees. Like crumbs leading to Grandma's great big gun.

Professor Rosenblatt was not used to forests. Or fields. Or

124

lakes. Or nature of any kind. They'd walked for a few minutes and he was already tired. He skidded off another moss-covered rock and hugged a tree trunk to stop himself from falling.

'All right?' Gamache asked, reaching out to steady the older man and to pick up his briefcase, again. He'd offered to carry it but the professor had politely, but firmly, declined and took it back, again.

And so their progress through the forest became a sort of minuet, with Professor Rosenblatt lunging from tree to tree, like a drunk groping his way across a dance floor.

Lacoste and Beauvoir were now a distance ahead, almost swallowed up by the trees.

'This is not my natural habitat,' said the professor, unnecessarily. 'I prefer four walls, a computer and a plate of madeleines.'

Gamache smiled. '*Chocolatines* for me.'

'*Oui*. They'd do, in an emergency. I don't suppose . . .'

'Sadly, no,' said Gamache with a smile.

Far up ahead Rosenblatt could hear, between his raspy gasping breaths, the two officers talking. Words familiar from television shows drifted back to him.

DNA. Forensics. Blood work.

He wondered how the boy had died, though at that moment he was concentrating on not dying himself, as he huffed and wheezed and stumbled through the forest.

And then, in the gloom, Rosenblatt saw something that made his heart leap. One of the trees moved. He stopped and removed his glasses, wiping sweat from his eyes with the back of his hand.

Being a scientist, Professor Rosenblatt knew it could not possibly be a tree, walking. But he also knew that this forest contained other unbelievable things.

And then his vision adjusted, and he saw that it wasn't, of course, a tree at all, but another Sûreté officer, dressed in his moss-green uniform. And off to the side was another one.

And coming around that hill, still another.

And then his eyes adjusted some more, and focused on what it was they circled. And guarded.

He thought he was prepared, but as he stared at the towering jumble of vines in front of them all rational thought escaped and left him light-headed.

'Ready?' Isabelle Lacoste asked.

One by one they went inside. First Inspector Beauvoir, then Chief Inspector Lacoste. Then it was Professor Rosenblatt's turn.

He hesitated and realized with some surprise that he was afraid. Afraid of what he'd find. Afraid it wasn't what he thought it was. Afraid it was.

Gamache held back the thick vines at the opening so that the professor could squeeze through on his hands and knees, pushing his briefcase ahead of him.

The Sûreté officers had turned on their flashlights but they didn't provide much light. And then there was a thump and huge floodlights were turned on.

Michael Rosenblatt brought his hand to his forehead, shielding his eyes from the glare. And then his gaze traveled up. And up. And up.

And his mouth went slack. He held his breath and then released it in a long, long exhale, at the tail end of which were two words, barely audible.

'He didn't.'

And then Professor Rosenblatt dropped his briefcase.

CHAPTER 12

'My God,' Rosenblatt whispered.

But he didn't seem to Gamache, who stood beside the elderly professor, like a man who'd seen his God. Just the opposite.

'Can I go closer? Am I allowed to touch it?'

'Yes. But be careful,' said Lacoste.

He handed his briefcase, no longer all that important, to Gamache and approached the gun. Slowly, carefully. His hands out in front of him, as though worried he might scare it off.

'The main thing we need to know from you, Professor,' said Lacoste, as they followed him, 'is whether it can be fired. We'd need to disable it.'

'Yes,' said Rosenblatt, in a dream state.

He walked up to the etching, and stopped. Considering the monster. Then he laid his palms flat on it. Feeling the cold metal. Almost expecting to feel a pulse.

He leaned into it, and Gamache thought he heard a whisper, but couldn't make out the words.

Then Professor Rosenblatt stepped back. And back again. And another step. Craning his neck, dropping his head back until it could go no further. His mouth open, his eyes wide, he tried to take in the magnitude of what he was seeing. Not simply the size of the weapon, but the very fact of it.

He turned his head to look along the barrel as it disappeared into the darkness. Not even the floodlights could reach to the end.

Gamache watched as the professor closed his eyes, took a couple of deep breaths, then with one last exhale he turned to his companions.

'I need to find the firing chamber, to see if it's armed.'

He was all business now.

'It'll be around here,' he said, walking to the rear of the gun. 'Did you open this?'

He pointed to a round metal door, large enough to walk into.

'We tried, but couldn't make it open,' said Lacoste. 'We stopped, afraid we might inadvertently fire it.'

Professor Rosenblatt was nodding. 'You wouldn't have. The firing mechanism is somewhere else. This is the breech. If there's a missile, it would be in here.'

They watched as the professor ran his hands over the latches and handles and knobs.

'Careful,' warned Beauvoir, but Rosenblatt didn't respond. He was too focused on the mechanism.

'Do we know for sure he knows what he's doing?' Lacoste asked Beauvoir.

Before Beauvoir could answer, they saw the professor reach out and grasp a lever. Leaning into it, the elderly man pulled but nothing happened.

'I need help,' he said. 'It's stuck.'

Beauvoir joined him, and between them they pulled and pulled until it gave with such suddenness both men leapt back.

There was a whirring, grinding sound, then a loud hiss.

Gamache tensed. Afraid Rosenblatt had just set it off, but not at all sure what to do if he had.

Then the massive door swung open, like a mouth. Like a maw. Inviting them in.

The four of them stared. Gamache could hear heavy breathing and knew it came from Jean-Guy. Not because the effort had winded him, but because he was staring into his nightmare.

While Gamache was afraid of heights, Beauvoir was terrified of holes. Armand stepped over to him.

'Stay here,' he said. 'If the door closes, please open it again.'

Beauvoir didn't answer, but continued to stare.

'Do you need to write that down?' asked Gamache.

'Huh? *Pardon?*' said Jean-Guy, coming out of his reverie. 'Right. Wait, are you going in there?'

He waved to the opening, where Professor Rosenblatt was already standing.

'I am. And if we need to climb up on the thing?'

'I'll go,' said Beauvoir, with a smile.

'You'd better.'

Gamache followed Rosenblatt and Lacoste into the chamber.

In the beams of their flashlights, Gamache could see the professor's face. His eyes. Bright, but not overexcited. He seemed almost calm, in control.

This was his natural environment. The belly of the beast. This was where the little professor belonged.

'Incredible,' Rosenblatt murmured, shaking his head. 'No electronics.' He looked back at his companions. 'It's like a Meccano set.'

'But is it armed?' asked Lacoste. She was beginning to get antsy. She'd never suffered from claustrophobia, but then she'd never been crammed into the firing chamber of a giant weapon with two other people before.

'No,' said Rosenblatt, and pointed toward the great long tube stretching out in front of them.

Rosenblatt was studying the wall of the borehole.

'Empty. There's never even been a missile in here. It's unmarked.'

Gamache reached out and touched the side. It felt slightly greasy.

'It's been prepared,' he said.

Rosenblatt looked at him and nodded. 'You know guns.'

'Sadly, yes,' said Gamache. 'We all do. But never anything like this.'

'No one has known anything like this,' said Rosenblatt, and even by the limited beam of the flashlight Gamache could see the wonder in the professor's eyes.

'Can it be fired?' Lacoste asked.

'I need to find the firing mechanism before I can answer and for that, we need to leave.'

He did not need to say it twice. Lacoste was out in a flash, following the professor around to the side of the machine.

'That's interesting. The trigger should be here.' He placed his fist in a large hole. 'But it's missing.'

'Maybe it's somewhere else,' Beauvoir suggested.

'No, it would have to be here, given the configuration inside.'

He looked behind him, toward the back wall of the camouflage netting, and shook his head.

'But the main thing is,' said Lacoste, 'it isn't armed, and even if it was, it can't be fired.'

'Not without the mechanism, no.'

'What would it look like?' Gamache asked.

'The trigger would have cogs that fit onto this wheel.' The professor pointed to a circle with teeth, about a foot wide. 'There's nothing electronic on this thing. Not even the guidance system. It's all done manually.'

'Could it have fallen off?' asked Beauvoir, looking on the ground.

'This isn't a LEGO set. Things don't just fall off. It's intricate, perfectly made. Each piece fits snugly, exactly.'

'So, no?' said Beauvoir.

'No,' said Rosenblatt. 'If it's gone, someone took it, and by the looks of it, not recently. I need to see the etching again.'

The elderly man spoke with determination and Gamache realized that while he was afraid of heights, and Beauvoir was afraid of confined spaces, Professor Michael Rosenblatt was afraid of the etching.

They walked back to it, and Rosenblatt stepped back, taking in the winged monster as it reared and bucked. Its seven heads were straining, its long necks intertwining like serpents. There was a woman on its back, holding reins. Controlling the beast. She stared out at them, a strange expression on her face. It wasn't wrath, thought Gamache. It wasn't vengeance or blood lust. It was more sinister. Something Gamache couldn't quite define.

Professor Rosenblatt whispered under his breath.

'What did you say?' asked Gamache, who was closest to the scientist.

Rosenblatt pointed to what looked like scales on the monster's body.

Gamache stepped closer, then, putting on his glasses, he bent in. Straightening up, he looked at the professor.

'Hebrew?'

'Yes. Can you read it?' asked Rosenblatt.

'No, I'm afraid not.'

Rosenblatt looked again at the creature. At the detailing, which was not scales at all, but words. And he read, out loud.

"עַל נַהֲרוֹת בָּבֶל—שָׁם יָשַׁבְנוּ, גַּם בָּכִינוּ."

Then he turned to his companions in this dark place. He looked both triumphant and terrified. As though his worst fear and greatest wish were one and the same. And had come true.

'By the waters of Babylon,' he said, *'we sat down and wept.'*

The blood rushed from Gamache's face. In front of him the gun glowed, unnaturally, supernaturally, in the flood-lights. Shadows were thrown on the canopy, a false sky above, a grotesque constellation.

'Now,' said Professor Rosenblatt, 'I can tell you what this is.'

They sat in the living room of the Gamache home, around the fireplace where flames leapt and danced and threw cheerful light on the somber faces.

It had been cold in the forest, and the decision was made to return to someplace warm. And private.

They sat with mugs of tea, warm and comforting, and plates of madeleines Armand had picked up at Sarah's bou-langerie as they'd passed by.

'What you've found,' said Professor Rosenblatt, 'is Project Babylon. When we spoke this morning and you described it, I barely believed you. Project Babylon is a tale physicists told to scare each other. It's a Grimms' tale for scientists.'

He took a deep breath and tried to cover his discomfort by reaching for another pastry. But his unsteady hand betrayed him.

Gamache couldn't decide if the tremble was caused by fear or excitement.

'What you have is a Supergun. No, not "a" Supergun, it's "the" Supergun. The only one of its kind. Within the armaments community it's a sort of legend. For years we'd heard rumors that it'd been built. Some people tried to find it, but gave up. Then the talk died away, as time passed.'

'When you first saw it,' said Gamache, 'you whispered, "He didn't." Who did you mean?'

Armand leaned forward, forearms on his knees, his large hands forming a sort of bow in front of him. Like a ship plowing through the seas.

'I meant Gerald Bull,' said Rosenblatt, and seemed to expect some sort of reaction. A gasp, perhaps. But there was nothing beyond rapt attention.

'Gerald Bull?' Rosenblatt repeated, looking from one to the other to the other.

They shook their heads.

'*Look on my works, ye Mighty*,' said Rosenblatt as he drew his battered leather briefcase toward him. '*And despair.*'

'Oh no,' sighed Beauvoir. 'Now we have two of them.'

'"Ozymandias",' said Gamache, looking at Jean-Guy with despair. 'The professor was quoting a sonnet by Shelley—'

'—of course he was.'

'—that speaks of arrogance, of hubris. A king who thought his achievements would stand for thousands of years, but all that remained of him was a broken statue in the desert.'

'And yet he was finally immortalized,' said Rosenblatt. 'Not because of his power, but because of a poem.'

Beauvoir looked about to say something smart-ass, but stopped. And thought.

'Who was Gerald Bull?' he finally asked.

Professor Rosenblatt had unbuckled the briefcase and, after sorting through the contents, brought out some papers.

'I found these in my files after we spoke. I thought they might be needed.'

He put the papers, held together by a staple, on the coffee table.

'This is Dr Bull.'

Isabelle Lacoste picked them up. What the professor had brought was yellowed and typewritten. There was also a grainy black-and-white photograph of a man in a suit and narrow tie, looking put upon.

'He was an armaments engineer,' said Rosenblatt. 'Depending on who you speak to, Dr Bull was either a visionary or an amoral arms dealer. Either way, he was a brilliant designer.'

'He made that thing in the woods?' asked Lacoste.

'I think so, yes. I think it was part of what he called Project Babylon. His goal was to design and build a gun so powerful it could launch a missile into low Earth orbit, like a satellite. From there it would travel thousands of miles to its target.'

'But don't those exist?' asked Beauvoir. 'ICBMs?'

'Yes, but the Supergun is different,' said Rosenblatt.

'The Meccano set,' said Lacoste. 'No electronics.'

'Exactly.' The professor beamed at her. 'No computer guidance systems. Nothing that depends on software or even electricity. Just good old-fashioned armaments, not that far off the artillery used in the First World War.'

'But why was that such an achievement?' asked Gamache. 'It sounds like a step back, not forward. As Inspector

134

Beauvoir says, if there're ICBMs that can send nuclear warheads thousands of miles accurately, why would anyone want or need Gerald Bull's Supergun?'

'Think about it,' said Rosenblatt.

They did, but nothing came to mind.

'You're too mired in the present, in thinking that newer must be better,' he said. 'But part of Gerald Bull's genius was recognizing that ancient design could not only work, but in some cases, work better.'

'Did he also build a giant slingshot?' asked Beauvoir. 'Should we be looking for one of those?'

'Think,' said Rosenblatt.

Gamache thought, and then he looked around their home. At the useless smartphone on the desk in the study. At the dial-up connection that barely worked.

He looked at the crackling fireplace, feeling its heat, and he thought about the woodstove in the kitchen. In Clara's kitchen. In Myrna's bookstore.

If the power went out they'd still have warmth and light. They could still cook. No thanks to modern technology. That would be rendered useless, but they'd have power because of old, even ancient, tools. Woodstoves. Wells.

Three Pines might be primitive in many ways, but unlike the outside world, it could survive a very long time without power. And that itself was powerful.

'The weapon needs no power source,' said Gamache slowly. Coming to the realization, and the implication. 'It can send a missile into orbit without even a battery.'

Professor Rosenblatt was nodding. 'That's it. The brilliance and the nightmare.'

'Why nightmare?' asked Beauvoir.

'Because Dr Bull's Supergun meant any terrorist cell, any

135

extremist, any crazy dictator could become an international threat,' said the scientist. 'They didn't need technology, or scientists, or even electricity. All they'd need was the Supergun.'

He let that sink in, and as it did even the cheery fireplace couldn't take the chill out of the room, or wipe the alarm from their faces.

'But maybe he didn't do it,' said Lacoste. 'Maybe he wasn't successful. Maybe Bull abandoned it because it doesn't work.'

'No,' said Professor Rosenblatt. 'He abandoned it because he was killed.'

They stared at him.

'How?' asked Gamache.

'He was murdered in 1990. Some describe it as an assassination. He was living in Brussels at the time. Five bullets to the head.'

'Professional,' said Lacoste.

Rosenblatt nodded. 'The killers were never caught.'

Gamache's eyes narrowed in concentration.

'I seem to remember this,' he said. 'Gerald Bull was a Quebecker—'

'Actually, he was born in Ontario and studied at Queen's University. It's all in there.' Rosenblatt waved at the papers he'd brought them. 'But he did much of his work here in Quebec. At least, at first.'

'Did you know him?' asked Gamache.

'Not really. He was at McGill for a short while. Considered a bit of a crank. Difficult.'

'Unlike physicists?' asked Gamache, and saw Rosenblatt smile.

'I'm afraid I'm not brilliant enough to be difficult,' he said. 'That's reserved for geniuses. I was just an academic, teaching students about trajectory. Or trying to. When sophisticated systems came in, students realized they didn't really have to know these things. Computer programs would do it all for them. I might as well have been using a slide rule and an abacus.'

'Dr Bull never came to you for advice?' Gamache prodded.

Now Rosenblatt laughed outright. 'Advice? Gerald Bull? No. And he wouldn't have come to me anyway. I was much too lowly.'

The two men regarded each other before Gamache finally smiled and dropped his eyes. But Michael Rosenblatt took warning, and wondered if he might have just overdone it.

'The chatter after he'd died was that Bull had in fact built the Supergun,' said Rosenblatt. 'And it was ready to be tested. But no one knew where it was. And it was all just gossip. People like drama but no one really believes it.'

'Why was he killed?' Beauvoir asked.

'No one knows for sure, of course,' said Rosenblatt. 'The assumption was he was killed to stop him from building the gun.'

'*By the waters of Babylon*,' Gamache quoted, his eyes on the elderly scientist, '*we sat down and wept*. There's more to tell, Professor. We'll find out eventually, you know. Why was that etching, the beast, carved into the gun? Why did Gerald Bull put it there? And why that quote?'

Professor Rosenblatt looked around in a glance that would have been ludicrously furtive had they not been talking about a gun whose very existence had killed at least two people. Its maker and Laurent. And whose intent was to kill far more.

Michael Rosenblatt realized, too late, that he had vastly underestimated all three of them. And certainly Gamache. It was true, they would find out eventually.

But perhaps, he thought, his mind racing, not everything.

He might as well tell them. But perhaps, he thought, not everything.

'Gerald Bull was a Renaissance man,' he said, and heard Beauvoir snort. He turned to the Inspector. 'The Renaissance created amazing works of art, of innovation. But it was also a brutal time. I'm not unaware of the fact that this is a weapon.'

'Of mass destruction,' said Gamache, who was also having none of this glorification of an arms designer, an arms dealer.

Professor Rosenblatt studied him to see if there was any other agenda, anything else behind the exact words Gamache had just chosen. But there didn't seem to be.

'True. But he was also a classicist. A man who loved music and art and history. Dr Bull knew perfectly well what he was building. Stories circulated within the armaments community that he'd not only built the Supergun, but carved a seven-headed beast on it, as a reference to the Book of Revelation.'

He looked at them. Isabelle Lacoste was thinking, trying to remember her Bible classes as a child. Beauvoir shook his head impatiently. And Gamache just stared in a way the professor found disconcerting.

'The Whore of Babylon?' said Rosenblatt.

'Just tell us,' said Beauvoir, his patience at an end.

The professor took out his iPhone, punched at the screen, then put it on the table. Beside the golden madeleines glowed the image of a monster rearing up with seven heads on long serpentine necks springing from the body.

And riding the monster was a woman, not looking out to where the beast was taking her, but staring back at whoever was staring at her.

'Who's the Whore of Babylon supposed to be?' Beauvoir demanded.

Professor Rosenblatt was about to answer, but then turned to Gamache. 'I think you know.'

Gamache hadn't taken his eyes off the image. 'The Antichrist.'

Beauvoir sputtered in amusement. 'Oh, come on,' he said, his handsome lean face breaking into deep lines of laughter. 'Really?'

He looked at them, his eyes finally resting on the elderly scientist.

'Are you seriously saying that thing in the forest is the devil?'

'I'm not saying that, but you asked about the Whore of Babylon and that's the answer. You can look it up yourselves or ask any biblical scholar. There're all sorts of interpretations about what the beast and the seven heads represent, but most come to the same conclusion. She's heading for Armageddon.'

'As was Gerald Bull,' said Lacoste. 'In building the Supergun he was courting the end of the world.'

'Well now,' said Rosenblatt. He looked down at his feet, then up at her. 'The community is divided on that. Many, probably most, think Dr Bull was a mercenary. An arms dealer. A one-stop shop. He'd design, build and sell any weapon to the highest bidder.'

'And the others?' asked Gamache. 'The minority?'

'They think Dr Bull was a hero. That he was very clear

about why he was building the Supergun, and who he was making it for. They believe he carved the beast on it as a sort of gesture. Like pilots in the Second World War often painted frightening images on their planes.'

'He called it Project Babylon,' said Gamache. 'Why?'

'Who was the devil in the late 1980s?' Rosenblatt asked.

'The Soviet Union,' said Lacoste, remembering her history.

'The Cold War was waning,' said Gamache. 'Yeltsin and President Gorbachev were bringing in glasnost.'

'Exactly,' said Rosenblatt. 'But there was someone else. An ally who was fast becoming an enemy. A wolf in sheep's clothing, to use another biblical image.'

'Babylon?' said Gamache. 'Are you saying Gerald Bull built that thing for Saddam Hussein?'

He didn't even try to keep the incredulity out of his voice, and he could only imagine the look on Jean-Guy's face.

'You don't believe it?' asked Professor Rosenblatt. The words fell into the silence in the room and drifted into the fireplace, to be burned.

'Would you?' asked Isabelle Lacoste, regarding the elderly man and wondering just how crazy he might be. The gun itself was hard enough to swallow, but she could at least see it, touch it. She knew it was real. But this was a step too far.

'I don't suppose it really matters if you believe it or not,' said Rosenblatt, gathering up his papers. 'You asked me here to tell you what I know. That's what I know.'

He got up and Gamache rose with him.

'You didn't believe the boy either,' said Rosenblatt quietly. 'And look what happened.'

Gamache felt himself go numb, for a moment. As though

140

the life had been snuffed out of him. And then he took a breath and sat back down.

'Please,' he said, indicating the seat beside him. Professor Rosenblatt hesitated, then took his seat again. 'Tell us what you know about Project Babylon and Gerald Bull.'

Professor Rosenblatt looked at them, still seeing disbelief, but now also seeing a willingness to try. To be open to the possibility that what he was about to tell them was the truth.

'It was no secret that Saddam wanted to destroy Israel,' said Rosenblatt. 'And start a full-scale war. He wanted to control the whole region.'

Gamache nodded, remembering the late 1980s, early nineties. To Beauvoir and Lacoste it was history. To him, and Rosenblatt, it was a memory.

'To be fair, there are all sorts of theories about Project Babylon,' said Rosenblatt. 'Some more outlandish than others.'

No one looked at Beauvoir who, with a mighty effort, was keeping his mouth shut.

'Some even believed Dr Bull was building the Supergun for the Israelis. To hit Iraq first. They're pragmatists. They believe in God, but how do you fight the devil? With prayers? Well, Gerald Bull was the answer to a prayer.'

'But the Israelis have all sorts of sophisticated weapons,' said Lacoste. 'Why would they need the Supergun?'

'They wouldn't,' said Gamache. 'But Saddam Hussein would.'

Across from him, Armand saw Beauvoir's brows come together as logic began to penetrate disbelief.

'Yes,' said the scientist. 'A weapon of mass destruction that could be assembled anywhere, the middle of a desert, for instance. Without need of electronics or expertise.'

'How would the missiles be aimed?' Gamache asked, remembering images of Israeli citizens wearing gas masks and huddling in their homes as the sirens wailed during the Gulf War.

'There's a guidance system,' said Professor Rosenblatt. 'But without electronics it's difficult to be completely accurate, especially at a distance. It's the one possible flaw in Bull's design.'

'Flaw?' asked Gamache. 'I'd call it more than that, wouldn't you?'

The professor, under the sharp gaze, reddened.

'And that means?' Gamache pushed.

'It means from a distance the Supergun could not be guaranteed to hit just military targets.'

'It means more than that,' said Gamache. 'It was never designed to hit military targets, was it?'

'Then what was it designed to hit?' asked Lacoste.

'Cities,' said Gamache. 'The biggest, crudest bull's-eye. It was meant to destroy Tel Aviv and Jerusalem. It was designed to kill men, women, children. Teachers, bartenders, bus drivers. It was meant to wipe them out. To bomb Israel back to the Stone Age.'

'Or Baghdad to the Stone Age,' said Lacoste. 'If the buyer was Israel. After all, that inscription on the etching was in Hebrew.'

Beauvoir had been quiet, except the initial grunts as he fought to keep scathing comments in.

'What are you thinking?' Armand asked him.

'I'm thinking about Armageddon,' he said.

'The movie?' asked Lacoste, and saw him smile.

'*Non.* If that thing in the woods works, this Bull fellow made a gun that would fling a missile into orbit with the intention, the hope, of wiping out entire cities. Anywhere.'

Professor Rosenblatt nodded. 'Anywhere.'

It was now clear who the real monster was. Not the Whore of Babylon, not even the Supergun. But the man who had made them.

Gamache and Beauvoir left the house a few paces behind Lacoste and the professor.

Rosenblatt was heading home to pack a few things and return to the B and B, to be on hand to help. Lacoste and Beauvoir were going back to the Incident Room, to see if the forensics reports were in. And Gamache was going to join Reine-Marie at the bistro.

Beauvoir fell in beside Gamache.

'Do you believe him?' asked Beauvoir. 'About the Iraqis?'

He was unconsciously mimicking Gamache by clasping his hands behind his back and falling into the rhythm of his walk.

'I'm not sure,' said Gamache.

'Well, even if it's true, it can't possibly matter anymore. The intended target, or buyer, is long gone. Saddam Hussein was executed years ago. Any danger is long gone.'

'Hmmm' came from Gamache.

'What is it?'

'Someone killed Laurent to keep the gun a secret,' Gamache reminded him. 'I think the danger might've been dormant.'

They walked for a few more paces in silence.

'But now it's back,' said Jean-Guy.

'Hmmm,' said Gamache again. Then after a few more paces, 'Did you notice where that gun is pointed?'

Beauvoir stopped then and looked toward the stone bridge and the forest.

'It's not pointing to Baghdad, that's for sure,' said Beauvoir.

'No. It's pointing south. Into the United States.'

Beauvoir turned to stare at Gamache, who was watching the elderly scientist get into his car.

'I wonder what Project Babylon was really about,' said Gamache. 'And if it really died with Gerald Bull.'

CHAPTER 13

As Chief Inspector Lacoste approached the old railway station, she noticed a nondescript car parked off to the side.

A man and woman were sitting in the front seat, and as the doors opened her heart sank.

Journalists, she thought. Much as a doctor might think, plague. But the thought was fleeting, disappearing as soon as she got a good look at them.

'Chief Inspector Lacoste?' the woman asked, after inelegantly slinging a large cloth handbag over her shoulder.

'*Oui.*'

'Oh good. We wondered if we had the wrong place.'

She looked so relieved that Isabelle was relieved for her.

'I told you I knew where we were going,' said the man. 'Not a wrong turn all the way down.'

'Which is why you're the navigator,' said the woman.

'No. I'm the navigator because you insist on driving.'

'Only after—'

The woman put up her hands and whispered to the man, loudly enough for Lacoste to hear it, 'We can talk about this later.'

Isabelle Lacoste, far from being put out, almost smiled. These two reminded her of her parents, and were about the same age. Mid-fifties, she guessed. Sensibly, if unimaginatively, dressed. The woman wore a cloth coat of decent cut, though slightly baggy, while the man had on a raincoat, with the lightest dusting of doughnut sugar down the front.

The woman's hair was obviously dyed at home, and due for another treatment. And the man's hair was combed over, in an attempt to hide what could not be hidden.

'My name's Mary Fraser.' Her hand, extended in greeting, revealed chipped nail polish. 'This is my colleague, Sean Delorme.'

He smiled and shook hands. His cuticles were nibbled and torn.

'We're from CSIS,' she said cheerfully.

Had Mary Fraser said they were from the moon it would have been more believable. Isabelle Lacoste tried not to show her surprise.

'Are we supposed to tell her that?' Sean Delorme asked, averting his face from Lacoste and putting his hand to his mouth. Again, trying to hide the obvious.

'What else are we going to say?' whispered Madame Fraser. 'That we're tourists?'

'Okay, but we should have consulted.'

'We had the whole drive down—'

Now it was the man's turn to put up his hand to stop the bickering.

'We can talk about this later,' he said. 'But if we get into trouble, it's your fault.'

They spoke to each other in English but had spoken to Lacoste in heavily accented, textbook good, French.

Perhaps, thought Lacoste, they didn't think she spoke English. She decided not to disabuse them of that thought.

'*Un plaisir*,' she said, shaking their hands. 'CSIS, you say? The Canadian Security Intelligence Service?'

She had to be sure. If two people looked less like spies, and even less like intelligence agents, it was these two.

The man, Sean Delorme, looked around, then leaned closer to Lacoste. 'Can we talk privately?'

His eyes darted around, as though they were in Berlin in 1939 and he had the codes.

'Of course,' said Lacoste, and unlocking the door into the Incident Room, she led them inside just as Beauvoir arrived.

Lacoste made the introductions.

Like her, Beauvoir looked at them and asked, obviously needing to clarify, 'CSIS? The spy agency?'

'We prefer intelligence,' said Mary Fraser, but she didn't seem displeased to be called a spy.

'What brings you here?' asked Lacoste, taking them over to the conference table.

'Well,' said Delorme, dropping his voice to barely above a whisper. 'We heard about the gun.'

Lacoste half expected him to tap the side of his nose.

'You'll have to forgive Monsieur Delorme,' said Mary Fraser, giving her colleague a filthy look. 'We're not often allowed out of the office.'

Now he gave her an equally filthy look.

'Where is your office?' asked Lacoste.

'Ottawa,' said Ms Fraser. 'We're at headquarters.'

'May I see your identification?' asked Beauvoir.

Delighted by the request, they were completely oblivious to the possible insult.

They brought out their wallets but had trouble getting

their laminated ID cards out. Mary Fraser was even having trouble finding hers.

As the two squabbled, Jean-Guy and Isabelle exchanged a grimace. Ottawa, and CSIS, could not have thought much of the find in the woods if this is what they sent.

Finally they handed the ID cards over to Beauvoir and Lacoste, who confirmed the two smiling middle-aged people across the conference table were Canadian intelligence agents.

'How did you hear about the gun?' Lacoste asked, sliding the cards back.

'Our boss told us,' said Delorme.

'How did he hear?' she tried again.

'I don't really know.' Delorme looked at Ms Fraser, who shook her head.

'Frankly, we just do as we're told, and we were told to come here to look at the gun.'

Almost certainly this was the result of General Langelier 'thinking about it', thought Lacoste. He must've called someone in National Defence, who called CSIS, who sent it down the line until they ran out of line and came to these two.

'Why you?' asked Beauvoir. 'Not that we aren't thrilled to have you.'

'You know,' said Ms Fraser. 'We were wondering the same thing. We work in the same section, Sean and I. Have for years. Mostly filing.'

'But some fieldwork,' Delorme jumped in.

'Putting records on computer. Cross-referencing,' she said. 'Seeing if any connections were missed. We're quite good at that.'

'We are,' he admitted. 'We see things others don't.'

'Best not to tell them we see things,' she said, and Delorme laughed.

'Well,' said Lacoste, warming to them. 'I imagine you'd like to see the gun.'

She sounded to her own ears like a 1950s housewife discreetly offering to show guests the facilities.

'Do you wish you were out there?' Reine-Marie asked, as her husband took a bite of the maple-smoked ham, apple and Brie sandwich, on a *pain de campagne*.

He looked out the bistro window, toward the stone bridge.

'You mean in the damp, cold woods at a crime scene?'

'Yes.'

'A little.'

'Monsieur Gamache,' said Reine-Marie, 'you're crazier than even my mother thought.'

'Your mother loved me.'

'Only because you made her own children look sane. Except Alphonse, of course. He really is nuts.'

Henri was curled under their bistro table. The shepherd's head, resting on Armand's shoes, was smattered with flakes of crusty bread.

'Isabelle's doing a good job?' Reine-Marie asked.

'Not just a good job, a remarkable job. She's completely taken control of the department. Made it her own.'

Reine-Marie watched him for signs of regret hiding beneath the obvious relief. But there was only admiration there for his young protégée.

'Jean-Guy seems to be accepting her as his boss,' she said, buttering a piece of fresh baguette from the basket that came with her parsnip and apple soup.

'I think it's still a bit of a struggle,' said Armand. 'But he at least respects Isabelle and knows he couldn't possibly be made Chief Inspector, after what happened.'

'You mean after he shot you?' Reine-Marie asked.

'That didn't help,' Armand admitted. He picked up his sandwich again, then put it down. 'I was threatened yesterday by a young agent.'

'I saw him put his hand on his billy club,' said Reine-Marie, lowering her spoon.

Armand nodded. 'Fresh out of the academy. He knew I was once a cop and he didn't care. If he'd treat a former cop like that, how's he going to treat citizens?'

'You look shaken.'

'I am. I'd hoped by getting rid of the corruption the worst was over, but now . . . ' He shrugged and smiled thinly. 'Is he alone, or is there a whole class of thugs entering the Sûreté? Armed with clubs and guns.'

'I'm sorry, Armand.'

She reached across the table and placed her hand on his.

He looked down at her hand, then up into her eyes, and smiled.

'It's a place I no longer recognize. *To everything there is a season.* I'm thinking of talking to Professor Rosenblatt about his job at McGill.'

'You think he's not who he claims to be?'

'Oh, no, not at all. I'm sure Isabelle and Jean-Guy checked him out. No, this is personal interest.'

'Really? Thinking about becoming a physicist?' asked Reine-Marie. When he didn't answer, she looked at him closely. 'Armand?'

She knew he wasn't considering studying science, but now she understood what he was considering.

If the big question facing both of them was *What next?* could the answer be *University*?

'Would that interest you?' he asked.

150

'Going back to school?'

She hadn't really thought about it, but now that she did she realized there was a world of knowledge out there she'd love to dive into. History, archeology, languages, art.

And she could see Armand there. In fact, it was a far more natural fit than the Sûreté ever seemed. She could see him walking through the hallways, a student. Or a professor.

But either way, he belonged in the corridors of academe. And so did she. She wondered if the killing of young Laurent had finally, completely, put paid to any interest he had in the disgrace that was murder.

'You like the professor?' she asked, going back to her soup.

'I do, though there seems a strange disconnect between the man and what he did for a living. His field was trajectory and ballistics. The main people who'd benefit from his research would be weapons designers. And yet he seems so, so, gentle. Scholarly. It just doesn't seem to fit.'

'Really?' she asked, trying not to smile. It was what she'd just been thinking about him. A scholarly man who pursued murderers. 'I guess we're not all what we seem.'

'He does seem to know his stuff, though. He identified the weapon immediately. He said it was a Supergun.'

'A Supergun?'

He'd wondered if she'd laugh. Sitting in the warm and cheerful bistro, with fresh warm bread and parsnip and apple soup in front of them, the very word sounded ridiculous. 'Supergun.' Like something out of a comic book.

But Reine-Marie didn't laugh. Instead she remembered, as he did every hour of every day, Laurent. Alive. And Laurent, dead. Because of the thing in the woods. No matter its name, there was nothing remotely funny about it.

'It was built by a man named Gerald Bull,' said Armand.

'But what's it doing here?' she asked. 'Did Professor Rosenblatt know?'

Armand shook his head, then gestured out the window. 'Maybe they can tell us.'

Reine-Marie looked out and saw Lacoste and Beauvoir walking across the dirt road, to the path into the woods. And with them were two strangers. A man and a woman.

'Who are they?' asked Reine-Marie.

'At a guess, I'd say National Defence, or maybe CSIS.'

'Or maybe more academics,' suggested Reine-Marie.

Once again, Jean-Guy Beauvoir attached the huge plug to the huge receptacle and heard the clunk as the huge flood-lights came on.

He kept his eyes on the CSIS agents and wasn't disappointed.

They'd gone from standing shoulder to shoulder, holding their briefcases like commuters at a train station, to looking like two people who'd lost their minds.

Their eyes flew wide open, their mouths dropped, their heads in unison slowly, slowly tilted back. And they stared up. Up. Had it been raining they would have drowned.

'Holy shit,' was all Sean Delorme could say. 'Holy shit.'

'It's real,' said Mary Fraser. 'He did it. He actually built it.' She turned to Isabelle Lacoste, who was standing beside her. 'Do you know what this is?'

'It's Gerald Bull's Supergun.'

'How did you know?'

'Michael Rosenblatt told us.'

'Professor Rosenblatt?' asked Sean Delorme, recovering enough to stop saying 'holy shit'.

'Yes.'

'How did he know?' said Delorme.

'He's seen it,' said Beauvoir. 'He's here.'

'Of course he is,' said Mary Fraser.

'I asked him to come,' said Beauvoir.

'Ahhhh,' said Mary Fraser, turning away. Her eyes dragged back to the giant gun. But she wasn't looking at the weapon. The CSIS file clerk was staring at the etching.

'Unbelievable,' she said under her breath.

'The stories were true then,' said Delorme, turning to his colleague.

Mary Fraser took a few tentative steps forward and leaned into the image.

'That's writing,' she said, pointing to, but not touching, the etching. 'Arabic.'

'Hebrew,' corrected Lacoste.

'Do you know what it says?' Delorme asked Lacoste.

'*By the waters of Babylon*,' said Isabelle.

'*We sat down and wept*,' Mary Fraser finished the quote, taking a step away from the image. 'The Whore of Babylon.'

'Holy shit,' said Sean Delorme.

Gamache and Henri walked toward the edge of the village. Henri had his ball, and Armand had his script.

He looked down at the title, smeared with dirt from the grave Ruth had dug for it. But it hadn't rested in peace. He'd dug it up and now it was time he read it.

She Sat Down and Wept.

It could be a coincidence. Almost certainly was. That the title of a play by a serial killer was so similar to the phrase carved onto the side of the weapon of mass destruction.

Coincidences happened, Armand knew. And he knew not

to read too much into them. But he also knew not to dismiss them altogether.

He'd planned to read the play at home, in front of the fireplace, but he didn't want to sully his home. Then he thought he'd take it to the bistro, but decided against that too. For the same reason.

'Aren't you giving it more power than it deserves?' Reine-Marie had asked.

'Probably.'

But they both knew that words were weapons too, and when fashioned into a story their power was almost limitless. He'd stood on the porch, holding the script.

Where to go?

To a place already sullied beyond redemption, he thought. Though the only place that came to mind was the forest, where a boy had been murdered and a gun designed to kill *en masse* had sat for decades. But there were too many people and he didn't want to have to explain himself.

So if not a place that was damned, there was only the alternative. The divine. A place that could withstand the onslaught of John Fleming.

He and Henri walked to the edge of the village. They climbed the stairs to the doors of the old chapel, always unlocked, and stepped inside.

No one was in St Thomas's Church but it didn't feel empty. Perhaps because of the stained-glass boys, there in perpetuity. Sometimes Armand would go up to St Thomas's just to visit them.

He sat now on the comfortably cushioned pew and put the play on his lap. Henri lay at Gamache's feet, his head on his paws.

The two of them looked at the window, created at the

end of the Great War. It showed soldiers, impossibly young, clutching guns and moving forward through no-man's-land.

Armand came here sometimes to sit in the light thrown by their images. To sit in their fear and to sit in their courage.

This place was sacred, he knew, not because it was a church but because of those boys.

He felt the weight of the script on his legs, and the weight of memory. Of what Fleming had done. It came crashing, crushing, down until the script felt like a slab of concrete, pinning him to those memories.

And he heard again the testimony of the shattered officers who'd finally found Fleming. And seen what he'd done. And Armand saw, again, the photographs from the crime scene. Of the demon another demon had created.

The seven-headed monster.

Armand dropped his eyes to the script, red and gold light spilling from the boys onto the title page.

He gathered his courage, took a breath, and opened the script.

CHAPTER 14

———

'I see you're back. Do you mind if I join you?'

Jean-Guy Beauvoir sat down across from Professor Rosenblatt at the bistro. The elderly scientist smiled, clearly welcoming the company.

'I just unpacked my things at the B and B and thought I'd come over for lunch,' said Professor Rosenblatt.

'You're making notes,' said Jean-Guy, looking at the open notebook. 'On the gun?'

'Yes. And trying to remember all I can about Gerald Bull. Fascinating character.'

'I see you also stopped by the bookstore.'

A slim volume sat on the table between them.

'I did. Wonderful place. I can't resist a bookstore, especially a secondhand one. I found this.'

He gestured to the copy of *I'm FINE*.

'I was actually going to buy something else, but some old woman stood by the cash register and said she wanted every book I chose. This was the only book she let me buy. Fortunately I'm a fan.'

Beauvoir smirked. 'You like the poet who wrote *I'm FINE*?'

'I do. I think she's a genius. *Who hurt you once/so far beyond repair/that you would greet each overture/with curling lip.*' Rosenblatt shook his head and tapped the book. 'Brilliant.'

'Ruth Zardo,' said Beauvoir.

'Ahhh, I see you know her too.'

'Actually I was introducing you. Professor Michael Rosenblatt, may I present Ruth Zardo and her duck, Rosa.'

The elderly scientist looked up, startled, into the pinched face of the old woman who'd essentially bullied him into buying her book.

He struggled to his feet.

'Madame Zardo,' he said, and practically bowed. 'This is an honor.'

'Of course it is,' said Ruth. 'Who are you and what are you doing here?'

Rosa, nestled against Ruth, stared beady-eyed at Professor Rosenblatt.

'I, well, I was just—'

'We asked him here to help,' said Beauvoir.

'With what?'

'With what we found in the woods, of course.'

'And what was that?' she demanded.

'It's a—' Rosenblatt began, before Jean-Guy cut him off. Ruth glared at the professor. 'Have we met?'

'I don't think so. I'd have remembered,' he said.

'Well,' said Jean-Guy, looking at the empty chair at their table, then at Ruth. 'Good-bye.'

Ruth gave him the finger, then limped away to join Clara at a table by the fireplace.

'Well,' said the professor, regaining his seat. 'That was unexpected. Is that her daughter?'

'The duck?'

'No, the woman she's sitting with.'

The very idea of Ruth giving birth shocked Beauvoir. He was still struggling with the thought that she'd been born. He imagined her as a tiny, wizened, gray-haired child. With a duckling.

'No, that's Clara Morrow.'

'The artist?'

'Yes.'

'I saw her show at the Musée d'art contemporain de Montréal.' His eyes narrowed. 'Wait a minute, did Madame Morrow do a portrait of Ruth Zardo? The old and frail Madonna? The one who looks so loathsome?'

'That's the one.'

Professor Rosenblatt glanced at the other patrons. At the beamed and cheerful bistro, at the comfortable armchairs. He looked toward the bookstore, then, in the other direction, the boulangerie that carried moist madeleines that tasted like childhood.

Then he looked out the window to the old, solid homes, and the three tall pines like guardians on the green. Then back to Ruth Zardo sharing a table and a meal with Clara Morrow.

'What is this place?' he asked, almost beneath his breath. 'Why did Gerald Bull choose to come here, of all places?'

'That's one of the questions I came to ask you, Professor,' said Beauvoir.

'*Salut*, Jean-Guy,' said Olivier, standing at the table with his notepad and pencil. '*Bonjour*,' he said to the professor.

'Olivier, this is Professor Rosenblatt. He's helping us with our investigation.'

'Oh, really?'

'I believe I spoke to your partner, Gabri,' said Rosenblatt. 'I've arranged for a room at the B and B.'

'Wonderful. Then we'll be seeing more of you.'

Olivier waited, clearly hoping for more information. But what he got was their lunch orders.

Jean-Guy, after a mighty struggle with himself, asked for the grilled scallop and warm pear salad. He'd promised Annie to eat more sensibly.

'Maybe Gerald Bull coming here is karmic,' said Rosenblatt, after Olivier left. 'Yin and yang. Two halves of a whole?' he offered when he saw his companion's scowl.

'Oh, I know what it means, but you don't believe in that sort of thing, do you?'

'You think because I'm a scientist I don't have a faith?' Rosenblatt asked. 'You'd be surprised how many physicists believe in God.'

'Do you?'

'I believe for every action there's an equal reaction. What else is yin and yang? Heaven and hell. A peaceful creative village, and a dreadful killing machine close by.'

'Where else would the devil go, but to paradise?' asked Beauvoir.

'Where else would God go, but to hell,' said Rosenblatt.

The elderly man raised his hands, blotched with age, and lifted first one then the other.

A balance.

'*Merci, patron*,' said Jean-Guy, leaning back to make room for Olivier to put down his plate.

The scallops were large and succulent and grilled golden brown. They lay on a bed of grains and fresh herbs and roasted pine nuts and goat cheese next to a warm grilled apple. He was about to ask about the pear but was distracted by the bacon club sandwich with thin, seasoned fries put before the professor.

He is smart, thought Beauvoir.

'Can I tempt you?' Rosenblatt asked, pushing his plate a millimeter closer to Jean-Guy.

'*Non, merci*,' said Jean-Guy, taking a fry.

The professor smiled, but then it faded.

'Who're they?'

Beauvoir followed Rosenblatt's scowl and saw Isabelle Lacoste standing in the doorway of the bistro with Sean Delorme and Mary Fraser.

Across the room, Mary Fraser turned to Lacoste. 'Is that him?'

'Professor Rosenblatt, *oui*,' said Lacoste. 'Would you like an introduction?'

Isabelle pretended not to hear the urgent whispers of *Non, merci* behind her as she wove between the tables.

'They're coming this way,' said Rosenblatt in an urgent whisper. Beauvoir half expected him to bark, 'Quick, hide.'

'There you are,' said Isabelle, as though seeing Beauvoir was a surprise and not part of the plan. 'We were just coming in for a late lunch too. I don't believe you've met. Professor Michael Rosenblatt, may I present Mary Fraser and Sean Delorme. They've just arrived from Ottawa. They're also interested in what we found.'

Rosenblatt had once again struggled to his feet, though with far less gusto than for Ruth Zardo. He didn't exactly curl his lip at the newcomers, he was far too courtly for that. But it was close.

'We haven't met,' he said. 'But I believe we've corresponded.'

'Yes' was all Delorme said, while Mary Fraser remained silent, though she did shake the professor's hand. More, Lacoste felt, out of habit than desire.

Lacoste looked around and spotted a table in the corner, a distance from Beauvoir and the professor.

'I think that one's free,' she said, and watched as the CSIS agents practically climbed over the other tables to get to it.

Chief Inspector Lacoste had asked Olivier not to mention that she'd called ahead and reserved it.

'They work for CSIS,' said the professor, turning his back on them. 'But of course, you know that. I think it would be a stretch to call them intelligence agents.'

'Then what are they?' asked Beauvoir.

'File clerks,' said Rosenblatt.

'How do you know them? And how come they know you?'

'I've petitioned the government for the files on Gerald Bull and Project Babylon for years. I was planning to write a major paper on him to mark the twentieth anniversary of his assassination. Those two are in the department that keeps the dossier on Dr Bull, but they won't release the information.'

'Why not?'

'That's a good question, Inspector.'

He glanced behind him, and saw Mary Fraser swiftly drop her eyes. Then Rosenblatt returned his attention to Beauvoir.

'How did they react to the Supergun?'

'They were as surprised as you were,' said Beauvoir.

'I wonder if that's true.'

'He was brilliant, you know,' Mary Fraser said. 'Gerald Bull. The youngest person to get a Ph.D. in Canada. At the age of twenty-two. Twenty-two. He was light years ahead of the rest. But there was something wrong with him. He had no brakes. He drew no line. And if he saw one, he was determined to cross it.'

Isabelle Lacoste listened. The two CSIS agents were taking turns telling the story. It was now clear to Lacoste why they'd been sent.

Mary Fraser and Sean Delorme might not know much about being spies, but they knew a great deal about Gerald Bull. They were tasked with gathering, and guarding, that knowledge. And now they were letting it out.

Or, at least, some of it.

'Dr Bull worked with the American government, he worked with the Brits. He was involved with the High Altitude Research Project,' said Sean Delorme, speaking, Lacoste noticed, without need of notes. 'He was with McGill University in Montréal for a while. And then he moved to Brussels and went out on his own.'

Delorme took his glasses off and polished them with one of the linen napkins.

'It was a disaster,' he said, putting his glasses back on. 'Gerald Bull went from being a scientist, a designer, to being an arms dealer.'

'And Canada lost control of him,' said Chief Inspector Lacoste.

'I think any control we thought we had over him was an illusion,' said Mary Fraser. 'I think Gerald Bull was always beyond control because he was beyond caring.'

'That man isn't much better,' said Sean Delorme, indicating Michael Rosenblatt across the bistro. 'We have a file on him too, you know. Not very thick, of course. Did he tell you he helped design the Avro Arrow? One of the most sophisticated jet fighters in the world, before the project was scrapped. He's no stranger to the arms race and arms deals. Don't be taken in by him.'

*

'Do you seriously think Gerald Bull could have created the Supergun without the government knowing?' asked Rosenblatt.

'I don't know,' said Beauvoir. 'He seems to have built it outside this village without anyone knowing.'

'Given that that's the quality of agent at work, do you wonder?' Rosenblatt waved toward Lacoste's table.

The scientist seemed to want it both ways. The government knew and de facto supported Bull's research, while at the same time, the government was too incompetent to know anything.

When Beauvoir pointed this out, Rosenblatt shook his head.

'You misunderstand me,' he said. 'I think the Canadian government supported Dr Bull's research, encouraged it even. Poured money into it. Knew perfectly well what he was building. And I think the papers filed away at CSIS will prove all that.'

'But then?' asked Beauvoir.

'But then when Bull suddenly moved to Brussels and cut ties with Canada, they went, pardon the term, ballistic. They panicked. Listen, I'm no fan of Gerald Bull's ethics. I think he would have done just about anything to make a fortune and prove himself right. To rub the nose of the establishment in what he created.'

'And which establishment was that? The other armament designers?' Beauvoir asked.

'You carry a gun,' said Rosenblatt, looking at the holster attached to Beauvoir's belt. 'Best not to be hypocritical.'

But his smile softened the statement.

'I guess we're all hypocrites, to a degree,' Rosenblatt admitted. 'I worked on ballistics and trajectory, and it wasn't for the fisheries department.'

Beauvoir smiled, nodded and took a forkful of grilled scallop. It turned out to be delicious. The only possible improvement would be to deep-fry them, he thought.

'We all draw lines,' the professor was saying. 'Even those who design weapons. Things that are too horrible to do, even if they can be done.'

'This is a world with nuclear bombs and chemical weapons,' said Beauvoir, putting his fork down. Suddenly no longer hungry. 'How much more horrible can it get?'

To his relief, Professor Rosenblatt didn't answer. Instead the elderly professor looked out the old windowpanes, to the quiet little village. 'I can't believe he built it. He was begged not to, but he thought the other designers were just jealous.'

'Did you know Dr Bull?' Beauvoir asked.

'As I told you, only by reputation. I wasn't in his league, but I was a part of that community, even if it was just at the edges, the academic part.'

'And were you jealous?' asked Beauvoir. 'Were the other designers jealous?'

Rosenblatt shook his head. 'We were frightened.'

'Of what?'

'That what Gerald Bull said could be done really could. And that he'd actually do it. He was assassinated to stop him, there's little doubt of that. I think the CSIS files will prove it. But they didn't realize it was too late. The die was cast. The weapon built.'

'*Oui*,' said Beauvoir. 'But who did he build it for and why did he build it here?'

'He's a crackpot,' said Mary Fraser, looking across the bistro at the elderly man's back. 'Has all sorts of strange ideas about Gerald Bull. And about us. He's got a sort of persecution complex. Thinks we're keeping information from him.'

'Well, we are,' said Delorme.

'Yes, but it isn't personal,' said Mary Fraser. 'It's all covered under the Security of Information Act. We can't release it, even if we want to. Which reminds me, who have you told about the Supergun besides him?'

'It's in our official report on the crime,' said Lacoste. 'But that's confidential. We haven't made any announcement.'

'Good. Please don't until we get a handle on the thing.'

'Yes, we need to put this on lockdown,' said Delorme, obviously enjoying using that phrase perhaps for the first time in his career.

'I can understand keeping the Supergun confidential for now, but why has the information on Gerald Bull been kept a secret?' asked Isabelle Lacoste, taking a forkful of her warm duck salad. 'The man's long dead.'

'I don't really know,' said Mary Fraser. It seemed she'd never asked herself that question. Her job, after all, was to analyze the files, not question the content.

'You've obviously read the files,' Lacoste pressed. 'You're probably more familiar with Gerald Bull than anyone else in the world. What do those files say?'

'They say he was a common arms dealer, probably a sociopath,' said Mary Fraser. She was talking about Gerald Bull, but continued to look at Rosenblatt. 'He didn't care who he sold his weapons to, or how they'd be used.'

'All Dr Bull wanted was boatloads of money and the chance to prove his theories right,' said Delorme. 'And if, in the process, hundreds of thousands of people died, it wasn't his concern.'

'If he'd succeeded, God knows what would've happened

in the region,' said Mary Fraser, turning back to look at Lacoste.

'Then his client really was Saddam?' asked Lacoste.

'The field agents believed it,' said Mary Fraser.

'But even if they were wrong and he sold to the Israelis or the Saudis, it would still be a goddamn mess,' said Delorme.

'Armageddon,' said Mary Fraser. Somehow she managed to say it without making it sound ridiculous, even in this most peaceful of places.

'How did you know about the etching on the gun?' Lacoste asked. 'The Whore of Babylon.'

Sean Delorme leaned across the table with enthusiasm. 'It's all part of the legend. That's what's so amazing. Our job is to collect information and file it.'

'We'd come across stories about the etching in some field agent reports from the late eighties,' said Mary Fraser. 'The agents were trying to keep track of Dr Bull. While they were pretty sure his client was Saddam Hussein, they couldn't pin it down.'

'There were all sorts of wild rumors,' said Delorme. 'Makes for entertaining reading but not useful intelligence.'

'One rumor that kept coming up was that Bull had commissioned a drawing for the side of the Supergun,' said Fraser. 'The Whore of Babylon. From the Book of Revelation.'

'Satan. Armageddon,' said Delorme.

'Pure Bull,' said Mary Fraser, shaking her head.

'Did you mean to say that?' Delorme turned to her. 'Very clever.'

Lacoste, watching these two, thought the play on Dr Bull's name was more obvious than clever, but the CSIS agents seemed amused.

'What I meant was that Dr Bull was famous for these grand gestures,' said Mary Fraser. 'But they were always empty. The more extravagant the claim, the emptier the bubble.'

'And a Supergun etched with the Whore of Babylon was pure Bull,' said Delorme, sneaking a smile, still amused by the obvious, and now worn, joke.

'No one believed it?' asked Isabelle Lacoste. 'It was a step too far. Just like the boy who was killed. Laurent Lepage. No one believed him either.'

'Obviously someone believed it,' said Mary Fraser. 'They were both killed.'

Isabelle Lacoste walked over to Gabri's B and B with the two CSIS agents, to make arrangements for them to stay there.

It would be crowded, but it would also be interesting. Throw the agents and the academic together, and see what happened.

Like Mary Fraser and Sean Delorme, she found it odd that Professor Rosenblatt should be so obsessed with a long-dead arms dealer. But she also found it odd that Mary Fraser claimed not to know the difference between Arabic and Hebrew, written on the etching.

And she found it even odder that Sean Delorme had made his way straight to Three Pines, when getting lost was almost a prerequisite for finding the place.

The Supergun was definitely strange, but it wasn't the only strange thing going on.

CHAPTER 15

———

'You're back,' said Reine-Marie.

She turned from the computer to look at Armand and Henri, who were standing at the door into the study.

'*Oui*,' said Armand. 'What're you up to?'

'Research,' she said, getting up to greet them. 'How bad is the play?'

He tossed it onto the table by the door. 'As a play? It's not bad at all. In fact, Antoinette was right. It's brilliant.'

He looked like he'd just eaten something foul.

'I didn't finish it, but I will later. Just needed a break. Drink?'

'Please,' she said, returning to the computer. He heard the printer working and glanced in on his way to the cleaning closet, where they hid their best brands from Ruth.

'Lysol or Mr Clean?' he called.

'Actually, a Spic and Span sounds good. But a light one.'

He handed her a gin and tonic, with extra tonic and a wedge of lemon, and noticed she had the McGill site up and was reading.

Armand slipped a CD into the stereo and the

unmistakable voice of Neil Young came out. Then he took his Scotch and a book over to an armchair.

He read the familiar first lines of the book and felt the calm come over him, like a comforter. He lost himself, even momentarily, in the familiar world of Scout and Jem and Boo Radley.

Reine-Marie found him half an hour later sitting by the window, his finger in the book, staring into their garden and listening to the music. Henri by his side.

'Happy?' she asked.

'Peaceful,' he said. 'Find any interesting courses?'

'*Pardon?*'

He waved to the sheaf of printouts in her hand.

'You were looking on the McGill site. Are you also going to check out the Université de Montréal? They have some terrific courses. Will you audit classes, or go for a degree?'

'I wasn't looking up courses, Armand. I was looking up Gerald Bull. For a man whose work was supposedly secret, there's a surprising amount out there about him if you know the keywords, like Project Babylon. The public search engines like Google have a fair amount, all saying much the same thing. But it gets really interesting once you go into the private records.'

'Private?' he asked, sitting up.

'I'm an archivist,' she reminded him. 'Like a priest, we never really retire.' She held up the sheaf of papers. 'And I have the codes to the private McGill archives.'

'Bless you,' said Armand, reaching for the printouts and his glasses. 'What did you find?'

'Well, Gerald Bull was considered a bit of a failure in both his own academic record and his work. He seems to have been a great big pain in the *derrière*. According to his personnel file at McGill, he sort of muddled along, alienating everyone who came into contact with him. He was a big personality, with big and what were considered crazy ideas. No one wanted to work with him.'

'Why didn't they get rid of him?'

'They did eventually, though it's couched in all sorts of diplomatic, nonactionable terms. But they kept him on for a long time in the hopes that one of his outlandish ideas might work.'

'Which, of course, it did,' said Armand. He studied the papers, then looked up at her. 'But by then he was long gone. When was he born?'

Reine-Marie scanned her notes. 'March 9, 1928.'

Gamache did a quick calculation. 'That would put him well into his eighties now. Almost ninety.'

Reine-Marie looked at him, puzzled. 'But he's dead. You know that. Dr Bull was killed in 1990, at the age of' – she worked it out – 'sixty-two.'

'Yes,' said Armand, leaning back in his chair.

'What're you thinking?'

'Doesn't matter. It's ridiculous.'

'You're wondering if Gerald Bull is still alive?' she asked, astonished.

'I've spent too many years being suspicious,' he said with a smile. 'Forget I said anything.' He held up his weak Scotch. 'Blame it on the Lysol.'

'Armand, there is something odd in the files.'

She took a couple of the sheets from his hands and lowered her glasses from the top of her head where they rested, to her eyes. Words and sometimes whole lines had been blacked out, redacted, on the pages. Even the secret files continued to hold some secrets.

'I'm used to seeing this,' she said. 'Notes and papers are sent to the archives, but are edited by security first. It's often the personal diaries of politicians or scientists, so I wasn't particularly surprised.'

'No,' said Armand. 'Neither am I. Dr Bull was doing research that obviously had weapons applications.'

'Right. What surprised me is this.'

Reine-Marie sifted through the pages. She'd put a pen behind her ear and her glasses had now slipped down her nose. She looked like Katharine Hepburn in *Desk Set*. All smart and efficient and completely unaware of how beautiful she was. Armand could watch her all day long.

Reine-Marie found what she was looking for, and handed him one of the sheets. It had been heavily blacked out.

'It's part of an internal report on Dr Bull's work. It was written after his murder. Look at that.'

She pointed to one line. He put on his glasses and read it, then reread it, his brows drawing together. He sat up straight in the chair.

The censor had missed one reference to the Supergun. Not a huge omission, since Dr Bull's effort to create one was a kind of open secret.

'Do you think it's a typo?' she asked.

'I hope so.'

He looked back down at the report. At the word. That should have been blacked out.

'Superguns.' Plural.

Jesus, he thought. Could there be more than one of them?

Reine-Marie pushed her glasses back up her nose and took the pen from behind her ear.

Katharine Hepburn was gone. Spencer Tracy was gone. This was no comedy. Armand and Reine-Marie looked at each other. Then Armand got up, and started pacing. Not frantically. He took long, measured, almost graceful steps, up and down the living room.

'It might mean nothing,' he said. 'It might be just a typo, as you said. Almost certainly is. Let's stick to what we know to be true.'

'Well, according to the files, we know Dr Bull worked at McGill, doing research into long-range artillery. We know he moved to Brussels in the early eighties and was killed there on March 20, 1990.'

'Do the reports you found say who was responsible?'

'The main theory is Mossad. Gerald Bull was apparently also working on the Scud missile program for the Iraqis. But the main thrust of his work was to build a cannon for Saddam that could shoot a missile into low orbit.'

'And from there travel just about anywhere,' said Armand.

'Project Babylon,' said Reine-Marie. 'The Supergun was for the Iraqis after all.'

'Gun or guns,' said Armand. 'He was killed on March 20, 1990, you say?'

'Yes. Why?'

Armand took a few more agitated paces, then stopped and shook his head. 'It doesn't make sense. I know it doesn't.'

'What doesn't?'

'John Fleming's first murder was in the summer of 1990.'

There was a pause as Reine-Marie absorbed that, and tried to compose herself. 'Are you suggesting there's a link? How could there be?'

Armand sat down, his knees touching hers. 'Gerald Bull built Project Babylon, and etched onto it not just the Whore of Babylon but lines from a psalm, *"By the waters of Babylon, we sat down and wept."*'

He looked across their living room to the front door, where the goddamned play lay.

'John Fleming writes a play quoting the same line, or near enough. *She Sat Down and Wept.*'

'It's a famous line, Armand.' She tried to sound supportive without sounding patronizing. She could see the intensity in his eyes. 'There've been lots of literary references to it, even music. Didn't Don McLean write a song with that lyric?'

Then she saw what he was thinking and felt her concern spike.

'You're wondering if John Fleming could be Gerald Bull? But surely that couldn't be hidden.'

He picked up the blacked-out sheets. 'You can hide anything, depending on who "you" are.'

Reine-Marie leaned forward and took both his hands in hers. She spoke slowly, quietly. Holding his gaze. 'You've just been reading the play. It's brought up all sorts of memories of John Fleming. Do you think it's possible that your grief for Laurent has somehow gotten all mixed up with the trauma of the Fleming trial? I don't know what happened there, and maybe one day you'll tell me, but this isn't making sense, Armand.' She paused to let her words sink in, penetrate, and perhaps even overpower this delusion. 'The two aren't connected, except by a very common quote from the Bible. Do you see that? Fleming has gotten under your skin, or up your nose,' she smiled, and saw a small upturn at the corners of his mouth, 'but however he got there, he's in your head and you have to get him out. He doesn't belong there, and he doesn't belong in the murder of Laurent. It's just muddying things.'

Armand got up and stood by the fireplace, his back to her, looking at the flames. Then he turned around.

'You're right, of course. John Fleming is in his early seventies now. Far too young to be Gerald Bull. That was foolish of me. My imagination run wild again.'

He ran his large hands through his hair and smiled an apology.

'Still, I'd like to know more about that play. How it came into the possession of Antoinette's uncle, for instance.'

'Does it matter? Antoinette said he probably picked it up at a flea market. People collect strange things. Maybe he collected the macabre. Items associated with crimes or criminals.'

'But neither Brian nor Antoinette mentioned a collection,' said Armand. 'Why would an engineer who showed no interest at all in the theater buy any script, never mind one by the most brutal killer in the country?'

Reine-Marie stared at him. It was, she had to admit, an interesting question.

He took a deep breath and shook his head, then smiled at her. 'You have a lot of patience, *ma belle*.'

'Not as much as you might think.'

He smiled again. 'Nor should you. You've put up with all this for far too long. It's supposed to be over.'

He kissed her and walked to the door, inviting Henri along.

'I think I'll get some fresh air. Clear my head.'

'It has gotten a little crowded in there. Why don't I meet you at the bistro for tea in, say, twenty minutes?'

'*Parfait*. By then the eviction notices will have been served.'

CHAPTER 16

~

It was getting dark by the time the Gamaches returned home from the bistro. They found Ruth in the living room sipping Scotch from a measuring cup and eating left-over casserole while Rosa nibbled on a wild rice salad.

Reine-Marie sat down next to the poet while Armand went into the kitchen to wash up and prepare dinner.

'We've been waiting for you.'

Gamache leapt, startled, then grabbed his chest.

'Jesus,' he gasped. 'You scared me half to death.'

'Something's very wrong, *patron*,' said Isabelle Lacoste, getting up from her chair, 'when seeing Ruth is normal and we're the ones who frighten you.'

He laughed, recovering, though he'd been genuinely alarmed.

'I thought we locked the door,' he said.

'Ruth walks through walls,' said Jean-Guy. 'You should know that by now.'

'What did you want to see me about?' Gamache dried his hands on a dish towel and turned to face them.

'The forensics are back,' said Isabelle, getting herself a

beer and taking her seat again. 'They found one set of fresh prints on the missile launcher. Laurent's. But there were also smudges. Our killer touched it, but wore gloves.'

'What did you find on Laurent's stick and cassette tape?' asked Gamache.

'All sorts on the stick, including yours. But on the cassette we only found three sets. Laurent's own, of course, as well as his parents'. You were right. The cassette must've belonged to the Lepages.'

'Doesn't necessarily mean anything,' said Armand, joining them at the long pine table.

'No,' Beauvoir agreed. 'But it could mean everything. It could mean that the cassette dropped from the murderer's pocket in the struggle, or as he picked the boy up. If not, then how did it get there?'

Armand nodded. It made sense, of course. It might not be a smoking gun, but it was a pointing finger. Right at Al Lepage. With some surprise Armand realized he felt protective of Al Lepage. Perhaps because he liked the man and felt Laurent's father was suffering enough without the added weight of suspicion.

But suspicion was inevitable and often turned out to be true. People were almost always killed by someone they knew, and knew well, which compounded the tragedy and was probably why, Gamache thought, so many murder victims did not look frightened. They looked surprised. While Gamache liked Al Lepage, and sympathized with him, he'd arrested enough grieving family members for murder to know that Laurent's father was a legitimate suspect.

And he wasn't the only one who thought so. While he and Reine-Marie were at the bistro they'd heard the conversations, the rumors. Suspicion was settling on Laurent's father.

176

'We've interviewed the Lepages once,' said Jean-Guy. 'And searched the house. But we'll go out again tomorrow.'

Gamache nodded. He understood that Beauvoir and Lacoste did not need to report to him, and they weren't. They were simply informing him. It was a courtesy, not a requirement.

'I saw you taking some people into the woods.'

'Yes. Mary Fraser and Sean Delorme,' said Lacoste. 'CSIS. Low-level functionaries.'

'File clerks,' said Jean-Guy, opening the fridge and taking out a ginger ale.

'But they know a great deal about Gerald Bull,' said Lacoste.

She told him what they'd told her about the arms dealer.

'They also know our Professor Rosenblatt,' said Jean-Guy. 'And he knows them. There's not a lot of love lost.'

'Why not?' asked Armand.

'He thinks they're hiding something,' said Jean-Guy. 'He suspects the Canadian government might've been more involved with Gerald Bull than they're willing to admit.'

'His work or his murder?' asked Gamache.

'I'm not sure,' said Beauvoir. 'But he did say Fraser and Delorme might not have been as surprised about the Supergun as they appeared. He doesn't trust them.'

'And they don't trust him,' said Lacoste. 'They think it's odd that the retired professor is so obsessed with a long-dead arms dealer. And so do I.'

'What do you make of the CSIS people?' Gamache asked.

'They seem straightforward enough,' she said. 'A little out of their depth perhaps.'

'What is it?' asked Gamache. 'You're smiling.'

'They remind me of my parents,' said Lacoste. 'Bickering

and a little baffled. They're sort of endearing. But they're also not fools. They're very good at what they do, it's just that what they do is filing, correlating. Not fieldwork.'

'So why were they sent?'

'Probably because they know more than anyone else about Gerald Bull and his work,' said Beauvoir.

'Did you call them in?' he asked Lacoste, who shook her head.

'They just showed up. I think General Langelier at CFB Valcartier must've called someone at CSIS. He said he'd try to find us someone who could help. But I don't think anyone really believed that what we found was Project Babylon. I think if they did believe it they'd have also sent some higher-ranking intelligence agents. I expect some to arrive any moment now.'

She gazed out the window at the quiet village.

'They want to keep the existence of the Supergun secret, which might suit their purposes—'

'But it makes investigating Laurent's murder almost impossible,' said Jean-Guy. 'But I guess we have no choice.'

'Mmmm,' said Gamache. 'There's something I think you should see.'

He got up and returned a minute later with the papers he and Reine-Marie had left in the living room. Had Ruth read them? Had she learned about Gerald Bull and Project Babylon? And realized that was what was hidden in the woods?

Armand had the uneasy feeling that she probably had, though she didn't say anything when he picked them up. Which in itself was suspicious.

Returning to the kitchen, Gamache handed a page to Isabelle.

'Madame Gamache found these in a search of the archives,' he explained. Jean-Guy was reading over Lacoste's shoulder. 'Much of the information has been redacted, but they missed one reference.'

Jean-Guy got there first and looked up from the page into Gamache's thoughtful eyes.

And then, a moment later, Lacoste hit it. The one word. The one letter.

'A typo?' she asked.

'Maybe. We wondered the same thing.'

'And if it's not?' asked Beauvoir, sinking back into his chair. 'If there's another one?'

'Or two, or three?' said Lacoste.

Gamache held up his hand. 'We don't know if there are more. I think we need to keep this quiet for now.'

'Not even tell CSIS?' asked Lacoste.

'They're presumably the ones who blacked it out,' said Gamache. 'They must already know.'

'There was something else strange. Arabic and Hebrew. They look quite different, don't they?'

'Very,' said Gamache. 'Why?'

'Would you expect CSIS agents to know the difference?'

'I would,' he said, and studied her for a moment. 'Why're you asking? Is it the etching?'

'Yes. Mary Fraser found the writing, but she thought it was Arabic.'

He stared at her, not sure what to make of that.

'And there's something else,' she said. 'They didn't get lost.'

'*Pardon?*'

'Mary Fraser and Sean Delorme,' said Lacoste. 'They drove down from Ottawa and came straight to Three Pines.'

Gamache grew very still. The village itself was lost. Hidden in the hills. It was not on any map, or GPS. And yet the CSIS agents had come straight there. Which meant they might already have known where the village was.

Though invited to stay for dinner with the Gamaches and Ruth, and Rosa, the Sûreté officers declined.

'I think we'll go to the bistro, *patron*,' said Beauvoir. 'See what people are talking about.'

'You know what they're talking about, numbnuts,' snapped Ruth. 'Al Lepage.'

'And are you helping spread the rumors, Ruth?' Armand asked.

She glared at him, then shook her head and went back to her drink.

'Should she be . . . ?' Beauvoir tipped his hand up to his mouth.

'It's tea,' said Armand as they walked to the front door. 'We put it in the Glenfiddich bottle.'

'And she doesn't know?' asked Lacoste.

'If she does, she doesn't say,' said Gamache. 'Thank you for coming over and keeping me informed.'

'Always, *patron*,' said Lacoste. 'Why don't you join us for breakfast at the B and B? We'll see if our little social experiment of throwing the professor and the CSIS agents together has produced anything.'

'Like an explosion?' he asked, and agreed to meet them for breakfast.

'Oh, dear.'

Mary Fraser sat straight up in bed the next morning and stared at the softly closing door. The footsteps retreated down the corridor of the B and B and she heard a tap next door.

The owner, Gabri, was bringing up morning coffee. And news.

And now Mary felt like bringing up too.

'It's all over the village,' he'd said as he put the cup of strong, rich coffee on the bedside table and fluffed up her pillows. 'About the gun. *Crème?*'

'What gun?' Mary Fraser had asked, hauling herself upright and pulling the warm duvet over her flannel nightgown, for modesty.

The large, friendly man had walked to the door and now he turned and gave her an astute look. Then a quick and forgiving smile.

'You know which gun. The one in the woods. The one you're here to see.'

'Oh. That one.' She could think of nothing more intelligent to say.

'Yes, that one. They're calling it a Supergun.'

'Who're "they"?' she asked.

'Oh, you know. "Them."'

He left to deliver the morning coffee and spread the word. The word being 'Supergun'.

'Oh, dear,' she whispered. And then amended that to '*Merde.*'

'*Merci,*' said Sean Delorme, coming out of the bathroom, razor in hand, foam on his face, to thank the innkeeper for the coffee. And the news.

Once the door had swung shut, he sank down on the side of the bed and stared at the closed door. Then out the window, where fresh air was blowing in from the

181

mist-covered forest and across the village green. Below, he saw villagers stopping to talk. Hands were waving, gesturing. He could almost hear them.

Huge, one was saying, spreading his arms wide.

The other nodded. And pointed. Into the woods.

Despite the fresh, slightly pine-scented air, the CSIS agent smelled a foul odor.

'Fuck, fuck, shit.' He took a deep breath and sighed. 'Oh, dear.'

'Well.'

Michael Rosenblatt sat in bed and sipped coffee and watched the commotion on the village green.

'Well, well, well.'

He reached for his iPhone, then remembered it didn't work in this funny little village. Still, it wasn't the worst thing.

The worst thing was on the lips of everyone in Three Pines.

Professor Rosenblatt almost felt sorry for the CSIS agents. Almost.

Armand Gamache came out of the washroom in his bathrobe, a towel in hand, rubbing his hair dry. Then he stopped. And stood motionless in the middle of their bedroom.

A word had drifted in through the wide-open window, fluttering the curtains as it went by. And that word was 'Supergun'.

He shifted his gaze to Reine-Marie, whose eyes were wide with surprise.

'Did you hear that, Armand?'

He nodded and, looking out the window, he saw two villagers walking their dogs and talking, animatedly.

He thought he must have misheard. Surely they said Superman. Or Superglue.

One gestured toward the forest.

Or Supergun.

Clara Morrow was woken up by the phone. She answered, dazed, on the first ring.

'Hello?'

'Did you hear?' Myrna asked.

'Hear what? The phone waking me up?'

'No, what people are saying. Meet me in the bistro.'

'Wait, what's this about?'

'The Supergun. Hurry.'

'The what?' But Myrna had hung up.

Clara showered and dressed quickly, her curiosity and imagination fueling each other. But as wild as her imagination could be, it could never have conceived of what she was about to hear.

Isabelle Lacoste sat on the edge of her bed in the B and B. She thought about what she'd heard. And what it meant.

Then she gave one curt nod and went into the bathroom to shower and prepare for the day.

There was going to be hell to pay.

Ruth Zardo heard the soft knock on the back door.

She was in the kitchen. The coffee was perked on the old stove and she had the toast and jam out.

The knock did not startle her. She'd been expecting it. Rosa, however, looked up from her feed with some surprise. Though ducks often looked surprised.

Ruth opened the kitchen door, nodded and stepped back.

'You heard, Clément?' she asked.

'*Oui*,' said Monsieur Béliveau. 'Worse than we feared.'

'It's called Project Babylon, of course. What else would it be called?'

'How do you know that?' the old grocer asked the old poet as he sat at her kitchen table. 'No one else is saying that.'

'I saw it in some papers last night, over at the Gamache place.'

'You're not the one who . . . ?'

'Told everyone?' she asked, joining him. 'Of course not. We promised each other we wouldn't. Besides, we didn't know anything. Not really.'

Monsieur Béliveau looked at her, and she dropped her eyes to the white plastic table.

'We knew enough, Ruth. More than enough.'

'Well, why would I say anything now, after all these years?'

'To take the focus off Monsieur Lepage.' Clément paused before speaking again. 'To protect him.'

'Why would I do that? I don't even like the man.'

'You don't have to like him to protect him. Do you think he did it?' Monsieur Béliveau asked.

'Do I think Al Lepage killed his own son?' asked Ruth. 'It would be a terrible thing. But terrible things happen, don't they, Clément?'

'*Oui.*'

Monsieur Béliveau was quiet for a moment, looking out the kitchen door to the rectangle of freshly turned earth in her backyard. She followed his gaze.

'The Fleming play,' Ruth said. '*She Sat Down and Wept.* A reference to the psalm, of course.'

'Babylon,' he said. 'You buried it?'

'I tried to, but Armand came and asked for it.'

'You gave it to him?' It was as close as she'd seen the grocer come to anger.

'I had no choice. He knew I had it.'

Clément Béliveau nodded, his eyes drawn back to the dark hole in the bright green grass. A dead thing among the living.

'Does he know?'

Ruth shook her head. 'And I won't tell him. I'll keep my word.'

Though words, Ruth knew, were what had gotten them into trouble in the first place.

'Project Babylon,' said Monsieur Béliveau under his breath. *'And now it is now. And the dark thing is here.'*

CHAPTER 17

~

Jean-Guy arrived in the dining room of the B and B to find Isabelle Lacoste sitting alone at a large table by the fireplace, rereading the printouts on Gerald Bull that Madame Gamache had found and Gamache had given them the night before.

Gabri had laid, and lit, the fire. An autumn fog had descended, rolling down the cold mountains to pool in the valley. It would burn off in an hour or so, but for now the cheerful little fire was welcome.

'*Salut*,' said Beauvoir, sitting down. 'Did you hear? Someone leaked the news about the gun.'

He took a warm crumpet from the basket on the table and watched as the butter melted into the holes. Then he smeared it with marmalade. His uncle, a devout Québécois separatist, had introduced him to the pleasures of crumpets and marmalade, apparently unaware he was consorting with, and consuming, the enemy.

But allegiances, Jean-Guy knew, lived in the head, not the stomach. He took a huge bite and nodded when Gabri offered to bring a café au lait.

'I did hear,' said Lacoste.

'Makes the investigation into Laurent's murder easier,' said Jean-Guy. 'We can now talk about what he found. But I know two people who're going to be mighty pissed. Speak of the devil.'

Mary Fraser and Sean Delorme appeared at the door of the dining room and looked around.

Isabelle Lacoste waved them over.

'Would you like to join us?' she said.

'News of Gerald Bull's Supergun is all over the village,' said Sean Delorme without preamble. 'How did that happen?'

He glared at them.

'We have no idea,' said Beauvoir. 'We were just talking about it. We're as shocked as you. Fortunately, no one's talking about Dr Bull. Just the gun.'

'"Just" the gun?' asked Delorme. 'Isn't that enough?'

'It could be worse,' said Professor Rosenblatt.

The scientist had arrived in the dining room wearing gray flannels, a tweed jacket and bow tie. He looked around at the tables set for breakfast, with crisp white linen, sterling silver, and fine bone china. The fireplace lit with a modest fire.

The walls were thick and the windows mullioned and Rosenblatt had the impression if he waited long enough the stagecoach would come by.

But he wouldn't take it. This was far more interesting than any other place he could possibly think of.

'I won't join you,' said Professor Rosenblatt, as though he'd been invited. 'You have things to talk about.'

'Like the news,' said Jean-Guy.

'Yes.' Rosenblatt shook his head. 'That's a shame.'

But he didn't look at all upset.

'Please,' said Lacoste, smiling at the professor and indicating a chair. 'The more the merrier.'

'Merrier' did not describe the gathering, no matter how many there were.

Professor Rosenblatt took a seat and looked at the unhappy faces of the CSIS agents. 'Now, what were we talking about?' He put a white linen napkin on his lap and looked around at them. 'Ah yes, the leak.'

Now there's a shit-disturber, thought Beauvoir with some admiration. What seemed interesting was the amount of shit this professor emeritus was able to disturb.

Beauvoir shifted his gaze to the CSIS agents, whose faces were now masks of cool civility.

And why were they so disturbed?

'Did you do it?' Mary Fraser asked. Her hair was still damp from the shower and she wore a gray sweater and black skirt, and pearls, in what looked like an effort to dress things up, but only managed to make her look even more dowdy.

'A moment ago you were accusing that young man.' Rosenblatt indicated Beauvoir. 'And now me? Who else are you going to blame? Him?'

He looked at Gabri, making his way across the wide-plank floor with the café au laits. The innkeeper wore an apron with gingham frills, which drove Olivier nuts.

'It's fun,' Gabri had said to his partner. 'It makes me happy.'

'It makes you gay.'

'Yes. Otherwise no one would ever know.'

Gabri arrived at their table, distributed the coffees and stood poised for their breakfast orders.

Professor Rosenblatt asked him for a few more minutes to consider the menu. Lacoste and Beauvoir said they'd wait a little longer as well, but the CSIS agents ordered, obviously anxious to finish as quickly as possible.

'There're only so many people who could've leaked the information about the Supergun,' said Delorme once Gabri had left. 'And most of them are sitting at this table.'

He looked around and Beauvoir was struck by how very hard the man was trying to be threatening, and how very unsuccessful it was. He just seemed petulant.

'Whoever did it will face the full weight of the law,' said Mary Fraser.

She managed to be somewhat more threatening, though perhaps not in the way she intended. It was as though they'd disappointed a favorite aunt.

Jean-Guy wondered if they'd be recalled to Ottawa and some real agents sent down. He hoped not. He quite liked these two.

'*Bonjour*,' said Armand Gamache, walking over to the table and taking off his jacket. 'Bit of fog this morning. The fire's nice.'

He held out his large hands, momentarily, toward the hearth.

'*Patron*,' said Gabri, coming in from the kitchen. 'I thought I heard you. Café?'

'*S'il vous plaît*,' said Gamache, and looked at the people already at the table.

Beauvoir and Lacoste had gotten to their feet to greet him. He smiled at them, then shook the elderly scientist's hand.

'Professor,' he said with a smile.

Gamache turned to the other two.

'May I introduce you?' said Lacoste. 'Mary Fraser and Sean Delorme are down from Ottawa. They're with CSIS. This is Armand Gamache.'

Delorme had risen and took Gamache's hand, while Mary Fraser remained seated, staring at the newcomer.

Trying, thought Jean-Guy, to place him. He knew that look. Here was a familiar face, a familiar name. But in an unfamiliar setting.

And then she had it. 'Of course. Gamache. Of the Sûreté.'

It sounded much like Renfrew, of the Mounties.

'Late of the Sûreté,' he said, taking the empty chair beside her. 'My former colleagues are being kind to include me. My wife and I have retired to the village.'

Beauvoir marveled at Gamache's ability to make himself sound insignificant. But he could also see the wheels turning in Mary Fraser's mind. For a moment she looked less matronly and far shrewder. And then it was gone.

'It must be upsetting to have all this commotion just when you thought you'd left it behind,' said Mary Fraser.

'Well, I can pop in and out of the case. It's different when it's not your responsibility.'

Gabri came out with eggs Benedict for Sean Delorme, and for Mary Fraser, crêpes stuffed with apple confit and drizzled with syrup. On the side were thick strips of maple-smoked bacon.

'A very good choice,' said Armand, leaning toward her conspiratorially.

Mary Fraser all but blushed, and then to cover her reaction she pointed to the papers by Lacoste's hand.

'Are those about Project Babylon?'

'A little. Mostly they're about Gerald Bull.' Lacoste held them up. 'Redacted, so most of the information on Project Babylon has been removed.'

'Where did you get them?' asked Rosenblatt, taking a sheet and scanning it.

'Archives.'

'How did you get them?' he asked. 'I've been trying for years.'

'And if you'd joined the Sûreté you might've been successful,' said Lacoste. She caught Gamache's eyes and saw his appreciation. She was not going to mention Madame Gamache.

Rosenblatt frowned, but didn't say anything. Mary Fraser picked up the pages and scanned them, pausing at the black-and-white photograph of Gerald Bull.

'Did you ever meet him?' Lacoste asked, and Mary Fraser shook her head.

'This is a common photo of him though,' she said. 'Just about the only one I've seen. For a man with an outsized ego, he didn't like to have his picture taken.'

Mary Fraser put the photo down and turned to the typed pages.

'Interesting reading,' said Isabelle Lacoste. 'The details are blacked out, but the reports confirm that Gerald Bull would sell anyone anything. Not just the Iraqis.'

'I think it's over to you,' Rosenblatt said to the CSIS agents. 'Unless you'd like me to answer.'

Mary Fraser looked annoyed, but realized she really had no choice.

'The papers are correct. Gerald Bull went completely off the rails in Brussels. He took on contracts with anyone and everyone. All the legitimate powers who once worked with him backed off. He was like the Black Death.'

'Tell them about the Soviets,' said Rosenblatt, obviously enjoying himself.

Delorme shot him what he must've thought was a withering look but managed to be just comical.

'Bull used the Soviets and South Africans as conduits for his weapons and designs,' said Fraser. 'But as you know, his biggest contract was with the Iraqis. He was completely amoral.'

'Let's not be disingenuous here,' said Lacoste. 'We've been doing our own research. Saddam got a lot of his weapons from the West. Dr Bull was far from alone.'

'The region's a quagmire,' Mary Fraser admitted. 'We supplied Saddam, but stopped when we realized what he was capable of. Gerald Bull did not. He saw a business opportunity, a market, and he jumped in. We deeply regret selling Saddam any weapons, but who knew he'd turn out to be a sociopath?'

Professor Rosenblatt looked about to say something, so Sean Delorme jumped in.

'No one's proud of the choices we made, but at least we were trying to keep order. But Gerald Bull was a whole other beast. He was beyond any form of control. He'd slipped below the official channels and was into the dark region of arms suppliers. There were no rules or laws, and no boundaries. If governments were making a mess of it, you can imagine the damage the arms dealers were doing. We're pretty sure the gun was destined for the Iraqis. Bull apparently convinced Saddam that he could make him the only superpower in the region.'

'And you had no idea this was happening?' asked Beauvoir.

Sean Delorme shook his head and a long strand of the combover came loose. 'Informants told us they thought Gerald Bull was having parts of the cannon made in different factories around the world, but he was killed before he could assemble it.'

'Then what's that?' Beauvoir pointed toward the forest.

The CSIS agents shook their heads in unison. More combover came loose, exposing Sean Delorme's skull if not his thoughts.

'I don't know,' said Mary Fraser. 'I mean, we know what it is. It's a Supergun. But we don't know how it got there.'

'And why someone had to murder a nine-year-old boy to keep it quiet,' said Gamache.

'Thank God it doesn't work,' said Lacoste.

'But why doesn't it work?' asked Professor Rosenblatt. 'Don't get me wrong, I'm as relieved as you, but, well . . .'

'Where's the key?' said Beauvoir.

'The what?' asked Delorme.

'The key,' said Professor Rosenblatt. 'The missing firing mechanism.'

'But there's something else missing,' said Beauvoir. 'Something you haven't mentioned.'

'What?' asked Delorme.

'The plans,' said Professor Rosenblatt.

He no longer looked like he was enjoying this. Now he was deadly serious, his eyes bright and his voice grave. This was not a man who was there for amusement.

'*Oui*,' said Beauvoir, nodding. 'When I make a model plane, I have plans. You can't tell me Gerald Bull made it up as he went along. He might've been a genius, but no one could do that. He must've had drawings.'

The CSIS agents fell silent.

'Well?' asked Beauvoir.

'No plans were ever found,' said Mary Fraser. 'And not for lack of trying. Dr Bull's apartment had been broken into several times before he was killed. As a warning for him to stop his activities, but also, we suspect, to search for his schematics.'

'You suspect?' said Lacoste. 'So it wasn't CSIS?'

'No. We don't know who broke into his home.'

'Probably the same people who killed him,' said Delorme.

'It was a professional hit,' said Mary Fraser, the words coming out with disconcerting ease. And familiarity. 'Bullets to the head to be sure of the kill.'

And Isabelle Lacoste looked with fresh eyes at this middle-aged, slightly drab woman. Was she familiar with this method through training or personal experience? Was it possible she knew much more about the murder of Gerald Bull than she was saying? This conversation was obviously redacted.

Lacoste did a quick calculation. Mary Fraser was probably in her mid-fifties. Gerald Bull was murdered in Brussels twenty-five years ago.

Fraser would have been in her late twenties.

It was possible. Most soldiers were that age, or younger.

'Are you sure he's dead?' asked Gamache, and all eyes swung to him.

'Pardon?' said Mary Fraser.

'Gerald Bull. Did CSIS see the body? Did anyone at the Canadian Embassy identify it?'

'Yes, of course,' said Delorme. 'He's dead. Five bullets to the head will do that.'

Gamache smiled. '*Merci*. I was just wondering. And John Fleming?'

Now the CSIS agents really did stare at him, though both Lacoste and Beauvoir dropped their eyes to the table.

'I beg your pardon?' asked Mary Fraser. 'John Fleming?'

'Yes,' said Gamache, his voice conversational, friendly even. 'How is he connected?'

Mary Fraser looked first at her colleague, then over to the Sûreté agents. There was an awkward silence.

'You do know we're talking about Project Babylon,' she said.

'*Oui*,' Beauvoir jumped in. 'We found a play by John Fleming and it seemed a coincidence, that's all.'

'You found it at the site of the gun?' asked Sean Delorme, trying to follow, trying to find the logic.

'Well, no,' Gamache admitted.

'Then why're we talking about this?' Mary Fraser looked at the Sûreté officers, obviously asking for clarification. None was coming. They'd lapsed into embarrassed silence.

Armand Gamache, however, had not.

'So as far as you know, John Fleming has no involvement at all with Gerald Bull and Project Babylon?' he asked, looking from Mary Fraser to Sean Delorme and back again.

'I frankly don't even know who you're talking about,' said Mary Fraser, getting to her feet. 'I think this conversation has run its course. Thank you for your company and your help. Will you excuse us?'

'I have work to do too,' said the professor. 'Notes I'd like to reread. I'd also like to borrow those' – he pointed to the redacted pages – 'if you don't mind. I'll give them back to you.'

'It would be good to get your opinion, sir,' said Lacoste, handing them to the elderly scientist.

Professor Rosenblatt chose the spacious banquette by the window and immediately started reading.

After Gabri took their breakfast orders, Isabelle turned to Gamache.

'What was that about?'

'What?'

'John Fleming.'

'I just wanted to see their reaction,' said Gamache.

'And you saw it,' said Lacoste. 'They think you're nuts.'

'And you?' he asked, the smile softening. 'What do you think?'

Isabelle Lacoste looked into his shrewd eyes. 'I've never known you to ask a stupid question, sir. You might sometimes be wrong, but not foolish. I think you genuinely believe there might be a connection.'

'But you don't?'

He looked from Lacoste to Beauvoir, who dropped his eyes.

'I just don't see it,' Isabelle admitted. 'Bull and Fleming use a popular biblical quote on their creations, but that doesn't mean they worked together or knew each other.'

Gamache looked over at Beauvoir, who was fidgeting a little.

'I agree with Isabelle. I think you blew your credibility with those people. I could see the way she looked at you.'

'Yes,' said Gamache, sitting back. 'That was interesting. A bit too dismissive, wouldn't you say? She never even asked who I meant by John Fleming.'

Once again, Lacoste and Beauvoir exchanged a quick glance, not lost on Gamache.

'What do you make of the CSIS agents?' Lacoste asked, her voice overly cheerful. Changing the subject.

'I think they know a great deal about a gun no one thought had been built by a man long dead,' said Gamache.

'So do I,' said Lacoste. 'They're not quite as bumbling as they appear. Do they really spend their days filing?'

'And reading,' Beauvoir said to Gamache. 'I told you it was dangerous.'

'I don't think the sports page will kill you, *mon vieux*.'

Their breakfasts arrived. Crêpes and sausages for Gamache and Beauvoir, and eggs Florentine for Lacoste.

A basket of warm, flaky croissants was placed on the table by Gabri, who smiled at Lacoste.

Beauvoir looked from Isabelle to the retreating apron of Gabri.

'He and I shared a very special night,' said Lacoste.

Armand slowly lowered his cutlery. 'It was you. You told Gabri about the Supergun,' he whispered so that Professor Rosenblatt wouldn't hear. 'And asked him to spread it around.'

Isabelle Lacoste gave a very small shrug. '*Oui.*'

'You did it?' asked Beauvoir. 'Why?'

'Everyone agrees the gun would be dangerous if it fell into the hands of people who wish us harm, but let's not be blind,' she said. 'It's also dangerous in the hands of our own people. Especially if it's a secret. But I didn't do it for reasons of national security. Honestly, I'm not smart enough to understand all the working parts of that beast.'

Gamache doubted that. He'd always had great respect for his young protégée, and never more than now.

'You said it earlier, Jean-Guy,' she continued. 'It's almost impossible to investigate Laurent's murder unless we can talk about the motive. The gun. Our duty is to Laurent, not CSIS. Besides, if the murderer wants the Supergun to be a secret, the best thing we can do is not comply. Get it out there. See if it rattles the killer. And, as you taught us, Monsieur Gamache, a rattled killer will make himself known.'

It was true. But what struck both men wasn't her reasoning, but her calling Gamache 'Monsieur'. It was the first time she had not called him Chief Inspector.

It was natural, healthy. It was true. But to Armand Gamache it felt like having a tattoo scraped off.

'And what else did I teach you?' he asked.

'Never use the first stall in a public washroom,' said Lacoste.

'Besides that.'

'That a murderer is dangerous,' she said. 'And a rattled murderer is even more dangerous.'

Gamache got up. 'That was a big boot you used, Chief Inspector. You hit CSIS where it hurts. In their secret parts. But we can at least see their reaction. You also delivered a swift kick to the killer and he's still invisible to us.'

'I'm hoping this will make him act,' said Lacoste, also rising. She examined his face. So familiar from so many conversations just like this. Except he'd always been the one making the decisions.

'Did I make a mistake?' she asked.

'If you did, it was one I'd also have made,' he said, and smiled. 'It's dangerous, but necessary. This is not a time for timidity. Or secrets.'

'Except ours,' said Beauvoir.

CHAPTER 18

M ichael Rosenblatt looked up from his French toast and
saw the Sûreté officers get up to leave.

He'd been reading and making notes and eating. The trip
to this little village had been a revelation. The village itself
had been a revelation. As had the excellent French toast and
sausages and maple syrup almost certainly made from the
sap of trees he could see out the window.

But mostly that gun had been a revelation. When he'd
crawled through that tiny opening on his hands and knees
and looked up, he half expected to hear the celestial choir
singing, 'Ahhhh.'

There was Gerald Bull's Supergun. Bathed in light.

Goddamned Gerald Bull. Dead, but never gone. How had
he done it?

How had he built the goddamned gun?

Professor Rosenblatt looked at the papers by his plate,
then over to his notebook, slightly stained by drops of maple
syrup. One word had been written large, and circled.

How.

Then he wrote, *Why?*

That too seemed a good question.

But now that he thought about it, he added another.

Who?

Professor Rosenblatt put down his pen and watched Gamache say good-bye to his colleagues.

John Fleming. When the former Chief Inspector had said that name it had rattled the professor. He hadn't heard it in years. He knew, of course, who Gamache meant, and he could see the CSIS people knew too. The serial killer. A man gone badly wrong.

But to make the connection between Fleming and Bull? It seemed incredible.

Professor Rosenblatt watched as Gamache and the Sûreté officers parted. He could see the expressions on the young officers' faces as they looked at Gamache. With some concern and a great deal of affection.

Here was a nice man, Rosenblatt felt, and he realized that he did not himself know many nice people. Clever people, smart people, accomplished people, certainly. But not very nice. And not always good.

'I hope I'm not disturbing you,' said Gamache, walking across the wide-plank floor to the professor's table.

'Not at all, please.' Rosenblatt indicated a seat in the booth across from him.

'Did you sleep well?' Armand asked, sliding in.

'Not so well,' admitted Rosenblatt. 'New bed. New Supergun.'

Gamache grinned. The professor did, in fact, look tired. But his eyes still glowed with intelligence.

Here is a formidable man, thought Gamache.

Here is a formidable man, Rosenblatt knew. While his assessment that Gamache was a nice man hadn't changed, it had broadened. To include what else he now knew about

Armand Gamache, having done some research the evening before.

The large and thoughtful man across from him had turned in, and on, his superiors. He'd killed. And almost been killed.

Rosenblatt had learned those eyes, as kind as they appeared, had seen things few others had. And the hand that shook his, as warm as it was, had done things.

And would again, if need be.

Michael Rosenblatt was both comforted and a little frightened by Armand Gamache.

'You obviously spent some time in the night thinking about the gun,' said Gamache. 'The CSIS agents have their strengths but they're not scientists. I'd like to hear what you make of Gerald Bull's creation.'

Professor Rosenblatt shook his head and exhaled. 'As a scientist? It's even bigger than I imagined possible. Incredible. Powerful, but also elegant.'

'Elegant?' said Gamache. 'An odd word for something destined to become a weapon of mass destruction.'

'It's not a moral judgment, it's just a description of the mechanics. Mostly what we mean by elegant is that it's simple. Easy to use.'

'It's simple?'

'Oh, yes. The best designs are. That's its genius. It looks complex because it's so big. But there aren't all that many moving parts, so it would be fairly easy to manufacture and assemble. And fewer things to break down. Like a slingshot is elegant, or a bow and arrow. Or the gun you wore.'

'I rarely wore a gun,' said Gamache. 'Hate the things. They're very dangerous, you know.'

'You don't believe in the theory of the balance of terror?' asked Rosenblatt.

'Prime Minister Pearson's phrase to describe the Cold War?' said Gamache. 'I think he used it as a condemnation and warning, not as a goal.'

'Maybe,' said Rosenblatt. 'But it has worked, hasn't it? When both sides can destroy each other, neither side is willing to pull the trigger.'

'Until you give that weapon to a madman,' said Gamache.

Rosenblatt's face grew grim and he nodded. 'That's the flaw in the argument.'

'So Gerald Bull's gun is elegant,' said Gamache. 'But is it still relevant, or have time and technology passed it by?'

'A slingshot will still kill,' said Rosenblatt.

'And so will a bow and arrow. But it's not an advantage when faced with a nuclear bomb.'

Rosenblatt thought for a moment. 'I feel I should agree that the ICBMs of today are more dangerous than what Bull designed thirty years ago, but the fact is, they aren't. What Gerald Bull built might be less sexy, but it gets the job done.'

'The question is, what was the job?' said Gamache.

'Yes, that is a good question.'

'If the Supergun is really just a huge cannon,' said Gamache, 'would it fire only conventional missiles or could it be adapted?'

'It would fire anything put into it.'

Gamache paused to absorb that statement, said so matter-of-factly.

'Including a nuclear warhead?'

Rosenblatt shifted a little in his seat and nodded.

'Chemical weapons?' asked Gamache.

Another nod.

'Biological weapons?'

Now Rosenblatt leaned forward. 'It would shoot a

Volkswagen into the lower atmosphere. It would carry whatever the person firing it wanted.'

That was followed by silence.

'So what's it doing here?' Gamache asked.

More silence, until Rosenblatt finally spoke, quietly. 'I don't know.'

'Guess.'

'I won't guess. I'm a scientist. Guessing isn't part of what I do.'

Gamache smiled. 'Of course it is. Scientists come up with theories all the time. What are they except best guesses? Try. It's not as though you haven't been sitting here wondering the same thing.'

Professor Rosenblatt took a deep breath. 'It could be a prototype, something to show buyers. That might explain why the firing mechanism is missing. It's not meant to be fired. It's meant as a sort of mock-up. A sales tool.'

'Or?'

'Or it's meant to be fired. Did you notice where it's pointed?'

'Into the United States,' said Gamache. 'Which theory do you think is most likely? A mock-up, or built to be used?'

Rosenblatt shook his head. 'The missing firing mechanism is a puzzle. Was it never made? Was it removed?' He looked into Gamache's face. 'I honestly don't know.'

Armand Gamache wasn't sure he believed the scientist, but he knew he would not, at this point, get a clearer answer.

'The good news is we found the Supergun before it could be fired, if that was the intention,' said Gamache. 'Unfortunately, it cost Laurent Lepage his life.'

Professor Rosenblatt looked closely at his companion. 'You're retired. What's your interest in this?'

'Laurent was my friend.'

Rosenblatt nodded. The statement was simple. Elegant. And as powerful as the gun.

'And now you're out for revenge?' asked Rosenblatt.

Gamache tilted his head slightly. 'I hope that's not it.'

Now it was Rosenblatt's turn to tilt his head. 'But you're not sure.'

'Anything interesting in the papers you borrowed?' Gamache asked, his voice clipped.

Rosenblatt looked at him for a moment, then dropped his gaze to the pages.

'A shame about the blacked-out bits, but I don't think there's really anything in here that isn't common knowledge.'

'Common?'

'Since Bull's death and with the passage of time, some information has come out about his work,' said Rosenblatt. 'I'm sure you've found some yourselves now that you know the keywords. But there're still some things only people in the field know, or guessed.' Rosenblatt paused a moment. 'Theorized.'

'And what field would that be?'

Rosenblatt realized, too late, that his initial impression had been right. Here was a dangerous man. And he'd led him into dangerous territory.

Rosenblatt's formidable mind raced, but kept coming back to the same place.

He could lie, but it would be found out eventually.

'The field of armament design,' said Professor Rosenblatt, and noticed that Gamache showed absolutely no surprise.

'It would have to be, wouldn't it?' said Gamache, being equally open with Rosenblatt. 'After all, why else would you be here?'

The two men stared at each other. Not challenging, not

204

threatening each other. There was no power struggle. Just the opposite.

There was recognition.

Here was someone else best in his field. And that field was pitted, and weedy, and pocked with land mines. You didn't get to the other side without some wisdom, and without some wiles. And without some scars.

'What are you asking me, monsieur?'

'I'm asking if you worked with Gerald Bull.'

Gamache saw the eyes flicker, wanting to drop, to break contact. But they held, and Michael Rosenblatt gave one curt nod.

'As I told your young colleague, Inspector Beauvoir, we worked at McGill at the same time, but I'm afraid I wasn't completely honest. We did work together, not in the same department but on some of the same projects. Though no one really worked with Gerald Bull. It might start out that way, but eventually you found yourself working for him.'

'Were you working for him when he came up with the plans for the Supergun?'

'No. I left when he began using the Soviets as a back door to sell his arms. He wasn't very smart.'

'Is that why you left? Fear you'd get caught?'

'No. I left because it was wrong. It's one thing to design weapons for your own country, it's another to sell them to the highest bidder. Gerald Bull was the consummate salesman, and completely without a conscience.'

'Why did you just say that he wasn't very smart?' asked Gamache.

'He made some stupid choices, like cozying up to the Soviets. He had an outsized ego that told him he was smarter than other people.'

'The ego lied?' asked Gamache.

'Shocking, I know. Dr Bull was bombastic. The perfect personality for a man who sold cannons and Bull was, as I said, a great salesman.'

'Why would he have the Whore of Babylon etched into the cannon? Was it a sort of calling card? A signature? Did Dr Bull put it into all his designs?'

'Not that I know of. It was probably another sales tool. What else would appeal to a crazy despot like Saddam but a weapon etched with a symbol of the apocalypse? And one from ancient Iraq, no less. It was perfect.'

'But this wasn't Saddam's gun, was it?' said Gamache. 'Gerald Bull didn't build it in Iraq, he built it in Québec. And he etched the Whore of Babylon on it. Why?'

'Maybe it supports the mock-up theory,' said Rosenblatt. 'He built it to show the Iraqis. After all, by then all the intelligence agencies in the world were interested in Bull and Project Babylon but they'd never think to look for it here. He could show it to the Iraqis and once the order was in, he could dismantle it, and ship it piece by piece to Baghdad.'

Gamache listened to this curiously detailed hypothesis. He had to admit, it fit. Québec was a showroom. Though there was still another possibility. The other one.

'Or it could've been meant for Québec all along,' said Gamache. 'Saddam couldn't strike US soil with a Scud. Maybe the goal was never to hit Israel, or Iran, or any target in the region. Maybe the target was the US. Maybe those weapons of mass destruction that the Americans were so sure were there were actually here.'

Maybe, maybe, thought Gamache. All maybes.

It was frustrating. Though he felt they were getting closer. Maybe.

Gamache leaned against the banquette and looked across the table at his companion, remembering something else Reine-Marie had discovered while researching Gerald Bull.

'Dr Bull got his Ph.D. very young,' said Gamache. 'In physics. A remarkable achievement. But I understand his marks weren't very good.'

'I wouldn't know about that. I didn't know him as a student.'

'No. But you knew him afterward. He'd have been about twenty years older than you, is that about right?'

'About.' Now Rosenblatt was watching Gamache closely. He'd not be tricked again, but he couldn't shake the feeling they were again wandering into the minefield.

'His marks weren't terrific,' said Gamache, musing almost to himself. 'And you've described him a few times as a great salesman. Not a great scientist. But a salesman.'

And now Michael Rosenblatt knew he was indeed in the middle of the minefield. Drawn there by this calm, reasonable, kindly man.

And he waited for the next, inevitable, question.

Gamache leaned forward and seemed almost apologetic.

'Was Gerald Bull smart enough to design the Supergun? Or was he just the salesman? Was there another genius at work we don't know about?'

Ka-boom.

CHAPTER 19

—

Clara Morrow turned into the Lepages' driveway. It was long and rutted, as most of the dirt drives were in this area.

She glanced down at the passenger-side footwell, where a casserole covered in foil sat, along with an apple crisp. Still warm. She could smell the brown sugar and cinnamon, and wondered if it was a bad thing that she was salivating. And tempted to turn around. And eat it all herself.

She parked in front of the small farmhouse.

A curtain moved in an upstairs window and she saw Evelyn's face, a look of distress glancing across it, as though Clara was a germ and Evie an open sore.

An old mongrel dog, Harvest, lay on the grass. He struggled to his feet, his tail wagging slowly.

'Clara,' Evie said, coming to the screen door, forcing a smile that looked painful.

'I didn't want to disturb you,' Clara said, cradling the dishes. 'But I know how much energy it takes to get out of bed in the morning, never mind shop and cook. There're a couple bags of groceries in the trunk. They're from Monsieur Béliveau. And Sarah sent some croissants and baguettes from her boulangerie. She says you can freeze them. I wouldn't know. They never last that long in my house.'

Clara saw a hint of a genuine smile. And with it a slight relief, a loosening of the tight bands holding Evie Lepage in, and the world out.

Armand Gamache watched the old scientist leave the B and B dining room.

As soon as Gamache had asked about Gerald Bull's real contribution to Project Babylon, Michael Rosenblatt had looked at his watch and slid awkwardly out of the banquette.

'I really must go. Thank you for the company.'

Armand had got up too.

Professor Rosenblatt offered his hand and Gamache, stepping into the handshake, had whispered in the scientist's ear.

Then stepped back to look into the startled face.

Rosenblatt had turned and strolled away with forced leisure, and Armand had returned to the banquette, and his coffee, and his musings.

Had Gerald Bull designed his Supergun? Or was he just the clever front man? Was there another genius behind that one? Someone younger, smarter? And far more dangerous?

And perhaps still alive. According to Reine-Marie, Gerald Bull had been sixty-two when he'd been murdered. Gamache knew that most scientists did their best work, their most dynamic and creative work, by the time they were forty.

Did Bull have a silent partner? A scientist, a physicist, an armaments designer? Did they make the perfect team? One staying in the shadows, scribbling plans for a gun unlike any other? An elegant weapon? While the other schmoozed, moved about in powerful circles, made deals? Found buyers. Found Saddam?

Both brilliant and both commanding different fields.

Gamache did the math. Michael Rosenblatt would have been in his mid-forties when Gerald Bull was killed. The design of the Supergun must have been made half a decade earlier, perhaps more. Putting Rosenblatt in his thirties.

It fit. Was Michael Rosenblatt the father of the monster in the woods?

Armand Gamache noticed that Rosenblatt had left so quickly he'd forgotten the redacted papers. Armand gathered them up, and thought maybe it hadn't been an oversight. Maybe there was nothing in them that could possibly be news to the elderly scientist.

Gamache sipped his coffee, and thought.

He had a sense that Rosenblatt was a scientist with a conscience. The question was, had Rosenblatt's sense of right and wrong come too late? Had he already contributed to the balance of terror?

Or perhaps his sense of what was right was different from Gamache's.

'*We sat down and wept,*' Gamache had whispered into Rosenblatt's ear, as they'd said good-bye. And then he provided the next line of the psalm. The one not written on the weapon. '*When we remembered Zion.*'

Dr Bull and Professor Rosenblatt might have their weapons of mass destruction, but so did Armand Gamache. And judging by the look on Rosenblatt's face as they'd parted, he'd made a direct hit.

Had Rosenblatt had a hand in creating Project Babylon, and then, when he realized that it was intended for Saddam, and that Saddam intended to use it against Israel, had he also had a hand in trying to stop it? By killing Gerald Bull. Perhaps he hadn't actually pulled the trigger, but who else would have intimate knowledge of Bull's movements, except a close colleague? A whispered word was all it would take.

Mossad, the CIA, the Iranians, CSIS would do the rest.

But that was a twenty-five-year-old murder case. Armand Gamache's responsibility wasn't to the gun, and it sure wasn't to Gerald Bull. It was to Laurent. Who'd warned them all, and been ignored.

Isabelle Lacoste was running out of village and villagers to interview.

The Sûreté investigators could finally talk openly about the Supergun, and while wildly interested, the villagers were not even remotely helpful.

Most had been either too young at the time the gun was built, or hadn't lived there then. Like Myrna. And Clara. And Gabri and Olivier.

And now Isabelle took the black-and-white photograph of Dr Bull and her questions into the general store, to speak with the last person on her list. The second oldest resident, Monsieur Béliveau, while Jean-Guy got the short straw and was interviewing the oldest resident.

'Like some, numbnuts?'

Ruth tilted the Glenfiddich bottle toward Beauvoir.

'You know I don't drink anymore,' he said.

'This isn't alcohol. I took it from the Gamaches',' she said. 'It's tea. Earl Grey. They think I don't know.'

Beauvoir smiled and accepted, though part of him still felt uncomfortable seeing the amber liquid flow from the Scotch bottle into his glass. He smelled it. There was no medicinal scent of alcohol.

Nevertheless, he pushed the glass away from him and slid the photograph he'd had copied toward her.

It was black and white, and showed a substantial man in a suit and narrow tie, a coat slung over one arm. The image of a businessman, whose business was in trouble. While the stance might be casual, there was no mistaking the anxiety in his face, as though he'd heard a shot in the distance.

'Do you know this man?'

Ruth studied it. 'Should I?'

'You know about the gun?'

'I heard something. Everyone's talking about it.'

'That man built it. His name's Gerald Bull.'

'Then it's true. About the gun, I mean.'

Jean-Guy nodded.

'They're calling it a Supergun,' said Ruth.

Again he nodded. 'Bigger than any weapon I've ever seen.'

'Laurent was telling the truth,' said the old poet.

To Jean-Guy's eyes she'd never looked older.

'It was built in the mid to late eighties,' he said. 'You were here then. Do you remember anything? It must've made a racket in the forest. You couldn't miss it.'

'It's a question only a city person would ask. You think the countryside is silent, but it isn't. It would put New York City to shame some days. Chain saws are going around here all the time. Clearing land, cutting down trees, sawing off branches hanging too close to Hydro lines. People getting wood for the winter. Between the chain saws and the lawnmowers it can be deafening. And don't get me started on the frogs and beetles in spring. No one would notice, or remember, a particular racket in the woods thirty years ago.'

Beauvoir nodded. 'He didn't hire locals?'

'Well, he didn't hire me,' said Ruth. She slugged back the tea.

Monsieur Béliveau looked more morose than ever.

'*Désolé*, I wish I could help. I was here at the time and running the general store, but I don't remember anything.'

'The gun is huge,' Chief Inspector Lacoste said. 'Massive. Whoever built it would've needed help clearing the land and bringing in the pieces, and then assembling it. Can you remember any activity in the forest?'

'*Non*,' he said, shaking his head.

She waited for more, but no more was offered. She would have to go in and get the information, pull it from him.

'If he was going to hire someone to clear the site, who would it have been back then?'

'Gilles Sandon did a lot of work in the woods,' said Monsieur Béliveau. 'But he's too young. And Billy Williams has a backhoe and is handy with a chain saw, but he's had the municipal contract for forty years. Keeps him pretty busy.'

Lacoste had already spoken to both men. Neither knew Gerald Bull. Neither knew anything about the gun. Neither had been hired to clear the land or bring in strange machinery back in the mid to late 1980s.

'Most everyone around here has a chain saw and cuts wood for the winter. Most do odd jobs for cash.' He shook his head. 'Not exactly skilled labor.'

'No.'

'How's this supposed to help find who killed the Lepage boy?' asked Monsieur Béliveau.

Isabelle Lacoste picked up the photograph.

'I'm not sure,' she admitted. 'But that gun and Laurent's death are connected. He was killed because he found it. I don't suppose you remember anyone, a stranger, coming here in the last few years, asking about a gun in the woods?'

'*Non, madame*, no one came into my store asking for a Supergun.'

His morose and serious tone made his answer all the more ludicrous.

She put the photograph of Dr Bull back into her pocket. They were doing the forensics, doing the interviews, collecting all the facts. But it wasn't a fact that had killed Laurent. It was fear. Someone was so frightened of what the boy had found, by what the boy would do or say, that they had to kill him.

It took a certain type of person, and a certain type of secret, to kill a child. And a great, big, stinking, putrid emotion.

Chief Inspector Gamache had taught her that.

Yes, collect evidence, collect facts. Absolutely. The facts would convict him, but the feelings would find him.

Clara had put the shepherd's pie and apple crisp in the fridge. They'd been her own comfort food, after Peter had gone. She'd followed the casseroles back to sanity. Thanks to the kindness of neighbors who kept baking them, and kept bringing them. And who'd kept her company.

And now it was Clara's turn to return the comfort and the casseroles and the company.

'Where's Al?' she asked. The large man was usually at home, fixing something or sorting baskets of produce.

'In the fields,' said Evie. 'Harvesting.'

Clara looked out the kitchen window and saw Al Lepage, his gray ponytail falling down his broad back as he knelt in the squash patch.

Immobile. Staring down at the rich earth.

It seemed far too intimate a moment, and Clara turned back to Evie.

'How're you doing?'

'It feels like my bones are dissolving,' said Evelyn. And Clara nodded. She knew that feeling.

Evie left the kitchen and Clara and the dog followed her. Clara thought they were going into the sitting room, but instead Evie lumbered up the stairs and stood at a closed door. Harvest had stayed at the bottom of the stairs, looking up at them, either too old to climb, or no longer motivated, without the reward of the boy to play with.

'Al won't come in here,' she explained. 'I have to keep the door closed. He doesn't want to see anything to do with Laurent. But I come up, when he's outside.'

She swung the door open and stepped inside. The bed was as Laurent had left it, unmade. And his clothes were scattered about, where he'd tossed them.

The two women sat side by side on Laurent's bed.

The old farmhouse creaked and groaned, as though the whole home was in mourning, trying to settle around the gaping hole in its foundation.

'I'm afraid,' said Evie, at last.

'Tell me,' said Clara. She didn't ask, 'Of what?' Clara knew what she was afraid of. And she knew the only reason Evelyn had allowed her past the threshold wasn't because of the casseroles she carried in her arms, but because of something else Clara carried. The hole in her own heart.

Clara knew.

'I'm afraid it won't stop, and all my bones will disappear and one day I'll just dissolve. I won't be able to stand up anymore, or move.' She looked into Clara's eyes. Clung to Clara's eyes. 'Mostly I'm afraid that it won't matter. Because I have nowhere to go, and nothing to do. No need of bones.'

And Clara knew then that as great as her own grief was, nothing could compare to this hollow woman and her hollow home.

There wasn't just a wound where Laurent had once been. This was a vacuum, into which everything tumbled. A great gaping black hole that sucked all the light, all the matter, all that mattered, into it.

Clara, who knew grief, was suddenly frightened herself. By the magnitude of this woman's loss.

They sat on Laurent's bed in silence, except for the moaning house.

It was a boy's room. Filled with rocks, that might be pieces of meteors, and bits of white that might be plastic, or might be bones from saber-toothed tigers or dinosaurs. There were pieces of porcelain, that might be from an ancient Abenaki encampment. Had the old tribe enjoyed high tea.

The walls were covered with posters of Harry Potter and King Arthur and Robin Hood.

Up until that moment Clara had been shocked by Laurent's death and appalled that it was murder. But she hadn't really thought of him as a person. She'd only known Laurent as the strange, annoying little boy who made up stories and demanded attention.

And so Clara had averted her eyes whenever he burst in erupting with another fantastic tale.

But now she sat on his Buzz Lightyear bedspread. And saw his shoes, flung off in different directions. And socks, balled up and tossed to the floor. And books, loads of books.

Who read anymore? What child, what little boy read? But Laurent's room was filled with books. And drawings. And wonder. And a grief so thick she could barely breathe.

This was the real Laurent, and he was lost forever.

Clara stood up and walked to the bookcase, and gripped it, her back turned to Evie so that Laurent's mother wouldn't be subjected to Clara's own suddenly overwhelming sorrow.

She was face-to-face with Babar and Tintin and the Little Prince. Leaning against the books was a series of small framed drawings of a nimble lamb. Pen and ink on white paper. The lamb was dancing. What was the word? Gamboling, she thought. Nine frames were lined up, leaned up against the books. The later ones were more sophisticated, with some watercolor added. All of the same lamb in a field. And in the distance, a ewe and a ram, watching. Guarding. On the back of each was written, Laurent, aged 1. Laurent, aged 2, and so on. The first lamb, the simplest, had just 'My Son' written on the back and a heart.

Clara looked at Evie. She had no idea this woman had such skill. While his father was the singer in the family, Laurent's mother was the artist. But there would be no more lambs. Laurent Lepage had stopped aging.

'Tell me about him.' Clara walked back to the bed and sat beside Evie.

And she did. Abruptly, in staccato sentences at first. Until in dibs and dabs and longer strokes, a portrait appeared. Of an unexpected baby, who became an unexpected little boy. Who always did and said the unexpected.

'Al adored him from the moment he was conceived,' Evelyn said. 'He'd sit in front of me and play his guitar, and sing. His own songs, mostly. He's the creative one.'

Clara remembered Al sitting on that chair at the funeral.

The guitar on his lap. Silent. No songs left. Clara wondered if, like her art, his music was now gone forever. That great pleasure consumed by grief.

'He didn't do it, you know.'

'Pardon?' said Clara.

'I've heard the gossip, we've seen how people look at us. They want to say something nice, but they're afraid we did it. Do people really think that?'

Clara knew that grief took a terrible toll. It was paid at every birthday, every holiday, each Christmas. It was paid when glimpsing the familiar handwriting, or a hat, or a balled-up sock. Or hearing a creak that could have been, should have been, a footstep. Grief took its toll each morning, each evening, every noon hour as those who were left behind struggled forward.

Clara wasn't sure how she'd have managed if the grief of losing Peter was accompanied not by shepherd's pie and apple crisp, but by accusations. Not by kindness but by finger-pointing. Not by company and embraces and patience, but by whispers and turned backs.

Al Lepage, the most social of men, the most jovial, had spent most of his time since the tragedy kneeling in a field. And no one had gone to get him.

'They don't know what they're saying,' said Clara. 'They don't realize the harm they're doing. People are afraid and they're grabbing at whatever they can no matter how ridiculous.'

'We thought they were friends.'

'You have friends. Lots of them. And we're defending you,' said Clara.

It was true. But it was possible they could have done a better job. And Clara realized, with some shock, that part of her wondered if the gossip wasn't perhaps, maybe, just a little ... true.

'Well, they have something else to talk about now,' said Clara.

'What do you mean?'

She hasn't heard, thought Clara. These two really were isolated. It was like a moat had been carved around them.

'The gun,' she began, watching Evie, who was looking blank.

Beyond Evelyn, out the window of Laurent's bedroom, Clara saw a familiar car drive up and park beside her own. Behind it came two Sûreté squad cars. On seeing the look on Clara's face, Evie turned, then rose stiffly to her feet.

'The police.' She looked at Clara. 'Why? What was it you were saying about a gun?'

CHAPTER 20

'Al?' said Evie, approaching the large man planted in the field. 'The police are here.'

Al Lepage remained kneeling on the ground but straightened up. And then he very slowly hauled himself upright. He turned and stared at his wife as though not quite understanding what she was saying.

Evie put out her hand and he took it in his massive hand. And she led him back to the house.

'Al,' said Clara as he passed, but while he looked at her, he said nothing.

Clara wasn't sure what to do. It seemed invasive, and perhaps even ghoulish, to stay. She didn't want to appear to be simply curious, collecting gossip. But to leave felt like running away, abandoning them.

She decided to stay. Laurent's parents had been left on their own far too often and far too long.

'Monsieur, madame,' said Isabelle Lacoste. 'I'm afraid I'm going to have to ask to search your home again.'

She glanced at Clara and gave the tiniest of nods of acknowledgment.

'Why?' asked Evie. 'Has something happened? Is this about the gun?'

'Gun?' said Al. His slack face tightened up, and his eyes came back into something like focus. 'What gun?'

'I was just telling Evelyn,' said Clara. 'But I didn't get to the details. I don't think Al knows.'

The two Sûreté officers looked at Laurent's father, wondering, of course, whether that was true.

'I don't understand,' said Al.

If he did know about the Supergun, thought Beauvoir, he was doing a pretty good imitation of someone who was completely ignorant.

'The thing that was hidden under the netting,' said Lacoste. 'In the woods. Where Laurent died. It's a gun.'

'A cannon, really,' said Beauvoir, studying them. 'A missile launcher. It's called a Supergun.'

'Laurent was telling the truth,' said his father, staring at Lacoste, his eyes pleading for something, though she didn't know what.

Forgiveness? For ignorance? For her, and her news, to go away.

'I didn't believe him. I laughed at him.'

'We both did,' said Evie.

'No, you wanted to go and see, in case it was real.'

'But then he told us about the monster,' Evie reminded him. 'There was no way to believe that.'

'Christ,' said Al. It sounded more like a plea, a prayer, than a curse. 'Oh no.' Lepage shut his eyes and hung his head, shaking it slightly. 'I can't believe it.'

'You're not the only ones who didn't believe him,' said Lacoste. 'None of us did.'

While she spoke kindly, Chief Inspector Lacoste never

lost sight of the fact that she might be speaking to Laurent's killer.

'May we search your house?' Inspector Beauvoir asked.

Both Evie and Al nodded and followed them inside.

The agents who came with them began the search on the main floor, while Lacoste and Beauvoir went upstairs to the bedrooms.

While Lacoste searched Al and Evie's room, Jean-Guy went through Laurent's, opening every drawer, looking behind the posters tacked to the walls. He got on his hands and knees and looked under the bed, under the mattress, under the pillow, under the rug. He searched the closet and the pockets of Laurent's clothing. Anywhere and everywhere a clever child could hide something. But there was nothing.

Laurent might be inquisitive, creative, but he was not by nature secretive. In fact, he seemed to want to tell everyone everything.

Nothing was hidden.

On the bedside table was a collection of rocks, with quartz and fool's gold running through them. And a book, splayed open.

Le Chandail de Hockey, by Roch Carrier. One of Jean-Guy's favorite stories growing up. About a Québécois boy, a rabid Canadiens fan, who's sent a Toronto Maple Leafs hockey sweater by mistake, and has to wear it.

Jean-Guy picked up the book and saw that Laurent was nearing the end of the short story. He replaced the book exactly as he'd found it, his hand lingering on the familiar illustration on the cover.

'Find something?' asked Lacoste.

'Nothing.'

'You okay?'

'Fine.'

Isabelle picked up one of the tiny lamb drawings, reading what was written carefully on the back. My Son. And then a heart. She replaced it. This was a job that had to be done, but it never stopped feeling like a violation.

'You?' Beauvoir asked.

'Nothing much.'

She'd found that Al had an enlarged prostate, and Evie waxed her facial hair, and one of them needed suppositories. They found that Al read books on solar power and historic fiction, and Evie read about organic gardening and biographies.

There was no television in the home and one old desktop computer.

Lacoste had turned it on and did a search and read emails from clients and family and friends. Condolences that petered out in the last few days.

After the search they met the Lepages and Clara in the sitting room of the small farmhouse. Clara had made tea, and offered the officers some, but they declined.

The room was dominated by a large brick fireplace fitted with a woodstove. Two old sofas faced each other across the hearth, each with a knitted afghan folded across the back. The floors were hardwood, and pocked and scratched. Braided rag throw rugs were scattered here and there on the floors. The old dog lay with its head on its paws by a rocking chair.

A guitar was propped on a stand next to the chair.

Beauvoir walked over to the stereo and looked at the LPs and cassettes.

He pulled out a vinyl album and recognized the smiling man on the cover. With a full head of red hair, a bushy red beard, wearing a plaid lumberjack shirt and jeans with peace signs sewn in. He had everything but a joint.

He also recognized the background, with three tall pine trees.

The album was called *Asylum*.

'You?' asked Beauvoir, unnecessarily.

Al nodded. Evie took her husband's hand.

'You're American, is that right?' asked Lacoste. 'A draft dodger?'

Al nodded. 'There were lots of us.'

'I know,' said Lacoste. 'It wasn't an accusation. Why did you come here?'

'To get out of the war,' said Al.

'No, I mean, why here specifically?'

'I walked across the border from Vermont. I was tired. It was dark. I saw the lights of the village. So I stopped. Stayed.'

His speech was almost infantile, in spare declarative sentences.

'When was this?' asked Lacoste.

'Nineteen seventy.'

'More than forty years ago,' said Beauvoir.

'Do you know anything about that gun in the woods?' Lacoste asked.

'No. I hate guns.'

'Did Laurent say anything more after he found the gun? Did he talk to anyone else about it?' asked Beauvoir.

Both Al and Evie shook their heads.

'No?' asked Beauvoir. 'Or you don't know?'

'If he spoke to someone else he didn't tell us,' said Evie. 'But he must've, right? Was he killed because of the gun?'

'We think so,' said Lacoste. 'Can you think of anything Laurent said, anything at all, that could help?'

'He came home, we had supper. Laurent read and Al and I did the vegetable baskets, then we went to bed. It was a normal night.'

'And next morning?' asked Lacoste.

'Breakfast, then he was out the door and on his bike as always.' Evie shut her eyes and both Lacoste and Beauvoir knew what she was seeing. The back of her little boy as he ran out into the sunshine. Never to return.

'We looked in his room but didn't find anything,' said Beauvoir. 'Has anything changed in there? Is there anything new?'

'Like what?' Evie asked.

Like the firing mechanism to a weapon of mass destruction, thought Beauvoir. Or plans for Armageddon.

'Just anything,' he said. 'Did he bring anything home recently?'

'Not that I noticed.'

Isabelle Lacoste reached into her pocket, brought out an evidence bag, and placed it on the table between them. And waited for a reaction.

Al picked it up and his brows came together. 'Where did you find this?'

'Is it yours?'

'I think so.'

Evie took the cassette out of his hand and read the label.

'Pete Seeger. It's ours.'

'How can you be sure?' asked Beauvoir.

'Who else would have this?' she asked, holding it up. 'Besides, the label's torn where it got stuck in the cassette player in the truck.'

'One of Laurent's favorites?' asked Lacoste.

Evie smiled slightly. 'No. He hated it. It took a couple of

months for Al to pry it out of the machine, so it was all we played when we were driving.'

'He liked it at first,' said Al.

'Yes, but even I grew to hate it. Where did you find it?' Evie asked.

'On the ground by the gun,' said Lacoste. 'Did you notice it missing?'

Both Al and Evie shook their heads.

'Why would Laurent take it there?' Evie asked.

'Well, either he did or his killer did,' said Beauvoir.

It took a moment for the implication to penetrate, but when it did Al Lepage stood and faced Beauvoir.

'Are you accusing us? Me?'

'I'm stating what must be obvious,' said Beauvoir, also getting to his feet. 'Why would Laurent have a cassette with music he hated?'

'To hide it?' asked Evie, standing beside her husband. Holding his hand not for comfort but to stop him from doing something they'd all regret.

Here was a man who might hate violence, Beauvoir knew, but who was capable of it.

'We've heard the rumors,' said Al. 'They think I killed my own child. Some are even saying Laurent wasn't mine. That Evie . . . ' He was overcome and couldn't go on. The massive man stood within six inches of Beauvoir, staring at him. Not angry anymore, but desperate. If Al Lepage was a mountain, they were witnessing a landslide.

'Al,' said Evie, pulling him away. 'It doesn't matter what people say. We have to help the police find out who did this to Laurent. That's all that matters.' She turned from her husband to Lacoste. 'You have to believe it wasn't us. Please.'

The other Sûreté agents came up from the basement and shook their heads. Nothing.

Chief Inspector Lacoste picked up the cassette. 'Thank you for your time.'

'May I take this with me?' asked Beauvoir, holding up Al Lepage's record. 'I'll be careful with it.'

Al waved at him, dismissing the man, the record, the question.

Clara walked with Lacoste and Beauvoir to the cars.

'You don't really think Al or Evie had anything to do with Laurent's death, do you?' she asked.

'I think people can do terrible things,' said Beauvoir. 'Lash out. Hurt or even kill someone they love. That man is coming apart.'

'From grief,' said Clara.

'From something,' said Beauvoir.

Once in the car, Beauvoir turned to Lacoste. 'Did you notice anything strange about the Lepages?'

Lacoste had been quiet, thinking. Now she nodded.

'Neither of them asked about the gun,' she said.

Beauvoir nodded. 'Exactly.'

They spent the balance of the afternoon following up on the interviews and checking facts and details.

Isabelle saw Gamache leave his home with Henri, first glancing in the direction of the old train station, then turning away and walking out of sight.

A few minutes later she found him on the bench above the village, Henri sitting by his side.

'You aren't avoiding me, are you?' she asked, joining Gamache on the bench. 'Because this isn't a very good hiding place.'

He smiled. His face creasing with amusement.

'Perhaps I am,' he admitted. 'It's not personal.'

'It's professional,' she said, and nodded. 'It must be strange not to be in charge of the investigation.'

'It is, a little,' he admitted. 'It's hard not to slip back into the old roles. Especially since—' He spread his large hands, and she understood the enormity of his struggle. 'Laurent.'

She nodded. This murder had hit home.

'You need your space, Isabelle. It's your investigation. I have no desire to return, but—'

'But it's in the blood.'

She glanced down at his hands. Those expressive hands. That she'd held, as he lay dying. As he'd sputtered to her what they both knew would be the last thing he'd say.

Reine-Marie.

She'd been the vessel into which he'd poured his final feelings, his eyes pleading with her to understand.

And she did.

Reine-Marie.

She'd held his hand tightly. It was covered in his own blood and that of others. And it mingled with the blood on her hands. Her own, and others'.

And now catching killers was in their blood.

Chief Inspector Gamache hadn't died. And he'd continued to lead them for many investigations. Until the time had come to come here.

He'd done enough. It was someone else's turn.

Hers.

'You and Madame Gamache seem happy here.'

'We are. Happier than I ever thought possible.'

'But are you content?' Isabelle probed.

Gamache smiled again. How different she was from

Jean-Guy, who'd come right out and demanded, '*Are you going to stay here doing nothing, or what*, patron?'

He'd tried to explain to Jean-Guy that stillness wasn't nothing. But the taut younger man just didn't understand. And neither would he have, Gamache knew, in his thirties. But in his fifties Armand Gamache knew that sitting still was far more difficult, and frightening, than running around.

No, this wasn't nothing. But the time was coming when this stillness would allow him to know what to do. Next.

What next?

'Please take the Superintendent's position, *patron*. There's a lot left to do at the Sûreté. A mess still to clean up. And you saw those two recent recruits. The new agents have no discipline, no pride in the service.'

'I did notice that.'

'If those are the ones coming up through the ranks, we'll be back where we started within ten years.' She turned to fully face him. 'Please, take the job.'

He looked down at the village.

'It's so beautiful,' he said, almost under his breath.

She followed his gaze and looked at the cottages, the gardens, the three soaring evergreens on the village green. And she knew those weren't what made this village so attractive.

Gabri came out of the bistro and headed to the B and B. He spotted them on the ridge and waved. Sarah stood at the door of her boulangerie and flapped a towel embedded with flour. They could see movement through the window of Myrna's New and Used Bookstore.

Isabelle suddenly felt horrible, for making him feel this shouldn't be enough.

Gamache lifted his gaze from the village to the rolling

mountains covered in a forest that had taken root thousands of years ago. The brilliant autumn leaves interspersed with pines.

'Look at it,' he said, shaking his head slightly, almost in disbelief. 'I sometimes sit here and imagine the wildlife, the lives, going on in that forest. I try to imagine what it must've been like for the Abenaki, before the Europeans came. Or for the first explorers. Were they amazed by it? Or was it just an obstacle?'

He spent a moment imagining himself an early explorer.

He'd have been amazed. He was even now.

'Not surprising the gun wasn't found,' he said. 'Even if you knew it was there, and were looking for it, you'd probably never find it. You could walk within a foot of the thing and still miss it.'

Isabelle Lacoste stared across the village to the vast forest.

'What's shocking is that it was found at all,' he said.

'What's shocking is that it's there,' said Lacoste, and saw him nod.

'After you left this morning I asked Professor Rosenblatt about that.'

He told her about the two theories put forward by the scientist. That the Supergun was either a display model to show potential buyers, or it was placed deliberately to hit targets in the United States.

'But either way, why here?' she asked. 'Why not the forests of New Brunswick or Nova Scotia? Or somewhere else in Québec along the US border? Why here?'

She pointed to the ground.

Armand Gamache had been sitting there wondering the same thing. Someone had planned this, probably for a very long time. And then placed it. Carefully. Intentionally. Here.

'Three Pines isn't on any map,' he said. 'That would be an advantage when trying to hide something, but at the same time the village would provide services and workers when needed.'

'Except according to all our interviews, no local worked on the site,' she said.

'No one willing to admit it.'

'*Oui*,' said Lacoste.

Armand Gamache returned his gaze to the forest. He wasn't sitting there with Henri simply marveling at the wildlife it contained. He was also scanning it. For new growth among the old. For holes in the canopy.

For evidence of one reference in the redacted notes the censors had failed to find. And black out.

'Professor Rosenblatt read the notes Reine-Marie printed out,' said Gamache.

'Did he find them interesting?' asked Lacoste.

'He didn't seem to. And he either missed, or chose not to mention, the plural.'

The one letter among hundreds, thousands. Like a single tree in a forest. But one that changed everything.

'The *s*,' said Lacoste. 'Superguns.'

Then she too looked across at mile after mile of forest.

'We told the Lepages about the gun,' she said. 'Today, when we searched their place again.'

'Did you find anything?'

'No, though they admitted the Pete Seeger cassette was theirs but didn't know how it got near the gun. But that's another interesting thing. When we told them about the Supergun, they seemed surprised but neither of them asked any questions about it. Not one.'

'They might be absorbed in grief,' he said. 'People don't

behave normally when there's been a death, especially a violent one. Especially a child.'

'True.' After a few moments she spoke, under her breath. 'Why here?'

'The gun?' he asked.

'No, the man. I asked Al Lepage that question. Why did he come to Three Pines, when he was dodging the draft.'

'And what did he say?'

'He said he'd walked across the border from Vermont and saw the lights of the village.'

Now she turned to look at her former boss. His brows were raised, but he said nothing.

'But he couldn't have, could he?' she said. 'The forest is too thick. No one would just walk across the border, unless they wanted to get lost in the woods. He'd have to have known where he was going.'

Gamache nodded.

'He'd have to have had a guide. Someone who brought him here.'

They looked again at the old village. And the tall pine trees planted for one purpose. To signal to those seeking sanctuary that they were safe.

They'd made it to Three Pines.

CHAPTER 21

R eine-Marie and Armand knocked first, then let themselves into Clara's home. Some of the other guests had
already arrived, though 'guests' made it sound too formal.
They'd received a call late that afternoon from Clara inviting them for a potluck.

'And the luck,' said Clara, 'is that Olivier and Gabri are
taking the night away from the bistro and are providing a
main course and hors d'oeuvre.'

'We'll bring a salad,' said Reine-Marie.

'Salad?' Clara had said. 'What's that?'

They arrived with an apple crumble and a container of
Coaticook vanilla ice cream.

Olivier and Gabri showed up at the same time, with Ruth
and Rosa.

'Here's our casserole,' said Gabri, putting it on the
counter as though he himself had made it.

'Looks delicious,' said Reine-Marie. 'What is it?'

'Rock Cornish game hens,' said Olivier, when it appeared
Gabri was about to fabricate the ingredients. 'With wild
cranberry and' – he looked at the crumble on the counter –
'apple stuffing.'

'Exactly,' said Gabri.

'Well, if you're the luck, I suppose she's the "pot",' said Myrna, coming into the kitchen from the living room and pointing to Ruth.

'That would make you the kettle,' said Ruth.

'She's calling the kettle black,' said Gabri.

'I know, I got it,' said Myrna.

'What's that?' asked Ruth, turning around and listening to the strange sound.

'Something you've never used,' said Clara. 'The door-bell.'

'A doorbell?' Ruth asked. 'I thought they were a myth, like Pegasus.'

'And boundaries,' said Gabri.

Clara reappeared a moment later with Mary Fraser and Sean Delorme.

'I think you know some of the people here,' said Clara.

They nodded to Gamache and Jean-Guy, then Clara introduced them to Reine-Marie and Ruth, who said, 'They don't look like spies.'

'And you don't look like an invited guest,' said Clara. 'Yet here you are.'

'We didn't know what to bring,' said Mary Fraser. 'We picked this up at the general store.'

Clara took the bottle of apple cider.

'Thank you,' she said, putting it in the fridge alongside the clinking row of other cider bottles.

'So, what were you up to today?' asked Armand, as he and Reine-Marie walked with the newcomers into Clara's living room. 'I didn't see you in the village.'

'Oh, we were about,' said Sean Delorme. He lowered his voice. 'Doing some legwork on the you-know-what.'

'The gun?' asked Ruth. 'That great big goddamned thing in the forest where Laurent was murdered?'

That fell like a brain aneurysm on the gathering. Everyone in the living room stopped moving, talking, breathing.

'Yes,' said Delorme. 'That would be the one. Nice duck.'

Rosa, in Ruth's arms, thrust her beak toward the CSIS agent, who stepped back.

'What have you found out about it?' asked Myrna. She'd returned to the sofa and was sitting beside Professor Rosenblatt.

'We can't say much,' said Mary Fraser, who obviously wished she didn't have to say anything. She shot a withering look at Rosenblatt, who refused to wither. He sat contentedly holding a glass of Scotch, like a benign grandfather among precocious children.

'Don't worry,' said Delorme. 'We're on it.'

'Don't worry?' asked Ruth. 'There's a huge fucking missile launcher in our backyard and apparently the only thing between us and Armageddon is some guy who's afraid of a duck.'

Sean Delorme gave a strained smile and squirmed slightly. But Gamache thought his discomfort stemmed as much from the social situation as Ruth's caustic comment. Delorme seemed more at home with people on paper than in person. And Mary Fraser, while perhaps better at covering it up, looked like she was searching for someplace to hide. Or a file to read.

She drifted, naturally, over to the bookcases and read the spines.

The phone rang and Clara left to answer it.

'Don't mind Ruth,' said Olivier, taking Delorme's arm with one hand and Mary Fraser's with the other and steering them to the drinks table. 'She's one sneeze away from the asylum.'

'We're already there,' shouted Ruth.

Armand turned his attention to the old poet.

Ruth had said 'Armageddon'. Not 'catastrophe', not 'disaster', but the one word associated with the gun. With the etching. With the Whore of Babylon, marching toward the end of the world.

But no one had been told about the etching. Was it a coincidence, or did she know something? It was the sort of word she'd use, and certainly the sort of event she evoked.

'Speaking of asylum,' Beauvoir said to Ruth. 'Do you have a record player at home?'

'Is that a non sequitur?'

'No. I have Al Lepage's record and I'd like to hear it, but it's only on LP.'

'Come over if you must after dinner,' she said. 'I have a record player somewhere.'

It was as gracious an invitation as he'd had from Ruth.

Myrna excused herself to see if she could help in the kitchen, and Armand and Reine-Marie took her place beside Professor Rosenblatt.

Gamache hadn't spoken with him since that morning when the elderly physicist had left the breakfast table with Armand's question ringing in his head.

Did Gerald Bull create the Supergun, or was he just the salesman, and someone else the actual designer? Did Dr Bull have a silent partner, who'd survived assassination because Bull had taken all the credit? And all the bullets.

Gamache hadn't tried very hard to track down Rosenblatt and continue that conversation. He knew, from years of investigation, that sometimes a difficult question was best left to burrow into a person. And sit there, barbed.

He suspected Professor Rosenblatt had been avoiding

him, and that was fine with Gamache. Let the question fester. For now.

'Professor,' said Gamache, with a cordial nod. 'I'm not sure you've met my wife, Reine-Marie.'

'Madame,' said the professor.

'We've been discussing taking courses at either McGill or the Université de Montréal,' said Armand. 'I know Reine-Marie has been anxious to talk with you about that.'

'Oh, really?' Rosenblatt turned to her.

Taking her cue, Reine-Marie started chatting with Rosenblatt about McGill, while Armand walked over to Jean-Guy.

'Interesting group,' said Jean-Guy, surveying the gathering. 'Was it your idea to invite everyone?'

'Not at all,' said Armand. 'I'm as surprised as you.'

'That's too bad,' said Clara, returning from the phone call.

'What is?' asked Jean-Guy.

'I invited Antoinette and Brian, but Brian's in Montréal at a meeting of the Geological Survey and she just called to ask for a rain check. I think she wants a quiet evening to herself. *Les Filles de Caleb* is on, you know.'

'Yes, I know,' said Armand. 'We're taping it. For Reine-Marie, of course.'

'Of course,' said Clara. 'I'm taping it too.'

It was a repeat of the old Québécois drama that had gripped the nation years ago, and was even more of a hit now. Few strayed far from the television on nights it was on.

'It's been a difficult time for Antoinette,' said Armand. 'Is she still getting grief from members of her play group?'

'I don't think they call it a play group,' said Clara, laughing. 'But the answer is yes. They're still pissed at her for choosing the Fleming play without telling them. A lot of bad blood there now, I'm afraid.'

John Fleming, Gamache knew, had a habit of creating blood, most of it very bad.

'A shame she didn't come tonight. This is nice,' he said, looking around the gathering. 'Been a while.'

'I haven't been in the mood for entertaining,' said Clara.

'So what brought this on?' asked Jean-Guy.

'Seeing the Lepages this afternoon,' said Clara. 'They were so sad, and so alone. It made me miss this.'

She looked around her living room. The hubbub of conversation had increased, as guests mingled and chatted. Isabelle Lacoste had arrived and was offering around a platter of cheeses. But instead of crackers the cheese sat on top of thin slices of apple. It was actually, Clara had to admit, inspired and delicious.

'I came home and decided I'd had enough of my own grief. I wanted to move on.'

'Is such a thing a choice?' asked Gamache.

'In a way,' said Clara. 'I think I might've gotten stuck. I haven't even been able to paint. Nothing.' She waved toward her studio. 'But after seeing the size of their loss, mine suddenly seemed manageable. And this' – she looked around the room – 'is how I decided to manage it. With friends. I called up Evie and invited them, but she said they couldn't.'

Evie Lepage had made it sound as though they had another engagement, which Clara supposed was true in a way. They were bound to their home and engaged to their grief.

Evie had hesitated, though, and Clara could hear that part of her wanted to come. To try. But the grip was too strong, the loss too new, the desire to isolate too powerful. And then there was the guilt.

Clara knew how that felt.

'The painting will come back,' said Armand. 'I know it.'

238

'Do you?' she asked, searching his eyes for the truth, or evidence of a lie.

He smiled and nodded. 'Without a doubt.'

'*Merci*,' she said. 'Ruth's helping me.'

'Ruth?' both Armand and Jean-Guy asked at once. Neither had realized Clara had a creative death wish.

'Well, to be honest, more as a cautionary tale.' Clara looked over at the old poet, who was having an animated conversation with a painting on the wall.

In the foreground they saw Reine-Marie with a fixed smile on her face as Professor Rosenblatt entertained her with anecdotes from the world of algorithms.

'I think I'll just see if Madame Gamache needs rescuing,' said Jean-Guy, and walked off.

'Not that I'm not delighted,' said Armand, turning back to Clara, 'but I'm wondering why you invited them?'

He looked toward Mary Fraser and Sean Delorme, then over to Rosenblatt.

'They don't know anyone here,' she said. 'I thought they might be lonely. Especially the professor. I wanted them to feel welcome. We all want that.'

'True. And the fact they have information about the Supergun?'

'Totally irrelevant. Never entered my mind. But now that you bring it up, since they won't talk, what can you tell us?'

'Us?'

'Me. Spill.'

He smiled. 'Sorry, I can't tell you anything you don't already know.'

'But I know nothing. None of us does.'

'Someone does, Clara. The gun was built here, just outside Three Pines, for a reason.'

'Exactly. Why? What's its purpose? Does it work? Who built it?'

Unfortunately they were all questions he genuinely couldn't answer.

Reine-Marie Gamache, relieved of physicist duty, wandered over to where Isabelle Lacoste was talking with Mary Fraser.

Someone who seemed less like an intelligence agent would be hard to find, though Mary Fraser did look very intelligent, thought Reine-Marie, but not exactly sharp. More the slow, steady, often frightening mind, that took its time and arrived at a conclusion others might miss or did not want to see.

Having worked in archives and research all her professional life, Reine-Marie knew and admired that type of mind, though they could be a little frustrating to work with. They were often stubborn. Once a conclusion was finally reached they were loath to leave it, since it had taken so long to get there.

'Lots of people spent lots of time in the early nineties looking, but the plans were never found,' Mary Fraser was telling Isabelle Lacoste.

'Who were these people?'

Mary Fraser gave Reine-Marie a swift glance.

Reine-Marie veered away, recognizing this was not a conversation she should interrupt.

'Arms dealers hoping to sell the plans,' said Mary Fraser, once Madame Gamache had walked out of earshot. 'Or intelligence agencies hoping to suppress them.'

'Including CSIS?' asked Isabelle Lacoste.

'Yes. We looked for them but weren't successful. After a while most agencies gave up, thinking either the plans to Dr Bull's Supergun never existed, just another of his fantasies, or, if real, it had become obsolete, overtaken by advances in technology. Project Babylon would be just an oddity now. Everyone lost interest.'

'Except you.'

'And him.' She pointed to Professor Rosenblatt, now deep in conversation with Jean-Guy Beauvoir.

'But now we have the Supergun,' said Lacoste. 'It proves everyone wrong, and Gerald Bull right. The plans just got valuable, didn't they?'

'I don't think "valuable" quite covers it,' said Mary Fraser. 'With the discovery of the gun they just got priceless.'

She sounded triumphant, as though the accomplishment was her own. And in a way it was. The find had vindicated her and Delorme. Thrust them into the spotlight at CSIS. They'd gone from low-level functionaries correlating useless information in the basement to valuable resources. Priceless in their own way.

'Governments would pay a great deal for the plans?' asked Isabelle.

'Not just governments. Anyone with money and a target.' Mary Fraser glanced quickly over to Professor Rosenblatt. 'Have you wondered why he's still here? He's identified the gun, done what you asked. He's supposed to be retired. Shouldn't he be at home, or in Florida, or somewhere else? Relaxing.'

'What do you think?'

'I think weapons of mass destruction are a strange hobby,' said Mary Fraser. 'Don't you?'

Isabelle Lacoste had to agree.

'He worked for Gerald Bull, did he tell you that?' said Delorme, looking across the room to where Rosenblatt and Beauvoir were talking.

'He did,' said Gamache.

'He insinuates that he was more than just some assistant, but he hasn't contributed a thing to the field.'

Again with the 'field', thought Gamache. For something that was supposed to be covert, that field seemed surprisingly large and crowded.

'Was he good at what he did?' Armand asked.

'Rosenblatt?' said Delorme. 'We studied him, you know, thinking with Dr Bull dead then Rosenblatt might be the next best thing, and perhaps even better. But all his research hit dead ends.'

'I thought he helped design the Avro Arrow jet fighter,' said Gamache.

'Peripherally, yes. But it wasn't a contribution someone else couldn't have made. And the Arrow was scrapped, so again, we're back to nothing. Professor Rosenblatt has nothing to show for fifty years' work. Had he never lived, it wouldn't have mattered.'

It was such a brutal thing to say, and said so casually, that Gamache found himself reassessing this man. Perhaps it was just the unthinking utterance of a socially and emotionally inept person. Or maybe it was more than that. Maybe he genuinely loathed the man.

'Michael Rosenblatt's genius is attaching himself to brilliant people,' said Delorme. 'He's a leech. And now he's trying to take credit for the Supergun.'

'Credit?' asked Gamache. 'Can such a word be applied to such a thing?'

'You might not like it,' said Delorme, 'and I might not, but the Supergun is a remarkable achievement. That's just a fact. What we don't really know is what Gerald Bull planned to do with it. The problem is that it's an ever-changing world.

Friends become enemies, and the weapons you sold them are suddenly killing your own people.'

'*Non,*' said Gamache. 'The problem is that these weapons are built in the first place and people like Gerald Bull have no allegiances.'

'There've been weapons since there's been man,' said Delorme. 'Neanderthals had them. It's the nature of the beast. Whoever can make a better one wins. Where do you think weapons come from?'

They grow in a field, thought Gamache, though no one was suggesting hammering their swords into plowshares.

'We can't predict the future,' said Delorme. 'So we do our best to choose our allies.'

'And your weapons,' said Gamache. 'You said "we". I thought you were a file clerk.'

'I'm sorry, I meant the collective "we".'

'Of course, forgive me.'

But for just a moment, Sean Delorme no longer looked or sounded like a low-level office worker. He no longer seemed maladroit or ill at ease. An unexpected edge had appeared in this rather dull, almost comical, clerk.

There was an act going on here, Gamache was sure of it. Sean Delorme was alternately plodding and sly. A slightly muddled bureaucrat one moment, and in the next he was implying he was himself involved in the secretive world of arms dealing.

Was it more fantasy? Like Laurent playing soldier on the village green?

Was Sean Delorme playacting in a dangerous field? And then going home for dinner?

Armand Gamache looked at Sean Delorme and suddenly felt some concern that what had happened to Laurent, what happened to Gerald Bull, might happen to him. That reality would come calling. And once found, it would take his life. As it had taken theirs.

'You said almost everyone had stopped looking for the Supergun,' said Gamache.

'True.'

'Almost,' Gamache repeated. 'Almost everyone. But some would have kept going?'

Who kept going when every reasonable person gave up, Gamache wondered, though he already knew the answer.

The unreasonable. That's who. The fanatics.

'Who is still looking for the gun?' Gamache asked.

'This is all just theory, supposition.'

'Then theorize.'

Delorme sighed. 'Okay. The people who stopped looking were probably those who went on to other interests. They brokered other deals, found new clients, created new weapons. But there are some who can't do that.'

'Why not?' asked Gamache.

'They don't have the skills. There are some within the arms community who are bottom feeders. They live off the ideas of others. They're opportunistic. Mercenary. They're like grave robbers or treasure hunters. They don't have to amass the treasure, they just have to find it. And steal it.'

'Surely stealing from an arms dealer can't be a good idea.'

'No, but if the reward is big enough it might be worth the risk. And in this case, there was no risk. The man who designed the Supergun is dead.'

'Is he?'

Sean Delorme's head fell to the side, as though the

question had shoved him off-kilter. 'Are we back there? We told you over breakfast, Gerald Bull took five bullets to the brain. He's dead.'

'*Oui*, you did. But suppose Dr Bull was a great salesman, but not a great designer.'

Delorme opened his mouth to speak, but Gamache held up his hand.

'Hear me out. Isn't there a certain amount of evidence suggesting just that? That Bull might've had the idea, but someone else had to actually design the gun? They'd make the perfect team. Gerald Bull would find a buyer and someone else would draw up the plans.'

Sean Delorme was silent, taking this in. Then he smiled, breaking into a huge, goofy grin.

'You're kidding, right? Having fun with me?'

Gamache said nothing.

'Come on, there's no proof of that at all. And who would it be? And please don't say John Fleming.'

Again, Gamache remained silent, but looked across the room. And Delorme's smile faded.

'You don't think ... ' He glanced over toward Rosenblatt. 'But that's ridiculous. He's not nearly smart enough.' He lowered his voice. 'If he's still here, it's for a whole other reason.'

Gamache remembered Delorme's description of Rosenblatt. A leech. And his description of those who'd spent decades searching for the Supergun. As people who fed on the work of others. Leeches.

'The gun no longer matters, does it?' said Gamache. 'Once it was found, anyone looking for the Supergun would have shifted their search. After all, the gun's being guarded. No one can steal it, or fire it.'

'But someone might build another one,' said Delorme.

'If they had the plans,' said Gamache.

And if the gun was here, the plans might be too.

They'd assumed Laurent had been murdered by someone who knew the gun was there and wanted to keep its location secret. After all, who else would believe his ridiculous story?

But suppose Laurent was murdered by someone who'd spent decades searching for it? And when a dirty little boy came flying out of the woods yelling about a gun bigger than a house, with a monster on it, one person believed him. A plan had begun to form. For murder.

And Gamache now had an answer to a question that had been bothering him. It seemed inexplicable that a Supergun, a massive missile launcher, could be found in the woods of Québec and CSIS only send two file clerks.

No squad of soldiers. No team of scientists.

Gamache now knew it was because they didn't need anyone else. The gun was essentially a sculpture. All but useless. What CSIS needed were people who could find the plans.

And that task fell to two middle-aged bureaucrats who knew more about Project Babylon and the beast marching to Armageddon than anyone else.

With the possible exception of an elderly physicist.

Michael Rosenblatt sipped his Scotch and looked over at the fresh young Sûreté Chief Inspector, speaking with Mary Fraser, the dried-up CSIS agent.

And they were looking at him, but averted their gaze when he met their eyes.

Then he shifted his glance to the retired Chief Inspector speaking with Delorme.

They too were looking at him. The CSIS agent quickly looked away, but Armand Gamache held his eyes.

Professor Rosenblatt suddenly felt hemmed in.

Turning to his companion, he said, 'I wonder why they're still here.'

'The CSIS agents?' asked Beauvoir. 'To gather information about the gun, of course. Why else?'

'Yes,' said Rosenblatt. 'Why else.'

Dinner was served, with the platters of game hens and bowls of grilled vegetables and baskets of sliced baguette put on the long pine table in Clara's kitchen. The room was lit with candles, and in the middle of the table sat an exuberant centerpiece.

Myrna had spent the afternoon collecting arching branches of bright fall leaves, and smaller branches still bearing tiny red crab apples. She'd collected pine cones from under the trees on the village green. Sticks and cones. A tribute to the boy who'd spent his whole life protecting Three Pines.

CHAPTER 22

〜

O nce dinner was over and the dishes done, the guests
went their separate ways.

'Coming, numbnuts?'

'I just want to get the record, I'll be over in a minute.'

And he was. Within minutes Jean-Guy was carefully tip-
ping the vinyl record out of the sleeve.

'Here, give me that.' Ruth grabbed the LP from him and
almost dropped it on the floor.

Finding the A-side, she put it on the turntable, surprising
Beauvoir by fitting the small hole onto the post effortlessly.
But he stopped her before she swung the arm of the record
player over the precious disc and scratched it.

'Let me do that.'

'Have you ever done it before?' Ruth demanded, shoving
him aside with a sharp elbow.

'Hey,' he said. 'That hurt.'

'You want to know hurt? Wait 'til your ears get a load of
that.' She jabbed her finger at Al Lepage's record, now going
round and round on the turntable. Ruth lifted the arm and
expertly, delicately, lowered the needle to the vinyl.

A rhythmic crackling came from the speakers.

And then the first song started with a simple guitar. Classical, melodic. And then a drumbeat, like a metronome. At first a slow march, then it gathered speed, intensity. It picked up more instruments as it began to race along. A piano, strings. Horns. The drum became almost militaristic, building to a vigorous, energetic, stirring crescendo.

And weaving through it was the voice.

Beauvoir sat on the lumpy old sofa and stared at the turn-table, marveling at Al Lepage's deep, gravelly voice.

As the first song wound down, Jean-Guy turned to Ruth. 'That was incredible. Even you must see that.'

'Did you listen to the lyrics?'

'I think so.'

'Well, if you thought they were great, more than your nuts are numb. Excuse me, I have to pee.' She rocked herself out of the chair. 'I've been drinking tea all night.'

When she left, Jean-Guy carefully lifted the arm and replaced the needle at the beginning of the record.

A soldier and a sailor met in a bar, Al sang in his raspy voice. *The one said to the other, there you are.*

Jean-Guy listened as the soldier and sailor talked about war and love, parted ways, then ended up on different sides of a conflict.

Ruth was right. It was painful, but not in the way Al Lepage probably intended. The story was clichéd, embar-rassing, cringeworthy. The rhymes were either obvious or tortured. But the music and voice obscured that, cam-ouflaging it. Making it appear better than it was. Perhaps, thought Beauvoir, like the man himself.

The next song was on. The music was powerful, with piano and banjo and harmonica. A fusion of folk and rock and country.

Now Al was singing about a dog who gets lost and is just about to curl up and die when he's found by a pack of wild dogs and saved. He's accepted into the pack but, too late, he realizes they're wolves and he's expected to kill other animals. As they do. Not because they're cruel but because it's in their nature. Just as he's about to kill a little lamb, his heart in despair, he sees a light through the trees and runs toward it. A door opens, and it's his family. Calling to him. Waiting for him.

Jean-Guy sat on the sofa marveling how a story that should have been, could have been, very moving had been rendered ridiculous by infantile and clunky lyrics and silly attempts to force words to rhyme. Beauvoir was not sure 'dog' rhymed with 'ideologue'.

It was a shame. Lepage's ideas, his voice, his music were powerful. His lyrics, on the other hand, were *merde*. They should never have been shared. Beauvoir wondered how the record had fared.

Jean-Guy was having fun finding words that rhymed with *merde*, when Ruth reappeared. And glared.

'Had enough?' she asked. 'If you keep listening, your brain will turn into something soft and smelly.'

'How do you know? Have you heard it before?'

The mad old poet walked over to her stereo and returned to the sofa holding Al's record. Her own copy.

'How'd you get this?' Beauvoir asked, taking it from her.

'It's self-produced. I bought one and listened to it once to be polite, but it's crap.'

And yet, thought Jean-Guy, she'd kept it. The record didn't end up in the church rummage sale. Or the dump. And since when was Ruth polite? Or perhaps the question should be, when did she become impolite?

'He used to busk on the street in Cowansville, when he first arrived,' said Ruth. 'Sometimes he'd play in the *boîtes à chansons* in Montréal, but mostly he sang in the coffeehouses around here. That was before Gabri and Olivier opened the bistro.'

'He doesn't play there now, though, does he?' asked Beauvoir.

'No,' said Ruth. 'He stopped singing, thank God.'

Jean-Guy put the album facedown. He didn't want to look at the smiling young man with the bushy red beard, who had no idea what heartbreak was waiting for him a few decades down the road.

'How did Al Lepage get across the border?' Jean-Guy asked.

'He ran, I guess. Probably chased by a gang of music lovers.'

'Lepage claims he walked across the border from Vermont. But how'd he find Three Pines? He didn't just stumble into it, did he? He had to have had help.'

'Maybe he was meant to find Three Pines,' she said, getting up again and gathering Rosa in her arms.

'You don't believe that.'

'You have no idea what I believe,' she snapped, then softened her expression as she made for the stairs to her bedroom. 'Turn off the lights when you leave.'

'Are you going upstairs to heave?' he called after her and heard, out of the darkness, a chuckle.

Jean-Guy leaned back and listened to the music, trying not to hear the lyrics. Something about—

Buy, buy this good apple pie.

Oh no, thought Beauvoir, surely not.

Drove my Honda, which I'm fonda . . .

He tuned out the lyrics and replaced them with the conversation after dinner, when he and Isabelle had walked to the Gamaches' from Clara's so he could pick up the record and they could have a brief discussion about the evening.

'What I find strange,' Isabelle had said, as they sat in the Gamaches' living room, 'is that neither the CSIS people nor Rosenblatt picked up on Dr Bull's poor academic record and that maybe there was someone else, the real designer, working behind the scenes. I mean, it was right there. Even Madame Gamache found it.'

'Thank you, dear,' said Reine-Marie.

'*Désolé*. But you know what I mean. These people are supposedly experts on Gerald Bull, and professionals at deciphering information, and yet they miss that?'

Armand nodded. 'Why do you think that is? Beyond the obvious answer that Reine-Marie is far smarter than all of them.'

'*Merci, mon cher*,' said Madame Gamache. 'You know, a lot of geniuses did poorly in school. Maybe that was Dr Bull.'

'Maybe,' said Jean-Guy. 'But I think the CSIS people, and perhaps even Professor Rosenblatt, didn't miss it. They were just hoping we would. I think they know perfectly well someone else was involved with Project Babylon.'

'And that's why they're still here,' said Armand, nodding.

'To look for the plans or the person?' asked Isabelle.

'Both,' said Beauvoir.

'You think the person who designed Project Babylon is here in Three Pines?' asked Lacoste.

'I don't,' said Beauvoir. 'Not really. But maybe. I don't know.'

'Impressive,' said Lacoste.

Jean-Guy smiled tightly and got up. 'I'm heading over

to Ruth's place with Al Lepage's record. I want to hear it. Coming?'

'No, I'm going back to the Incident Room to see if any reports have come in. Both the Canadian government and the Americans are looking into Al Lepage. Does it seem odd that he arrived in Québec already having a French surname?'

'What strikes me as odd,' said Beauvoir, 'is that he said he walked across the border and just stumbled into Three Pines.'

'How else would you find it?' asked Reine-Marie. She thought for a moment. 'He was a draft dodger, right?'

The Sûreté officers nodded.

'From what I remember, they were welcomed in Canada,' said Reine-Marie. 'I'm not sure they really had to sneak across the border.'

'They were pardoned too,' said Armand. 'By Jimmy Carter. Many returned.'

'But not Al Lepage,' said Isabelle Lacoste.

'I'll ask Ruth if she knows anything,' said Beauvoir.

'One other thing you might check out tomorrow,' said Armand, as he walked them down the path. 'Where the CSIS agents disappeared to today. They weren't in the village and I don't think they were at the site of the gun.'

That had been an hour ago, and now Jean-Guy found himself alone in Ruth's living room, listening to Al Lepage's record.

When it was finished he placed the needle on the spinning vinyl again, but not at the beginning. Sitting back down, he listened, again, to the saga of the dog in the woods. The listener was meant to come away with the heartwarming image of the family not giving up hope, and the dog finding home. But what stayed with Jean-Guy was the image of an animal getting in touch with its true nature. Willing to kill if it had to.

The call came into the Incident Room in the old train station the next morning. It was from the local detachment of the Sûreté.

'Since you're already here, Chief Inspector, I thought you'd want to know.'

'Know what?'

'A body was found this morning.'

Lacoste grabbed a pen and motioned to Beauvoir, who came over.

'Who?'

She wrote the name on her notepad, and next to it the word *murdered*. And heard Jean-Guy whisper, '*Merde*.'

'Where?' Lacoste wrote an address. 'Is there a team there?'

'The first response just reported in. I've told them not to touch anything.'

Inspector Beauvoir had moved over to his desk and she could hear him calling for a Scene of Crime unit from Montréal.

'Bludgeoned to death at home,' the local agent said. 'The place has been ransacked. Looks like robbery. I've dispatched an ambulance, of course, but it's too late.'

'Call the coroner,' said Lacoste.

'Already done. She'll meet you there.'

'Good.'

She hung up and looked down at her notepad, where a name was written and circled.

Ten minutes later they were kneeling beside the body of Antoinette Lemaitre.

CHAPTER 23

'I recognize her,' said Sharon Harris, the coroner. 'She runs the Knowlton Playhouse, doesn't she?'

Dr Harris and Isabelle Lacoste were kneeling beside Antoinette, who was lying on her back, staring at the ceiling. Surprised. Jean-Guy Beauvoir was crouched on the other side of the body.

'*Oui*,' said Chief Inspector Lacoste. 'The Estrie Players.'

'They were doing the Fleming play,' said Dr Harris, her gloved hands swiftly checking the body. 'Community's in a bit of an uproar about it.'

The coroner grimaced as she spoke Fleming's name, as though she'd put a rotten trout into her mouth. Here was a woman who worked with corpses in all states of decay and what disgusted her? The very mention of John Fleming.

The grimace was, Lacoste knew, involuntary. Like being tapped on the kneecap. Flinching at the mention of Fleming was a healthy human reaction.

'Not much damage that I can see,' said the coroner. 'I don't want to move her until your forensics people have arrived, but from what I see she's been dead less than twelve hours, but more than six.'

'Between nine thirty last night and two thirty this morning,' said Beauvoir. 'And cause of death?'

'At a guess, I'd say that.' The coroner leaned close to Antoinette's head and pointed to the back of her skull where her purple hair was clotted and matted a deep red.

'It looks like a single catastrophic blow. Crushed the skull. She probably didn't know what hit her.'

'And what did?' asked Lacoste.

They looked around and quickly found blood staining the corner of the hearth.

Beauvoir leaned closer. 'Looks like it.'

He stood and stepped aside so that the coroner and Lacoste could get a better look. They stared at the stone corner, then back to Antoinette, glassy-eyed and shocked.

'She was either pushed or fell backward, hitting her head,' said Lacoste, and both Dr Harris and Inspector Beauvoir nodded agreement.

'Murder,' said the coroner. 'But perhaps not intentional. Looks like she might've surprised someone robbing her home.'

'There doesn't seem to have been forced entry,' said Lacoste. 'But that could mean nothing.'

As often as she'd been to this area of Québec, it still amazed her that people didn't lock their doors. Perhaps when they went to bed, but beyond that anyone could walk in and out. Sometimes people survived. Sometimes they did not.

But the fact that the door was unlocked did suggest Antoinette Lemaitre hadn't yet gone to bed. And she was still in her street clothes, not pajamas.

'She was supposed to go to Clara Morrow's for dinner last night,' said Beauvoir. 'But she called to cancel.'

Sharon Harris looked up. 'How do you know?'

'We were there,' said Lacoste.

'You know her?' Dr Harris motioned to the body.

'Not well,' said Lacoste. 'But yes. What time did Antoinette call Clara?'

Beauvoir thought. 'Not sure exactly, but it was before dinner and we ate at seven thirty.'

'Did Clara say why Antoinette canceled?' asked Lacoste.

'No, she just said she thought Antoinette wanted a quiet night to herself after all the stress of the Fleming play. Brian, her partner,' Beauvoir explained to Dr Harris, 'had a meeting in Montréal. Something to do with his job. So Antoinette had the place to herself.'

'I believe he's the man in the kitchen,' said Dr Harris. 'He found her.'

Beauvoir turned to the local agent guarding the scene. 'Is that true?'

'Yessir. When we arrived he was next door, but we brought him over. He's pretty shaken up. He was her *conjoint*.'

'What did he tell you?' asked Lacoste.

'Not much,' said the agent. 'It was all we could do to keep him upright.'

Both looked down again at the dead woman.

They hadn't known Antoinette well. Beauvoir had seen her and Brian in the bistro a few times, and once at dinner with the Gamaches.

The Gamaches, he thought. He'd have to tell them.

Knowing the victim was both a help and a hindrance. It meant they knew something of the victim's habits, her personality. But it also meant they came at it with preconceptions.

Jean-Guy studied Antoinette Lemaitre and realized he hadn't liked her.

She'd been childish and coquettish in a way that creeped him out. Antoinette did not behave like a woman in her forties. She wore too much makeup, had spiky hair dyed purple and clothes that were too young and too tight and too short. She could be willful and bossy.

He looked again at the blood, sticky on the hair and carpet.

But his main objection had little to do with her appearance and more to do with the fact she'd chosen to produce a play by a serial killer. He wondered if her murderer had had the same objection.

'She doesn't seem to have been violated,' said Dr Harris, standing up.

'Anything under her fingernails?' asked Lacoste.

'No flesh or hair. Whoever did this seems to have taken her by surprise. This' – Dr Harris gestured at the room – 'wasn't done in a fight.'

They looked around at the overturned furniture, the drawers pulled from the desk and cabinets and dumped on the floor. The books splayed in piles on the carpet. Some even lay on Antoinette's body.

'What does it look like to you?' Jean-Guy asked Lacoste.

'Not vandalism. Nothing's broken. No spray-paint or excrement. I agree with Dr Harris, it looks like she disturbed a robber.'

'A pretty desperate or persistent robber, wouldn't you say?' he asked. 'Most just grab the TV and run. Maybe pull out a few drawers looking for money.'

Lacoste considered. '*Oui.*'

It just wasn't adding up, though. A robber generally waited for the home to be empty, or the person to be asleep. But the lamps were still on. Whoever did this knew the owner was probably at home and almost certainly awake.

And most of the mess was made after Antoinette was dead by someone who knew he wouldn't be disturbed. And who was not disturbed by having just killed someone.

And that bothered Jean-Guy Beauvoir. A lot. Most robbers were just that. Robbers. They had no desire or stomach for murder. This was different. Someone had killed Antoinette, then spent hours searching her home while her body cooled.

The Scene of Crime team arrived and got to work. Jean-Guy directed them while Chief Inspector Lacoste walked around the rest of the house. Looking into rooms but not touching anything.

It was a modest single-story home with a basement. Even that had been ripped apart. It must've taken hours. The further she got into the house the more convinced Lacoste became this was not a simple robbery, and Antoinette Lemaitre not a random target.

Carpets had been ripped up, floorboards lifted. Paneling hung from the walls. A chair stood in the middle of the hall beneath an opening in the ceiling. Lacoste got on it and shone her light into the attic. She heard scampering and got off the chair.

If she had to she'd go up, but that was one of the perks of being Chief Inspector. She could assign someone else to do that now.

'The forensics team and Scene of Crime are doing their job,' said Beauvoir, joining her. 'Time to talk to Brian.'

Jean-Guy had spoken with him briefly on his way to find Lacoste.

'How does he seem?' Lacoste asked.

'Stunned. Numb.'

But neither was under any illusion. As they walked back

down the hallway, both seasoned homicide investigators knew they were about to speak to their main suspect.

Brian Fitzpatrick got to his feet when they entered. He was about to say something, but then looked as though he'd forgotten how to speak.

'I'm so sorry, Brian,' said Isabelle Lacoste. 'This is terrible.'

He nodded. His eyes darted from one to the other.

'What happened?' he asked, sitting back down on his chair at the Formica table.

Lacoste looked at the agent from the local Sûreté detachment, standing bored by the doorway.

'Can you make a pot of coffee?' she asked. The agent looked put out, but agreed.

The kitchen had also been ransacked, though the damage did not seem as great. Mostly flour, sugar and cornflakes spilled out onto the counter, and drawers opened and emptied.

It seemed more pro forma, as though the robber-turned-killer had run out of steam or was running out of time. Or conviction.

Brian looked at them, all eyes, wide and red.

'What time did you find her, Brian?' Lacoste asked.

'I left Montréal about seven thirty this morning, so I got here about nine.'

'You were in Montréal last night?' asked Lacoste.

'Yes, at a meeting. I stayed over. I wish I hadn't.' He had that haunted look people got when alternate endings began to appear. Endings in which they did something different. What might have been, if only . . .

'What did you find when you got home?' Lacoste asked.

Jean-Guy had assumed the role Chief Inspector Gamache favored in interrogations, of just listening. And watching.

Occasionally contributing, but mostly absorbing what was being said, or not said.

'The door wasn't locked—'

'Did that surprise you?' asked Lacoste.

'Not really. Antoinette would've been up and working by nine. She'd have unlocked the door already. But it did seem strange that the curtains were still closed.'

'She was a translator, is that right?' said Lacoste.

'Yes. She works from home.'

There was a conflict of tenses that would resolve itself with time.

'So you opened the door,' Lacoste prompted.

'I yelled "Hi," but there was no answer. Of course.' He seemed to deflate a little at those last two words. 'I hung up my coat and walked toward the living room and saw—' he gestured, but Chief Inspector Lacoste did not fill in the blank. 'Everything was all over the place. I think I sorta went blank. Froze. And then I panicked and started shouting for Antoinette. I ran into the room and must've tripped because I ended up on the floor. That's when I saw ...'

'Saw what, Brian?' asked Lacoste quietly when the silence had gone on.

'Her foot. I'm not sure what happened next. I've been sitting here trying to put it together but it just seems like ...' He struggled for the word. 'I remember seeing her face, and her eyes. And knowing. I think I might've touched her because I remember feeling cold. And then thinking I was about to pass out. It was just too ...'

He stared out the kitchen window and seemed to have ground to a halt, overwhelmed.

'What did you do then?' Lacoste asked.

She had the impression that had she not prompted him,

Brian would have spent the rest of his life staring out that window. Stuck.

Lacoste glanced over at Jean-Guy, who also sat very still, absorbing it all.

'I panicked,' said Brian softly, not meeting their eyes. 'I ran away. I had to get out. I went over to Madame Proulx's place next door. She called the police.'

'Did you come back here?'

He shook his head. 'Only when the police arrived. They asked me to come back with them, and they put me in here.'

The coffee was ready and Beauvoir poured them each a mug. When they'd taken a sip of the strong coffee, Lacoste resumed the interrogation. She made it sound like a conversation, but only a fool, or a man numb with grief, could mistake it for that.

'Can you tell us what you did last night?'

'I was in Montréal. The monthly meeting of the Geological Survey. We go through our reports.'

'Last night?'

'No, yesterday afternoon but I stayed over. Some of us go out for drinks and dinner after. We always do.'

'Can you give us the details, a phone number of someone who was there?'

'Yes.'

Beauvoir took it down.

'What time did you finish?'

'About eight, eight thirty. Not late.'

'Where did you stay? A hotel?'

'No, we have a pied-à-terre. Just a studio. I stay there when I'm in town for meetings and will have a few drinks.'

'Can anyone vouch for you?' asked Lacoste.

'Vouch for me?' he asked, and then it dawned on him, as it did every suspect eventually. That they were suspected. But unlike many, Brian didn't get angry or defensive. He just looked even more frightened, if that was possible.

'I was alone in the apartment. There's no doorman. I let myself in and didn't go out again.'

'Did you call anyone?'

'Just Antoinette.' He pressed his lips together and took a ragged breath.

'What time was that?'

'When I got in, about three in the afternoon. Just to say I'd arrived safely. She told me we'd been invited over to Clara's for dinner, but she thought she might cancel.'

'Did she tell you why?' Beauvoir asked, speaking for the first time in the interrogation.

'She said she thought a couple of people might drop by later.'

'Who?'

'People from the theater,' he said. 'They wanted to talk to her. I think they wanted to fire her, but I didn't say anything.'

'What did she think it was about?' Lacoste asked.

'She thought they'd changed their minds and were going to do the play after all.' His hand went to the copy of *She Sat Down and Wept* on the kitchen table. It was covered in scribbled notes. 'She couldn't believe everyone had quit.'

Once again Brian gave them names, and once again Beauvoir took them down.

'Emotions were running high about the play,' said Lacoste.

Brian nodded. 'It was a mistake, of course. We shouldn't have been doing it.' He looked at her then, focusing completely for the first time. 'You don't think it had anything

263

to do with—' He gestured out the kitchen door toward the living room. 'But that's ridiculous. It's just a play. No one cares that much.'

'They cared enough to quit,' said Lacoste.

But enough to kill?

'Who knew you'd be in Montréal?' she asked.

'I don't know,' said Brian, thinking but obviously not grasping the significance of the question. 'I think people knew I went in every now and then, but I don't think I told anyone I was going in yesterday.'

Lacoste caught Beauvoir's eye. Did Brian really not know he'd just been given a chance to take the heat off himself?

Antoinette was killed by someone who knew he wouldn't be interrupted. The murderer therefore didn't know about Brian, or knew Brian was in Montréal, or was Brian.

Had he told them lots of people knew he'd be away, that would open up the list of suspects. But he hadn't. Which showed he was innocent or stupid, or so sure of himself he chose to play stupid.

They went through the rest of the questions and Brian gave answers, some halting, some incomplete, some thorough. What emerged was the image of a man numb with grief, who'd been a hundred kilometers away when Antoinette was killed. Who had nothing to do with it. Who wished he'd been there. Who couldn't think of anyone who wanted her dead.

'I know you have to look at all possibilities, but it was a robbery, wasn't it?' Brian finally asked. 'It must've been. Look at the place.'

When the Sûreté investigators didn't answer, he looked more confused than ever.

'You're not saying someone killed Antoinette on purpose, are you?'

264

'It's a possibility,' said Lacoste.

'Who would do it?' he demanded. 'Why? I know she could rub people the wrong way, but she never got anyone that upset.'

'You can't think of anyone?' asked Lacoste.

'Of course not,' said Brian. 'This must've been a terrible accident. Someone came to rob the place, and Antoinette found them. Jesus, what're you saying?'

'We're saying it was probably robbery, but we have to be sure,' said Lacoste, her voice soothing. Certain.

Her calm seemed to have its effect. Brian took a deep breath and regained his composure.

'I'll help in any way I can. What can I do?'

'You can prove you were in Montréal,' said Beauvoir.

This time Brian didn't miss the implication, but instead of getting defensive he just nodded and gave them the address of the apartment building, the number of the superintendent, the names of neighbors.

He gave them the codes to their computers, their banking, their phones.

'Antoinette used the last four digits of your phone number?' said Beauvoir as he looked down at what he'd written.

'I know, too obvious,' said Brian. 'I told her that but she wanted something she could remember.'

'And yours?' asked Beauvoir. '0621 for everything?'

'Yes. Something I could never forget. June twenty-first. Our first date. Ten years ago.'

Jean-Guy Beauvoir concentrated on the page, on the numbers, on the pen as he wrote it down. And tried not to look into Brian's red, wondering eyes.

Like Brian, he too used his first date with Annie as his code. Something he would never, could never, ever forget.

How would he feel if he found Annie . . . ?

Chief Inspector Gamache had told them to crawl into the skins of the victim and the suspects, but he'd warned his investigators that it was difficult to do, and it was dangerous. Jean-Guy had never really understood the need, or the danger.

But now he did.

He'd gotten into Brian's skin but had overshot the mark and ended up in his broken heart.

As they left, Jean-Guy picked up the copy of the play from the table. Brian explained it was Antoinette's. He'd taken it with him to Montréal, having left his own copy in the theater.

Beauvoir was not a superstitious man, or claimed not to be. But even to this rational man, the play seemed heavier than just paper.

They interviewed all the neighbors, none of whom saw or heard anything, and left Madame Proulx, next door, 'til last. She was middle-aged and plump and worried, her large, red hands intertwined and fidgety.

'What did Brian Fitzpatrick say to you exactly?' Isabelle Lacoste asked as they took seats in the comfortable living room. 'When he arrived this morning.'

'That something had happened and he needed to call for help, but he was trembling too hard, so I called.'

'Did he say anything else?'

'Only that Antoinette had been hurt. I asked if we should go over to help and he looked so frightened, I knew.'

Her eyes moved from one to the other. 'She's dead, isn't she?'

'I'm afraid so.'

And then she did something rarely seen anymore in Québec. She crossed herself.

'Did you see anyone arrive at their place last night?' Isabelle Lacoste asked.

'No, I had the curtains drawn and was watching television. *Les Filles de Caleb*.'

Lacoste nodded. It was what all the other neighbors had said. Everyone had drawn the curtains and settled in front of the television to watch the rerun of the wildly popular show.

A werewolf could tear apart the living room and this woman wouldn't budge while that show was on. Lacoste was beginning to wonder if the killer had chosen the time for that very reason.

'Do you know who did it?' asked Madame Proulx.

'*Non*, not yet, but we will,' said Lacoste.

She tried to reassure Madame Proulx, but without a suspect arrested the reassurance was hollow.

At least Laurent Lepage's murder hadn't appeared random. It seemed clear from the beginning that he was killed not because he was Laurent, or a child, but because of what he found in the woods. There was a reason.

But the murder of Antoinette Lemaitre seemed senseless. There was no obvious motive. And into that void there streamed all sorts of suspicions. And understandable terror.

Lacoste could see exactly what Madame Proulx was thinking. *It could've been me.* Followed closely by, *Thank God it was the woman next door.*

'What did you think of Antoinette?' Lacoste asked.

'She was okay. She's friendly without being overly familiar, if you know what I mean.'

'Did you like her?' Lacoste asked.

There was a hesitation and Madame Proulx shifted in her

La-Z-Boy. 'I warmed to her. I liked her uncle, Guillaume. We'd chat over the fence in the summer while he gardened.'

'Sounds like you didn't really like her, though,' Lacoste gently pushed, though it didn't take much.

'She was difficult,' Madame Proulx admitted. 'As soon as she moved in she started complaining. About the kids playing street hockey and the noise from family barbecues. She behaved like it was her *seigneurie* and we were all *habitants*, if you know what I mean.'

Lacoste did. *Les Filles de Caleb* was having its effect, down to the old-fashioned description of lord and peasant. But while the words were from a TV script, the emotions seemed genuine. Madame Proulx did not take kindly to the city woman bossing them around. It was what they'd heard, in various versions, from the other neighbors, once they'd gotten past being polite about the recently, and violently, deceased.

'Can you think of anyone who might've done this?' Lacoste asked, and saw Madame Proulx's eyes widen.

'No. Can't you? Isn't that your job? You have no ideas?'

'We have some,' said Lacoste, bringing out the reassurance yet again, and yet again it had a marginal effect. 'But I need to ask. No especially violent feuds with neighbors?'

'None. It was annoying, nothing more. And she looked odd. Those clothes. She was like a spoiled child.'

She turned shrewd eyes on the investigators.

'You don't think it was just a robbery?'

'We're looking at all possibilities.'

Madame Proulx took in, apparently for the first time, the script in Beauvoir's hand, and she rose to her feet. Not swiftly, not even struggling out of the comfortable chair. There was a grace and ease about all her movements. And there was also certainty.

'I would like you to leave, and take that with you.'

There was no need to ask what 'that' was.

'You're aware of the play?' Beauvoir asked, holding it up. He thought for a moment Madame Proulx was going to cross herself again. But she didn't. Instead she straightened up completely and stood, tall and formidable, facing both him and John Fleming's creation.

'We all were. It's a travesty. How she couldn't see that is beyond me. I'm not a prude, if that's what you're thinking. But it's not right.'

No philosophical debate, no discussion of the evils of censorship. Just a clear statement of fact. Producing the Fleming play wasn't right. But exactly how wrong it was wasn't yet clear.

At the door Beauvoir asked about Brian.

'We liked him,' said Madame Proulx, apparently speaking for the whole neighborhood. 'Now if he killed her we could understand. But he seemed to really care for her.' She shook her head. 'Happens a lot, doesn't it? You look at a couple and wonder what they see in each other. You never know, if you know what I mean.'

Beauvoir did know. You never knew.

They got in the car and headed back to Three Pines.

'Why did you take the play with you?' Lacoste asked Beauvoir as he drove.

'It's been nothing but trouble,' he explained. 'And whoever killed Antoinette was looking for something. Maybe it was the play.'

'But there're lots of copies out there.'

'True, but that's the original. I thought it was worth a read.'

Isabelle Lacoste nodded. He was right. She wished she'd thought of that.

There were times when she felt completely up to the job of Chief Inspector. And times when she knew it should have gone to this man.

'Is there anything else I missed?' she asked him.

'You don't miss much, Isabelle,' said Beauvoir. 'And what you do, I pick up. And vice versa. It's what makes us a strong team.'

'Do you miss Monsieur Gamache?' she asked.

'It's no reflection on you, but I'll always miss Chief Inspector Gamache.'

'So will I,' she said. They drove a few more miles before she got up the courage to ask a question that had been bothering her since her appointment.

'Should you have been made Chief Inspector?'

She immediately regretted asking. Suppose he said yes?

'I would've liked it,' he said at last. 'But I wasn't expecting it. Not after all that happened.'

'You mean the drinking?' she asked. 'And the drugs? Or when you shot Chief Inspector Gamache?'

'When you say it like that it sounds pretty bad,' said Beauvoir, but he smiled as he said it. They both knew pulling the trigger was the one thing he did right. He'd saved Gamache's life, by almost taking it.

Few, if any, would have had the courage to shoot. Lacoste wasn't sure she would have.

'You could've stopped me, you know,' he said. 'You had me in your sights, just as I had him. You had no idea why I was about to gun down the Chief. Why didn't you stop me?'

'By shooting you?' she asked.

'Yes. Others would have. Anyone else would have.'

'I almost did. But you pleaded with me to trust you.'

'That's it?'

'It wasn't your words, it was your voice. You weren't angry or deranged. You were desperate.'

'You trusted your instincts?'

She nodded, gripping her hands together to stop the trembling that always overcame her when she thought of that horrific day. Having Beauvoir in her sights, her finger on the trigger. And hesitating. And watching him not hesitate. Watching him gun down Chief Inspector Gamache.

It had felt as though she herself had been shot.

Then seeing Chief Inspector Gamache's body leave the ground. Then hit the ground.

'You trust your instincts,' Jean-Guy said. 'That's why you'll make one of the great leaders in the Sûreté, Isabelle. And why I will be your loyal right hand for as long as you need me.'

'And would you shoot me?'

'In an instant, *patron*.'

She laughed. Then realized it was the first time he'd called her *patron*.

The Fleming play sat in the backseat like a passenger. Listening to them. Absorbing the talk of murder.

CHAPTER 24

———

'*Bonjour*,' said Armand Gamache.

He'd found Mary Fraser alone in the small library at the back of the B and B. She was in a comfortable chair, her back to the corner bookshelves and her feet on a hassock, stretched out toward the mumbling fire in the grate.

Her sweater was pilled and her big toe stuck out of one stocking. She did not bother to conceal it, nor did she seem at all embarrassed by this sartorial underachievement.

What she clearly did not want him to see, though, was the file she was reading. She closed it as soon as Gamache entered and splayed her hand over it. It was done without haste, almost languidly. But still the result was a closed and secret document.

'Old school?' he asked, indicating the dossier. 'Before everything was put on computer? Or maybe some things are best left as hard copies. More easily managed. And destroyed.'

He sat down in the other comfortable chair in the library.

Mary Fraser took her feet off the hassock and replaced them in her shoes. She crossed her legs and looked at him.

'What a funny thing to say, Monsieur Gamache,' she said, a cordial smile on her face. 'Most of our files are still paper. To be honest, I prefer it that way.'

272

'*Fahrenheit 451*?' he asked.

She looked baffled, and then she caught the reference and looked at him as his third-grade teacher, Madame Arsenault, had when he'd finally said something clever.

'I wasn't planning to burn it,' she said.

'Though you could.'

'Of course. Can I help you?'

'I'm just wondering why you're not more interested in the Supergun.'

His voice was pleasant, matter-of-fact, but his sharp eyes studied her.

Her indifferently dyed hair. Her face without makeup, except some lipstick and slightly clotted mascara. She didn't wear contacts, preferring glasses in unfashionable frames. She hid nothing. Not wrinkles, not flawed eyesight, not even the hole in her pantyhose. And that was one of Mary Fraser's great advantages, he was beginning to think. Being able to make artifice look genuine. Giving the impression all was revealed, when in fact very little of substance was revealed.

This CSIS woman had appeared like Mary Poppins, descending on the village to make everything all right. Only everything wasn't all right. He knew it. And she knew it.

No, he didn't trust Mary Fraser, but he did find her interesting.

Now she was giving him an equally assessing look.

'And I'm just wondering why you're so interested,' she said. 'In the gun.'

'Then we're even, madame.' He sat back, crossing his legs. Settling in. 'You know more about the Supergun than you've told us so far. I'd like to hear it.'

'Why should I tell you anything?'

'Because you're afraid, and you need all the allies you can get.'

'I'm not afraid.' She also sat back, wriggling a bit into the soft corner of the large chair. As a small creature might in a warm den.

'You should be afraid. Someone's found Bull's gun and is almost certainly looking for the plans,' said Armand. 'You're afraid they've already been found.'

'They haven't been.'

'How do you know?'

'It's been three days since the gun was found. If the plans had been there, the killer would have started sending out feelers, looking for buyers. Setting up an auction.'

'How do you know he hasn't?'

It was just the two of them and the real Mary Fraser was beginning to appear, seeping out from the ladder in the stocking, the undyed roots of her hair, the clotted mascara. The file clerk was receding. But then, the real Armand Gamache was also appearing. The kindly retired cop was receding.

She gave him a patient smile. 'We know.'

'You don't know everything. You didn't know about the gun.' But even as he said it he wondered if that was true.

'We knew Dr Bull was working on it, of course, but not that he'd actually built it. That came as a surprise.'

'An unpleasant one, I'm guessing.'

'Well, not necessarily. After all, we now have the world's only Supergun. It might come in handy.'

'Until another one's built,' said Gamache. 'Where are the plans?'

'Nowhere. They were destroyed by Gerald Bull.'

'Then why are you so worried?'

'I'm not.'

274

'Then why are you still here?' he asked.

She had nothing to say to that.

'And why are you reading a file on Dr Bull?'

Her hand splayed further, to better conceal the cover.

'You're not a fool, Madame Fraser, so why are you pretending to be?'

'Am I?'

'Word is spreading about the Supergun. The villagers now know, and while they've been asked to keep it quiet, it's just a matter of time before it breaks out of this valley. And then journalists, gawkers, other scientists will arrive. And who knows who else might come out of the shadows. Come looking. Time is not on your side.'

'It wasn't just anyone who leaked the news, Monsieur Gamache. It was Isabelle Lacoste.'

Gamache sat absolutely still. Trying not to give anything away. Not a word, an expression, a twitch.

'That was foolish of her,' said Mary Fraser. 'She has no idea of the world she's entered, and neither do you. You think you do, but you don't. There are no rules, monsieur. No laws. No gravity. Nothing binding us, holding us down or back.'

'I thought you were a file clerk.'

She looked at the manila folder on her lap. 'I am. And what are files? They're information. Knowledge. And what is knowledge?'

He didn't need to answer that, and neither did she.

'Why are you here?' he asked. 'Why you?'

'Be careful' was all she would say.

'Did you know Gerald Bull?' Gamache asked. 'Did CSIS kill him?'

There was silence. He leaned forward and looked into the bland, unremarkable face.

'Did you?' he asked.

'You have not been careful, Monsieur Gamache.'

He got up and bowed slightly. She remained where she was. But as he leaned toward her she whispered, 'Don't think it's escaped our notice how strange it is that a senior officer would take early retirement in the middle of nowhere, and shortly afterward Project Babylon is found.'

Gamache straightened up, genuinely surprised. But the real surprise came next. Standing up and facing him, Mary Fraser's soft face became rigid.

'And don't think it's escaped our notice that a grown man claims to have been friends with a nine-year-old boy. You are either a pervert or you wanted something from that poor child. And I will find out which. I have my eye on you.'

Gamache knew his mouth had just opened slightly, but he couldn't help it.

Was she really threatening him? Was this more artifice? A posture? Or did this woman genuinely believe he might be mixed up in this?

Were they on the same side? He knew what his role was, and wasn't, in this. But he could not figure her out. Mary Fraser appeared socially inept, a little bumbling, maladroit. Soft-spoken and bookish. But she was also fiercely intelligent, and strong.

Armand Gamache never, ever, made the mistake of demonizing strong women. Indeed, he'd been raised by one, married one, promoted one. But he was far from certain he trusted this one.

He took a few steps back and examined her, trying to figure out if she was sincere in her suspicions of him or just trying to toss the rock back.

'What's at Highwater?' he asked.

'Are you threatening me?' she asked. And she looked genuinely alarmed.

It was not the reaction he'd expected.

He'd hoped to speak to Lacoste and Beauvoir first, but when he saw them leaving Three Pines that morning, he'd made the call himself to Agent Yvette Nichol, a former colleague in the Sûreté. He asked her to track the movements of the CSIS investigators the day before through their cell phones. She reported back half an hour ago.

Instead of spending the day examining Gerald Bull's Supergun, or searching for the plans, the pings from their cell phones indicated Mary Fraser and Sean Delorme had driven twenty miles away, to the village of Highwater, right on the Vermont border.

'Is what I said threatening?' Gamache asked. 'I had no idea. My apologies.'

He left, feeling her eyes on his back until he was out the door of the small library.

He knew where he was going next.

He didn't get there.

Armand Gamache got as far as the front porch of the bed and breakfast when he saw Lacoste and Beauvoir return. Their car slowed, pulled over, and Jean-Guy leaned.

'We need to talk,' both men said at once.

'I'll come over to the Incident Room,' said Gamache. He could tell by their faces that something had happened.

As the car pulled away, he noticed a copy of Fleming's play on the backseat, its cover covered with scribbled notes.

Lacoste and Beauvoir were waiting for him beside the car as he walked across the bridge to the old railway station.

'What's happened?' he asked.

'You first,' said Lacoste as they went inside and took seats at the conference table.

'I know where the CSIS agents went yesterday,' said Gamache. 'I asked Agent Nichol to track their cell phones. I realize I was overstepping—'

Lacoste smiled and held up a hand to stop the apology. 'Please, don't. We want your help.'

Gamache gave a curt nod. 'They went to a place called Highwater. It's in Québec, close to the border with Vermont, about thirty kilometers from here.'

'Do you know it?' Jean-Guy asked, getting up to consult the huge map tacked to the wall.

'No,' he said, joining Beauvoir along with Lacoste. He pointed it out, having already looked it up. 'I've never been there. I gather it's pretty small.'

'Hmmm,' said Lacoste. 'Any idea what they were doing there? Meeting someone?'

'Could be,' said Gamache, as they returned to their chairs. 'They stayed in one place for most of the day, then came straight back. Your turn.'

'Antoinette Lemaitre's been murdered,' said Isabelle Lacoste, and saw the shock on Gamache's face. 'I know she was a friend of yours.'

He sat back in his chair and stared at them. Taking it in. 'What happened?'

'The place was ransacked,' said Beauvoir. 'Looks like she interrupted a robbery, or it was made to look like that. She seems to have fallen and hit her head on the corner of the fireplace. Dr Harris says it happened last night between nine thirty and two thirty in the morning.'

'She was supposed to be at Clara's,' said Armand. 'But she called to cancel. I wonder if the killer—'

278

'—also thought she'd be at Clara's and the place would be empty?' asked Lacoste. 'Could be.'

Beauvoir excused himself to make some calls while Lacoste told Gamache, succinctly, the story as they understood it so far. Gamache was quiet, focused. Not taking notes, but taking it all in.

'We asked the neighbors if they saw anything but they were all watching *Les Filles de Caleb*.'

'Maybe Antoinette asked her guests to come at that time for that very reason. She wanted to make sure no one saw them arrive,' said Beauvoir, returning.

'But why would it be a secret if it was just members of the theater company?' asked Gamache.

'Because it wasn't,' said Beauvoir. 'I called them just now. Neither has heard from Antoinette since they quit. So either Antoinette lied to Brian or he lied to us.'

'But he must've known we'd find out,' said Lacoste. She thought for a moment. 'It's more likely Antoinette lied to him about who was coming over.'

'And why?' said Gamache. 'Who could her visitors have been?'

'And did they kill her?' said Beauvoir. 'It seems likely. But they were running a risk. Suppose Antoinette told Brian who was really coming over?'

'They must've known she wouldn't tell him the truth,' said Lacoste. 'Which means it was something she wanted to keep secret.'

'Something shameful?' suggested Beauvoir, tossing out ideas. 'Something illegal or unethical? An affair?'

They stared at each other. Then Gamache's eyes were drawn to the script. So much seemed to circle back to it. The goddamned play.

Beauvoir followed the glance. 'Yes, we were wondering the same thing. Could her death have something to do with the Fleming play? Were they looking for it? Does that explain the mess in their home? Brian had taken it to Montréal, but they couldn't have known that.'

Gamache got up. 'I've almost finished reading it. There's nothing hidden in the plot that I can see. Do you need me for anything? I was going to drive to Highwater, but it's getting late, and with this news, I think I'll stay here. Do you mind if I tell Reine-Marie?'

'No. In fact, we might as well tell everyone,' said Lacoste, joining him. 'I'll come with you and start the interviews.'

'There's something else you need to know, Isabelle.'

He stopped, and she turned to him. 'I asked Mary Fraser about Highwater. They know that we know they were there.'

'And her reaction?'

'She asked if I was threatening her.'

'Huh,' said Lacoste. 'That's strange. I wonder what she meant.'

'I wonder what's in Highwater.'

'I'll look it up when I get back to the Incident Room.'

'You have other things to do,' he said. 'I can look it up. I still have my security codes.'

'Oh, the damage you could do, *patron*,' Lacoste said, with a smile.

'Funnily enough, Mary Fraser seems to think the same thing. She all but accused me of being involved in Laurent's death and somehow involved in the hunt for Gerald Bull's Supergun.'

'If she thinks that she's crazy.'

'She's complex,' he said. 'I was talking with an old friend at CSIS just a week or so ago. I'll call her up again and have

Mary Fraser and Sean Delorme checked out, on the quiet of course. But there's something else. They know you were the one who leaked the information about Project Babylon.'

Isabelle Lacoste's eyes widened, just a bit, and she sighed. 'Well, bound to happen. I'm not worried.'

But she looked worried. As well she should be, thought Armand as they walked into the quiet village and parted ways. He was beginning to think Mary Fraser was not some-one you wanted on the other side. The question was, which side was she on?

CHAPTER 25

———

C lara Morrow sank onto the chair in the bistro. She'd been having drinks with a few friends, including Myrna, when Isabelle Lacoste had come in.

They could tell by her face that she had news that would not be good. But neither Clara nor anyone else in the bistro thought it could be quite that bad.

Antoinette was dead. Murdered.

Like everyone else in the room, Clara had gotten to her feet on hearing the news. Then she'd sunk back down, staring at Myrna, who'd also dropped to her seat.

'What's happening here?' asked Clara.

'It's the goddamned play,' said Ruth, a few tables over. 'She should never have decided to produce it.'

They fell silent again, thinking of the play and its author.

It felt as though a long, elongated shadow had slipped between the bars of Fleming's cell, stretching toward them. Like a finger. Thin and grotesque.

And last night, it had arrived.

Clara and Myrna went over to join the old poet, who was scribbling in her notebook. Lines of poetry, Clara saw, but couldn't read the words. Gabri and Olivier were already at the table.

Professor Rosenblatt sat at a corner table, watching them from the outer edge of their universe. Clara motioned to him and he got up and joined them. There seemed safety in numbers, though they all knew safety was comforting but an illusion.

Chief Inspector Lacoste pulled a chair over to their table.

'What happened?' Olivier asked.

She told them what she could.

'Do you have any idea who did this to Antoinette?' Myrna asked.

They spoke in hushed tones.

'Not yet.'

'Or why?' asked Clara.

Again, Lacoste shook her head. 'When Antoinette called last night and said she wasn't coming for dinner, did she say anything else?'

Clara thought about that. 'She said she was tired and thought she'd have a quiet evening to herself.'

'What impression did you get?' Lacoste asked.

Clara shook her head. 'I'm sorry, but I got no impression at all beyond what she said. She wanted an evening to herself, with Brian away and all.'

'How did you know he was gone for the night?'

'She told me when I called to invite them that afternoon.'

'Did anyone else know he'd be away?' Lacoste looked around the gathering. Everyone was shaking their heads. 'Did you know Brian had regular meetings in Montréal?'

'We knew he had to go in every now and then,' said Olivier. 'And that they have a small apartment in the city, but I don't think we knew when he went.'

'Oh, my God, poor Brian,' said Gabri. 'Does he know?'

'He found her,' said Lacoste. 'This morning.'

'I'll call him,' said Gabri, getting up and going to the phone. 'See if he wants to come stay with us for a few days.'

'Is her death connected to the gun?'

That question was asked by Professor Rosenblatt, who up to now had sat quietly.

'We don't know,' said Lacoste.

'But how could it be?' asked Myrna. 'Antoinette had nothing to do with it, did she?'

'Not that we know of,' said Lacoste.

'It was the play,' Ruth repeated. 'It was John Fleming.'

'Someone might've killed Antoinette because they were angry about the play,' conceded Lacoste. 'And then made it look like robbery. It seems the most likely motive. But it wasn't John Fleming. He's in prison. Has been for years.'

'Has he?'

'What're you saying, Ruth?' Clara asked.

'You of all people should know.' The old poet turned to her. 'Creations are creatures, and they have lives of their own. That play is Fleming and Fleming is a murderer.'

'*And what rough beast, its hour come round at last,*' said Rosenblatt, looking down at Ruth's notebook, '*Slouches towards Bethlehem to be born?*'

Ruth glared at him and closed her notebook with such a snap they all jumped.

After breaking the news to Reine-Marie about Antoinette, and talking about it until there seemed little more to say, Armand went into the study and started searching the files for information on Highwater.

It seemed an innocuous little village. Like many

communities, it was settled along the border with Vermont and had once thrived with lumber mills and a train station. But, like many small communities, it had shrunk once the railway had closed the station. And now it was almost invisible.

He spent a couple of hours but found absolutely nothing remarkable about Highwater. Absolutely no reason two intelligence agents should spend the day there.

But something was there. Something, or someone, had drawn Mary Fraser and Sean Delorme to Highwater.

He wandered out of the study and his eyes fell on his own copy of the Fleming play. He grabbed a day-old copy of *La Presse* and settled in. Then he got up to see if Reine-Marie was all right. She was in the kitchen, making dinner.

'Can I help?' he asked, though he knew the answer.

When upset, Reine-Marie liked to chop, to measure, to stir. To follow a recipe. Everything in order. No guessing, no surprises.

It was creative and calming and the outcome was both comforting and predictable.

'No, I'm fine. And yes, I mean that sort of FINE,' said Reine-Marie, making reference to the title of one of Ruth's poetry books, where FINE stood for Fucked up, Insecure, Neurotic, and Egotistical.

He laughed, kissed her and returned to the living room, picking up a *New Yorker*. But his eyes were drawn to the play on the table by the door.

Finally he poured a drink for Reine-Marie and one for himself, then he picked up the goddamned play, and read.

He had to remind himself that there was nothing supernatural about what he held in his hands. Nothing malevolent. It contained only the power he gave it.

Armand forced himself to read a few more pages, then looked over at the bookcases lining their walls crammed with cherished volumes.

Where once his grandparents put up crucifixes and images of the benediction on their walls, he and Reine-Marie put up books on theirs. History books. Reference books. Biographies. Fiction, nonfiction. Stories lined the walls and both insulated them from the outside world and connected them to it.

He laid the script on the sofa and got up, browsing the shelves. Reading the familiar titles. Touching the covers.

Renewed, he returned to the play. And plowed onward.

A few minutes later the phone rang and Gamache realized he was gripping the play so tightly it took an effort to let it go.

'Chief?' said Lacoste. There was excitement in her voice.

'*Oui?*'

'Can you come over to the Incident Room? We've found something.'

'About the Lemaitre case?'

'Yes, but something else too.'

'I'll be right there.'

He asked Reine-Marie to hold dinner for a few more minutes and explained where he was going.

'Invite them back if you'd like,' she called after him. 'There's plenty.'

She was four courses upset and considering an *amuse-bouche*.

'Adam,' said Gamache, taking the younger man's hand in a grip that was strong and enveloping. 'A sight for sore eyes.'

'Chief,' said Adam Cohen with delight.

'Are you one of the investigators on the Lemaitre case?'

'Oh, God no, sir. They won't let me near the place,' said Agent Cohen. 'Chief Inspector Lacoste barely lets me leave my desk at headquarters.'

'And yet, here you are in Three Pines. You'll have to come down more often. I normally have to content myself with my son-in-law.'

Gamache gestured toward Jean-Guy Beauvoir.

'I'm afraid your daughter has shown questionable taste, sir.' Agent Cohen lowered his voice in the pretense of a whisper.

'It runs in the family,' said Gamache. 'Her mother did too.'

He examined the young agent. Cohen had washed out of the academy and taken a job as a prison guard. But he'd come to Gamache's aid during a terrible time, when everyone else was deserting the Chief, and Gamache had not forgotten. He'd managed to get Cohen back into the academy, tutoring him until he'd graduated.

Gamache had asked Lacoste, as one of her first acts and his final one, to take on Adam Cohen as a trainee and protégé. To take care of him.

'What are you doing here?' Gamache asked.

'Chief Inspector Lacoste asked me to look into Antoinette Lemaitre's family. I tried to send what I found, but the internet connection here is so weak I decided to bring it down myself to make sure it arrived.'

'He gnawed through his chain,' said Beauvoir, leading everyone over to the conference table.

Gamache sat down and looked from one to the other to the other, finally settling on Isabelle.

'What have you found?'

She leaned forward. 'The home Antoinette Lemaitre was living in was in her name, but before that it belonged to her uncle.'

Gamache nodded. He knew that. Brian had told them.

Armand noticed that in front of Agent Cohen there was a page, facedown.

Cohen, Gamache realized, had more than a little bit of the dramatist about him. He must have studied under Jean-Guy Beauvoir.

'Guillaume Couture's family was from the area,' Agent Cohen reported. 'He built the house on some of the land they owned. There were no other relatives. He retired in the early 1990s.' Cohen's fingers moved to the edge of the paper. 'He died in 2005. Cancer. But before he retired he held a fascinating job.'

'He was an engineer,' said Gamache. 'Antoinette said he built overpasses. Not dull, but not what I'd describe as fascinating.'

Adam Cohen turned the page over.

It was a grainy black-and-white photograph blown up from a smaller image. It showed a group of men standing in what looked like a tube.

Gamache put on his glasses and leaned closer.

'That,' Adam Cohen pointed, 'is Guillaume Couture.'

The nondescript man grinned, almost maniacally, into the camera. His hair was lank and he wore glasses with thick black frames and an ill-fitting suit and tie. Two men stood on either side of him. The one in a cap was caught looking down and away from the camera, while the other appeared disinterested, even disdainful. Impatient.

Gamache felt his cheeks grow cold. He looked up from the photograph into the glowing eyes of Agent Cohen.

Then Armand took off his glasses and looked from Beauvoir to Lacoste.

They were staring at him in triumph. And for good reason.

'*Voilà*,' said Lacoste, putting her finger right onto the churlish face of the third man in the picture. 'The connection.'

It was Gerald Bull.

Gamache took a deep breath, trying to take it in. 'Guillaume Couture knew Gerald Bull.'

'More than knew him, sir,' said Agent Cohen. 'The picture's from Dr Couture's obit. Not the one in the newspaper, but the one in the McGill Alumni News.'

'Guillaume Couture went to McGill?' asked Gamache.

'No. He graduated from the Université de Montréal,' said Cohen. 'But he worked at McGill.'

'In what department?' Gamache asked.

'Dr Couture was a mechanical engineer,' said Chief Inspector Lacoste. 'But he was seconded to the physics department, to work on the High Altitude Research Project.'

'HARP,' said Adam Cohen, leaning back, then deciding that was far too casual, he sat forward again. 'The forerunner of Project Babylon.'

'Antoinette's uncle worked with Gerald Bull,' said Gamache.

CHAPTER 26

D inner was served, starting with parsnip and apple soup, with a drizzle of walnut-infused oil on top.

'Olivier gave me the recipe,' said Reine-Marie, turning down the light in the kitchen.

Candles were lit, not so much to create a romantic atmosphere for herself and Armand, and Isabelle and Jean-Guy and young Mr Cohen. It was for the calm that came with twilight, and tea lights, and the small flickering flames. If the topic of conversation was harsh, at least the atmosphere could be gentle.

They'd returned to the Gamache home for dinner, and to continue what they'd started in the Incident Room.

'Was there any evidence in Antoinette's house of her uncle's association with Gerald Bull?' Armand asked.

'Nothing,' said Jean-Guy. 'In fact, there was no evidence of her uncle at all. *Nada*. Not a photograph, not a card. No private papers. If we didn't know Guillaume Couture was Antoinette's uncle and had once lived in the place, we'd never have discovered it in that house.'

Gamache took a couple of spoonfuls of soup. It was smooth and earthy and just a touch sweet.

'Delicious,' he said to Reine-Marie, but his mind was elsewhere.

'Some people aren't nostalgic,' Lacoste said. 'My father's like that. He doesn't keep papers or letters.'

'Maybe Antoinette just wanted to make the house her own,' said Jean-Guy. 'Heaven knows she was self-involved enough. Her uncle's things might not have been welcome in the seigneurial home.'

'But not even a photograph?' said Reine-Marie. 'They were close enough for him to leave her his home and she didn't keep anything belonging to him? Seems like a purge.'

Armand agreed with Reine-Marie. It suggested a cleansing far deeper than simply making a place her own.

'Maybe that's what the killer was doing,' said Isabelle. 'Maybe he wanted to erase all evidence of Dr Couture and his connection to Gerald Bull.'

Gamache remembered his conversation with Mary Fraser earlier in the day. And the file the CSIS file clerk was trying to conceal. But why hide a file on Gerald Bull? Everyone expected her to have one of those.

She was trying to hide the name on the file because it was unexpected. And Gamache thought he knew what it said. He'd been wrong. It wasn't Gerald Bull in that dossier, it was Guillaume Couture.

'More likely the killer was looking for something he thought Dr Couture would have in his home,' said Beauvoir.

'The plans for Project Babylon,' said Lacoste. 'Is that why Antoinette was killed? For something she never even knew she had?'

'But why would Guillaume Couture have had the plans?' Beauvoir asked. 'I can't imagine Gerald Bull would trust anyone with them.'

'Maybe Dr Couture stole them from Bull,' Lacoste suggested.

'Okay, let's say he stole them, then what?' said Beauvoir. 'Couture just hides them in his home. Why not sell them if they were that valuable?'

'Maybe he wanted to make sure no other gun was ever built,' said Cohen.

'Then why not destroy the plans?' asked Beauvoir. 'Why keep them?'

'We don't know that he did keep them,' Lacoste pointed out. 'We're pretty sure he didn't sell them because no other gun was ever built, but he might've destroyed them. We don't know, and the killer wouldn't know either.'

'But that would mean the murderer knew about the connection between Antoinette's uncle and Gerald Bull,' said Reine-Marie. 'Why didn't he look for the plans sooner? Why now?'

'Because the gun was found now,' said Lacoste. 'That's the catalyst. Until then the plans were worthless. But once a working model was found—'

'The plans become priceless,' said Reine-Marie. 'I get it.'

'There is another possibility,' said Gamache. 'That Gerald Bull never had the plans.'

They stared at him. They'd moved from the soup to fettuccine with grilled salmon, tossed with fennel and apple.

'His apartment in Brussels was searched several times before his death, and nothing was found,' Gamache explained. 'After his murder, people looked but the designs for Project Babylon never turned up. It was assumed that Bull, knowing he was in trouble, destroyed them. But suppose they weren't found on him because he didn't have them?'

'Because he gave them to Dr Couture,' said Lacoste.

'Or because Couture stole them,' said Beauvoir.

'Or,' said Gamache, 'because Gerald Bull never had the plans to begin with.'

'You think Gerald Bull was the "front of house",' said Lacoste. 'And Dr Couture the real genius?'

'I think it's possible Dr Bull did not have the plans because Dr Bull did not make the plans,' said Gamache. 'Do you still have the photograph, Adam?'

Agent Cohen jumped up and returned a moment later with the picture. He put it on the kitchen table and everyone leaned in.

'Do you want more light?' asked Reine-Marie.

'No, this is fine,' said her husband. The candlelight was indeed soothing. 'I think they might have been a perfect team,' he said, looking at the photo. 'Bull gregarious, out-going. Dr Couture quieter, a bachelor scientist. Devoted to his work.'

'His work being Project Babylon,' said Beauvoir.

'According to what you found out' – Gamache turned to Cohen 'Dr Couture started working with Gerald Bull at McGill, on HARP.'

'Right, but funding for the High Altitude Research Project was cut,' said Cohen. 'And Dr Bull left McGill.'

'What did he do then?' Gamache asked.

'He formed the Space Research Corporation,' said Cohen.

'And the SRC eventually developed the long-range artillery that became Project Babylon,' said Lacoste. 'By then it was a private company, run by Bull.'

'Gerald Bull became an arms dealer,' said Gamache. 'But not, perhaps, an arms designer.'

'That explains why Project Babylon was built here,' said Beauvoir. 'Because Guillaume Couture was here.'

'He built the prototype close to home,' said Lacoste. 'Where he could oversee it, but no one else could. In the middle of a Québec forest, where the Iranians, the Israelis, the Iraqis, our own people would never think to look. A gun that doesn't exist in a village that doesn't exist.'

'The last place on earth,' said Beauvoir. 'Three Pines.'

'And no one guessed that Gerald Bull wasn't the creator of Project Babylon?' asked Cohen.

'Why would they?' asked Chief Inspector Lacoste. 'And who would care? As long as he delivered.'

'And when he's murdered, Couture gets scared,' said Beauvoir. 'He hides the plans, or maybe destroys them, and goes to ground. Retires to his tomatoes and peppers, and tries to forget about the thing in the woods.'

'It was covered with camouflage netting,' said Gamache. 'An effort had been made to hide it. And the firing pin was removed. Who else but the designer could do that? Did you find the firing pin in Antoinette's home?'

'No, though to be fair, we weren't looking,' said Beauvoir. 'We'll go back and have another look.'

'If it was there, the killer probably took it,' said Gamache. 'But worth a look.'

'I'll double the guard on the gun,' said Lacoste, and headed to the telephone in the study.

The lights suddenly went on, full force, and Armand looked over at Reine-Marie, who was standing by the switch, then she returned to the table.

'Well, that killed the mood,' said Jean-Guy.

'I wanted a clearer look at this picture,' she said, bending over it.

'Do you recognize someone, Madame Gamache?' Adam Cohen asked.

'No, not the people, but the place looks familiar. Armand?'

The three men in the grainy enlargement were standing at the top of a very long tunnel that sloped downward. The walls appeared to be metal, with strips of more metal shooting down the sides and ceiling. Huge pot lights were attached to the top.

'I don't think this's a tunnel,' she said. 'I think they're standing at the top of a long cylinder.'

'The mouth of a gun, perhaps,' said Gamache.

'It would have to be a pretty big gun.'

'Well, we have a pretty big gun,' he said.

'I don't think it's a gun,' said Beauvoir, leaning over Madame Gamache's shoulder. 'It actually looks more like a stairway.'

'Or an escalator,' said Armand.

It did look vaguely familiar. A metro stop? An airport? It could be anywhere.

'Oh, this's killing me,' said Reine-Marie.

'Probably doesn't matter,' said Armand. 'The picture was obviously taken years ago.'

'What would happen if another one of those guns was built?' Reine-Marie asked.

Gamache was silent for a moment, then opened his mouth. But there were no words. Certainly none of the reassuring words she was hoping for. The candlelit words. And to Reine-Marie's horror, he simply closed his mouth and looked at her.

'Do you think the killer found the plans?' she asked quietly.

'I don't know,' said Gamache. 'Mary Fraser accused me of not understanding how dangerous the world of arms dealers is. And she's right. I don't think anything we've faced compares to it. The scale of death they deal in is almost beyond comprehension. They create and feed wars, they encourage genocide. For profit. And what a profit. The money must be in the billions. Lives are worthless, incidental.'

He spoke almost matter-of-factly, which only added to the horror of what he was saying.

'I think we have to assume the worst,' said Jean-Guy. 'That the plans have been found.'

The dinner broke up shortly after that. There didn't seem much else to say. They made arrangements for Adam Cohen to take Beauvoir's room at the B and B while Jean-Guy moved into the Gamaches' home. The young man seemed relieved not to have to drive back to the city.

After Lacoste and Cohen had gone and the dishes were done, Armand and Henri went for a walk.

'Mind if I join you?' Jean-Guy asked.

The three of them walked in companionable silence around and around the village green. It was a clear, cold night and they could see their breath. The sky was filled with stars, and moon shadows from the three huge pines stretched across the grass and landed at the bistro.

They could see Professor Rosenblatt sitting alone at a table. Gamache paused and thought. And knew it was time.

'Chilly night,' he said to Jean-Guy. 'I feel like something to warm me up.'

'I was thinking the same thing, *patron*.'

A minute later they were standing over the professor's table.

'*Bonsoir*,' said Armand.

'Hello,' said the professor, looking up and smiling.

Armand took the photograph from his pocket and placed

it on the bistro table, sliding it slowly forward, toward Michael Rosenblatt.

'I'd like an answer to my question now, *s'il vous plaît*,' said Gamache. 'Did Gerald Bull design the Supergun? Or did someone else? Someone smarter?'

He watched as the smile flattened. Flatlined. Died on Rosenblatt's face.

CHAPTER 27

'L ast call,' said Olivier from behind the bar.

There were two other occupants of the bistro, young lovers on a date, holding hands across the table. Gamache wasn't worried about them. They clearly were in their own world. One that, thankfully, did not include genocide, and warheads, and dark things hidden in deep forests. Gamache wanted to make sure the two worlds did not meet.

'Monsieur?' Gamache nodded toward Rosenblatt's cognac.

'Oh, I think not.'

The elderly scientist was slurring slightly, and now blood rushed, in a flush, to his face.

'Perhaps a glass of water, *patron*,' said Beauvoir, and Olivier returned with a pitcher and three glasses.

'I wondered when you'd find out,' said Rosenblatt. 'I probably should have told you.'

'*Oui*,' said Gamache. 'That would've been helpful, and might even have saved a life.'

'What d'you mean?' Professor Rosenblatt opened his eyes wide, then screwed them shut, in an attempt to focus.

It wasn't, Gamache thought, simply the alcohol. The man looked exhausted.

'A woman named Antoinette Lemaitre was killed last night,' said Beauvoir.

'Yes, I heard. Terrible,' said Rosenblatt. 'The people here seem to think it had something to do with a play. Must have been a very bad play.'

'She was Guillaume Couture's niece,' said Gamache.

Michael Rosenblatt stared at them as though they'd gone fuzzy.

'Guillaume Couture,' he repeated. 'I haven't heard that name in a long time.'

'How did you know him?' Beauvoir asked.

Rosenblatt looked surprised by the question. He glanced at the photograph, then from one to the other of his companions.

'We worked together, briefly. With Gerald Bull. Back in the McGill days.'

They waited for more. The young couple left, arm in arm, and Olivier began cleaning up.

And still they waited.

It seemed Rosenblatt had fallen into a stupor.

'Where did you get that?' He finally spoke, gesturing toward the picture.

'The McGill alumni magazine. It's from Dr Couture's obituary,' said Beauvoir.

Michael Rosenblatt nodded. 'I remember seeing the notice and the photo and wondering if anyone would put it together. But they didn't.'

'Put what together?' Gamache asked.

'Or maybe they did,' said Rosenblatt, either ignoring the question or lost in his own thoughts.

He seemed to be rallying, rousing. His voice was less dreamy. His eyes sharper.

Gamache wasn't sure this was such a good thing. His

defenses would soon go up again, and this man's barriers were thick and old and encrusted with a lifetime of evasions.

'He was very clever, you know. Switched on.'

'Dr Couture?' asked Gamache.

Rosenblatt laughed. 'No. Not him. Gerald Bull. Most scientists are sort of idiot savants. They know one thing very well, but fail in most other aspects of their lives. But not Dr Bull. He could be off-putting. Abrupt, impatient. But he could also be charming and clever. He was shrewd, you know. Picked up on things that others missed. It's a useful tool. He made connections. I don't mean social, though he did that too. He made intellectual connections. He could see how things fit together.'

'As a scientist?' asked Gamache.

Now Rosenblatt chuckled. 'As a scientist he was crap.' He reflected a bit on that, then amended what he'd said. 'Not crap really. He'd earned his Ph.D. He was workmanlike. No, you were right yesterday when you suggested his real genius was public relations. Getting people to agree to the disagreeable. But he was also ruthless.'

'Who designed Project Babylon?' asked Gamache.

Rosenblatt nodded toward the photograph. 'You already know.'

'I need you to confirm it.'

Even now, even when worn down and cornered, Gamache could see the elderly scientist twisting, so deep was the instinct and perhaps the training to evade.

'The plans may have been found,' Gamache said quietly.

'Ahh,' said Rosenblatt. The sound slipped out of him, like a long tail on a sigh.

He nodded a few times, carrying on some internal conversation. A debate. An argument. And then he spoke.

'Guillaume Couture designed Project Babylon. I suspect Gerald Bull conceived of the idea, but he needed someone smarter than himself to actually figure out how to do it. So he found Dr Couture ferreting away in the engineering department of McGill. Couture became Bull's chief designer and silent partner.'

Now that he'd started, Professor Rosenblatt couldn't seem to stop talking. It was such a stream of information and confidences that Gamache found himself wary. Not sure if this was the truth, half-truths, or a blockade of lies.

Though it fit with their own conclusions. Perhaps a bit too well.

'Gerald Bull essentially committed suicide when he put himself forward as the sole designer of Project Babylon,' said Rosenblatt. 'He was killed to stop him. No one knew about Guillaume Couture.'

'Except you,' said Beauvoir.

'Oh, I didn't know. Not until much later. All that research on Gerald Bull, it didn't fit, until I factored in someone else. Someone smarter.'

'Do you think Dr Couture would have kept the plans?' Beauvoir asked. 'After all, they're what got his boss killed.'

'It was his life's work,' said Rosenblatt. 'Guillaume was a nice man, in many ways a gentle man. But he was unbothered by a conscience. He had no imagination. No, that's probably unfair. He was myopic. Shortsighted. He only saw the challenge, the scheme. He didn't look beyond that, to what his plans would actually do.'

'So what does that mean?' Beauvoir demanded. 'Would he have kept the plans or not?'

'I think so,' said Rosenblatt. 'They were the work of a lifetime. Without doubt the highlight of his career.' He considered for a moment. 'You say the woman killed last night was his niece?'

'She lived in his home,' said Gamache.

In the background, the clock on the bistro mantel struck the hour. Midnight.

'And you didn't find the plans?' Rosenblatt asked.

Gamache shook his head and in the silence the clock continued to sound. One measured stroke after another.

'You think the killer has the designs for Project Babylon,' said Rosenblatt.

'I think it's possible. We have to assume he found them,' said Gamache.

The clock struck one last time, then stopped.

Michael Rosenblatt looked at it, then back at Gamache.

'The chimes at midnight, Chief Inspector,' he said quietly. 'It's later than we thought.'

Beauvoir saw a look pass between the two men and knew he'd missed some reference. But not the meaning.

They walked the professor back to the B and B and made sure he got up to his room. A light was on under Mary Fraser's door, and Gamache paused, then tapped.

'What're you doing?' Beauvoir whispered.

'The CSIS agents need to know that the plans might've been found,' Gamache whispered back.

'Just a minute,' came Mary Fraser's pleasant voice. The door opened and she stood there adjusting an unexpectedly frilly dressing gown. 'Oh.'

'You were expecting someone else?' Jean-Guy asked.

'Well, I wasn't expecting you,' she said. She had her glasses on and papers were spread out on the bed. Jean-Guy strained to get a look at them, but she stepped out and closed the door.

'What can I do for you? It must be late.' She peered at her watch. 'It's past midnight.'

It's later than we thought. Rosenblatt's words drifted into Beauvoir's mind.

'The plans might've been found,' said Armand.

The bookish woman who lived in a filing cabinet disappeared and a much sharper person stood before them, albeit in a frilly pink dressing gown.

'Come with me,' said the CSIS agent, and led them downstairs and into the farthest corner of the B and B's living room.

'Should we get Monsieur Delorme?' Gamache asked.

'No need,' she said, taking a seat. 'You can tell me and I'll pass the information on to him.'

Gamache and Beauvoir sat in the two remaining armchairs.

'You might have heard about another murder in the area,' said Gamache. 'A woman named Antoinette Lemaitre.'

'Yes, the owner of the B and B told me. He seems to be town crier.'

'Antoinette Lemaitre was Guillaume Couture's niece.'

Fraser stared at Gamache, the words sliding off her expressionless face to drop into silence. It took effort for an intelligent person to look that vacant, and Gamache suspected she was working very, very hard at that moment.

'Whose niece?' she asked.

'Please, madame,' said Gamache. 'We have no time for this. You know as well as I do that Guillaume Couture worked with Gerald Bull at HARP, and almost certainly on the Supergun.'

Once again he took the photograph out of his pocket. Unfolding it, he handed it to her. Her brows rose very slightly, creating tiny crevices in her forehead.

'You cannot possibly be an expert on Gerald Bull and not know that,' said Gamache.

Mary Fraser folded the picture in half and offered it back.

'Dr Bull had many colleagues. Including, might I remind you, Professor Rosenblatt.'

'True, but Professor Rosenblatt's niece wasn't just murdered and the home he once owned ransacked,' said Gamache, taking back the photograph. 'Time is running out and your evasions are wasting what little we have left. You seem to be treating this as some sort of game. We know all about Dr Couture.'

'You know nothing,' she hissed. 'You're mired in guesses, not facts. And don't you ever presume to lecture me about the importance of what we're doing. You gave up that right when you ran away to this quaint little village with its café au laits and village fêtes. Do you know what I see when I look at you?'

'Yes, you told me this afternoon. A suspect, maybe even a pedophile because I happen to have cared about a nine-year-old boy.'

Mary Fraser had managed to get under his skin and now the sore erupted.

'No,' she said. 'I see a hypocrite. You saw the chance to retire and you took it, knowing no one would blame you. I see a man bloated with croissants and fear, desperate to hide out in this little village, beyond harm and beyond reproach while the rest of us keep fighting. And then you pass judgment on me? You're a disgrace, monsieur.'

'That's it—' said Beauvoir.

'*Non*,' said Gamache, breaking eye contact with Fraser to look at Jean-Guy. '*Non*,' he said, regaining his own composure.

Then he turned back to Mary Fraser.

'I didn't come up here to discuss my choices,' he said. 'But to warn you that someone killed Antoinette Lemaitre then tore her home apart last night. We think he was looking for the plans to Project Babylon.'

'That's a big leap,' said Mary Fraser.

'Is it? We have every reason to believe Guillaume Couture designed the Supergun. Not Gerald Bull. Dr Bull was the salesman, and Dr Couture was the scientist. That's why the gun was built here, because Dr Couture knew the area. Knew the people. And knew no one would come looking for Project Babylon in a Québec forest. It was perfect. Until someone killed Gerald Bull.'

'These are all guesses,' she said.

'You seem resistant to the possibility,' said Gamache. 'Why is that? We have a direct line connecting Dr Couture to Gerald Bull—'

'—you have a grainy old photograph.'

'We have more than that,' he said, but Beauvoir noticed he stopped short of implicating Professor Rosenblatt.

The CSIS agent seemed perfectly composed. Her hands rested in her lap, but the fingers were tightly intertwined, turning the tips white.

'None of this is news to you, is it?' Gamache asked, tumbling to the truth. 'You knew all along. Was that the file you were reading this afternoon? The name you were trying to hide from me? It was Guillaume Couture.'

She sat up straighter, as though bracing herself.

'You came here knowing the connection with Guillaume Couture, but you didn't say anything,' said Gamache, his voice rising slightly. 'You didn't warn us, you didn't warn Antoinette Lemaitre.'

She was silent.

'We could have saved her.'

'You could do nothing,' she snapped. 'You've discovered more than I would have thought possible, but you have no idea what you've gotten hold of. Back off. Step away.'

'Why? So more people can die while you pursue whatever your own goals are?' he demanded. 'And what are they exactly?'

'You're right, we knew about Dr Couture, of course we did,' said Mary Fraser. 'But we all assumed Project Babylon died with Gerald Bull. There were rumors a gun had been built, but rumors are rife in the intelligence community, most put out as misdirection. We kept Couture under surveillance for a few years, but like you, he'd retired down here and grew tomatoes and roses and joined a bridge club, and faded away. The threat faded away.'

'Until the gun was found.'

'Yes. That was a surprise,' she admitted.

'Why didn't you tell us about Guillaume Couture when you first saw the gun?' Beauvoir demanded. 'Why didn't you tell us about his role in creating Project Babylon, and the fact he lived in the area and had a niece?'

She said nothing.

'You didn't want us to know,' said Beauvoir. 'You want—'

Gamache placed a hand on Beauvoir's arm, and he stopped talking.

Mary Fraser had not looked at Beauvoir when he spoke, but continued to keep Gamache in her sights.

'That was wise, Monsieur Gamache.'

Beauvoir was staring at Gamache, unclear why he'd stopped him.

'We're here on official business, Monsieur Gamache. For

CSIS. But there is someone you should be asking yourselves about. Michael Rosenblatt. Why is he still here?'

It was, Gamache thought, an evasion on her part. An attempt to redirect his attention. But it was also, he had to admit, a question that was making its way to the top of his list.

'Why do you think Professor Rosenblatt's still here?' Beauvoir asked.

'I have no idea,' she said. 'That's your concern, not mine. I have one brief, and that's to make sure no one else ever builds a weapon like the one we found in the woods. That's all I care about.'

'That's all?' asked Beauvoir. 'And the human cost?'

She looked at the younger man as though he'd said something adorable. A child learning to pronounce words he couldn't possibly understand.

'Do you know what I see when I look at you?' Gamache asked her.

'I honestly don't care,' Mary Fraser said.

'I see someone who's been tunneling in the dark for so long you've gone blind.'

'I thought it would be something like that,' she said, smiling. 'But you're wrong. I'm not blind. My eyes have simply adjusted to the darkness. I see more clearly than most.'

'And yet you can't see the damage you're doing,' he said.

'You have no idea the things I see,' she said, her voice hard and clipped. 'And have seen. You have no idea what I'm trying to prevent.'

'Tell me,' Gamache said.

And for the briefest instant, Jean-Guy Beauvoir thought she might. But then it was gone.

'You accused me of not understanding your world,'

Gamache said. 'And you might be right. But you no longer understand mine. A world where it's possible to care about the life of a nine-year-old boy, and to be enraged by his death. A world where Antoinette Lemaitre's life and death matter.'

'You're a coward, monsieur,' she said. 'Not willing to accept a few deaths to save millions. You think that's easy? Well, it's easy when you run away, as you've done. But I stay. I fight on.'

'For the greater good?' asked Gamache.

'Yes.'

He got up, suddenly repulsed, and stood in the middle of the charming room.

'I don't think what you do is easy,' he said. 'At least, not at first. I think it's soul-destroying. But once that happens, it gets easier. Doesn't it?'

Mary Fraser stood up then and faced him.

'Go to hell,' she said quietly.

'I will. If necessary. I expect I'll see you there.'

'Just know this, monsieur,' she said to his back. 'A coward not only dies a thousand deaths, he can cause them too.'

As they left, they noticed movement on the B and B stairs, and saw Brian standing there. Halfway up and halfway down. Frozen.

How much did he hear? Beauvoir wondered.

He heard it all, Gamache knew, judging by the look on Brian's face.

Wordlessly, Brian retreated upstairs. *All sorts of funny thoughts running through his head*, thought Gamache as he and Beauvoir left the B and B.

'Why did you stop me when we were talking with Mary Fraser?' Jean-Guy asked as they walked back home.

'I was afraid you were about to say something that should not be said. At least, not in that company.'

'That they knew about Couture and the plans and wanted to find them not for CSIS but for themselves,' said Beauvoir.

Gamache nodded.

'Do you think that's who Antoinette was expecting last night? Mary Fraser and Sean Delorme?'

'It's possible,' conceded Gamache.

'Who are these people, *patron*?'

'That, *mon vieux*, is a very good question.'

CHAPTER 28

⌒

Clara poured a coffee from the percolator in Myrna's New and Used Bookstore and brought it over to her seat in the bay window. Morning was struggling through the cracks in the heavy clouds, shooting columns of light onto the forest.

'I'm hearing rumors that Antoinette's death and Laurent's might be connected,' she said, and watched Myrna lower the newspaper just enough to stare at her. 'And might have something to do with that gun in the woods.'

Myrna crumpled the paper onto her lap.

'Really?' She took off her glasses. 'But how could that be? Antoinette's death was during a robbery probably, or maybe something to do with the play—'

Clara shook her head. 'The police don't think so anymore.'

'Who'd you hear this from?'

'Gabri. He was talking to Brian, who overheard Armand and Jean-Guy talking to that CSIS woman last night. Fighting with her, apparently.'

'Fighting?'

'Well, arguing. Gabri told me this in confidence. Shhhh.'

'Shhhh?' asked Myrna. 'Is that the sound of secrets escaping from you?'

The two women stared at each other, but hanging between them, like a hologram, was the gun. The big, goddamned gun. In the woods. Neither had seen it, but both women imagined what such a thing might look like. And wondered how it could kill so many people just by being.

'How could Antoinette have been involved with the gun?' Myrna asked.

'I don't know and Gabri couldn't tell me,' said Clara. 'It's strange that no one remembers it being built. You'd think some of the older residents might remember. Ruth, for instance.'

'Ruth? You expect Ruth to remember anything?'

'She is a bit of a loose cannon herself,' Clara admitted.

'Maybe she was left behind by the builders,' said Myrna. 'A failed first attempt.'

Clara gave a short laugh, then sighed. 'I wish we knew more. It's so easy to start imagining the worst.'

'It doesn't take much imagination,' said Myrna, her eyes drifting past Clara and out the window.

'What do you see?' Clara asked, turning to look.

She saw the village green, the three tall pine trees, the homes. She saw storm clouds and shafts of light and a gaggle of hungry birds and an elderly man sitting on the bench feeding them.

'I see answers,' said Myrna.

'I'll get it,' called Reine-Marie. She was in the study doing some research when she heard a tentative knock on the door.

It was so tentative she thought she must've misheard. But

311

then she heard it again. A more confident rap. When she opened the door, Brian Fitzpatrick was standing there.

'I'm sorry,' he said. 'Is it too early?'

'No, of course not. Come in. You must be cold.'

The clouds that had moved in overnight threatening rain had brought with them a cold front with winds and a chill that burrowed under the skin and into the bones.

'When Gabri came to pick me up last night, I tossed a few things into a suitcase, but I wasn't thinking straight,' said Brian, hugging himself. 'I have three pairs of shoes, but only one pair of socks. And no sweater or jacket.'

'Well, we have plenty of clothes we can lend you.' She kissed him on both cold cheeks.

'May I see your husband?'

'Of course.'

She led him into the kitchen where the woodstove was lit and a pot of coffee was perking. 'Armand.'

Armand looked up from his notepad, and Henri looked up from the stuffed moose he was chewing. Both got up immediately.

'Brian,' said Armand, shaking the man's hand. 'Sit down. I was just writing down some thoughts and then I was going to go over to the B and B to see you.'

He ushered Brian to a comfortable chair by the fire while Reine-Marie poured a coffee.

'Did you have breakfast?' she asked. 'I can make some bacon and eggs.'

'*Merci*. Gabri made me some toast. I'm not actually all that hungry.'

'I'm so sorry about Antoinette,' said Reine-Marie, bringing over the coffee and some orange juice. 'How are you?'

She couldn't not ask, but the answer was obvious in his

hollowed-out look. He just shook his head and lifted one hand, then dropped it to the arm of the chair.

It was also obvious that Brian wanted to speak to Armand alone.

Reine-Marie went upstairs and brought down sweaters and socks and warm flannel pajamas of Armand's for Brian. She put them on the table by the door along with a warm jacket, then called to Henri and, clipping the leash onto the shepherd, went for a walk.

'You heard us last night,' said Armand after Reine-Marie had left.

Brian nodded. 'I couldn't sleep. I heard you knock on the CSIS woman's door and followed you downstairs. I don't understand what's happening.'

'Antoinette's uncle was one of the architects of that gun we found in the woods,' said Gamache. No use hiding it since Brian had heard it all the night before anyway.

'Uncle Guillaume?' asked Brian. 'But he was an engineer. He built overpasses.'

'Antoinette talked about him then?'

'Not much, and to be honest, I didn't really ask. She seemed to like him, and he obviously liked her. You think she was killed because of him?'

'It's possible. We think he might have kept the designs for that gun and someone went there to find them, maybe thinking she wasn't home.'

'They're worth a lot of money. I heard you say that last night.'

Gamache nodded. 'That's right. Do you have any idea at all whether those papers were in the house?'

Brian shook his head. 'I feel useless. I think I should be able to hand them over to you, but all of this is news to me.

I have no idea what's happening. Did Antoinette know what her uncle really did?'

'We don't know that either. We do know that there's no evidence of him in your home. Can you remember anything? Even a photograph?'

Brian pursed his lips, thinking, then shook his head. 'There might've been and I just didn't notice. I don't think I'm all that observant. I wish I'd been home. I should've been home.'

'Whoever did this would've just waited until you were gone the next time,' said Armand. 'There's nothing you could've done.'

Gamache didn't say it, but he believed Antoinette's life was over as soon as Laurent found the gun and started telling everyone, and when the CSIS agents decided not to tell anyone about her uncle.

'Did anyone ever come asking about Guillaume Couture?' Armand asked.

'Not that I know of. He died before I met her.' Brian looked down at his coffee mug, as though he'd never seen one before. 'I don't know what to do.'

Armand nodded. He understood that with loss came the overwhelming feeling of being lost. Directionless.

'I can't go home,' said Brian. 'Not yet.'

Gamache knew he meant emotionally, but he also wouldn't be allowed home.

Not surprisingly, Lacoste had called first thing with the news that Mary Fraser and Sean Delorme had an injunction to search Antoinette's home themselves. Alone. Though Gamache had the feeling the injunction was just for show. He was pretty sure they'd already been there. Already searched. Without benefit or need of legal approval.

'I might go to the theater today,' said Brian. 'I think I'd feel close to her there. Better than sitting around the B and B all day. And I don't really want to talk to anyone, you know?'

'Let me drive you,' said Armand, getting up. 'I'm heading in that direction myself.'

At the door they found the clothing.

'Here,' said Armand. 'Put on one of the sweaters while I make a phone call.'

He went into the study, closed the door firmly, then called a private number in Ottawa. It was eight thirty. After a brief exchange he hung up.

By noon they should know more about Mary Fraser and Sean Delorme.

Brian was waiting for him at the front door, wearing Armand's favorite blue cashmere sweater.

'A bit big for you, I'm afraid,' said Gamache, rolling up the sleeves for him.

'Are you going to Knowlton too?' Brian asked.

'No, a few kilometers beyond. I can drop you at the theater then pick you up in a couple of hours, if that's all right.'

He didn't say he was going to Highwater. The fewer people who knew, the better.

As they drove away, Gamache saw Professor Rosenblatt sitting on the bench, bundled against the brisk wind and tossing bread to the birds. Autumn leaves, blown off the trees, swirled in a whirlwind about him, mixing with the excited birds and airborne bread so that it looked like nature had gone mad around the elderly physicist.

And once again, Armand was left to wonder why Professor Rosenblatt was still there instead of at home in front of his fireplace, safe and warm.

*

Clara and Myrna approached the bench and sat, one on either side of the professor.

'Good morning,' said Clara. She had to raise her voice to be heard over the howling wind. 'How did you sleep?'

'I'm afraid I had a little too much to drink last night,' he said. 'I came out here for fresh air.'

'Well, there's lots of that,' said Myrna, trying to keep her scarf off her face. On the other side of the professor, Clara was fighting with her hair.

Rosenblatt offered them some of his stale bread to toss to the chickadees and blue jays and robins.

'Ravenous,' he said. 'Now I understand where that expression comes from.'

The bread they threw was caught by the wind and tumbled across the green, chased by the leaves and the birds.

'I'm sorry about your friend,' said Rosenblatt, watching the commotion caused by the bread.

'It's awful,' said Clara. 'But what makes it worse is that no one is telling us anything. We wondered if you could answer some questions.'

'I'll try.'

'We heard that Antoinette's death might be linked to Laurent's,' said Myrna. 'Is that true?'

'I think the police suspect that might be true,' he said.

'But how?' Clara asked. 'The gun is somehow involved, right?'

'Yes. But I really can't tell you more. I'm sorry.'

'You can't, or you won't?' asked Clara.

'You're friends with Monsieur Gamache, why don't you ask him?'

Myrna smiled. 'Because he won't tell us.'

'So you're trying to get me in trouble, ladies?' It was said with amusement and charm, but also without any weakening on his part.

'You know something, don't you?' said Myrna. 'When Isabelle Lacoste told us about Antoinette you said something. A quote. About some rough beast, and Bethlehem.'

'I wish I could take credit, but I was just reading what your friend Ruth had written in her notebook.'

'It's a quote, right?' said Myrna.

'I believe so,' said Rosenblatt. 'Shakespeare probably. Isn't everything? Or the Bible.'

'It must've meant something to you, for you to not just read what Ruth had written, but to say it out loud,' said Clara. 'You must've agreed.'

Michael Rosenblatt pressed his lips together and lowered his head, either in thought or against the particularly violent gust that hit them.

'I don't know what's confidential and what's public knowledge.' His words were whipped away as soon as they were out of his mouth, but Clara and Myrna were close enough to catch them.

He studied Clara, obviously weighing some decision.

'I was at your solo show, you know, at the Musée d'art contemporain a year or so ago. I thought what you did with portraits was brilliant. You reinvented the form. Reinvigorated it. Gave it depth and a kind of joyful spirit missing in most works today.'

'Thank you,' said Clara.

'You obviously know that art has power,' he said. 'It can be freeing, but it can also be a weapon, especially when combined with something equally powerful, like war. Art's been used to inspire all sorts of things. Public statues of brave soldiers. Paintings of heroic sacrifice. But it's also been used to put the fear of God into enemies.'

'Why are you telling me this?' Clara asked.

'Because you've been kind to me and I can see that not being told anything is making a terrible situation even worse. I can't show you the gun or talk about it really, and I doubt it would help even if I could, but there is something you might be interested in, might even be able to help with.'

He brought out his iPhone, tapped the screen, then handed it to her.

'What is it?' she asked, looking at the photograph.

'An etching. It's on the side of the gun.'

Myrna got up and moved to the other side of her friend for a better look. Professor Rosenblatt brushed his finger along the screen and the image changed to show another view of the etching.

Both women stared at the serpent with seven heads, writhing and bucking. A woman on its back. She was even more terrifying than the monster. Hair flowing, back straight, she stared at Clara and Myrna and Professor Rosenblatt. Seeing not just them, but the village behind them and the whirlwind about them. But she herself was calm in the maelstrom. Confident.

A cold drop tapped the top of Clara's head, startling her. Then another. One fell on the screen, distorting the woman's face, making it even more grotesque.

'The Whore of Babylon,' said Myrna, and Professor Rosenblatt nodded.

The women looked at each other while Professor Rosenblatt took back the device and slipped it into his pocket, out of the rain. Out of sight.

'From the Book of Revelation,' said Clara.

They were both aware of the reference. And the symbolism.

318

It was a warning of catastrophe. Deliberate and inescapable. And complete.

'We should get inside,' said Professor Rosenblatt.

The rain was falling more heavily, in great big drops that splattered on the road, and on their backs, and on their heads as they hunched over and ran for it. The trees corkscrewed in the wind and they saw Reine-Marie with Henri racing to get home before the deluge.

The three of them hurried into Myrna's bookstore. Once inside she got towels to dry themselves off, stoked the woodstove, and poured tea, hot and strong.

Rain now beat against the windows. Rattling them.

'My God,' said Myrna, wiping her face. 'If that drawing was meant to terrify, it worked. Isn't the goddamned gun scary enough? Who needs to do that as well?'

'Can I see it again?' Clara asked, and Professor Rosenblatt gave her his iPhone. She stared at the image, making it larger, then smaller.

'It wasn't signed?' she asked.

'Nothing as convenient as that,' said the professor. 'Why?'

'Most artists sign their work in one way or another. There's writing on it though.'

'Yes, a biblical quote. In Hebrew.'

'The one you and Ruth quoted?' asked Myrna.

'No, another one. About Babylon.'

'Why was the Whore of Babylon put on the gun?' Clara asked.

'We think it was supposed to be a sales tool to appeal to the buyer.'

'And who was the buyer? The devil?'

'Pretty close.'

'Some rough beast,' said Clara, staring at the etching. 'Slouching toward Bethlehem.'

'And his route took him right through Three Pines,' said Myrna.

CHAPTER 29

———

The wipers on Gamache's car were working furiously, thumping and sweeping, thumping and sweeping away the rain, trying to clear a semicircle of visibility.

When they arrived at the theater, Brian bolted out. Armand waited in the car until he got inside, but saw Brian put his hands in the pockets of his jacket, then bring them out and try other pockets. Then he looked over at Gamache.

Armand turned the car off and dashed over, head down against the driving rain.

'Do you have the keys?' he shouted.

Once again Brian searched the pockets and shook his head. 'They're in my jacket. This's yours.'

Gamache tried the handle. It turned and the door opened.

'Thank God,' he said, quickly following Brian inside. 'But shouldn't this be locked?'

He closed the door against the beating rain.

'Antoinette sometimes forgets to lock it,' said Brian, running his hands through his wet hair. 'I'm okay now, you can go if you want to.'

'I think I might wait until the storm passes,' said Armand, feeling a little bad since he knew Brian desperately wanted time alone. 'I'll just wait in the theater for a few minutes.'

Brian went over to a panel and with a clunk turned on the stage lights, but not the house lights. While Armand took off his sodden overcoat and chose a seat in the darkness a few rows back, Brian sat on the sofa on the stage. Folding his hands on his lap, a calm seemed to come over him. He looked like a man meditating. Eyes closed, face tilted slightly upward, peaceful though not, Gamache supposed, at peace.

This was Brian's sanctuary and Gamache was aware he was an intruder. He felt like a voyeur. Watching an intimate act. An uninvited audience at a private play.

He averted his eyes, looking around the set.

It took him a while to realize what he was seeing. It started as a vague sense that something was different. Not wrong, not threatening, just a little different.

Brian wouldn't have noticed. His back was to the set and his eyes were closed. But Armand sensed it, then saw it.

There were more items on the set. The tatty furniture was the same, but there were more books on the shelves, and little ornaments filled some of the empty spaces.

Armand cocked his head to one side, looking at the items. They were too far away to see clearly, though one caught his eye. He stared at it, and then stood up.

Walking to the wings, he climbed the few steps to the stage and into the floodlights. Brian, hearing the footsteps, opened his eyes.

'Leaving?' he asked, with more than a little hope in his voice.

'Not yet,' said Armand, distracted, staring at the items on the bookshelf. Then he took a step to his left and bent down, reading the spines of the books. Some were dusty old volumes that had been there before, no doubt bought in bulk at a rummage sale and used for props in many productions. But there were a few others, including – he bent closer and put on his reading glasses – *Classical Dynamics of Particles and Systems*, *Barrier Trajectories* and one called *Applied Physics, Theory and Design*.

Straightening up, his eyes moved swiftly over the bookshelf, the desk, the chest of drawers, all meant to convey the living room of a boardinghouse in the Fleming play.

And then his eyes stopped. There, at the back of the desk behind a pen set, was a small photograph in a silver frame of a smiling man with a little girl in pigtails leaning against his knee.

Gamache brought out the photo of the three scientists and compared the faces. Both smiling. Both slightly disheveled. Both Guillaume Couture.

And the girl was almost certainly Antoinette Lemaitre, when she really was a girl and not a woman-child.

He reached for his cell phone and called Isabelle Lacoste.

'Antoinette brought her uncle's things to the theater,' he said. 'They're scattered around the set on the stage.'

'Are the plans there?' she asked immediately. 'The firing mechanism?'

'I don't know yet, I just discovered it.'

Brian had come over and was standing next to Gamache. He reached out for the framed photograph but Gamache stopped his hand.

'We'll be over right away,' said Lacoste. 'Don't touch anything.'

It was out before she realized what she'd said.

'We'll try not to,' said Gamache, eyeing Brian.

'I'm sorry, *patron*,' said Lacoste. 'Of course you won't.'

After he'd hung up, Gamache asked Brian if he could point out which props had been there for a while and which ones might be new.

Brian took his time, pointing to, but not touching, the pen set, the photo, some books, some bric-a-brac.

When he finished, he turned back to Armand. 'Did I hear you say Antoinette put these things out? That they belonged to her uncle?'

'She must have,' said Armand. 'The books were suggestive, but that photograph puts it beyond doubt. How about this?' Armand motioned to the ornament that had first caught his attention. Brian had pointed it out as something he'd never seen before. 'Are you sure this isn't from your props department?'

Brian gnawed on his lower lip. 'Pretty sure. It's kind of memorable, isn't it?'

It was that, Gamache agreed. And it was manufactured to be just that. Memorable. He was certain it hadn't been on the stage when he'd visited Antoinette a few days earlier. He'd have remembered.

It was, after all, a souvenir. Bending closer, he came eye to eye with the statue. It was small and tacky and cheap. He knew because he'd bought one himself, but not for himself. Or Reine-Marie.

They'd bought one each for their granddaughters when last they'd visited Paris. They'd taken the girls for a weekend away, to give Daniel and Roslyn time on their own.

In a series of clear images, Armand saw little Florence and her littler sister Zora in front of the Eiffel Tower. In the

Luxembourg Gardens. At a *laiterie* with dripping ice cream cones.

Then little Florence and littler Zora on the *train à grande vitesse*, the TGV, in profile, side by side, looking wide-eyed out the window, the French countryside zipping by at great speed as they hurtled toward Belgium.

And then little Florence and her littler sister Zora pointing to and laughing at the little bronze boy, peeing into the fountain in Brussels. The famous statue was called the Manneken Pis, which was also greeted with hilarity. Grandpapa had told them the story of the baby prince who, legend had it, in 1142 had peed on his enemies from a tree during battle. Legend also had it that somehow this act had led to victory. If only the arms dealers knew it wasn't arms that won a war.

The girls were so taken with the story and the silly statue that they'd pleaded for their own from a souvenir stand. It proved a little embarrassing to explain to their parents how the girls could have gone to the beautiful city of Brussels and their only memory, their only souvenir, was of a peeing boy.

But Gamache now remembered something else from that trip. They'd taken the girls to the Atomium, a huge reproduction of an atom, shepherding in the atomic age. It was possible to go inside, to visit rooms, to look out the windows, and to travel up and down on the quite singular, indeed unique, escalators.

And that's what Reine-Marie had remembered when looking at the picture of the scientists.

Once again Armand brought the photograph from his pocket and stared at it. Had there been a chair under him, he'd have sat. In his mind he replaced the three scientists with two teary, weary and bored girls and an exhausted Reine-Marie. At the top of the escalator. This escalator. At the Atomium.

That was where the photograph was taken. At the Atomium. This picture placed Guillaume Couture in Brussels with Gerald Bull. Proving he'd stayed on to work with Dr Bull while Project Babylon was being developed.

Anyone familiar with Gerald Bull's career, and the Atomium, would have seen that too.

Beauvoir and Lacoste arrived a few minutes later and Gamache showed them the new items on the stage set.

'Brian confirms these pieces weren't here before,' said Gamache. 'And they certainly weren't out when I was here last week.'

'Where is he?' asked Beauvoir, unpacking his forensics kit and putting on gloves.

'He's gone downstairs to the greenroom, to be alone.'

He also told them where the picture had been taken.

'Brussels,' said Beauvoir, pausing in his search of the books. 'Where Bull was murdered. But when Bull was murdered?'

'We can't be sure,' said Gamache.

'Antoinette might've hid all her uncle's things in the basement and then brought them here in the last few days,' said Lacoste. 'That suggests she knew her uncle was involved with Gerald Bull and the gun. Why else hide the things? Why else bring them here?'

'To get them out of the house, I agree,' said Beauvoir. 'But why only in the last few days? What happened then? She didn't do it when she took over his house. She didn't do it when Laurent was murdered. What happened to make her get the wind up?'

'The gun,' said Gamache.

'But it was found when Laurent died,' said Lacoste. And then it dawned on her. 'But no one knew what was under the netting. It was only three days ago that people found out it was Gerald Bull's missile launcher.'

Gamache nodded. 'I think when Antoinette heard, she panicked. She must've realized it was her uncle's gun and that was why Laurent was killed.'

'She was afraid she'd be next,' said Beauvoir. 'If the murderer found out about her uncle and his connection to Bull.'

'And she was right,' said Lacoste. 'But by the time she hid the things, it was too late.'

'Which means,' said Gamache, 'her uncle must've told her at least something about his work.'

'Probably to warn her,' said Lacoste.

'But how did the murderer find out about Dr Couture? And that his niece was living in his home?' asked Beauvoir.

'The photograph of them together in Brussels was published in his obituary, probably furnished by Antoinette, not realizing what it revealed,' said Gamache. 'Anyone looking for the plans would see the significance immediately.'

'But Dr Couture died years after Gerald Bull was murdered,' Isabelle pointed out. 'Was anyone still interested?'

'In a fortune?' asked Beauvoir. 'Even Professor Rosenblatt admitted there'd be people out there still looking for the mythical Supergun. What I'm not clear on is, after Laurent found the gun and was killed to stop him blabbing, why did the murderer wait a week or more to kill Antoinette and search her house for the plans? If he knew her uncle had worked on the Supergun, why not go there right away?'

Gamache took a deep inhale, held it a moment, then exhaled.

It was a very good question. There was a reason, of course. And perhaps the answer was—

'Maybe they aren't the same person,' said Armand. 'Maybe someone killed Laurent and someone else, on hearing of the find, came down to see it and look for the plans. They knew that Guillaume Couture was Antoinette's uncle, and if anyone had the plans to Project Babylon it would be him.'

'They?' asked Lacoste. 'You're thinking of Mary Fraser and Sean Delorme, aren't you?'

'I'm not sure what I'm doing could really be called "thinking",' said Gamache. 'But yes, they're a possibility. I put in that call to my contact in CSIS this morning. We should know more about them later today.'

Lacoste looked around the stage. They'd printed, swabbed and bagged the items they knew were from Antoinette's home but hadn't found the firing mechanism or the plans.

Gamache picked up a few of the bagged items and examined them. A pen set. A pair of bookends. The peeing boy.

'I don't suppose ...' Gamache turned the Manneken Pis around, and around.

'You think that's the firing mechanism?' asked Beauvoir, trying not to laugh.

'I think if a weapon's powerful enough to wipe out an entire region, and is worth billions, some effort might be made to disguise the one component that will make it work. And that' – Gamache handed the Manneken Pis to Jean-Guy – 'is not it.'

Beauvoir looked at it with distaste. 'It does look familiar. Don't Florence and Zora ... ?'

'*Oui*,' said Gamache. 'Reine-Marie bought them each one. Guess what you're getting for Christmas.'

They heard heavy steps on the stairs and turned around to see Brian emerging from the wings.

'I was sitting in the greenroom when I realized that Antoinette has a desk down there. I almost looked but then thought you might want to do it yourselves.'

'I'll go,' said Beauvoir, handing the small statue back to Gamache. 'I'm rethinking your gift now, *patron*.'

He came back up twenty minutes later, shaking his head. 'Just old scripts and crap. When's the team getting here from Montréal? It's a real rat's nest down there with costumes and props.' He looked out into the body of the theater. 'It'll take hours to go through this place. Maybe days.'

A few minutes later the forensics team arrived and began the arduous task of searching the theater.

Gamache drove through what was now drizzle. The dramatic dawn with its broken clouds and shafts of light had made way for the storm, which in turn became just a dreary, cold, rainy early autumn afternoon.

Now the wipers made a lazy, rhythmic motion as he drove south from the Knowlton Playhouse toward the Vermont border, listening to Neil Young on CD sing about the place his memory went when he needed comfort. All his changes were there.

Helpless . . .

Gamache had left Lacoste and Beauvoir and the forensics team at the theater and was following his GPS along the route Mary Fraser and Sean Delorme had taken two days before. Just south of Mansonville, he turned right and drove into Highwater.

Bounded by a hill on one side and a river on the other, it should have been a picturesque little village. Could have been. Would have been. Almost certainly had been a pretty little village, once. But now it felt abandoned, forgotten. Not even a memory.

. . . helpless.

It was far from the first run-down little community Armand Gamache had arrived in. He looked around and saw the old train station, shuttered. The transport link, like an artery, was severed and the once vital community had died. Slowly. The young people seeping away for jobs elsewhere, leaving aging parents and grandparents.

Gamache looked at his GPS. He was in Highwater, but the CSIS agents seemed to have traveled slightly beyond it. Turning right again, then left, he came to a line of high chain-link fencing and a gate with a rusty chain and a new lock.

Without compunction, or hesitation, Gamache reached into his glove compartment, brought out a small pouch of tools, and within moments the lock was open. He drove in, parked the car behind an old building, then taking the GPS and an umbrella with him, he started to walk.

Up.

The walk turned into a trudge along a narrow, muddy path. He tried not to slip but twice he lost his footing, dropped the GPS, and a knee, into the mud. On the second tumble, as he reached for the wet and soiled GPS, hoping it wasn't broken, he noticed tracks. Rails. Uncovering them, he realized he was walking in the middle of a set of railway tracks. Narrower than the ones used by passenger or freight trains. These were abandoned, overgrown, all but invisible to everyone except a man on his knees.

He stood, pausing to catch his breath. He was almost at the top of the hill. After a few more minutes' climb there was no more up left, only down. Bending over, he rested his hand on his knee. It was at times like this he realized he was no longer thirty, or even forty. Or even fifty. Straightening up, he looked around. The crown of the hill was wooded, but he could tell by the relatively new growth that it had once been clear-cut.

With the toe of his rubber boot, he uncovered the narrow rails and followed them until they ended at a concrete platform, half buried under years of dirt and roots and fallen leaves. Around it were other lumps, but those had been recently excavated. The huge pieces, like artifacts, sat half buried and half rusting in the drizzle. He examined them, taking photographs, and then returned to the platform.

A view that would once have thrilled him now left him queasy. He looked over the vast forest, his sight line skimming the treetops all the way to the Green Mountains of Vermont in the distance. Mist and low clouds clung to them and the world seemed washed of all vibrant color. He could hear, on the umbrella over his head, the drum of raindrops.

The Whore of Babylon had been here, and then moved on. Leaving behind a graveyard of giant severed limbs.

There was no mistaking what, when whole, they had once been.

CHAPTER 30

O nce again the investigators sat around the conference table in the Incident Room. Jean-Guy watched as Gamache put on his reading glasses and looked down at the report Beauvoir had handed out. Then Gamache took off his glasses and turned thoughtful eyes on his former second-in-command and Jean-Guy had to remind himself that Gamache was a guest and not in charge anymore.

As a joke he'd given his father-in-law a Walmart greeter's vest as career advice. Gamache had laughed with genuine amusement and once even wore it when his son-in-law and daughter visited, opening the door with, 'Welcome to Walmart.'

But now Jean-Guy regretted the vest and the implication that the Chief Inspector could not possibly be happy in retirement. That something else, something more, was expected of this man who had given his life to his job.

He remembered what Mary Fraser had said, the hurtful words. And realized he'd essentially said the same thing to his father-in-law with that vest.

Beauvoir didn't need to consult his own report. There was not much to say.

'We've interviewed Antoinette Lemaitre's friends, clients and the members of the Estrie Players. There's no doubt her decision to produce the Fleming play caused a lot of bad feeling. People were angry, to say the least.'

'Do you think the play had anything to do with her death?' Lacoste asked.

'No, I don't. We're checking alibis now, but so far everyone seems in the clear.'

'And Brian?' asked Lacoste.

'He's a little more difficult, of course. His prints and DNA are all over the crime scene, but you'd expect that. The clothes he was wearing also had her hair and some minute particles of skin and blood, but he found her, and he thinks he touched her body, so again—'

He put up his hands.

'His alibi checks out,' Lacoste read from the report.

'*Oui*,' said Beauvoir. 'His cell phone shows him in Montréal the whole time, but as we know, he could have deliberately left it there.'

'We know Antoinette took her uncle's things over to the playhouse the day she died, maybe even that evening,' said Gamache. 'Anyone see her do it?'

'No,' said Jean-Guy. 'We have witnesses though who saw her that afternoon at the grocery store, the bakery and the Société des alcools, where she bought two bottles of wine.'

'The autopsy reports a dinner of pizza, *tarte au chocolat* and red wine,' said Lacoste. 'Her blood alcohol was well above the limit, and there was an empty bottle in recycling.'

'And the other bottle?' asked Gamache.

'In the cupboard, unopened,' said Beauvoir.

Gamache pondered for a moment. 'What does it sound like to you?'

'Sounds like an alcoholic,' said Jean-Guy.

'Sounds like a woman letting herself go for a night,' said Lacoste. 'You guys have no idea how attractive sitting around in sweats eating junk and guzzling wine sounds to any woman. Nice dinner in Paris? Forget it. Give me pizza, wine, chocolates and sweatpants and I'm happy.'

Beauvoir and Gamache looked at her.

'Motherhood,' she explained. 'Annie will understand one day. And I bet if you ask Reine-Marie—'

'But she wasn't in sweats,' said Gamache. 'She was in her street clothes.'

'True,' said Lacoste. 'She had casual clothing in her closet. She could've changed.'

'But didn't,' said Gamache. 'Why not?'

'Maybe she meant to, but got into the wine right away,' said Beauvoir. 'And got so shit-faced she no longer noticed or cared what she was wearing. I think the wine was to numb herself. She was obviously afraid. Why else take those things to the theater?'

'But if she was so afraid, why did she let Brian go to Montréal?' asked Lacoste. 'If I was afraid, I think I'd want company.'

'Brian?' asked Beauvoir.

'Okay, he's no Rottweiler, but it's better than being alone if you're that afraid.'

'Why was the door unlocked?' asked Gamache. 'She was afraid enough to get her uncle's things out of the house, but then she gets home and leaves the door unlocked?'

'Habit?' asked Lacoste. But she was unsatisfied with that answer.

'Maybe we have it all wrong,' said Beauvoir, leaning back in his chair and crossing his arms in annoyance. 'Maybe she wasn't really afraid. Maybe she wanted Brian out of the way so she could meet someone.'

'A lover?' asked Lacoste, but shook her head and looked at Beauvoir, her eyes gleaming. 'No. A buyer. That's what you're thinking.'

'I'm wondering,' said Jean-Guy. 'It fits too, I think. Guillaume Couture tells his niece about Project Babylon and his role in creating it, to warn her. Tells her about the firing mechanism and the plans that he's hidden. But she's not really interested, it's an old gun her elderly uncle is babbling on about. But then, when it's found, she realizes what she has, and she knows it must be worth something to someone.'

'When she's approached,' said Lacoste, working her way through this scenario, 'she invites him—'

'Or her,' said Beauvoir.

'Or them,' said Gamache.

'Over. And makes it the one night she knows Brian won't be around.'

'Yes,' said Gamache. 'I think that's important. It's the one night he was away.'

'Then why did she take the things to the theater?' asked Beauvoir, then held up his hand. 'Wait. Don't tell me. It's to get them out of the house, so that the buyer can't find them without her. And she won't tell, without the money.'

He slammed his hand down on the conference table.

'Solved.'

'Aren't you leaving out one detail?' asked Armand.

'The name of the killer?' asked Jean-Guy. 'I got us this far, I think the Chief Inspector can do the rest, don't you?'

Isabelle Lacoste was leaning back in her chair, tapping a pen against her lips. No longer listening, which was wise, but thinking.

'The wine,' she said. 'Why would Antoinette drink a whole bottle before an important meeting? Wouldn't she want a clear head?'

'Maybe she needed courage more,' said Beauvoir. 'Besides, we don't know that she drank it all herself. The killer might've had a couple of glasses then washed up. Or Antoinette might've been nervous and drank more than she meant to. After all, she knew she was meeting someone who'd already killed at least one person.'

Lacoste was nodding. 'That could also explain her injury. It doesn't look deliberate. If she was drunk and got into an argument, a shoving match, let's say, with the buyer, she might've lost her balance.'

'And once she was out of the way, the buyer was free to search the house,' said Gamache. 'Not realizing Antoinette had taken everything away.'

'Well, now, there's another problem,' said Lacoste. 'The search of the theater turned up nothing. No firing mechanism, no plans. So where did she put them?'

They stared at each other.

'We seem to have hit a dead end,' said Lacoste. 'We obviously need more information.'

She looked over to Adam Cohen, who was sitting at a desk staring at his computer screen. *If he's playing games*, she thought, and getting up, she crossed the room.

'We're ready for your report.'

His hands rested on the keyboard but didn't move as he stared at what Lacoste was relieved to see was text. Documents, it seemed.

'Almost ready,' he said, distracted. Then he looked up. 'Sorry, sir. Ma'am. Chief Inspector.'

He bobbed slightly in what might have been a curtsy had he been standing.

'Come over when you're finished.'

She'd given him the thankless task of tracking down documents, materials to support their investigation. Dr Couture's will. Antoinette's tax returns.

'He'll be another few minutes,' she said, returning to the conference table. 'Did you ever hear back from your friend at CSIS?'

'I spoke to her just before coming here,' said Gamache. 'She doesn't know Mary Fraser or Sean Delorme personally but she looked up their records and confirmed that they work there. Their area of expertise is the Middle East, and Gerald Bull was indeed one of their dossiers.'

'If their field of expertise was the Middle East,' said Lacoste, 'wouldn't you expect her to know the difference between Arabic and Hebrew? When she saw the writing on the etching she thought it was Arabic.'

'I think she was playing dumb,' said Gamache. 'I suspect she does that a lot. She might have also wanted to see if you knew.'

'Well, her act worked,' said Lacoste. 'I told her.'

'No harm done,' said Gamache. 'I'm sure Mary Fraser speaks Arabic and Hebrew and knew exactly what it said. My source said Fraser and Delorme have been with CSIS since the beginning.'

'When was that?' asked Beauvoir.

'Nineteen eighty-four,' said Gamache, and saw both of them raise their brows.

'You're kidding. In 1984 Canada created a Big Brother?'

asked Lacoste. 'I hope at least one person appreciated the irony.'

But Beauvoir was looking less amused. 'They've been there that long and they're still file clerks?'

'That was the crux of our conversation. When my contact saw that, she also wondered, but it seems to be the truth.'

'I guess some people get lost in the system,' said Lacoste.

But Gamache knew the Mary Fraser he'd met the night before in the B and B might be the type to hide, but not the type to get lost.

'My friend did have one thought,' said Gamache.

'They aren't really file clerks?' asked Beauvoir.

'Oh, they are who they say they are,' said Gamache. 'My friend made sure of that. They're file clerks, but with, perhaps, some added value.'

'Meaning?'

'CSIS has a mandate to collect and analyze intelligence both domestic and international. That's why Fraser and Delorme were able to collect so much information on Gerald Bull's activities here and in South Africa and Iraq and Belgium. But to do that effectively, to know what information is real and what is, in Mary Fraser's word, misdirection, you need a field agent who knows what to look for.'

'A file clerk?' asked Lacoste, and Gamache smiled. 'Who can also be sent out on assignment.'

'It appears that's a possibility. My contact said it was something instituted early on, but then bureaucracy and civil service unions got in the way. Multitasking was out and jobs became more compartmentalized. Delineated. There was support staff and there were field agents. Two distinct areas.'

338

'But some of the originals might've quietly stayed on,' said Lacoste. 'Doing both jobs. Genuine file clerks part of the time, researching, analyzing, but going into the field too, to collect intelligence.'

'*You have no idea what you've gotten hold of*,' said Gamache. 'Remember Mary Fraser saying that, Jean-Guy?'

Beauvoir nodded. He'd never forget the chill in the room and had been surprised the words hadn't come out in a cloud of vapor.

'I don't think she meant the world of sorting and filing,' said Gamache. 'Now, my contact was quick to point out that there's no evidence to support this. It's all a bit of CSIS mythology, that these deeply covert agents exist. In fact, all the evidence points to Mary Fraser and Sean Delorme being exactly who they say they are. File clerks approaching retirement.'

'Finally being sent into the field,' said Lacoste. 'And being given one last chance to distinguish themselves. That's how they struck me when they first arrived. Two slightly bumbling, likable, but not very effective low-level bureaucrats, sent because they're the only ones who still know something about a long-dead arms dealer and his long-abandoned project. They were playacting at being real agents.'

'And do they still strike you that way?' asked Beauvoir.

'No.'

'Me neither.'

'Will your contact at CSIS dig some more?' asked Lacoste.

'She said she would, but I could tell it was getting more delicate,' said Gamache. 'And if Fraser and Delorme really are field agents, then it might be best left as is.'

They heard the sound of a printer in the background.

'Isn't the deputy head of CSIS a woman?' Beauvoir asked. 'She's not your . . . ?'

'There are a lot of women who work for CSIS,' said Gamache.

'Right,' said Isabelle Lacoste. 'As file clerks. But there is one high up enough to get this information. You said you'd been speaking with her recently.'

'This afternoon,' said Gamache.

'No, I mean before that. Did she offer you a job? Her job maybe, once she moves up?'

'We had a pleasant catch-up, that's all. We've known each other for years. Worked a few cases together.'

'Of course,' said Lacoste.

Beauvoir had been listening closely, watching his old boss. He'd make a very good intelligence officer, Jean-Guy realized. He suspected Gamache had been approached, maybe even for the top job, and was considering it.

Welcome to CSIS.

Gamache was just about to tell them what he'd found in Highwater, when Adam Cohen interrupted.

'I have information on Al Lepage,' he said, sitting down. 'Do you want me to give it to you now?'

Lacoste looked over at Gamache, who gestured to the young man to continue. Cohen seemed so anxious, any delay might make him combust.

'Laurent's father is not Al Lepage.'

'*Quoi?*' asked Beauvoir, rocking forward in his chair and leaning across the table toward Agent Cohen. 'Then who is Laurent's father?'

'No, sorry, I put that badly. I didn't mean biologically . . .' He could see he'd already confused them.

'Let me start again. Al Lepage is not his real name. We

sent his fingerprints to police across Canada and into the US, and since he was a draft dodger, we also sent them to the Department of Defense in Washington.'

'Right,' said Lacoste. 'It turned up nothing.'

'Which was strange,' said Cohen. 'He admits he's American, a draft dodger. There should have been something. But then I tried the Judge Advocate General's office. It's the legal part of the US Army, based in Washington, and look what I found.'

He handed a printout to Chief Inspector Lacoste, who read it, her face growing graver and graver. After taking a deep breath, she handed it to Beauvoir, and then turned to Cohen.

'Show me.'

She followed him to his computer while Beauvoir read, then handed the page to Gamache.

Al Lepage's real name was Frederick Lawson. A private in the US Army.

'Not a draft dodger,' said Gamache, looking at Beauvoir over his reading glasses. 'A deserter.'

'Keep reading,' said Jean-Guy, his face solemn.

Gamache did. He could feel his cheeks grow cold, as though a window had been left open a crack and an ill wind had slipped in.

'Not just a deserter,' said Beauvoir, when Gamache had lowered the page to the table. 'He was about to be tried for his part in a massacre.'

'The Son My Massacre,' said Gamache. 'You're too young to remember, but I do.'

Isabelle Lacoste had sunk into a chair and was scrolling through photographs on Cohen's computer. Beauvoir joined her, as did Gamache, reluctantly. He'd seen them once before, as a young man, barely more than a child.

341

Photographs of the atrocity were on the evening news in the late 1960s. It was something you never forgot.

The four of them, three seasoned homicide detectives and one rookie, looked at the pictures, almost too horrific to comprehend. Hundreds and hundreds of bodies. Little limbs. Long dark hair. Bright clothing put on by men, women, children, infants that morning, not knowing what was approaching over the ridge.

'Al Lepage was one of the soldiers who did this?' asked Lacoste.

'Frederick Lawson was,' said Agent Cohen. 'And he became Al Lepage when he came across the border.'

'Not running from a war he didn't believe in, but from justice,' said Beauvoir.

Beside him he heard Gamache take a deep, deep breath and then sigh.

'We now know Al Lepage's capable of killing a child,' said Beauvoir.

'What do we do with this information?' Adam Cohen asked Chief Inspector Lacoste.

'We keep it to ourselves for now,' said Lacoste. 'Until our investigation's over. And then we decide what to do.'

As they walked back to the conference table she glanced at Gamache, who gave her a subtle nod. It was what he'd do.

'What's this?' asked Beauvoir, reading another printout.

'That's the other thing I found,' said Cohen. 'You asked me to look into Dr Couture's will, which I did. He left everything to his niece. That's pretty clear, but then I got to wondering what "everything" was. The contents of his home, a twenty-thousand-dollar life insurance policy and a bit of savings, and the house itself. But the real estate search showed he once owned another property.'

'Just outside Three Pines?' asked Lacoste. 'Where the gun is?'

'No. A distance from here,' said Agent Cohen. 'In a place called Highwater.'

'Ahhhh,' said Gamache, putting his hands together on the table. 'That is interesting.'

'Isn't that where the CSIS agents went the other day?' asked Lacoste.

'And where I went after leaving you at the Knowlton Playhouse,' said Gamache. 'I retraced their route. And this is what I found.'

He handed his device with the pictures on it to Lacoste, and described what he'd done. And what he'd seen.

'But what is it?' asked Lacoste, handing the device to Beauvoir via Cohen, who snuck a quick peek.

'You remember the redacted information Reine-Marie found on Gerald Bull?' asked Gamache. 'Most of the interesting information had been blacked out, but there was the one word the censors missed.'

'Superguns,' said Beauvoir, his brows rising. 'Sssssszzzz.'

'Plural.' Gamache nodded toward the device in Jean-Guy's hand. 'I think that was another one of Gerald Bull's, or Dr Couture's, missile launchers. A much smaller version, maybe a test model before building the real thing.'

'Project Babylon wasn't one gun, but two,' said Lacoste. 'And the land belonged to Dr Couture?'

'Until he sold it to a numbered company,' said Cohen. 'I'm trying to track it down.'

'I think we'll find it's the Space Research Corporation,' said Jean-Guy. 'Gerald Bull's company.'

'I think you're right,' said Gamache. 'But why abandon what looked like a perfect site on the top of a hill looking directly into the US? Why move everything here? I've asked Reine-Marie to use her archive access and see what she can find out.'

'And I'll keep looking, if it's okay with you,' Agent Cohen said, looking at Gamache, then over to Lacoste, then back again, like a confused puppy.

Gamache however was not confused. He looked at Chief Inspector Lacoste, who nodded to Cohen.

'Can your contact at CSIS help?' Beauvoir asked Gamache. 'I know you don't want to press her, but it seems important to know what CSIS really does have on Gerald Bull. The agents clearly knew about Highwater, or suspected.'

But Gamache shook his head. 'If Fraser and Delorme are who we suspect, then they'll be monitoring things very closely. I don't want them to know that we know.'

'But you asked your contact at CSIS about their work and their real jobs,' said Beauvoir. 'Aren't you worried that Fraser and Delorme will find out about that?' He watched Gamache, then smiled. 'I see. You want them to find out that you've been asking.'

'I want them to think we've been, to once again use Mary Fraser's word, misdirected. I think the one thing they don't want us to find out about is that.'

He pointed to his device with the photographs of another Babylon.

Come hell or high water, he thought.

'Hello? *Bonjour?*'

They heard the voice before they saw the man, though they knew who'd called out. A moment later Professor Rosenblatt appeared around the big red fire truck that shared the space with the homicide unit. He wore a rumpled black raincoat and held a dripping umbrella that he'd furled up.

'Am I interrupting?' he asked, shaking his umbrella. 'I can come back.'

'Not at all,' said Lacoste. 'We were just finishing.' She got up and walked over to him. 'How can I help you?'

'This is so trivial I'm a little embarrassed.' And he looked it. 'I was just wondering if I could use one of your computers? My iPhone won't receive or send messages in the village.'

'No one's does,' said Beauvoir, joining them. 'It'd be relaxing if it wasn't so infuriating.'

The professor laughed, until his attention was caught by the image on Agent Cohen's screen.

'Is that—?'

Cohen quickly stepped in front of it.

'Why don't you use this computer, Professor,' said Lacoste, directing the elderly scientist to a desk across the room. 'It's hooked up but not in use right now. Need to check your email?'

He might have laughed again, but all humor had withered in the face of the fleeting image on Agent Cohen's computer.

'No, no one really writes to me. I wanted to look up a reference.' He turned to Gamache. 'You might know where it's from.'

'Is it obscure poetry?' asked Beauvoir.

'As a matter of fact, it is,' said Rosenblatt, and saw the alarm on Beauvoir's face. 'Though I don't think it's all that obscure. I just can't place it. The Bible, I think, or Shakespeare. Your friend Ruth Zardo wrote it in her notebook when we were told about that woman's murder.'

'One of hers, probably,' said Lacoste.

'No, I don't think so. Something about some rough beast moving toward Jerusalem.'

'It sounds familiar,' said Gamache.

'Oh, we're in luck,' mumbled Jean-Guy.

'But I don't think it's Jerusalem,' said Gamache.

'No, you're right,' said Rosenblatt. 'It was Bethlehem.'

The two men pulled chairs up to the terminal, and while the others investigated murders and massacres, they looked up poetry.

'Any luck finding the plans?' Rosenblatt asked, as they typed in a few words: *rough beast, Bethlehem*. Then hit search.

'Not so far,' said Gamache. 'We found some things belonging to Dr Couture, but no plans and no firing mechanism.'

'That's a shame.'

'Would you like to have a look?' Gamache asked, and brought over the box while they waited for the dial-up to download.

Professor Rosenblatt poked through the things without great interest until he came to the Manneken Pis. He picked it up and smiled.

'I bought one of these for my grandson. My daughter wasn't impressed. David spent six months urinating in public after that. That child could pee for Canada.'

He then picked up the desk set. Taking out the pens, he studied them, then rummaged through the box until he found the bookends. He turned one over, put it down and picked up the other. By now Lacoste and Beauvoir had joined the elderly scientist, watching as he toyed with the items.

'What are you—' Lacoste began but stopped, not wanting to break his concentration.

They watched as the professor manipulated the pieces,

and then there was a small click. Rosenblatt frowned, then, picking up the two pens, he inserted them into holes at the base of one of the bookends.

After studying it for a moment, he held it out, as a bright child might who'd made something for Mother.

'Is it . . . ?' Lacoste asked, taking it from him.

'The firing mechanism? I think so,' said the professor, as astonished as everyone else. 'Ingenious.'

Gamache stared at the piece in Lacoste's hand while she turned it over and over and around. It looked nothing like a pen set and bookends now. Just as the pen set and bookends had looked nothing like a firing mechanism.

'How did you know?' asked Beauvoir, taking it from her and also turning it around and around, studying it.

'I didn't, I just tried. A prerequisite for being a physicist, I think. Good spatial reasoning. But the first clue was the pens, of course.'

'The pens?' asked Beauvoir.

'They don't work,' Rosenblatt pointed out. 'No nibs. They wouldn't write.'

Lacoste and Beauvoir looked at each other, then over at Gamache, who was staring at the firing mechanism in Beauvoir's hand. Then he dropped his eyes to the computer screen, where the poem had appeared.

In his line of sight, forming a tableau, were the firing mechanism, the Son My Massacre, John Fleming's play on Beauvoir's desk, and the words on the computer:

> *And what rough beast, its hour come round at last,*
> *Slouches towards Bethlehem to be born?*

CHAPTER 31

'The clock is ticking,' Gamache said quietly as he and Rosenblatt took seats at the back of the bistro. 'Isn't it?'

Around them, young waiters set the tables for the dinner service. Out the window, dying leaves shuffled in the wind and rain, and two chipmunks sat up on their haunches, alert.

Were they hearing it too? Gamache wondered. On the wind.

The tick, tick, ticking of time running out.

'Yes,' said the old scientist. He raised a hand and caught the attention of a server. '*Chocolat chaud, s'il vous plaît.*'

'Have you considered a nice warm apple cider?' Olivier asked. 'Please?'

'Sounds good, *patron*,' said Gamache.

'And one for me too. Nonalcoholic. I'm still recovering from last night,' he said to Armand once Olivier had left. 'You know, I ordered a hot chocolate yesterday and they brought an apple cider.'

Professor Rosenblatt extended his hands to the fire in the hearth, rubbing them together as though the warmth was water.

'That was quite a trick,' said Gamache, when the cider

arrived. He stirred the drink with the cinnamon stick, the warm apple and cinnamon scent mixing with the musky wood smoke. 'Finding the firing mechanism.'

'A trick?' Rosenblatt studied the man in front of him.

They'd left the Sûreté officers to continue their research, galvanized by the findings, and Gamache had brought the elderly scientist to the bistro. People were beginning to arrive for drinks before dinner, but their table was tucked nicely away and few would even notice they were there. To be certain of privacy, Gamache had asked Olivier not to seat anyone too close.

'This isn't a magic act, you know, monsieur,' said Rosenblatt, as serious as Gamache had ever seen him.

'And you're not the magician?'

The professor pursed his lips, contemplating. 'Do you suspect me of something?'

'What's in Highwater?'

Now the lips went taut and a stillness came over Rosenblatt. Gamache could almost smell the man's mind working. It smelled a bit like apple.

Rosenblatt smiled, more with resignation than humor.

'You know about that?'

'Mary Fraser and Sean Delorme went there shortly after seeing the gun,' Gamache explained. 'We tracked their cell phones.'

Rosenblatt shook his head. 'File clerks.'

'Well?' Gamache asked.

'Highwater was the site of the first Supergun,' said Michael Rosenblatt. He watched Gamache as he spoke. 'You're not surprised.'

Gamache was quiet, waiting to see what Rosenblatt would say, or do, next.

'You went there, didn't you?' said the scientist, once again fitting the pieces together. 'You already knew. So why ask me?'

But his companion remained silent, and once again Rosenblatt put it together.

'It was a test? You wanted to find out if I'd tell you the truth. How did you even know I knew?'

'The redacted pages,' said Armand at last. 'You read them but didn't mention the plural. The censors took out everything, except one reference. Superguns. Everyone else who read those pages saw it. I couldn't believe you didn't too. So why wouldn't you point it out? There was only one answer. Because you already knew, and hoped I hadn't seen it.'

'Why wouldn't I want you to know?'

'That's a good question. Why didn't you tell us this as soon as you saw the gun in the woods? Didn't you think it might be important for us to know there'd once been another one, close by?'

Michael Rosenblatt took off his glasses and rubbed his face, then he replaced his glasses and looked at Gamache.

'I actually thought it didn't matter, but hearing you say it like that, I can see how it might seem suspicious. Not many knew about the other part of Project Babylon,' said Michael Rosenblatt. 'The two halves were called Baby Babylon and Big Babylon.'

'Two halves?' asked Gamache. 'Of a whole?'

'No, better to call them two parts, but not of a whole. One led to the other. The first was Baby Babylon, the smaller of the two.'

'The one in Highwater.'

'Yes. It was conceived by Gerald Bull through his Space Research Corporation. Baby Babylon was a sort of open secret, like a lot of products in the arms market. Secret enough to be enticing, but out there enough to attract interest.'

'And it did,' said Gamache. 'Didn't it?' he asked when Rosenblatt didn't answer.

'Of a sort. Baby Babylon was met with ridicule. It was called "Baby" but it was so huge, so ungainly, unlike anything else out there, that it was dismissed as the product of a mind as unstable as the weapon. A fantasist. No credible engineer or physicist thought it could be built. And, if it was, it couldn't possibly work. Only another unstable mind would commission it.'

'Saddam Hussein,' said Gamache.

'Yes. The fact Saddam was interested just confirmed everyone's suspicion that the idea was crazy.'

He turned his mug of warm apple cider around in a lazy circle.

'They were wrong,' said Gamache.

'Oh, no. They were right. Baby Babylon didn't work. It was top-heavy, couldn't sustain trajectory. With something like that, firing a missile into low orbit and having it travel tens of thousands of miles, if you're off by one one-thousandth of a degree at launch, you wipe out Paris instead of Moscow on impact. Or Baghdad.'

'Or Bethlehem.'

Rosenblatt didn't respond to that.

'How did they know it didn't work?' asked Gamache.

'They fired it.'

Gamache didn't, or couldn't, hide his surprise.

'Not into the air,' Rosenblatt hurriedly assured him.

'Then where?' asked Gamache.

'Into the ground.'

Now Gamache looked, and was, confused.

'When you were there, did you happen to notice railway tracks?' the professor asked. 'Not the Canadian National ones, but smaller, narrower?'

'Yes. I followed them up the hill.'

'Good. That's how Bull did it. As with everything else about Project Babylon, it was brilliant in its simplicity. They couldn't possibly test the missile launcher by actually launching a missile, so they put it on a flatbed on rails at the bottom of a hill and fired it into the ground.'

'What good would that do?' asked Gamache.

'The backward force,' said Rosenblatt. 'They measured the degree of incline, the speed and distance traveled, and the depth and trajectory of the hole in the ground. It was so simple it was genius.'

'It doesn't sound simple to me,' Gamache admitted. Rosenblatt had lost him at 'degree of incline'. Gamache considered what he'd heard.

'Wouldn't it make a lot of noise?' he asked. 'So much for secrecy.'

'Yes,' agreed Rosenblatt. Gamache waited for more, but nothing more came.

'It didn't work, you say?'

'They tried it a few times, apparently, but while the force could be corrected, they couldn't solve the trajectory problem. Eventually they abandoned the site.'

That sounded like the end of the story, but Gamache knew it was really just the beginning. They weren't even at the end now, thirty years later. But he had a feeling they were approaching it. Or it was approaching them.

'What happened next?' he asked.

'Project Babylon was closed down. Gerald Bull moved to Brussels and Guillaume Couture retired to his roses.'

'Except that Project Babylon wasn't over,' said Gamache. 'In fact, it got bigger. You say not many knew about the next phase?'

'That was the only thing that was disconcerting. Gerald Bull was guarded about the second weapon, Big Babylon. It was unlike him. He was a snake-oil salesman, a huckster. So when he was quiet about this second design, it got some people wondering.'

'If it was true,' said Gamache.

'If Gerald Bull was building an even more dangerous weapon, and playing an even more dangerous game. With even more dangerous people.'

'More dangerous than the Iraqis?'

Michael Rosenblatt didn't answer that.

Gamache thought for a minute. 'If Bull didn't talk about it, how did people find out?'

'Most didn't. And any information that did come out was patchy. A whispered word here and there. It's a community filled with whispers. They add up to a sort of scream. Hard to separate the good intelligence from the noise.' He paused, thinking back. 'They should've known.'

'CSIS? About the other half of Project Babylon?'

'Everything, they should've known it all. I think they did know. They just didn't believe it. They dismissed Gerald Bull as a fool, a dilettante, especially after Baby Babylon failed.'

'So did you,' Gamache pointed out.

'But I didn't have the entire intelligence apparatus at my disposal. I worked with the man, I knew he wasn't capable of actually creating the machines he was marketing. What I didn't appreciate was that Guillaume Couture was.'

Rosenblatt looked at Gamache.

'It honestly never occurred to anyone that Project

Babylon wasn't just a madman's delusion. Especially after Baby Babylon failed. But he did it. He actually built it.' Rosenblatt shook his head and looked into his fragrant cider, stirring it with his cinnamon stick. 'How did we miss it?'

'Did you miss it?'

'What's that supposed to mean?'

'If everyone thought Bull was such a buffoon, and his designs the product of a delusional mind, why was he killed?'

'To be sure,' said Rosenblatt. 'To be on the safe side.'

'Murder puts you on the safe side?' Gamache asked.

'Sometimes, yes.' Rosenblatt stared at the former head of homicide. 'Don't tell me you've never thought that.'

'And is this the "safe side"?' Gamache asked. 'We're half a kilometer from a weapon that could wipe out every major city down the East Coast, never mind Europe.'

Rosenblatt leaned closer to Gamache. 'Like it or not, the death of Gerald Bull meant Project Babylon did not end up in the hands of the Iraqis. They'd have won the war. They'd have taken over the whole region. They'd have wiped out Israel and anyone else who stood up to them. In a dangerous world, Monsieur Gamache, this is the safe side.'

'If this is so safe,' said Gamache, 'why are you so afraid?'

CHAPTER 32

———

Clara confided her suspicions to Myrna.

As she spoke she became more convinced. Some-times, on saying things out loud, especially to Myrna, Clara could see how ludicrous they were.

But not this time. This time they jelled.

'What should I do?' asked Clara.

'You know what you have to do.'

'I hate it when you say that,' said Clara, sipping her white wine.

Across from her Myrna smiled, but it was fleeting, unable to penetrate beyond what Clara had just told her.

They hadn't noticed the two men in the dark corner until one of them got up.

Clara nodded to Professor Rosenblatt as he walked by their table. He didn't stop but continued to, and out, the door. Then they turned their attention to the person left behind.

Armand was either staring after the scientist or into space. He seemed to make up his mind. Getting up, he walked to the bar, and placed a phone call, turning his back to the room as he spoke. Then he returned to the table, wedged snug into the corner.

Clara got up, followed by Myrna, and slipped into seats on either side of him.

'I think I've found something interesting,' said Clara. 'But I'm not sure.'

'She's sure,' said Myrna.

'Tell me,' said Armand, turning his full and considerable attention to her.

'Take a seat.' Isabelle Lacoste indicated the conference table in the Incident Room. Mary Fraser and Sean Delorme joined Inspector Beauvoir, who was already there.

'Project Babylon wasn't one missile launcher,' said Beauvoir without preamble. 'It was two. Why didn't you tell us this before?'

Gamache had called them from the bistro after Professor Rosenblatt confirmed there were two guns, christened with the unlikely names Baby Babylon and Big Babylon.

Mary Fraser was perfectly contained, in her drab way. Isabelle Lacoste had the impression that the middle-aged woman should have a ball of knitting in her lap like some benign presence, there to calm and soothe infants who were acting out.

'Was it?' asked Mary Fraser.

Isabelle Lacoste leaned slightly forward and, lowering her voice, she said, 'Highwater.'

It was like throwing a boulder into a small pond. Everything changed.

'But Baby Babylon didn't work—' said Mary Fraser.

'Mary,' Sean Delorme interrupted.

'They already know, Sean.'

Now it was his turn to stare at his colleague. 'You knew they'd found out about Highwater and you didn't tell me?'

'I forgot.'

'That's not possible,' he said, examining her.

'This isn't the time to discuss it.'

Her words mirrored their exchange when they'd first arrived in Three Pines. Their little tiff over driving. Then it had been almost endearing, now it was chilling. And by the look on Sean Delorme's face, he felt it too. With one more quick glance at his partner, he turned back to the Sûreté investigators.

'Have you been there?'

'Up the hill, following the tracks?' said Beauvoir.

Delorme shifted in his chair, took a breath, and nodded.

Mary Fraser, however, sat absolutely still, composed. Frozen.

'We knew about the one in Highwater, but not the other,' she admitted.

'You went there,' said Lacoste.

'Yes. To confirm that the pieces were still there and hadn't also been made to work. But I admit, Big Babylon came as a genuine shock.'

Neither Lacoste nor Beauvoir were swallowing this whole. There was very little 'genuine' about these two.

'Why didn't you tell us about Highwater?' said Lacoste.

'That a giant gun had been built, with our knowledge, on the border with the US thirty-five years ago?' asked Mary Fraser. 'Not exactly dinner table conversation.'

'This isn't a dinner table,' Lacoste snapped. 'This is a murder investigation. Multiple murders, and you had valuable information.'

'We had nothing,' said Mary Fraser. 'How does it help find your killer to know about a long-abandoned and failed experiment?'

Jean-Guy reached into the evidence box and brought out the pen set and the bookends and placed them on the table in front of him, then, without a word, Isabelle Lacoste picked them up, manipulating them.

The CSIS agents watched with mild curiosity that became astonishment as they realized what she was doing.

After the final piece clicked into place, she put it on the table in front of Mary Fraser. It was Sean Delorme who picked it up and examined it.

'The firing mechanism?' he finally asked.

'*Oui*,' said Lacoste. 'In case you didn't know, that' – she thrust her finger toward the assembled piece – 'is a pretty good representation of a homicide investigation. All sorts of apparently unrelated and unimportant pieces come together to form something lethal. But we can't solve a case if people are keeping information from us.'

'Like a big goddamned gun on the top of a hill,' said Beauvoir. 'The baby brother of the one in the woods.'

Mary Fraser took this in but seemed unmoved, and Lacoste suspected it was because to her secrets were as valuable as information. She was not designed to give up either.

'Where did you find it?' Sean Delorme held it up.

When Lacoste didn't answer, he looked back down at the thing in his hand. 'Well, wherever it was, I'm glad you did. This could've been big trouble.'

'Big trouble,' Beauvoir repeated. 'Maybe that's why it's called Big Babylon.'

'You think this is funny?' Mary Fraser asked in exactly the same clipped tone his teacher had used when he'd hit Gaston Devereau in the nose with a baseball. All that was missing was the 'young man?'

'Do you know what the bomb that destroyed Hiroshima was called?' she asked, confirming Beauvoir's image of her.

'Little Boy.' Mary Fraser let that sink in. 'Little Boy killed hundreds of thousands. Big Babylon would do worse. Unlike you, Gerald Bull knew his history and knew his clients would too. He also knew the power of symbolism. He comes from a long and proud tradition of making a weapon even more terrifying by appearing to belittle it.'

'Proud tradition?' asked Lacoste.

'Well, a long one.'

Lacoste walked to the window. 'If it's so dangerous, why haven't you called in the army? The air force?' She scanned the skies. 'There should be helicopters overhead and troops on the ground guarding the thing.'

She turned back to the CSIS agents.

'Where is everyone?' she asked.

Sean Delorme smiled. 'Don't you think it might be better not to advertise? The bigger the weapon, the greater the need for secrecy.'

'The bigger the secret, the greater the danger,' said Lacoste. 'Don't you think?'

Armand listened to Clara and Myrna, his face opening with wonder.

'Are you sure?'

'No, not really,' Clara admitted. 'I'd have to see them again. I was going to go over there.'

'You need to tell Chief Inspector Lacoste,' said Gamache. 'She and Inspector Beauvoir are at the old train station. Whatever happens, don't tell anyone else. Does Professor Rosenblatt know?'

'No. It didn't come to me until later.'

'Good.'

Clara stood up. 'Coming with us?'

They walked together to the door of the bistro.

'No, there's someone else I want to see.'

'Want to?' asked Myrna, following his gaze.

'Have to,' admitted Armand.

They parted, Clara and Myrna walking over the bridge to the Incident Room and passing the CSIS agents just leaving. Gamache walked the few paces to the bench on the village green and took a seat beside Ruth and Rosa.

'What do you want?' Ruth asked. Rosa looked surprised.

'I want to know why you wrote those lines from the Yeats poem when you heard that Antoinette had been killed.'

The rain had stopped, and water beaded on the wood. It now soaked into his jacket and the legs of his slacks.

'I happen to know the poem and like it,' said Ruth. 'I've heard you quote it often enough. About things falling apart.'

'True. But those weren't the lines you chose.'

'Fuck, fuck, fuck,' muttered either Rosa or Ruth. It was impossible to say which had just spoken. They were beginning to meld into one creature, though Ruth was more easily ruffled.

'You know more than you're saying,' said Gamache.

'True. I know the whole poem. *Turning and turning in the widening gyre/The falcon cannot hear the falconer.* What's a gyre?'

'I have no idea,' Gamache admitted. 'I think I looked it up once.'

Ruth stared into the late-afternoon sky as the clouds broke up and the sun broke through. Sparrows and robins and crows descended, gathering on the green.

'No vultures,' she said. 'Always a good sign.'

360

He smiled. 'You needn't worry. You'll live forever.'

'I hope not.' She broke up some bread and pelted it at the head of a sparrow. 'Poor Laurent. Who kills a child?'

'Who is slouching toward Bethlehem?' Gamache asked. 'Who is the rough beast?'

When she didn't answer, he stopped her hand before she could cast the morsel of bread, and held her gently, but firmly, until she looked at him.

'Yeats called that poem "The Second Coming",' he said, letting go of her thin wrist. 'It's about hope, rebirth. But that only happens after a death, after the apocalypse, after the Whore of Babylon has arrived in Armageddon.'

'Do you know how ridiculous you sound? You don't believe that myth, do you?'

'I believe in the power of the imagery. In the symbolism.' He stared at her. 'You know about the etching, don't you? About the Whore of Babylon on the gun. That's why you specifically quoted those lines about the beast slouching toward Bethlehem, waiting to be born. They're a reference to the Whore of Babylon.'

Her thin hand fell to her lap, still clasping the bread.

Her face was pale, her eyes stared ahead. Sharp. Searching. Her head cocked slightly to the side. Listening, Armand thought, for the voice of the falconer. Telling her what to do.

'Can we speak to you?' Isabelle Lacoste asked.

Jean-Guy was behind her and Clara stood behind him. Clara had gone to the Incident Room and told them everything, at Myrna's urging. Myrna had returned to her bookstore, but the others now stood on the porch, waiting for an answer.

'Please, Madame Lepage.'

Evie Lepage stepped back and let them into her home, surprised to see Clara with the Sûreté officers.

'I don't mean to be rude—' Evie began.

But Clara knew that's exactly what Evelyn meant to be. If she had a hatchet and some privacy, she'd have used that instead of words.

'—but I'm a little busy. Perhaps you can come back later.'

'You drew the Whore of Babylon on the missile launcher,' said Clara. She brought out her device and showed the picture to Evie. 'This is your work.'

'What?'

'I know,' said Clara. 'They know. I'm sorry but I've told them. Don't make this worse.'

'The Whore of Babylon?' Evie leaned closer to the image glowing on Clara's device. 'That was on the goddamned gun in the woods? The one Laurent found? Where he was found? Where he wa ...' She stumbled to silence, wide-eyed. Wild-eyed.

Clara lowered her arm and turned off the device.

'Yes,' said Isabelle Lacoste.

Clara studied Laurent's mother. She knew faces. Knew moods. Tried to capture both in her paintings. Her works appeared to be portraits but were actually of the layers of skin underneath, each stretching over a different, deeper, emotion.

If she were to paint Evie Lepage at this moment she'd try to get the emptiness, the bewilderment. The despair. And just there, barely visible in the depths – was that dread Clara saw? Was the mask stretched too tight, was the emotion too strong? Was it breaking through?

And if Clara was to do a self-portrait? There would be anger and disgust and, beneath that, compassion. And beneath that? In the darkness?

Doubt.

'I saw the drawings in Laurent's room, of the lambs,' said Clara. 'The ones you did for him every birthday. The same hand did both. It's unmistakable.'

But seeing Evie's alarm grow, Clara felt her own doubt expand, bloat, break through the other taut layers. Until doubt and dread stared at each other across the kitchen.

'It wasn't you, was it?' said Clara. Stating what would have been obvious had she not been blinded by her own brilliance.

'That picture,' Evelyn gestured toward the now dark device in Clara's hand, 'was on the gun?'

'Yes,' said Beauvoir.

'What is it? You called it the Whore of Babylon.'

'It's a biblical reference,' said Clara. 'From the Book of Revelation. Some interpret it as the Antichrist. The devil.'

It would have sounded melodramatic had two people not already been killed, including this woman's son.

Evie gripped the Formica countertop behind her.

'Can I see the drawings again?' Clara asked.

They followed Evelyn through the empty home, up the stairs, and into Laurent's room. There, leaning against the books, was the row of lambs with the ewe and ram on the knoll watching over their child. The drawings progressed from the very first, which simply said 'My Son', through to Laurent aged nine. In each the lamb grew slightly larger, grew up. And then it ended. The lamb to the slaughter.

'You didn't draw them, did you,' said Clara, seeing it now. 'Al did.'

Evelyn nodded. 'I thought I made that clear when you came the other day.'

'You might have, but I was so convinced it was you that I

never really heard what you were saying. It didn't occur to me that Al would do these.'

'Did you know your husband helped build the missile launcher?' Beauvoir asked.

'He couldn't have,' said Evie. 'Al hates guns, hates violence. He came here to get away from all that. There's no way he'd have had anything to do with whatever is in those woods. Not Al.'

The Sûreté agents did not tell her what they knew about her husband. That he was not only capable of violence, he'd been involved in one of the great atrocities of the past century.

'Where is your husband?' Lacoste asked.

'In the field,' said Evie. 'He spends all of his time out there now.'

Through Laurent's bedroom window, past Spider-Man and Superman and Batman on the sill, they could see the large man bending over, pulling his crop from the ground.

A minute later Clara and Evie watched as the Sûreté officers approached him. He stood up and wiped his large forearm across his forehead, then dropped his arms to his sides.

Then the Sûreté agents shepherded Al Lepage to the car.

CHAPTER 33

'I knew,' Ruth admitted.

'And Monsieur Béliveau knew,' said Gamache. 'That's why he's been visiting you so early in the morning when he thought no one would see.'

'He's a good man, Armand,' said Ruth, warning in her voice. 'Too good perhaps.'

'He's certainly good at keeping secrets.'

'Look, none of us knew what they were actually doing in the woods.'

'You must have suspected.'

'That they were building the biggest goddamned missile launcher this side of the River Jordan? Even I'm not that nuts. Who thinks that?'

'What did you think?' he asked.

She exhaled heavily, but didn't speak.

Gamache got up, and walked away.

'Where're you going, shithead?'

He kept walking.

'Asshat,' she called.

He didn't turn around.

'Armand?'

But by then it was too late. She saw the screen door of the general store swinging and heard the thwack, as it passed the threshold. Thwack as it came back.

And she heard the familiar squeak of the hinges.

Squeak. Thwack.

She picked up Rosa, holding the duck to her chest. Standing up, she turned to face the door.

The door opened again, squeak, thwack, and the two men walked toward her.

'I'm sorry, Clément, I didn't mean—'

The grocer held up his hand and smiled. 'It's all right, Ruth. We should've said something sooner. It's time.'

They took their seats, Monsieur Béliveau on one side of her and Armand on the other. The three of them stared ahead, as though waiting for a bus.

'I can't remember the exact date,' Monsieur Béliveau began without Armand prompting. 'Or even the year. Can you, Ruth?'

'All I remember is that it was spring. It must've been in the early eighties. I was working on my first collection of poetry.'

'Early eighties?' asked Gamache. 'As long ago as that?'

The grocer nodded. 'I think so. During a bridge game at Ruth's home, Guillaume Couture said he'd heard that some rich Anglo was going to build a home in the woods behind Three Pines.'

'And what did you think?'

'We thought nothing,' said Ruth. 'Why would we? If someone mentioned to you that they were building a home in the forest, what would you think?'

'I guess I'd just hope it wouldn't be too disruptive,' said Armand. 'That was why Dr Couture mentioned it to you, of course. To explain any noise and strangers. And no one noticed it wasn't a woodstove and a kitchen sink being taken into the woods?'

'We weren't paying attention,' said Ruth. 'It was off over there.' She waved behind her, toward the forest. 'At most we might've heard machinery, but if someone was building a home, you would.'

It would have seemed implausible, incredible. Impossible. How could they have missed a massive missile launcher being hauled into the forest right behind the village? But Gamache remembered what Professor Rosenblatt had said. Gerald Bull had the gun made in pieces, by different factories around the world. The final result was massive, but each piece might not be. It would be taken in a bit at a time and assembled there.

'Did you ever meet this rich Anglo?' asked Armand.

'Once,' said Monsieur Béliveau. 'In the hardware store.'

'Where the bistro is now,' said Ruth. 'Used to be a hardware store.'

'The fellow introduced himself,' said Monsieur Béliveau. 'He wasn't alone. There was a man with him. His project manager. Seemed a little odd that a log cabin, even a big one, would need a project manager. But we figured it was the sort of thing a rich Anglo would do. They wanted to know if there were any artists around.' The grocer looked uncomfortable. 'I sent them to Ruth.'

'To Ruth? Why?'

'I panicked.'

'Panicked?' asked Gamache. 'Why would you panic?'

Clément Béliveau looked down at his large hands, and rubbed an imagined stain.

'There was something about them,' he said into his hands.

'Something off. They looked okay, if you didn't look too close or too long.'

He picked up an apple from the grass. With an expert twist of his hands, the apple split in two. He offered one half to Armand.

The outer flesh was white and moist. Perfect. But the core was dark, decayed.

'After a while, in my profession, you can tell when something's gone rotten,' said the elderly grocer. 'Even if it's not obvious from the outside.'

Armand looked at the apple in his hand, then cocked his arm, tossing it as far as he could.

'I just wanted to be rid of them,' said Monsieur Béliveau, throwing his own piece, and watching it bounce into the tall grass by the pond. Then he looked at Ruth. 'I've regretted sending them to you ever since.'

Ruth patted his hand. 'You're one of the good ones, Clément. Always will be.'

'What did they want?' asked Armand.

'They wanted to commission a work of art,' said Ruth. 'I explained I was a poet and told them to go away. But they wouldn't leave until I gave them the name of an artist.'

'Evelyn Lepage,' said Gamache.

'Evie?' said Ruth. 'No. She was a child at the time. It was Al Lepage.'

Gamache closed his eyes for a moment. Of course, he thought. It couldn't have been Evie.

'How did you know he was an artist?' Gamache asked. 'Isn't he a musician?'

'If you can call it that. He drew a bit too,' said Ruth. 'If you look at the sleeve of his album, you'll see some of his drawings.'

'Did Lepage know what was being built?' Armand asked.

'How could he not?' demanded Ruth. 'Do you think he did it blindfolded? Maybe he thought he was drawing a horsie but ended up with a sign of the apocalypse.'

'You quoted Yeats's "The Second Coming",' Gamache pretended she hadn't just spoken. 'How did you know that the image Gerald Bull wanted was the Whore of Babylon. Did he tell you?'

Ruth shook her head. 'The other man did.'

Gamache drew his brows together, trying to remember. Then he had it.

'The project manager.'

'*Oui*,' said Monsieur Béliveau.

'After our first conversation, the project manager returned,' said Ruth. 'He wanted me to write a few lines of poetry inspired by the Book of Revelation. He was the one who quoted Yeats.'

'*And what rough beast, its hour come round at last,*' said Gamache.

'*Slouches towards Bethlehem to be born,*' Monsieur Béliveau finished the line.

'I told him to just put the Yeats poem on Lepage's drawing,' said Ruth. 'I couldn't do better. But he said they wanted something unique. Something inspired specifically by the Whore of Babylon.'

'Were you tempted?' asked Gamache. He hadn't meant to ask, it wasn't at all relevant, but he was curious. 'It's a powerful image.'

'It's a vile image,' she said. 'It's hounded women for centuries and been an excuse for witch trials and torture and burnings. So, no. I wasn't tempted. I was revolted.'

369

'Did you still think it was for someone's private home?' he asked.

'People have different tastes. Some like pastel flowers, some prefer demonic images. I'm not one to judge.'

Even Monsieur Béliveau raised his brows at that statement.

'Clara and Peter weren't in Three Pines then, but when Gerald Bull asked about an artist, why didn't you recommend your friend Jane Neal? She lived in the village.' He gestured to the small stone cottage next to Clara's. 'She was an artist. Surely she would've appreciated the work.'

'Jane was very private about her art,' said Ruth, turning to face him. Challenging him to challenge her.

But Armand didn't. He sat waiting. For more.

'Ruth,' Monsieur Béliveau said quietly. 'We have to tell him everything.'

'I didn't want to bring Jane into it,' she said at last.

'Why not?' Armand asked. 'Why suggest Al Lepage, someone you didn't like? Why give him the job and not your closest friend?'

Ruth looked cornered, desperate, and Armand wished he could help her but he didn't know how, except to say, 'The truth, Ruth. Tell me.'

'He looked perfectly normal, of course,' she said. 'They do, don't they? But he wasn't. He was like Clément's apple.'

'Gerald Bull?'

Ruth shook her head.

'Al Lepage?'

'No.'

Gamache thought. Who else?

And then he looked from Ruth to Monsieur Béliveau.

'The project manager,' said Armand.

'*Oui*,' said Clément Béliveau. 'He was small, slight. Easy to overlook in the company of Gerald Bull. But if you looked at him, really looked at him, you could see it. Or feel it. There was something wrong with him. Inside.'

Monsieur Béliveau sighed. Heavily. The very thought of the man a weight on the grocer's chest.

'I sent them over to Ruth.' He placed his large hand on her tiny one. 'I was afraid, and I just wanted to get rid of them. Of him.' He squeezed Ruth's hand. 'I've never forgiven myself that cowardice.'

'But who was he?' asked Gamache.

'You know him,' said Ruth.

Gamache thought, his lips moving slightly as he murmured to himself, going through the possibilities. Then he finally shook his head.

'I don't know who you mean.'

'The third man in that picture,' said Ruth.

'What picture?'

'The one you showed me. With Gerald Bull and Guillaume.'

'This one?' He reached into his breast pocket and pulled out the old black-and-white photo taken at the Atomium in Brussels.

There was the grinning, almost buffoonish Guillaume Couture. The taciturn Gerald Bull.

And one other. His head down and away from the camera.

'*Would I meet your eyes, and stand,/rooted and speechless*,' said Ruth. '*While the pavement cracked to pieces/and the sky fell down.*'

Gamache looked at her.

'I wrote it after he left.' She gestured to the photograph. 'After I sent him on. I did the same thing, Clément. I threw

371

them Al Lepage, in the hopes they'd take him and leave me. I'd have done anything to get rid of him. After Gerald Bull left, the project manager returned. Alone. He knocked on the door and that's when he asked if I could write a few lines to accompany the drawing of the Whore of Babylon. I told him I couldn't. I told him I wasn't really a poet. That it was just a lie I told myself.'

Her hands were trembling now, and while Monsieur Béliveau held one, Armand took the other.

'When he left I went up to St Thomas's,' she said, looking at the small clapboard chapel. 'I prayed he'd never come calling again. I sat there and cried for shame. For what I'd done. Then I wrote those words, sitting in the pew, and didn't write again for a decade.'

Gamache looked down at the black-and-white photograph. It seemed, in just that instant, that the third man tilted his face up. And looked straight at him.

Would I meet your eyes, and stand,/rooted and speechless.

The blood ran from his face and his hands grew cold and Armand Gamache knew who it was.

While the pavement cracked to pieces/and the sky fell down.

'It's John Fleming,' he said beneath his breath.

'Yes,' said Ruth, her cold hand squeezing his. 'The rough beast.'

CHAPTER 34

~

Ten lambs were lined up down the center of the conference table in the Incident Room, facing Al and Evie
Lepage.

'You drew the etching,' said Isabelle Lacoste. 'You knew
the gun was there. What did you do, Monsieur Lepage,
when your son came home and told you what he'd found in
the forest? A giant gun with a monster on it. We've been
looking for someone, just one person, who'd believe such
a far-fetched story. And we've found him. You. Did you
take him back there? Did you kill your son to keep your
secret?'

Al gaped at them, his blue eyes wide with terror.

'You knew if the gun was found, the etching would eventually be traced back to you,' Lacoste pressed on. 'And we'd
start asking questions. We'd find out who you really are. And
what you did.'

Evelyn turned to her husband. 'Al?'

Gamache sat across from the couple and waited for the
answer.

He'd been on the bench with Ruth and Monsieur Béliveau
when the vehicles drew up to the old railway station.

He'd been trying to absorb the news that John Fleming was once in Three Pines. Was in fact Gerald Bull's project manager. In a slight daze he watched Beauvoir and Lacoste get out of the car with Al Lepage, while Clara and Evie climbed out of the pickup truck. Evie ran to her husband's side while Clara hesitated, then walked back to her home.

Gamache turned back to Ruth and Monsieur Béliveau.

'When you sent John Fleming his way, did you know who Al Lepage really was?'

He hadn't directed the question specifically to either one, but both nodded.

'You helped him across the border.' It was a statement, not a question, and once again, they nodded.

'It was 1970,' said Monsieur Béliveau. 'We were involved in the peace movement, working to get draft dodgers across. We were approached about a special case.'

Ruth was silent, her thin lips all but disappearing.

'You didn't approve?' asked Gamache.

'I was conflicted,' she said. 'I couldn't decide if I thought Frederick Lawson was also a victim of the war or a psychopath.'

'A conflict,' said Monsieur Béliveau with a small smile. 'Your own civil war.'

Armand knew if he'd said such a thing Ruth would have lashed out at him, but with Monsieur Béliveau, Clément, she accepted what he said.

'Because I wasn't sure, and he hadn't been convicted, I didn't feel I could refuse,' said Ruth. 'But it didn't mean I had to like it. Or him.'

'It helped that we didn't have television at the time. The signal didn't make it into the valley,' said Monsieur Béliveau. 'We'd read the reports of the atrocity in the newspapers and

374

seen the photographs, but it wasn't until years later that we saw the newsreels.'

'If you'd seen film of the Son My Massacre,' Armand asked, 'would you have helped Frederick Lawson find sanctuary here?'

'We'll never know, will we?' Monsieur Béliveau looked at the tree-covered mountains. 'We set him up in the boardinghouse. It's now the B and B.' He gestured toward Olivier and Gabri's place. 'And helped him get work singing at local *boîtes à chansons*.'

'He changed his name,' said Ruth. 'No one else knew who he really was and what he'd done. But we did.'

'So when it came time to throw someone to the wolf you chose him?' asked Armand.

'Is that really necessary, monsieur?' asked Monsieur Béliveau.

'It's all right, Clément. He's just speaking the truth.' She turned back to Armand. 'Al Lepage or Frederick Lawson or whatever he chose to call himself was already damned. What I hadn't counted on was that in doing it, I was too.'

'That's not true, Ruth,' said Monsieur Béliveau.

'But it is. We both know it. I sacrificed him to save myself.'

'*Who hurt you once so far beyond repair*,' said Gamache, quoting her most famous poem.

'So far beyond repair,' Ruth repeated. She looked at Gamache and almost smiled. 'I was nice once, you know. And kind. Perhaps not the most kind, or the nicest, but it was there.'

'And still is, madame,' said Armand, stroking Rosa. 'At your core.'

He got up and excused himself. Lacoste and Beauvoir

needed to hear about this. He arrived at the Incident Room just as Lacoste was placing the ten lamb drawings down the center of the conference table, facing Laurent's parents.

Armand caught her eye and she came over, followed by Beauvoir.

'I was just speaking with Ruth.'

'Yes, we saw,' said Beauvoir. 'And Monsieur Béliveau.'

'She knew about the drawing of the Whore of Babylon. She's the one who recommended Al Lepage for the job.'

He told them what he'd discovered and then, from his breast pocket, he brought out the black-and-white photograph of the three men.

Isabelle and Jean-Guy looked at the familiar picture, then at him. Waiting.

'Gerald Bull had a man with him when he was here working on Project Babylon. A man he introduced as his project manager.'

Gamache tapped the photograph. 'This man. Ruth recognized him.'

His finger landed on the third man, whose face was turned away from the camera, and down.

'*Oui?*' said Lacoste, leaning in for a better look.

Beauvoir also studied it. He'd wondered about that third man and had harbored a suspicion that it was Professor Rosenblatt. But he couldn't make the contours of the face, the forehead, the chin fit. Even allowing for thirty years of food, and drink, and worry, it was not Michael Rosenblatt.

'Who is he, *patron*?' asked Beauvoir.

Isabelle Lacoste looked up from the picture and met Gamache's eyes.

'My God, it's John Fleming,' she said, barely above a whisper.

'Please,' said Beauvoir, with a dismissive snort. But Gamache hadn't laughed. Didn't correct Lacoste.

Jean-Guy looked more closely and remembered the coverage of the trial, years earlier. John Fleming had been both completely unremarkable and completely unforgettable.

And there he was again. Now that he knew, it seemed so obvious. And yet—

'How could that be?' he asked.

'I don't know,' said Gamache, putting the photograph back in his breast pocket. 'But I do know he's the one who commissioned Al Lepage to create the Whore of Babylon.'

They looked over at the couple waiting quietly at the table.

'Why don't you sit in, *patron*, while we interview him,' said Lacoste.

Armand took a seat across from Al Lepage. He looked at the deep blue eyes, the powerful shoulders, the scored and weather-beaten face. Lepage's bushy gray beard still had a hint of the bright orange it had once been. It was loose today, not bound by a hair band. It gave him an untamed, wild appearance. His long hair was also loose and tangled so that he appeared to be some sort of missing link. Close, but not quite human.

Except for the eyes. Sharp and intelligent.

Al Lepage looked almost relieved. A beast of burden fallen to its knees, still carrying the load, but going no further. The end of the road.

And then Lacoste had asked him outright if he'd killed his son to keep his secret. He'd created the Whore of Babylon, and now it was marching to his own personal Armageddon. If discovered, it would lead straight to Al Lepage, who led to Frederick Lawson, which led to a village in Vietnam and a massacre.

For an instant Al Lepage looked terrified. But then the expression retreated behind the beard and Gamache wondered if that was its purpose. It was a big, bushy mask behind which Frederick Lawson, the mass murderer, hid.

'What? What?' Lepage asked, looking from one to the other, apparently bewildered. 'Hurt Laurent? I could never—'

'Now, we know that's not true, don't we?' said Beauvoir, glaring at the man.

Lepage's breath came in short gasps as he looked from Beauvoir to Lacoste and finally to Gamache.

'Look, I admit I did the drawing. They offered me a lot of money, how could I refuse?'

He stared as though expecting them to understand.

'But I knew nothing about a gun. I hate—'

He stopped himself and looked at them again.

'You hate guns, you were about to say?' said Beauvoir. He shoved his device across the table and Lepage's large hand instinctively stopped it from sliding off. He looked down at the glowing image.

'Is that your etching?' asked Lacoste.

Lepage nodded.

'As you see,' said Lacoste. 'It's on the gun. The great big gun, where Laurent was killed.'

'I don't understand,' said Al. 'I admit I did the drawing. They were very clear what they wanted, but they didn't say what it was for and I didn't ask.'

'And you didn't notice the huge missile launcher you were using as a canvas?' demanded Beauvoir. 'How much acid were you dropping? Look, I know you think you can get out of this, but you can't. Stop wasting our time, stop making it worse for everyone.' Beauvoir glanced over at Evelyn, who was staring at her husband, dumbfounded. 'Start at the beginning. Tell us about the gun and the etching.'

The shaggy head dropped and lifted a couple of times in what might have been assent or despair.

'It was a long time ago,' Lepage finally said. 'Two men came to the boardinghouse and asked if I could do a commission. I thought they meant write a song. I agreed. But then they explained it was a drawing, and told me how much they'd pay. They gave me some special paper. One of the men said he'd be back in a few weeks. When he returned he seemed to like it. I bought the farm with the money and never saw him again.'

'You drew it on paper?' asked Lacoste. 'Not directly onto the gun?'

'I knew nothing about a gun,' said Lepage. 'No amount of money would have made me agree to that.'

'What were the men's names?' Lacoste asked.

'It was thirty years ago,' said Lepage. 'I can't remember.'

Lacoste looked at Gamache. The photograph was sitting facedown on the conference table in front of him. He slid it over to her, and she handed it to Al Lepage.

'Anyone look familiar?'

Lepage studied it, though Gamache had the impression he was really just trying to figure out what best to say. How much to admit.

'This is one,' he pointed to Gerald Bull. 'And this is the other. The one who came to get the work and to pay me.'

He was pointing at John Fleming.

Gamache listened to the words but also to the tone. Lepage seemed to be skimming across the surface of his feelings, reporting something factual that had no emotional content at all. And yet his etching of the Whore of Babylon

379

had reeked of pain and despair. It was not simply lines on a piece of paper, or a gun. Each of those etched lines came from some horrific place and Armand could guess where.

'Didn't you question why someone would want the Whore of Babylon?' asked Lacoste.

Al Lepage fell silent but they could hear him panting, like a man pursued.

'If you met him you wouldn't wonder.'

'What's that supposed to mean?' asked Beauvoir.

'He seemed like the sort of person who'd be drawn to that image.'

'As do you,' said Beauvoir.

He turned his laptop around so the Lepages could see the screen, then he hit a key and beyond the field of lambs in the foreground, a newsreel played out.

Beauvoir, Lacoste and Gamache couldn't see the images, but they could see their effect. Evelyn Lepage put her hand to her mouth. Al Lepage closed his eyes for a moment, then forced them open. Sounds, so small they might have come from an infant, escaped his throat.

Jean-Guy had muted the reporter's commentary so all the Lepages had were the pictures, made the more powerful by the silence.

Al Lepage's framed lambs had their backs to the Sûreté officers, and Gamache read the writing on the back of each. Laurent, aged 2, Laurent, aged 3, and so on. But it was the very first one that caught his attention.

'My Son,' it said. Just that. And a heart. My Son.

Son My.

Had this man killed again? His own son this time, and Antoinette Lemaitre? To keep his secret safe? It was a hell of a secret, and a hell of a crime.

'Al?' Evie said, when the newsreels ended in a freeze frame. 'Why're they showing us this?'

'She doesn't know?' asked Beauvoir.

Al shook his head then turned to her. He took her hand and looked down at it. So familiar. So unexpected. To have found her late in life, and fallen in love. And taken her hand.

'I'm not a draft dodger, Evie,' he said quietly. 'And my name isn't Al Lepage. It's Frederick Lawson. I was a private in the army. I deserted.'

His wife looked from him to the screen, then back.

'Oh no,' she whispered. 'It's not true.' She stared at him, searching his face. Then her eyes returned to the pile of bodies on the path, the bright green fields behind them and the little lambs in front. Her hand slid out of his.

No one moved, no one spoke. There was complete and utter silence, as though they too had been paused. And then it was shattered by a single word, screamed.

'Noooooooo.'

It came out of her like a blast furnace and she began pounding his chest, no longer making words but just sounds. Howling.

Lacoste started to get up but sat back down.

Lepage did nothing to defend himself, except close his eyes. It seemed he even leaned in to the fists, welcoming the beating. The Sûreté officers watched as Evelyn Lepage's life well and truly collapsed. Armand narrowed his eyes, not wishing to watch something so private, so intimate, so painful. But needing to see it.

He watched and wondered if little Frederick Lawson had raced through the woods, as Laurent had. A stick for a gun. Playing soldier. Fighting the enemy. Sacrificing himself in deeds magnificent and heroic.

One thing Gamache knew for sure. Little Frederick Lawson had not picked up his stick, pointed it, and slaughtered a village filled with old men, and women and children. So how did one become the other? How did a nine-year-old boy acting out heroics become a twenty-year-old man committing an atrocity?

Evelyn only stopped pounding on her husband's chest when she was too exhausted to go on.

'You did that?' she whispered.

'Yes.'

He tried to take her hand again, but she batted him away, flailing her arms.

'Go away, get back,' she demanded.

'I was a different man back then,' he pleaded. 'It was war, I was young. The platoon leader said they were Viet Cong.'

'The babies?' she said, her voice barely audible.

'I had no choice. It was strategic. They were the enemy.'

His voice petered out and with it the litany, the liturgy, the story he'd told himself every day, until he believed it. Until the miracle occurred, the transubstantiation. Until Frederick Lawson became Al Lepage. Troubadour. Raconteur. Organic gardener and aging hippie. Draft dodger.

Until a lie became the truth.

But the ghosts had pursued him over the border and across the years.

There had been no escape for Frederick Lawson after all. No second chance. No rebirth. His past had shown up one day, and knocked on his door, and asked him to do an etching. Looking into those dead eyes, Frederick Lawson knew this pretty village had offered him sanctuary but not pardon.

'There was one young girl—'

Al Lepage stopped, and Gamache thought he could go no

further. Hoped he could go no further. But Lepage gathered himself, and his burden, and moved on.

'She couldn't have been more than ten years old. She knelt on the ground in front of me, her arms out. She said nothing. Not a word, not a sound. No begging, no crying. There was no fear. None. All I could see in her eyes was pity.'

Pity, thought Gamache. That was the expression Lepage had put on the face of the Whore of Babylon. The emotion he couldn't quite name. It wasn't contempt, it wasn't arrogance, or amusement. It was pity. For the hell to come.

That was the root of that etching. The rot.

But Al Lepage wasn't finished yet.

'I was alone,' he said, his voice detached, filled with wonder. 'I could've let her go.'

Jean-Guy stood up suddenly. His face was contorted with rage and he looked about to pour it all over Lepage, but instead he walked swiftly, unsteadily away, knocking over a wastepaper basket and banging into a desk before making it to the bathroom.

Lepage lifted his eyes from the screen and looked at Gamache.

'But I didn't.'

CHAPTER 35

A fter an all but silent dinner, Armand retired to his study, closing the door.

Jean-Guy and Reine-Marie sat in the living room in front of a fire that popped and danced and threw gentle heat.

They exchanged pleasantries, but Reine-Marie had been around homicide long enough to know there was a time to talk and a time to be silent.

From the study they could hear talking.

'He's on the phone,' said Jean-Guy, putting down the newspaper.

'I hope so,' said Reine-Marie and saw her companion smile. 'Is everything all right? You both looked a little pale when you came in.'

'Sometimes you hear and see things you never really want to know,' he said. 'And can never forget.'

She nodded. Jean-Guy had called Annie as soon as he'd arrived back, and Armand had hugged her and then taken a shower. Something had happened. She knew Armand would tell her about it, if not today then one day. Or maybe not. Maybe it would go into that locked and bolted room.

'*Pardon*,' said Jean-Guy a few minutes later, when they could hear no more from the study.

He knocked, and without waiting for a reply he went in.

'Chief?' he said, closing the door behind him.

Gamache sat in his large, comfortable chair by the desk, a file box open on the floor and a dossier on his lap. The bookcase behind him contained not just books but photographs of the family in all stages. One, though, had been taken down and was now in Gamache's hand.

It was a tiny sterling silver frame with a photograph of the grandchildren, Florence and Zora.

Gamache was staring at it, one hand holding the picture, the other up to his face, gripping his face. Trying to hold the wretched, wrenching feelings in. But they escaped through his eyes. Leaving them red and glistening.

And now he closed them, at first gently, and then he squeezed his eyes tight shut.

Jean-Guy sat heavily in the armchair across from him and put his own hands up to his own face, to cover his own grief.

The two men sat there for a long time, without a word or sound, except for the occasional ragged gasp for breath.

Finally Beauvoir heard the familiar sound of a tissue tugged from the box.

'Oh God,' sighed Armand.

Jean-Guy lowered his hands and instinctively drew his arm across his wet face before reaching for a tissue.

Both men wiped and blew and finally stared at each other.

Armand was the first to smile.

'Well, that feels better. We must do this again sometime.'

'Is that why you came in here, *patron*?' asked Jean-Guy,

reaching for another tissue and wondering how many tears these books had seen while the rest of the world saw a calm, determined visage.

'No,' said Armand with a small laugh. 'That was a surprise. I came in because there's something I've known I should do for a while but haven't wanted to. But after talking to Ruth, there was no way out of it.'

'What's that?'

'I have an appointment at the SHU tomorrow morning. I need to speak to John Fleming.'

Gamache tried to make it sound like any other rendezvous, but couldn't quite pull it off. The hand holding the tissue trembled slightly, until he closed it into a fist, crushing the moist tissue.

'I see,' said Beauvoir. And he did. He knew slightly more than the public about the Fleming case. He'd followed the trial and he'd heard the rumors swirling around Sûreté headquarters. And he knew, though he was never told outright, that there'd been a secret trial. A trial within a trial, and the Chief Inspector had been part of it, though in what capacity Beauvoir didn't know.

'What'cha reading?' he asked, in an intentionally hyper-cheerful voice, and nodded toward the file on Gamache's knees. 'Is it about a serial killer?'

But he could see by the grim expression on Gamache's face that he'd overstepped, in the question and in the ill-timed attempt to lighten the mood.

'It is,' said Gamache. He closed the file, resting a heavy hand on it, then he looked at Jean-Guy. 'Why did you leave when Lepage was telling us about the Son My Massacre?'

'I was overcome,' he said. 'I was afraid I was going to either be sick or attack him. That something awful was going to happen. I couldn't believe anyone could do those things. And then the girl.'

His voice trailed off and he rubbed his face again.

He wanted with all his heart to tell this man everything, and he almost did. But then stopped himself.

'What did John Fleming really do, *patron*? What don't we know that you do?'

Gamache felt the file folder under his hand, but didn't look down at it.

As soon as they'd arrived home, Armand had gone to the locked room in the far corner of the basement. In the course of a long career investigating murder, he'd come across things that could not be used, were not pertinent. Other people's secrets, their shames, even their crimes.

He'd kept them in files in his basement, under lock and key, where he could guard them, and hide them, and get at them if he needed to. And today, he needed to. The rest of the basement had bright lights, but this room had just the single bulb hanging from the ceiling. It swung a little when Armand pulled the chain, dirt and dead bugs baked onto the bulb. The light revealed boxes neatly arranged, like bricks in a wall. And bricked up, at the very back, was the box he was looking for.

He'd brushed off the dust and spiderwebs and brought it upstairs into the study. And then he'd had a long, long shower. And dinner. Only later did he return to the box sitting so innocently on the floor of the study.

Gamache had opened the lid, half expecting a shriek to escape. But of course there was only silence, except for the comforting murmur of Reine-Marie and Jean-Guy in the next room.

Closing his eyes for a moment and steeling himself, he

opened the first file, and started to read. To remember. And then the screaming started. Not from the files, but from inside his own head as the sights and sounds from the trial of John Fleming burst out from where he'd locked them away.

He saw again the images and imagined the sounds. The crying and the pleading.

Had one of Fleming's victims knelt silently, not begging for mercy? Not screaming in terror, not crying out for her mother, her father, her God? Had she instead looked at him with pity?

'I can't tell you anything you don't already know, Jean-Guy. John Fleming killed seven people over the course of seven years. One in each decade of life. A woman in her twenties, a man in his thirties, and so on. Made him very hard to catch since the murders seemed completely unrelated and were a year apart.'

Beauvoir noticed that the Chief did not mention any victim younger than twenty, though Jean-Guy knew they existed.

'Their bodies weren't found until after he was arrested,' said Gamache.

'There's more, *patron*. What is it?' whispered Beauvoir. 'Tell me.'

He could see that his father-in-law wanted to.

'It's something to do with what Fleming did to them, isn't it?'

'Seven,' said Gamache. 'There were seven of them. But I didn't see the significance at the time. No one did. But now I know.'

'What? What do you know?'

'*By the waters of Babylon, we sat down and wept*. Babylon, Jean-Guy. The Whore of Babylon.'

'*Oui?*' said Jean-Guy. But even as he said it he could see Gamache step back, close the door. Somehow Jean-Guy had missed it.

'John Fleming committed his crimes in New Brunswick,' said Gamache, his voice businesslike again. 'And was brought to Québec, where it was felt he might get a fairer trial. He was sent to the Special Handling Unit where he's been ever since.'

Jean-Guy saw Gamache's hand tighten around the tissue.

Beauvoir got up and nodded. 'I'd like to come with you tomorrow.'

Gamache also rose. 'Thank you, *mon vieux*, but I think this is better done on my own.'

'Of course,' said Jean-Guy.

Next morning Jean-Guy Beauvoir was waiting by the car with two travel mugs of café au lait from the bistro and two *chocolatines*.

'Just because we're going to Mordor doesn't mean we can't enjoy ourselves on the way,' he said, opening the passenger-side door for Armand.

Gamache stood on the path, adjusted his satchel over his shoulder, and looked at Reine-Marie.

'Did you know about this?'

'That Jean-Guy meant to go with you all along?' she asked. 'No. I'm as shocked as you.' Though it was clear she was anything but surprised.

'I was wrong, Armand.' She took his hand and examined it for a moment, playing with the simple gold wedding band. 'When you said there was a connection between Fleming and Dr Bull I dismissed it. I'm sorry. I should have trusted you.'

'But never blind trust, *ma belle*,' he said. 'You were right to question. What I said sounded delusional. You weren't to know how brilliant it actually was.'

She laughed and shook her head. 'You're right, judging by past conclusions.'

Armand looked at Beauvoir, watching them. 'I'd better go before he eats both *chocolatines*.'

'There were also a couple of croissants a few minutes ago,' she said. 'You'd better hurry.'

'Can I talk you out of this?' Gamache asked Beauvoir, as he approached the car.

'Why don't you try, while I drive.'

'All right, Frodo. But just remember, this was your idea.'

Beauvoir drove out of Three Pines, amused that he was Frodo and hoping Gamache was Gandalf and not Samwise.

'Do you think Al Lepage knew about the gun?' Beauvoir asked after a few miles.

'I don't really know. I've been wondering the same thing. I suppose it makes sense not to have a stranger at the site of the Supergun, putting an etching on it. After all the secrecy, would Gerald Bull really do that?'

'Agent Cohen did some research,' said Beauvoir. 'There is a type of paper that can be used to transfer a drawing or writing into an etching. He might be telling the truth.'

'Hmmmm' was all Gamache would say.

It was a bright morning and they were driving directly into the sun. Jean-Guy put on his dark glasses, but Gamache preferred to just lower the visor.

'I finished reading the play,' said Beauvoir, looking in the rearview mirror at the satchel sitting on the backseat.

'And?'

'When I forgot who'd written it, I thought it was amazing.

I got caught up in the story, in the characters. The rooming house, the landlady, the boarders. Their lives. And I laughed – some of it was so funny I thought I'd pee. And then I hated myself.'

'Why?'

'Because John Fleming wrote it,' said Beauvoir. 'And when I was laughing, part of me wondered if maybe he wasn't so bad. Maybe he'd changed.'

He shot a glance at Gamache and saw him nod.

'You too?' he asked.

The nodding stopped.

'No. But I know more about him.'

'Then why were you nodding?'

'Because that's what Fleming does, what he wants. He tunnels out of his cell through other people's minds. That's one of the reasons I wanted to go alone today.'

'Because you're immune, *patron*?'

'No, I'm as susceptible as you, but at least there'd only be one of us with Fleming in our heads. And for me, well, he's already there. The damage is done.'

'But it could get worse,' he said. 'And that's why I'm here.'

After a couple of hours' drive, the walls of the penitentiary could be seen rising out of the landscape in the middle of barren ground. The forest had been clear-cut. The ground was leveled and shaved. Any man who escaped would be seen and stopped before he reached civilization.

But no one had ever escaped from here. It was impossible to break out without help from the outside, and no one on the outside wanted any of these men back.

If there were zombies in this world, they lived behind those walls. Men who, in another day and age, would have been executed for their crimes. The mass murderers, the serial killers, the psychopaths, the criminally insane, all made their home here. They lived a demi-existence, waiting for death. Ironically, many of them waited a very, very long time for the grim reaper.

Beauvoir parked the car and they sat there a moment, contemplating the bleak walls, and guard towers, and the one tiny door. It looked like a hole.

'Adam Cohen worked here?' asked Beauvoir.

'*Oui*. It's where we first met.'

Jean-Guy had not been overly impressed with Agent Cohen, but he knew Chief Inspector Gamache had taken a liking to him. And now he understood why. Anyone who could work here and keep any humanity, never mind the near naïveté that Cohen displayed, deserved respect.

'He must have hidden depths,' said Jean-Guy, getting out of the car. 'He does,' said Armand. 'And I suspect every man in here does too. The question is, what are they hiding so deep down?'

'And Agent Cohen?' asked Beauvoir, as they neared the odd little door. 'What's he hiding?'

'I'm not sure yet,' said Gamache. 'I'm still trying to figure out what you're hiding.'

Beauvoir stopped and looked at his father-in-law. 'What do you mean?'

'No need to get defensive.' Gamache smiled. 'I meant some people keep their darkness inside, and some hide their light. You, *mon ami*, almost certainly have a croissant in there.'

Jean-Guy laughed and the door opened. It was such a coincidence that for a mad moment Beauvoir wondered if it was cause and effect.

And then they stepped inside the godforsaken place.

CHAPTER 36

———

A rmand Gamache stared at John Fleming. On the drive there, on the long walk down the institutional-green corridor flanked by heavily armed guards, through the miasma of eye-watering disinfectant and the bangs and clangs and banshee cries, he'd come up with his plan.

Look the man in the eye. Let him know you're not disgusted, not sickened. Let him know you feel nothing.

He's just one more item on the to-do list. Another person to be interviewed in a homicide case. Nothing more.

Nothing more.

Nothing more, Gamache had said to himself as he'd taken a seat in the interview room. Jean-Guy positioned himself by the door beside the armed guard, out of Fleming's sight but where Gamache could see him.

But now that Fleming was sitting across the table, all planning, all questions, all strategy left Gamache. Even that thought swirled and disappeared down a drain.

His mind wasn't just blank, it was empty. He lowered his gaze from Fleming's eyes to Fleming's hands. So white. One flopped over the other.

And then an image crawled out of the drain, and another, of what those pale hands had done. With an effort that actually caused him pain, Gamache looked up.

> *Would I meet your eyes, and stand,*
> *rooted and speechless,*
> *while the pavement cracked to pieces*
> *and the sky fell down.*

All he saw now was the seven-headed beast. Not an etching. Not a metaphor. But the creature John Fleming had created. Armand Gamache knew something that had eluded the court, the cops, Fleming's prosecutors. Even his own attorneys.

He knew what John Fleming had in mind when he'd committed his crimes. The Whore of Babylon, who brought not simply the end of the world, but eternal damnation.

Gamache took a ragged breath and heard a slight wheeze as the air struggled through his throat.

Across from him, John Fleming's mouth curved up. Like a blade.

Gamache held Fleming's calm gaze and conjured Reine-Marie, and their children, and grandchildren, and Henri, and their friends. The chaos of Christmases. Quiet moments by the fireplace. Dancing at Annie and Jean-Guy's wedding in Three Pines. He called up meals at Clara's, and drinks in the bistro, and times spent on the bench in the village.

Those muscular memories pushed and shoved and stuffed the others back into their own bedlam. Armand Gamache sat in the sterile room and smelled old garden roses in summer, and heard laughter on the village green. He tasted strong café au lait, and felt the fresh morning mist on his face.

'I'm here,' he said, his voice strong, 'to talk to you about Gerald Bull and Project Babylon.'

He was rewarded by a blink. A moment of uncertainty. Of caution.

John Fleming hadn't been expecting that statement.

'I know you. You were at my trial,' said Fleming. 'You just sat and watched. Do you like to watch? Was it fun for you?'

Gamache's expression didn't change, but in his peripheral vision he saw Beauvoir stir and he could tell that Fleming sensed it too. A slight reaction. Exactly what he wanted.

It was the first time Gamache had heard his voice. Fleming had not testified at the trial. Armand was surprised by how soft the voice was. There was the hint of a speech impediment. Real? Or manufactured to make him appear more human, even vulnerable?

People instinctively let down their guard when they saw a limp, an illness, a flaw in someone else. Not out of compassion but because it made them feel superior. Stronger. Those people, Gamache knew, did not always last long. It was not a useful instinct.

'What do you want to know?' Fleming asked.

'I want to know how you came to be the project manager.'

'Dr Bull was looking for someone to coordinate the day-to-day work. Not a scientist. They might be precise, but they're not good at the big picture. I am.'

'But how did Bull hear about you?' Gamache asked, recognizing that Fleming had only partially answered the question.

'Word gets around.'

'Depending on the circles you move in,' said Gamache. 'Who recommended you?'

'It could've been any number of happy clients. I worked for an agency that specializes in discretion.'

'Which agency was that?'

'I don't think you're listening closely enough. Discretion, remember?'

'Why don't you want to tell me?' Gamache asked.

'Why do you want to know? Can it possibly matter?'

'I wasn't so sure before,' said Gamache. 'But now I'm beginning to wonder.'

The two men stared at each other.

'Tell me about the Whore of Babylon.'

And now there was a reaction. A thinning of the lips, a narrowing of the eyes. And then the razor smile again.

'I wondered when someone would come asking.' Fleming regarded Gamache as though he was Fleming's guest and not the other way around.

'And what's the answer?' Gamache asked.

'Who are you?' Fleming asked.

He hadn't moved since sitting down. Not a millimeter. His hands, his head, his body remained completely still, like a mannequin. As far as Gamache could tell, he wasn't even breathing.

There was only that one blink. And the smile. And the soft, flawed voice.

'*And what rough beast, its hour come round at last,*' said Gamache conversationally, '*Slouches towards Bethlehem to be born?*'

Was there, from across the table, the slightest pulse of alarm?

Gamache leaned forward and whispered, 'That's who I am.'

'How do you know about the Whore of Babylon?' Fleming asked.

'Which one?' Gamache countered, and again Fleming blinked. And paused.

He has to think, thought Gamache. Which means I'm in his head now. It was not an altogether comforting thought.

'You obviously found the gun,' said Fleming.

'Obviously,' said Gamache. And waited.

'Where did you find it?' asked Fleming.

'Where you left it, of course. It's not exactly mobile, is it?'

'Tell me where you found it,' said Fleming.

He'd become wary. He'd sensed something in Gamache. A slight hesitation, perhaps. A change of pallor, or breathing, or heartbeat. This man was a predator, with the heightened senses that went with a lifetime of stalking. And killing.

The only way to stop a predator was to be a bigger one, Gamache knew. He hadn't survived a lifetime of catching killers by being meek or weak.

'We found Baby Babylon in Highwater,' he said casually. 'Or at least what was left of the gun. The other was in the forest. As for the Whore of Babylon, well, it was hard to miss. Then we had a little chat with Al Lepage.'

He waited while Fleming digested this information.

'I told Bull he was the weak link,' said Fleming at last. 'But Bull trusted the man.'

'Dr Bull trusted you too. Seems he did not have good instincts,' said Gamache. 'As it turned out, Dr Bull was the weak link.'

Fleming studied him. Trying, Gamache sensed, to figure out how best to fillet him. Not, perhaps, physically, but intellectually, emotionally.

Gamache didn't take his eyes off Fleming, but he was aware of Beauvoir at the door, a look of anxiety on his face. Sensing trouble.

'Yes,' said Fleming. 'Gerald Bull had a good brain, but he had a huge ego and an even bigger mouth. Too many people were finding out about Project Babylon. He was even beginning to hint that Big Babylon had been built.'

Fleming shook his head slightly. It had the disconcerting effect of looking like the movement of a cheap wooden doll.

'Baby Babylon wasn't really a secret, was it?' said Gamache. 'It wasn't meant to be. We all knew about it.'

The strategic use of 'we' caught Fleming's attention.

'That was my idea,' he said. 'Build the gun on the top of a mountain, pointing into the States. Make it a "secret".' His pallid hands did the air quotes.

'So that all eyes would be on it.' Gamache nodded in appreciation. 'Not on the other one. The real one. And they said Gerald Bull was the genius.'

It was said sarcastically, and Fleming flushed.

'It fooled you, didn't it?'

Gamache lifted his hands then dropped them to the cold metal table, so like an autopsy bench.

'You don't really know who I am, do you?' said Gamache. It was like toying with a grenade. The guard at the door clutched his assault rifle tighter and even Beauvoir backed away a little.

'No one knew about Big Babylon,' said Fleming. 'No one. They thought the Highwater gun was the only one, and when it failed they thought we'd failed.'

'You proved all the critics right,' said Gamache. 'Project Babylon wouldn't work. They laughed and stopped paying attention, and you quietly went about building the real thing.'

It was, Gamache had to admit, genius. A massive act of *legerdemain*, and the sleight of hand had worked. They were able to hide the biggest missile launcher in history because everyone was looking in the wrong direction. Until Gerald Bull's ego roared to life.

'Of course, the real genius was Guillaume Couture,' said Gamache.

'You know about him?' said Fleming, assessing and reassessing his visitor. 'Yes. We'd make a fortune, thanks to Dr Couture.'

'Until Gerald Bull threatened the whole thing.'

Gamache took the photograph out of his pocket. He hadn't planned to do this. In fact, his plan was not to do this. But he knew his only hope of getting information out of Fleming was to imply he already knew it.

He smoothed the picture on the metal surface then turned it around.

Fleming's brows rose, and again his lips curled up. In his youth this man might have been attractive, but all that was gone, eaten away not by his age but by his actions.

Gamache tapped the photo. 'This was taken at the Atomium in Brussels shortly before Bull was killed.'

'That's a guess.'

'You don't like guesses?'

'I don't like uncertainty.'

'Is that why you killed Gerald Bull? Because he could no longer be controlled?'

'I killed him because I was asked to do it.'

Ah, thought Gamache. One piece of information.

'You probably shouldn't have told me that,' said Gamache. 'Aren't you worried that with the gun discovered, you might be next? I'd be worried.'

He was taking a risk, he knew. But since he was in Fleming's head, he might as well mess around and see what happened.

He saw fear in Fleming's face and realized that this loyal agent of death was afraid of it himself. Or perhaps not so much afraid of death as the afterlife.

'Who are you?' Fleming asked yet again.

'I think you know who I am,' said Gamache.

Now he was in uncharted territory. Beyond Fleming's head, beyond even that cavern that had once housed his heart, and into the dark and withered soul of the creature.

He was familiar with Fleming's biography. A church-going, God-fearing man, he'd feared God so much he'd fled him. Into another's arms.

That was why he'd made the Whore of Babylon. As tribute.

But now Gamache's thoughts betrayed him. Once again the images of Fleming's horrific offering exploded into his head. Gamache pushed, furiously shoving the pictures out of his mind. Across from him Fleming was watching closely, and now he saw what Gamache had taken pains to hide, was desperate to hide. His humanity.

'Why are you here?' Fleming snarled.

'To thank you, but also to warn you,' said Gamache, fighting to win back the advantage.

'Really? To thank me?' said Fleming.

'For your service and your silence,' said Gamache, and saw the creature pause.

'And the warning?'

Fleming's voice had changed. The slight impediment had disappeared. The softness now sounded like quicksand. Gamache had hit on something, but he didn't know what.

His mind raced over the case. Laurent, the missile launcher, the Whore of Babylon. Highwater. Ruth and Monsieur Béliveau. Al Lepage.

What else, what else?

The murder of Gerald Bull. Fleming had admitted to that. Gamache tossed it aside as done.

Fleming was staring at him, realization dawning that Gamache was a fraud, was afraid.

Gamache's mind raced. Guillaume Couture, the real father of Project Babylon. Was there more? Gamache scrambled. What was he missing?

What warning could possibly be issued? What could a confined man have done?

And then he had it.

'*She Sat Down and Wept*,' he said, and saw Fleming's face pale. 'Why did you write it, John? Why did you send it to Guillaume Couture? What were you thinking, you little man?'

Gamache reached into his satchel and dropped the script, with a bang, onto the metal table.

Fleming unfolded one hand and caressed the title page with a finger that looked like a worm. Then a look of cunning crept into his face.

'You have no idea why I wrote this, do you?'

'If I didn't, why would I be here?'

'If you did, you wouldn't need to be here,' said Fleming. 'I thought Guillaume Couture might appreciate the play. He gave me the plans, you know. Wanted nothing more to do with Project Babylon. I thought it poetic that the only clue to the whereabouts of the plans would rest with the father who abandoned them. Have you read it?'

'The play? I have.'

'And?'

'It's beautiful.'

That surprised Fleming and he examined his visitor more closely.

'And it's dangerous,' Gamache added, placing a steady hand on the play and dragging it toward himself, out of Fleming's reach. 'You should not have written it, John, and you sure as hell should never have sent it to Dr Couture.'

'It frightens you, doesn't it?' said Fleming.

'Is that why you did it?' said Gamache. 'To try to frighten us? Was this' – he poked the script as though it was *merde* – 'meant as a warning?'

'A reminder,' said Fleming.

'Of what?'

'That I'm still here, and I know.'

'Know what?'

As soon as the words escaped his mouth Gamache wished them back. But it was too late. He'd been wandering in the dark and now he'd walked off a cliff.

His only hope had been in keeping Fleming guessing, making him believe he knew more than he did. Was one of 'them'. But with that question he'd given himself away.

The guard backed up against the door, and Beauvoir's face went white. Gamache felt himself shoved in the chest by the force of Fleming's personality. The back of the chair stopped him. Had it not, he had the overwhelming impression he'd have fallen, fallen. Straight to hell.

Armand Gamache had been in the presence of malevolence before. Wretched men and women who'd tried to exorcise their demons by placating them. Feeding them terrible crimes. But of course it only made them more monstrous.

But this was different. If Project Babylon had a flesh and blood equivalent, it was John Fleming. A weapon of mass destruction. Without thought, or conscience.

'Who are you?' Fleming demanded.

His gaze traveled over Gamache, taking in his face, his throat, his chest. His hair, his clothing, his hands. His wedding ring. 'You're not a cop. They have to identify themselves. Not a journalist. A professor writing a book on me perhaps? But no. Your interest isn't academic, is it?' His eyes bored into Gamache. 'It's personal.'

Fleming sat back, and Gamache knew that he'd lost.

But it wasn't over yet. Not for John Fleming. His fun had just begun. Fleming tilted his head to one side, coquettishly. It was grotesque.

'You got in here, so you must have some pull.' He looked around before his eyes zipped back to Gamache. Studying him, like a butterfly pinned to cardboard. 'You're older, but not old enough to be retired.'

Fleming's gaze shifted to Gamache's temple.

'Nasty scar. Recent, but not immediate. And yet, you look healthy. Hearty even. Grain-fed. Free-range.'

He was toying with him, prodding him, but Gamache wasn't responding.

'Your physical health wasn't the issue, was it?' asked Fleming, leaning forward. 'It's emotional. You couldn't take it. You're broken. Something happened and you weren't strong enough. You let down people who were depending on you. And then you ran away and hid, like a child. Probably in that village. What was its name?'

Don't remember it, Gamache prayed. *Don't remember.*

'Three Pines.' Fleming smiled. 'Nice place. Pretty place. It was a kind of rock, with time moving around it, but not through it. It wasn't really of this world. Is that where you live? Is that why you're here? Because the Whore of Babylon was disturbing your hiding place? Marring Paradise?' Fleming paused. 'I remember there was a woman who sat on her porch and said she was a poet. She's lucky so many words rhyme with fuck.'

He didn't just remember Three Pines, every detail seemed etched in his memory.

'I'm not the only prisoner in this room, am I?' Fleming asked. 'You're trapped in that village. You're a middle-aged man waiting out his days. Do you lie awake at night, wondering what's next? Are your friends growing bored with you? Do your former colleagues tolerate you, but cluck behind your back? Is your wife losing respect for you, as you grip the bars and look at her through the prison of your days? Or have you dragged her into the cell with you?'

John Fleming was looking at him. Triumphant. He'd filleted Gamache after all. Eviscerated him. The man lay gutted before Fleming. And both knew it.

Fleming throbbed, emitting malevolence on a scale Gamache had never known before.

'Mary Fraser,' Gamache said, his voice low.

He felt a slight hesitation in the force of personality across from him, and he used it to push forward.

'She's in Three Pines,' said Gamache. 'Along with Delorme.'

He thrust the words at Fleming, then followed them with his body. Ignoring the throbbing in his head, he stood up and leaned forward, hands splayed on the cold metal table, only stopping when his face was within an inch of Fleming's.

Fleming also stood and closed the tiny gap between them, so that his nose was actually touching Gamache's. His fetid breath was in Gamache's mouth in a mockery of intimacy.

'I don't care,' Fleming whispered.

But what Fleming had done was confirm he knew who they were. Up until that moment it had been a guess on Gamache's part.

'They know everything,' said Gamache.

'Now that's not true,' said Fleming, and while Gamache was too close to see the smile, he felt it. 'Or you wouldn't be here. You might have the gun, but you haven't found what really matters. What only I can find.'

'The plans,' said Gamache. 'You took them from Bull when you killed him in Brussels.'

But by Fleming's reaction, he could see that was wrong. He thought quickly, trying not to be distracted by Fleming's face touching his. He stared into those eyes, their lashes almost intertwining.

And then Gamache moved away, back across the table.

'No,' he said. 'Dr Bull didn't have them. He didn't need them. They weren't his plans, after all. They were Couture's. The plans never left Québec.'

'You're getting closer,' Fleming said in a singsong voice, a parody of a children's game of hide and seek.

Fleming sat back down.

'That's why you're here, isn't it?' he said to Gamache. 'You have the gun but not the plans. Funny, isn't it? That little village has so many hiding places, and so much to hide. I wonder if it really is Paradise, or something else? What would hell look like? Fire and brimstone, or some beautiful place, in a glade or valley? Luring you in with the promise of peace and protection, before turning into a prison. The cheerful grandmother with the lock and key.'

Fleming examined Gamache.

'I know where the plans are. You might find them without me. Or you might not. Or . . . ' Fleming paused, and smiled.

'While you're turning over every stone, someone else might find the plans to Project Babylon. And then what?'

'What do you want?' Gamache asked.

'You know what I want. And you're going to give it to me. Why else would you be here?'

'You thought I was someone else,' said Gamache. 'Someone you've been waiting for all these years. Someone who terrifies you.'

He looked at the black-and-white photo of the fathers of Project Babylon. Two dead men and one imprisoned for life. But there had been someone else in Brussels that day, Gamache realized. There had to have been.

'Who took the picture?' he asked.

Fleming leaned back and folded his arms over his chest. But something had shifted. Fleming's fingers were closed tight around the bones of his arms. The sardonic smile was forced.

Gamache had hit on something.

'You helped create Project Babylon,' Gamache pressed. 'On the orders of someone who wanted you to keep an eye on Gerald Bull. The same person who took the photograph. Who was there with you all in Brussels. But you lied to them, didn't you, John? You told them about Highwater, but not the other. You killed Bull when he got too dangerous, started talking, starting hinting there was another gun. Then you stole the plans and hid them. Believe me, John, you don't want freedom. You wouldn't live a day outside these walls. You're a polio victim and this is your iron lung.'

'You think they'd harm me?' Fleming asked. 'I'm their creation. I might've made my own Whore of Babylon, but they made me. They need me to do what they will not.'

406

'They don't need you. You've been discarded, left here to rot.'

'How much more rotten do you think I can get?' asked Fleming with a grin, and Gamache could almost smell the decay. 'If I'm the child, what must the parent be like? If I'm a branch, imagine the taproot.'

The words seemed whispered directly into Gamache's ear, on warm fetid breath.

'There's a purpose to everything under the sun. Isn't that what you believe?' Fleming said. 'I have a purpose. And so do you. Now go back to your pretty little village with all those hiding places and think about that. And then I want you to come back and let me loose so I can give you the plans for Armageddon, and then disappear. Never bother you again. You said I've been waiting for someone, and you were right. I've been waiting for you.'

Gamache got up. It was over.

CHAPTER 37

Jean-Guy wanted to say something, but couldn't find any words that would make this better. And so he just drove while Gamache stared out the window.

The Chief had once told him about the behavior of gorillas when faced with an attack. They met it head on, staring down the enemy. But every now and then they'd reach out to touch the gorilla beside them. To make sure they were not alone.

Keeping his eyes on the road, Jean-Guy reached out and touched Gamache's shoulder.

Armand turned and smiled at Jean-Guy.

'You all right?' Beauvoir asked.

'Are you? At least I knew what we were in for.'

'Did you?'

'No,' Armand admitted with a tired grin. 'I thought I did, but you can't really prepare for that. Still, we learned some things. Fleming was the one who killed Gerald Bull.'

'On someone's orders. The "agency". I don't suppose there's much doubt which agency. He must mean CSIS.'

Gamache nodded but seemed distracted. 'Maybe. Probably. He certainly knew about Mary Fraser and Sean Delorme.'

'Was one of them in Brussels?' asked Beauvoir. 'Did Fraser or Delorme take that picture and then order the murder of Dr Bull?'

'I was wondering the same thing, though there are other possibilities.'

'Professor Rosenblatt,' said Beauvoir. The elderly scientist who stood on the edge of so much of what had happened in the past, and was happening now. He glanced over at Gamache, whose eyes were narrowed, following a path, but not the road they were on.

'Is there someone else, *patron*?'

'There is one other person, Jean-Guy. Another possibility.'

Beauvoir went through all the people in the case who were of the right age to have been active in Brussels in the early 1990s.

'Monsieur Béliveau?' he asked. 'He seems to know a lot about this, and really, what do we know about him? No one but Ruth even knew his first name.'

'I wasn't thinking of him,' said Gamache. 'I was thinking of Al Lepage.'

And as soon as he said it, Beauvoir could see the logic of it. In fact, it now seemed so obvious as to be almost unmissable.

Frederick Lawson might have snuck across the border with the help of Ruth and Monsieur Béliveau, but he'd been able to stay, to make a life for himself, to become Al Lepage, get married. How did a deserter about to be tried for a war crime manage that except with the blessing of the government, or one of its agencies?

Was that the price of admission to Canada? Every now and then Al Lepage would be called upon to do some of the government's dirty work?

Lacoste had let Lepage return to his home, but assigned agents to watch him around the clock.

'*Pardon*,' said Gamache, taking his phone out of his pocket, where it must have vibrated, because Beauvoir hadn't heard anything.

Gamache looked at who was calling, then answered.

'Chief Superintendent,' he said.

'I take it you're not alone, Armand,' said Thérèse Brunel. 'I have some news.'

'*Oui?*' By the tone of her voice he could tell he probably hadn't won the lottery.

'I had a call just now from the executive producer of the CBC national news.'

Gamache took a deep breath, steeling himself.

Beauvoir glanced over. The Chief was alert, tense.

'Go on.'

'It's what you think,' she said. 'They've found out about the gun.'

'How much do they know?'

'They know about Project Babylon, about Gerald Bull, they know the gun's somewhere in Québec, which is why they called me.'

'But they don't know where it is?'

'Not yet. They're holding the story until the six o'clock national radio news tonight. By then they might know everything. And even if they don't, it'll still hit the headlines like a bomb. Every journalist will be all over the story. They'll find out everything eventually. You might have a day from the time of broadcast, or you might have hours.'

'Can you stop it?' he asked.

'You know what's involved in censoring the press, Armand. I have an urgent request in for an injunction but

410

judges are loath to give them. We have to assume the story will run.'

Gamache looked at his watch. It was already one thirty.

'They don't know about Guillaume Couture?' he asked.

'No, but you found out within a matter of hours. They'll have that soon enough. Once it airs, someone in the village will talk. It's shocking that word hasn't leaked before now.'

Three Pines was good at keeping its secrets, thought Gamache. But this one was about to escape.

'*Merci.*' He hung up. 'Stop the car, please.'

Beauvoir pulled over and Gamache got out, bending over, one hand on the car, one on his knee, as though he was about to retch.

Jean-Guy hurried around the car. 'Are you all right?'

Gamache straightened up and caught his breath. Then he walked away, along the dirt shoulder of the back road.

'What's happened?' asked Jean-Guy, pursuing him, but stopping when Armand waved at him to give him space.

Beauvoir had only heard Gamache's end of the conversation, but it was enough to get the gist.

Armand turned to Jean-Guy, his face pale and haggard. 'We have four hours before word of the gun is all over the CBC national news.'

'Shit.'

Beauvoir felt his own stomach lurch. They both knew what that meant. Within moments of the broadcast it would be all over the internet, social media, other media. NPR, CNN, BBC, Al Jazeera. News of Gerald Bull's gun would be blasted around the world.

'They don't yet know where it is,' said Gamache. 'They don't know about Three Pines. I'm not sure they know about Highwater yet. But they will. And when they do . . .'

Pandemonium, thought Jean-Guy.

Beauvoir studied his father-in-law and felt light-headed.

'My God, you can't be considering . . .'

But he could tell by the expression on Gamache's face that was exactly what he was considering.

'You'd release Fleming?' asked Beauvoir, barely able to make the words audible.

'We have to find the plans before the broadcast. The problem won't be journalists or curiosity seekers. Every arms dealer, every mercenary, every intelligence organization, every terrorist group and corrupt dictator will hear about it. These people aren't bumbling opportunists. They're smart and motivated and ruthless. And they'll be coming here. Jesus, Jean-Guy, you know what'll happen if an arms dealer finds the plans before we do.'

'If, if,' shouted Jean-Guy. 'It might not happen, but we know for sure what'll happen if Fleming's let out of that hellhole. He'll kill again. And again.'

'Don't tell me what Fleming will do. You have no idea what that man's capable of. I do.'

'Then tell me, for God's sake. What did he do? What is that man capable of?'

'He made the Whore of Babylon,' shouted Gamache.

'The etching, I know.'

'No, the real thing. Out of his victims.'

Beauvoir stepped back, away from Gamache. From the words that had come out of his mouth and the image that came with them. Of what Fleming had done. Of what had been so horrific it was kept from the public.

'Ohhhhh' escaped Beauvoir, a sigh, as though his soul had withered and was sliding out.

'The children?'

'Everyone. All seven victims,' said Gamache, and bent down again, his hands on his knees.

Beauvoir sank to his knees in the dirt. He watched Gamache trying to catch his breath. He'd had no idea of the weight this man had been carrying all this time. The images he must have seen. There were even rumors of a recording. Gamache had stood in that courtroom and absorbed it so that no other citizen had to. A few sacrificed for the many.

Gamache straightened up, stiffly, until he stood tall and resolute.

'If there was any other way, Jean-Guy . . .'

'You can't let him out. I'm begging you.' Beauvoir, still on his knees, lifted his arms toward Gamache. 'It won't even do any good. He was probably lying to you. He might not even know where the plans are.' Beauvoir got up, angry now. 'You were too close, you couldn't see it. He was playing with you, messing with you.'

'You think I don't know that?' shouted Gamache. 'You think I don't know he was probably lying, and even if he does know where the plans are, he almost certainly won't tell us? I know that.'

'Then why do it? Why even consider it?'

'What happens if we leave Fleming where he is and those plans are found by another arms dealer?'

He stared at Beauvoir, challenging him. Daring him to go where Gamache himself stood. In the whirlwind.

The two men were ten feet apart, glaring at each other.

'You think,' growled Gamache, 'I want to release Fleming? To bring him to Three Pines? It sickens me. But we might have no choice. Fleming might not tell us where the plans are. And yes, he might escape. But I don't know

413

where the plans are. You don't know where they are. God knows I've been desperate to find them.'

'And Fleming probably doesn't either. He'd say anything to get out of there.'

'But he might. He might know. He could be our only hope.'

Beauvoir stared at him, appalled. 'You're pinning hopes on that creature? What if the lives he takes next time belong to Madame Gamache, or Annie, or your granddaughters? Would you be so cavalier then?'

'Cavalier? You think that's what I am? If those plans are found, how many more wives and husbands, children and grandchildren will be killed? Tens of thousands, maybe even hundreds of thousands. No one would be safe.'

It was a grotesque equation, and Gamache looked like he was about to pass out. He was contemplating being an accessory to a slaughter, for the greater good.

Mary Fraser had been wrong about Gamache. He'd done it before, and he'd do it again. Send a few to possible death, to save the many. Those decisions had finally torn him to shreds, and he'd crawled to Three Pines to heal. But not, it would appear, to hide.

Beauvoir opened his mouth, his breathing heavy, his eyes wide.

'Annie's pregnant, Armand.'

It took a moment for the words to penetrate Gamache's defenses, to get through his turmoil. But then his shoulders dropped, his face softened.

And he understood.

'Oh my God,' he whispered.

In long, swift strides he covered the distance between them, and gathering Jean-Guy in his arms, he held the sobbing man.

'We'll find the plans,' he repeated over and over, until Jean-Guy had calmed down. 'We'll find them.'

Though he didn't know how.

Armand drove the rest of the way home, giving Jean-Guy a chance to recover and to talk about the new baby. And Annie.

'Please don't tell Madame Gamache,' said Jean-Guy. 'Annie would kill me. She wants to do it herself.'

'I won't, but you have to tell her soon because she might pry it out of me. She's very cunning.'

As they talked about this happy news, Gamache could almost forget where they'd been, and what lay ahead. After a few miles they once again lapsed into silence.

Gamache went back over his interview with Fleming, struggling to bring it into focus.

'Fleming admitted he knew Mary Fraser and Sean Delorme,' he said, and Beauvoir nodded. Jean-Guy had also been replaying the meeting with Fleming, with growing urgency, pursued by the ticking clock and the realization of just how monstrous Fleming really was.

'But he said something,' said Armand. 'Something I thought at the time I needed to remember, but then it got lost.'

'Misdirection,' said Beauvoir. 'Fleming probably knew he'd said too much and tried to hide it under a pile of crap.'

'But what was it?' asked Gamache.

They racked their brains. Al Lepage? Brussels. The agency. What was it Fleming had said?

Jean-Guy got there first. It wasn't something Fleming had said. It was something Gamache said.

'The play,' he said. 'You mentioned the play, and put it on the table, remember?'

'That's it,' said Gamache. 'He asked if I'd read it.'

'You said it was beautiful, and that surprised him, but it was something else.'

Beauvoir reached behind him to the backseat and, picking up the satchel, he took out the worn and dirty script.

'He touched it and said if you'd really understood it, you wouldn't need to be speaking with him.'

'Yes, yes,' said Gamache. 'We wouldn't need to visit Fleming because we'd have the answer.'

'The hiding place of the plans is in the goddamned play,' said Beauvoir, looking down at *She Sat Down and Wept*. 'You read it, I read it. I don't remember anything about plans or papers or anything hidden, do you?'

Gamache thought, scouring his memory. The play was set in a boardinghouse. The main character was a sad-sack fellow who kept winning the lottery. He'd lose all the money and end up back there. Then win again. And lose again. It was excruciating but also sensitively observed, insightful and very funny.

'The winning ticket wasn't hidden or lost, was it?' asked Beauvoir.

Gamache shook his head. 'No, he kept it on the chain around his neck, remember? Where the crucifix once was.'

'Shit. What else, what else? Did anyone lose a key? A glove, anything?'

Beauvoir opened the script and turned the pages at random, with growing frenzy.

'Call Isabelle,' said Gamache. 'Tell her about the CBC news at six, and get her to have every copy of that play picked up.'

'Mary Fraser and Sean Delorme have one,' Beauvoir reminded him, as the phone rang.

'Leave them alone,' said Gamache. 'If they've read Fleming's play then they've also missed the reference. Let's keep it that way.'

Beauvoir got Lacoste on the line, put her on speaker and brought her up to speed.

'I know about the CBC,' she said. 'Professor Rosenblatt was just in here. He had a call from a journalist asking about the Supergun. They've obviously done enough research to know he's the expert on Gerald Bull.'

'What did he tell them?' Beauvoir asked.

'He says he told them he's long retired and the case of Dr Bull was long ago. They asked about finding Project Babylon and he said he thought that unlikely since it probably was never built and wouldn't work anyway.'

'Did they buy it?'

'Not for a moment,' said Lacoste. 'The professor's afraid he might have even made it worse by denying what they already knew to be true.'

'I don't think it's possible to make it worse at this stage,' said Beauvoir.

'Well, the good news is, so far they don't seem to know where the gun is, and I suspect they'll zero in on Highwater to begin with. They might even stop there.'

But they all knew that wasn't going to happen. 'You'll get all the copies of the play? But leave the CSIS agents out of it.'

'I'll get Cohen on it,' she said.

'No,' Gamache interrupted. 'Not Cohen. Can you get another agent to do it?'

'I can,' she said, her voice guarded. 'Why?'

'I'd like Agent Cohen to stay in the Incident Room. Do you mind? I'll explain when we get there.'

They hung up and Beauvoir glared at the phone, not daring to look at his father-in-law. He knew why Gamache wanted Cohen to stay behind.

It was a terrible thing he was about to do.

CHAPTER 38

'That's insane.' Then, after a tense pause, Isabelle Lacoste added, 'Sir. Even if we could get Fleming out of the SHU and bring him here, it would be like releasing a plague.'

'We have' – Gamache looked at the clock on the train station wall – 'three hours and five minutes until the news breaks and there's no going back. It takes two hours to drive to the SHU. Agent Cohen will have to leave now.'

'I can tell the time, *patron*,' said Lacoste. 'What I can't tell is if you've lost your mind. I understand the equation, I really do. But I agree with Inspector Beauvoir. There's a better-than-average chance Fleming's lying. That he has absolutely no idea where the plans are. And then what? Arms dealers might still find the plans before we do, and John Fleming will certainly kill again once he escapes. Because he will escape. And you know who his first victim will be?'

They looked over at Agent Cohen, who was watching them from across the room. He dropped his eyes and pretended to wipe something off his slacks.

'It has to be done,' said Gamache.

'Fleming gets what he wanted,' said Lacoste.

'And we get what we need. Look,' said Gamache. 'You

know what will happen if someone else finds the plans to Project Babylon first. Fleming will seem like a cartoon character compared to what would happen then.'

He glanced over at Adam Cohen.

'If I could go in his place I would, but only Adam can do what we need done. Only he can get Fleming out. He worked there for eighteen months. He knows the SHU, he knows the guards and the system. It gives me no pleasure, but this task falls to him. It has to happen, Isabelle.'

Gamache tried to mask his frustration. For years, decades, he'd consulted his team, but the final decision was always his. Now, though, he needed Isabelle Lacoste to agree, and to act.

'You're talking about getting John Fleming out of the SHU?' asked Adam Cohen. He was leaning toward them. 'I'm sorry, but I overheard.'

They turned to the young man and Gamache took a step toward him.

'Do you think you can do it?'

Cohen considered, then nodded.

'I think so.'

He looked both determined and about to run away. His eyes were wide, his pupils dilated, his skin was not just pale but gray. A man about to jump off a cliff, hoping he'd sprout wings.

'I'm sorry to ask, sir, but are you sure it's such a good idea?'

'We just need to know if you think it's possible,' said Gamache reassuringly. 'No decision has been made yet.'

'But John Fleming,' said Cohen. 'He's not ... ' Cohen searched for the right way to put it. 'He's not a normal person.'

It was such an understatement it was almost funny. But the look of sheer terror on the young man's face made amusement impossible.

'Let me go with him,' said Beauvoir. 'We can't send him alone.'

'I'm sorry to interrupt again,' said Cohen, again leaning into their conversation. 'There's one flaw in the SHU security. We were trained to expect riots, breakouts, but not a break-in. So it might work. But it needs to be someone they know and trust. Someone they'd never expect would cause trouble. Me. Alone.'

His words said one thing, but his eyes were begging them to disagree. To not send him there at all, and certainly to not send him alone.

'Excuse us,' Lacoste said to Agent Cohen with exaggerated courtesy, and took the other two deeper into the Incident Room. 'We have to come to a decision.'

She looked at Beauvoir, at Gamache. She glanced over at Agent Cohen, then up to the clock.

'All right. We'll send him to the SHU. As you said, it'll take two hours for him to get there, and we have just over three until the broadcast. We don't have to decide about Fleming until later, but Agent Cohen will at least be in place.'

Gamache and Beauvoir nodded and Isabelle Lacoste walked back to Adam Cohen.

'This is not sanctioned,' she said. 'If you go, you need to be aware of what will almost certainly happen. Even if we're successful, and you get Fleming out and return him, we will all be fired and probably brought up on charges. Do you understand?'

'My uncle has a poutine stand,' he said. 'I think I can get us all jobs there.'

He spoke with such sincerity, Beauvoir didn't know if Cohen was serious. And he didn't know whether to laugh or cry. Or to tell him the real truth. That young Adam Cohen might very well lose more than his job.

Chief Inspector Lacoste wrote up a letter of authorization, printed it out on Sûreté letterhead, and handed it to Agent Cohen. Then they walked him to the car.

'If you haven't heard from me by six you need to go into the SHU, do you understand?' said Chief Inspector Lacoste. 'The moment the Gerald Bull story airs on CBC.'

'Yes, sir. Mom. Ma'am.'

'Oh God,' Beauvoir whispered.

'You'll be fine, son,' said Armand. 'Just don't give Fleming any information. Not your name, not where you're taking him. Nothing. He'll try to engage you, just ignore him.' He put out his hand. '*Shalom aleichem.*'

Adam Cohen looked surprised and pleased. He took Gamache's hand. 'And peace be upon you too, sir. How did you know?'

'I was raised by my Jewish grandmother,' said Gamache.

'*B'ezrat hashem,*' said Cohen, releasing Gamache's hand and getting into the car.

They watched him drive off.

'What did he say to you?' Beauvoir asked.

'He said, God willing,' said Gamache.

'I don't think God has much to do with anything that's happening,' said Lacoste. Then she turned to the two men. 'If the location of the plans really is hidden somewhere in that play, we need to go through it, closely and quickly.'

'I've been thinking about that,' said Gamache. 'Both Jean-Guy and I have already read it and found nothing.'

'You need new eyes,' said Lacoste. 'Do you want me to read it?'

'No, I want the village to read it,' said Gamache. 'A play's meant to be performed.'

'We're going to put on the play?' asked Beauvoir. 'Wait a minute. It can be done. Mom can do the costumes and we can use Uncle Ned's barn.'

'Calm down, Andy Hardy,' said Gamache. 'I meant a read-through. We need people to read it while we listen.'

'It's not a bad idea,' said Lacoste. 'But it'll take time. An hour and a half at least by the time you even start. By then it'll be almost six o'clock. If you're wrong—'

'If we're wrong we have Agent Cohen in place,' said Gamache.

'Well, it might all work,' said Lacoste. 'Don't these things usually turn out well?'

Gamache gave a single gruff laugh. 'Always.'

He started walking rapidly toward the village. 'I think we should do it in our home. More private. I'll round up some people we know we can trust. What is it?'

He'd noticed her hesitation and stopped.

'And who can we trust?' she asked.

'What do you mean?'

'Let me ask you this,' she said. 'If someone arrived in Three Pines two weeks ago and met you walking Henri or sitting on your porch with Madame Gamache, would they know who you were and what you'd done?'

He smiled slightly. She had a point.

Who could know that Myrna hadn't always run a used bookstore, but was once a prominent psychologist in Mon-tréal? Who knew the woman with wild food-infested hair was a great artist?

How many of the people in Three Pines were on their second or third acts? People had hidden depths, but they also had hidden pasts and hidden agendas.

Who could really be trusted?

Jean-Guy had asked about Monsieur Béliveau. It seemed unlikely he had anything to hide, but was it any more unlikely than that the quiet man walking the shepherd with the extravagant ears had once hunted murderers for a living? Or that the burly organic gardener was a war criminal?

'Someone here killed Laurent,' Lacoste reminded him. 'And Antoinette. Someone is not who they appear to be.'

'Once again, though,' said Gamache, 'we have no choice. We need help. We need their help,' he said, gesturing toward the village.

He waited, poised to act, until Chief Inspector Lacoste gave a curt nod, then he hurried across the bridge.

'I'll get the scripts,' said Beauvoir. 'You coming?'

Isabelle Lacoste was standing still. She met his eyes and shook her head.

'No, I think you and the Chief are enough.' She looked at her computer where, like Beauvoir's, the screen saver was rotating photographs of Laurent and Antoinette. 'I have work to do here. You look for the plans, I'll look for the murderer. We've gotten sidetracked by the gun. More misdirection, and I fell for it.'

'Not complete misdirection,' said Beauvoir. 'Laurent wasn't killed because he was Laurent, he was killed because he found the weapon, and Antoinette was killed because her uncle designed it. The gun is at the center of everything that's happened.'

'True, but the focus has become finding the plans, and we've taken our eyes off the murderer. He's in here

424

somewhere.' She tapped the dossier on her desk. 'Mary Fraser said we don't understand her world, and she's right. This is the world we understand. This is what I should've been doing all along. I need to go back over the basics. The interviews, the forensics. Who knows, we might end up at the same place.'

'*B'ezrat hashem,*' he said, and left while Lacoste opened the dossier and began reading.

There was more than one path to the truth.

Armand went to the bookstore first. There he found Ruth, Myrna and Clara and invited them over to his place. He was vague and they were curious. It was a perfect fit.

Next he went to the bistro, where he found Brian having a beer with Gabri. It was now just past four. Gamache hesitated a moment, then invited them both. Brian might be a suspect, but he was also their greatest asset. He knew the play inside out and backward.

'Bring Olivier,' said Armand over his shoulder, as he hurried to the bistro door.

He was about to leave when he noticed Professor Rosenblatt in a corner, gesturing to him.

'What's happening?' he asked when Gamache arrived at his table. Lowering his voice, he said, 'Is it something to do with the CBC story?'

Gamache could have kicked himself. He'd been so intent on who to invite he hadn't properly scanned the room for who not to. Rosenblatt was certainly a retired professor. Their background check bore that out. But Gamache was far from convinced he wasn't more than that. Just as Mary Fraser and Sean Delorme were almost certainly file clerks. And much more.

'Can I help?' asked the elderly professor.

'*Non, merci*. I think we have it covered.'

Rosenblatt examined him, then looked around the bistro at the people chatting over drinks.

'They have no idea what's coming their way once word of the gun gets out.'

'None of us can tell the future,' said Gamache. It was an intentionally banal response. He just wanted to get away and wasn't interested in wasting precious time on some esoteric conversation.

'Oh, I think some can, don't you?'

Something in his tone made Gamache refocus and give the scientist his attention. 'What do you mean?'

'I mean some can predict the future because they create it,' said Rosenblatt. 'Oh, not the good things. We can't make someone love us, or even like us. But we can make someone hate us. We can't guarantee we'll be hired for a job, but we can make sure we're fired.' He put down his apple cider and stared at Gamache. 'We can't be sure we'll win a war, but we can lose one.'

Gamache was very still, examining the scientist. Then he sat down.

'So many people make the mistake of thinking wars are fought with weapons,' said Rosenblatt, almost to himself. 'But they're really fought with ideas. The side with the most ideas, the best ideas, wins.'

'Then why kill the person with those ideas?' asked Gamache. 'I take it we're talking about Gerald Bull. Someone thought he was the genius and had him shot in the head.'

'You know the answer to that. To stop anyone else from getting him. Having him on our side might not guarantee we'd win a war, but giving him to an enemy just about guarantees we'd lose it.'

426

'And when it became apparent you got it wrong?' asked Gamache.

'Me?'

'A manner of speech, monsieur. I meant nothing by it.'

'Of course.'

'When it was clear the wrong person was killed?' asked Gamache. 'That Gerald Bull wasn't the ideas man at all, but just a fake front?'

'Ah, then there's a problem. A big one. A very big one. That would need to be taken care of.'

'Are you saying what I think you are?' said Gamache. It was the closest Michael Rosenblatt had come to admitting involvement in the death of Gerald Bull. And more.

'I'm saying nothing. I'm an old man, who can't even dress himself.' He looked down at his disheveled clothing.

'You are not your clothes, monsieur,' said Gamache. 'They're a costume. Perhaps even a disguise.'

'I'm glad you think so.' Rosenblatt looked amused, but then his face turned serious. 'You think I had something to do with it? I've been sitting here thinking about what would happen if those plans are found. All those lives lost. I think only very old men appreciate what a terrible thing it is to die before your time.' He leaned across the table toward Gamache. 'It is not something I could ever be part of.'

'Unless it was to save even more lives,' suggested Gamache.

'Maybe that's what old men are for. To make decisions that no young man can.' He was watching Gamache closely. 'Or should have to. I'm old enough to be your father. I wish I was. Perhaps you'd trust me then. I have no children of my own.'

'But David? Your grandson?'

When Rosenblatt didn't answer, Gamache nodded.

'Fictitious?'

'I find people are less suspicious of grandfathers,' Rosenblatt admitted. 'So I created David. But I've spoken of him so often, I can almost see him. He's skinny and dark-haired and smells of Ivory soap and bubblegum, which I give him behind his mother's back. Some days he's more real to me than people who actually exist.'

Michael Rosenblatt looked down at his hands. 'That goddamned gun in the woods is real but my grandson isn't. What a world.'

Armand glanced at the clock, ticking. 'There's something you should know. I spoke to John Fleming this morning.'

It was Rosenblatt's turn to grow very still.

'I know he worked with Gerald Bull,' said Gamache. 'I know he was here in Three Pines. I know he was in Brussels with Dr Bull and Guillaume Couture. And I know he killed Gerald Bull. But I also believe it was not his idea.'

Gamache once again brought out the old photograph of the three men, the unholy trinity.

'I showed this to you once before. There's Dr Bull, Dr Couture, and John Fleming. But someone else was there that day, wasn't there? The person who took this picture and ordered the death of Gerald Bull.'

'It wasn't me.'

'Maybe. Maybe not.'

'It doesn't matter what you think. It was long ago. It's done.'

'It's not done,' Gamache snapped, lowering instead of raising his voice, so that it came out a growl. 'What has happened here is a direct consequence of that decision that day. The war wasn't won, it went dormant. And now it's flaring up.'

428

'You must understand—' Rosenblatt began.

'I don't need justifications, I need clear answers. Who was there that day? Who took this picture? Was it you? Who's behind all this?'

'It wasn't me,' said Rosenblatt. 'I swear. If I had anything to tell you I would. The thought of those plans falling into someone else's hands sickens me.'

'John Fleming is coming here,' said Gamache, his voice struggling back to normal. He picked up the photograph and got to his feet.

'What?'

'If we don't find the plans by six, he'll be brought here. And all will be revealed. The plans, and everything else.'

'You can't,' Rosenblatt rasped. 'The man's a monster.'

'*Oui*. Man-made. And whose idea was he?'

CHAPTER 39

They sat on chairs in a semicircle in the Gamache living room. Fortunately the play didn't have a huge cast. A few boarders at the rooming house, the landlady, and the proprietor of the hardware store next door.

'You want us to read this out loud?' asked Monsieur Béliveau, holding the script as though it was written in urine.

'Actually, I like the idea,' said Gabri.

'You would,' said Clara.

'No, really. I know from my time on the stage—' He paused dramatically, daring them to make a rude comment. For some reason, the silence seemed even more insulting. '—that something can sound completely different when lifted off the page by a good actor.'

'If only we had one of those,' said Ruth.

'Well, we have nothing to lose,' said Olivier.

'That's the spirit,' said Myrna.

But Gamache and Beauvoir knew that wasn't true. They had the most precious of commodities to lose. Time. It would be five thirty by the time they finished reading Fleming's play. There would be no time for anything else.

Armand had told them in broad strokes why they were there. They divvied up roles, leaving Gamache and Beauvoir as the audience, then began the read-through.

Some, like Ruth, simply read their lines, while others, like Clara, threw themselves into their roles. Gabri, who'd allowed himself to be talked into the male lead, shot annoyed glances at Clara when it became clear she had a hidden talent.

The other revelation was Monsieur Béliveau, who started off quite stilted but, inspired by Clara's all-in performance, rose to the occasion and by the second act had everyone in stitches as the comic-relief owner of the hardware store that had everything except what the other characters really wanted. Milk. Every character went into the hardware store looking for milk.

It became a leitmotif of the play.

What was not revealed, however, was the whereabouts of the plans.

When the final word was spoken and silence descended, they looked over at Armand and Jean-Guy, who were leaning forward in their chairs hoping to catch that one vital word or phrase.

But there were no more words. They'd run out of play.

Gamache pulled out his device, which kept accurate time. It was five twenty-three. Thirty-seven minutes left.

He looked at Brian. 'Anything?'

'I'm sorry, nothing struck me.'

'Anyone?' asked Gamache.

They all shook their heads.

Gamache got up and thanked them sincerely.

'There's something you need to know,' he said. He'd debated telling them about the CBC broadcast, but decided they'd hear it themselves soon enough. 'The CBC is about to air a story on Gerald Bull's gun being found.'

They looked surprised, but not yet shocked.

'What does that mean?' Myrna asked.

'Well, they don't know where it is,' he said, and saw relief in their faces. 'But it's just a matter of time. Once they find out, then everyone will come here.'

'Everyone?' asked Myrna. 'Who's "everyone"? Journalists, of course, but who else?'

'People looking for the plans,' said Gamache. 'That's why we asked you here, and that's why we need to find them ourselves first. You've just read the play, most of you for the first time. If anything should strike you later, please let us know right away. And, of course, it's vital you tell no one about this. Jean-Guy?'

He invited Beauvoir into the study and closed the door.

Gabri left to go back to the B and B and Olivier headed over to the bistro, which would be busy at this time of day.

Brian helped Reine-Marie clear the coffee mugs while Clara and Myrna put the furniture back, and Ruth did nothing.

'May I borrow her?' Monsieur Béliveau asked with his exaggerated politeness, indicating Ruth.

Ruth got up. 'No need to ask them. I don't even know who they are.'

'We have a no-returns policy,' Clara warned him.

'And she was already broken when we found her,' said Myrna, picking up a chair.

Ruth scowled at them and Monsieur Béliveau looked perplexed, then he nodded.

'I know,' he finally said. 'I think I was there when it happened.'

It was Clara and Myrna's turn to be perplexed as the two elderly villagers left.

Gabri stood in the doorway of the small library at the very back of the B and B, staring.

What he saw was so ordinary and yet it was riveting.

Mary Fraser was reading.

That was it. Just sitting there. Looking down at her lap. Not at a book, but at a script. The script.

There was nothing even remotely remarkable about it. Except for the intensity with which she was looking at the page.

Sean Delorme sat in the wing chair, watching her, studying her as she studied the play.

And then he looked up. At Gabri. And then he got up and walked slowly, deliberately toward him.

Gabri took a step back as this previously nondescript, dull man came toward him. There was no weapon in his hand, not even a threatening expression on Delorme's face, but Gabri found his heart pounding. Sean Delorme stopped at the doorway and the two men stared at each other across the threshold.

Then Delorme slowly, wordlessly, closed the door until it clicked shut. And then there was another sound, as a bolt was drawn across.

Gabri stared at the wooden door. His last image of the small library fused into his memory. Of Delorme's dark eyes and beyond him, Mary Fraser continuing to read. As though her life depended on it.

From the study Beauvoir phoned across to Lacoste at the Incident Room.

She confirmed that Cohen was at the SHU. 'He's in his car, waiting.'

'Good' was what Beauvoir said, but good was not what he felt. 'Anything in the case files?'

'No, nothing yet,' she said, and hanging up, she went back to them. Like the play, she knew her answer was right in front of her if only she could find it.

Isabelle Lacoste had gone over and over the notes. The interviews. The evidence from both murders.

Antoinette Lemaitre had been killed either by someone she'd invited into her home, or when she'd surprised an intruder. It was someone who knew about Project Babylon, and knew Brian would be in Montréal. Someone who knew that her uncle was Guillaume Couture and that Dr Couture had been Gerald Bull's main designer. Perhaps even knew he was the real architect of Project Babylon.

Someone who thought the plans were hidden in his home. Someone who might've been looking for them for years.

The gun couldn't be sold. Not anymore. But the plans could.

Lacoste stopped herself.

Sidetracked by the goddamned plans again, she thought, and gave a heavy sigh.

But still, she'd come close, before veering off. Where had she gone astray?

All right, she told herself. Let's set aside Antoinette's murder and go back to the first one. Laurent's death.

She herself had been in the bistro when the boy had raced in with yet another ridiculous story, so clearly a product of his imagination.

Isabelle Lacoste tried to remember what he'd said and done.

Laurent had run in and come up to their table, jabbering excitedly, announcing to the room that he'd found a huge gun in the woods. With a monster on it.

When no one paid attention, Laurent had tugged at Gamache's arm to follow him.

Instead, the Chief had driven him home. In the car, Laurent had entertained him with more tales about the gun, and about winged monsters and alien invasions and whatever else his fertile imagination produced.

A day later, Laurent was dead.

Who else had he told? His parents. His father. The one person who would know it wasn't a fantasy, though Lepage claimed not to know what Dr Bull and the others were building. Was that one more lie in a life that was itself a fabrication? Did he kill his own son to shut him up, knowing that if the massive gun was found, with his etching, questions would be asked and Frederick Lawson might be revealed?

Is that what happened? Or had Laurent run into someone else in the hours after Gamache had dropped him off? Someone who knew Laurent was telling the truth. Someone who had Laurent show him the gun, and then killed him there and placed his body by the side of the road, to make it look like an accident.

She was missing something. Or misinterpreting something. There was something she wasn't seeing.

That's when Beauvoir called and reported that they'd found nothing in the play. Her heart dropped. It wasn't their only hope, but it was their best one.

She went back to the file folder and began reading again.

And then she forced herself to stop. She knew the case. Had just refreshed her mind. Now it was time to use her mind. Isabelle Lacoste closed the file, swung her chair around, and stared out the window. Forcing herself to do nothing. Except the most important thing. Think.

Gabri had called from the bistro and asked Gamache to meet him there, leaving Beauvoir alone in the study.

Jean-Guy hadn't meant to pry but, once alone, his eyes had strayed to papers on Gamache's desk. Letters. Offers. Stacks of them. The top one was from the UN to head up their policing division, with a particular focus on Haiti.

For reasons he couldn't explain, Jean-Guy's heart dropped. Haiti was close to Gamache's own heart. It was a job that demanded diplomacy, and patience, and respect. And French. It would be dangerous, but it would be fulfilling, to train the local police in that shattered nation. It was a perfect fit for the Chief.

Then Beauvoir refocused and returned to the script in a desperate, last-ditch attempt to find something in the play.

It seemed more and more likely that Fleming was lying, at least about the play. Probably about the plans too.

The words swam in front of Jean-Guy's eyes and nothing was going in. He read and reread the same passage. It was like the recurring nightmare where he had to get away, but couldn't run.

He looked at the words and willed his mind to settle down. But all he could think of was Annie and the baby and a world where a goddamned gun was in the hands of a madman. And another madman was on the loose, freed by them.

Jean-Guy forced himself to close his eyes. And from his mind he pulled the fresh memory of the play being read by Clara and Myrna, Madame Gamache and Brian and Gabri. Ruth and Olivier and Monsieur Béliveau. Their familiar voices lulled him, like his grandmother's voice reading to him at bedtime about the hockey sweater.

Slowly the scenes came alive, the characters came alive, in front of him. Beauvoir could see them. The boarders, the shopkeeper. Vivid. At once funny and heartbreaking, and surprisingly human.

John Fleming was describing a group of people who were being offered a second chance. A lifeboat. But who didn't recognize it for what it was, because it wasn't offered in the form they wanted.

They wanted a burning bush, a bolt of lightning. A lottery win.

It reminded Jean-Guy of Three Pines. Of the travelers who came upon the village unexpectedly. They sat in the bistro, having stopped just to relieve themselves and get something to eat. They drank their café au laits and ate their *pain au chocolat*, and consulted their maps. Never once looking up, and around.

And then they left, climbing out of the lifeboat and back into the ocean. And they swam away. In search of the job, the person, the big house that would save them.

But every now and then someone did look up. And around. And saw that they'd arrived. They'd made it to shore.

Jean-Guy had sat in the bistro, or on the bench, or the porch of the Gamaches' home with Annie and seen that look on new faces, on a few faces. Not many, but it was unmistakable and unforgettable when it happened. It wasn't joy, it wasn't happiness. Not yet. It was relief.

He recognized it because he himself had washed ashore. Here.

Jean-Guy opened his eyes and sat up straight.

*

Armand Gamache stared out the bistro window at the B and B. Gabri had quietly told him about seeing Delorme and Fraser in the library there, with the Fleming play.

'I've never seen anyone read like that before,' he said. 'She was so focused and he was like her watchdog. A pit bull.'

'Sean Delorme?' asked Gamache.

'I know,' said Gabri. 'That's why I thought you should know. He wasn't at all happy that I'd seen them.'

Gamache was keenly aware of the clock on the mantelpiece behind him, ticking down. And Michael Rosenblatt, in the corner. Cornered.

Someone had told the CSIS agents about the significance of the play and Gamache could guess who.

Armand looked out over the village and with a great effort cleared his mind and heard again the voices of the villagers reading the Fleming play. Armand stood very still, in the window, his hands clasped behind his back, his eyes closed.

'Jesus,' he whispered after a couple of minutes. 'Could it be?'

Mary Fraser looked up from the script, the blood rushing from her face, then rushing back.

She felt faint, light-headed.

'What is it?' asked Delorme.

'Jesus,' she mumbled. 'I'm an idiot.'

She lifted the script off her lap as though offering it to Delorme, but kept it for herself.

'Fleming was here, in this village.'

'We know that,' said Delorme.

'The play is set here,' she said, excited. 'We missed it because Three Pines has changed, not a lot, but enough so that it wasn't immediately recognizable.'

*

438

Jean-Guy was reaching for the phone when it rang. Before he could say '*Allô*,' Gamache said, 'The play is set in Three Pines.'

'I just realized it myself,' said Jean-Guy. 'The B and B was a boardinghouse when Fleming was here. He set the play there. But what does it mean? We still don't know where the plans are. Nobody lost anything in the play.'

'True, but every character was in search of something, and they all went to the same place hoping to find it. Remember?'

'Milk,' said Beauvoir. 'The hardware store.'

'Which is now the bistro.'

'I'll be right over.'

Gamache took Olivier and Gabri aside, well aware that Rosenblatt was watching, and no longer caring. It no longer mattered. There was no 'longer' left.

It was twenty to six.

'The B and B was a boardinghouse when you moved here, right?'

The two men nodded, attentive, alert, picking up on the urgency.

'And this was a hardware store?'

'*Oui*,' said Olivier.

'You obviously did major renovations,' said Gamache. 'Did you find anything in the walls, the floors?'

Please Lord, please Lord, he thought.

'All sorts of things,' said Gabri. 'We took the place down to the studs. The walls were insulated with old newspapers and mummified squirrels.'

'The papers,' said Gamache, speaking clearly, deliberately. 'Where are they?'

'We put them in the blanket box over there.' He waved at

the pine chest in front of the fireplace. They'd been using it as a coffee table and footstool for years.

'We always meant to read them,' said Gabri, following Gamache over there. 'Some are really old.'

Beauvoir arrived and joined them at the blanket box.

'They found papers when they did the renovations,' said Gamache, kneeling in front of the box. 'They're all in here.'

'Let me help.'

They looked up and into the eyes of Professor Rosenblatt.

'Please,' said the elderly scientist.

Gamache and Beauvoir exchanged a quick glance, then Gamache nodded. They emptied the contents of the heavy wooden box onto the area rug. Behind them the fire in the grate mumbled and popped as though sensing something flammable nearby.

Gabri and Olivier joined them on the floor and Professor Rosenblatt sat on the sofa as they divvied up the pile.

'Carefully,' said Gamache. 'No panic, look at everything carefully. The plans might appear to be something else. Examine a piece of paper, then set it aside, then take the next—'

But they were already racing through the great mound of papers.

The phone rang and Olivier got up to answer it.

'It's for you.' He held the receiver out to Jean-Guy.

'Take a message.'

'The message is "Fuck you",' said Olivier, returning to the hunt. 'I think you can guess who that was. She wants the two of you to share a Lysol.'

After a minute or so, Gamache looked at Beauvoir. 'I think you should go see her.'

'I was thinking the same thing,' said Beauvoir, getting up.

440

'Who?' asked Rosenblatt, setting aside a copy of the *Québec Gazette* from 1778.

'Ruth,' said Gabri.

'He's going to help her clean? Now?'

Olivier shrugged.

'Keep looking,' said Gamache, kneeling by the over-turned blanket box. He could feel the fire behind him and hear the clock above him.

CHAPTER 40

'What is it?' Beauvoir asked, taking a seat next to Ruth in her living room.

Monsieur Béliveau sat across from them on a lawn chair that looked familiar because it had once belonged to the grocer.

Ruth's home was furnished with what she described as 'found' objects. Found, that is, in other people's homes.

'I know where the plans are.'

'Where?' he asked.

She leaned forward and tapped the play, which was sitting on a plank of wood held up by a stack of books found in Myrna's bookstore.

'The play?' demanded Jean-Guy. 'We already know that.'

'Not the play, numbnuts,' she snapped. 'This.'

She thumped the cover and now his eyes widened in frustration.

'For Christ's sake, what are you saying?'

But then he saw what she'd been indicating. Not the play itself, but the title.

'*She Sat Down and Wept?*' he said. 'You think the title's the key?'

'It's a reference to Babylon, isn't it?' said Ruth. 'And what would Fleming want to immortalize? What would give him the most pleasure?'

'A moment of despair,' said Monsieur Béliveau.

'I don't understand.'

'He came asking for help and I sent him to Al Lepage,' she said. 'I'd have done anything to get him away from me.'

Beauvoir was listening, nodding. None of this was new, so why was she repeating herself? Once again, she tapped the title.

She Sat Down and Wept.

'Why did he call it that?' Ruth asked. 'We just read it. At no stage does any woman actually sit down and weep. No one does. So why call it that?'

Gamache looked at the mess on the floor of the bistro. Old newspapers and magazines were scattered everywhere. But no plans.

What was he missing? It was ten to six and they were no closer to finding the designs for Project Babylon.

He looked at the play, the goddamned play, which he'd tossed onto one of the armchairs at the bistro. Had Fleming lied? It seemed likely now.

She Sat Down and Wept. She Sat Down and Wept.

It was, he had to admit, a strange title. No one in the play, man or woman, ever sat down and cried. Or stood up and cried. No one wept at all.

And the actual biblical quote was *By the waters of Babylon, we sat down and wept.* We sat down, not she. It was a misquote. But Fleming knew the Bible, so it must've been done on purpose. With a purpose. Gamache remembered Fleming caressing the play with that one finger. But he wasn't just touching the script, he was stroking the words of the title when he'd said, 'You have no idea why I wrote this, do you? If you did, you wouldn't need to be here.'

'This' wasn't the play, it was the title.

She Sat Down and Wept.

Gamache forced himself to sit in the armchair, the play on his lap. Olivier, Gabri and Rosenblatt stared at him.

'Aren't you going to do something?' Gabri demanded. 'Have you just given up?'

'Shhh,' said Olivier. 'He is doing something. He's thinking.'

'Ahhh,' said Gabri. 'That's what it looks like.'

What did it mean? Gamache asked himself, tuning out the rest of the world.

Fleming hid the plans, then he wrote the play. A play set in a fictional Three Pines. His eyes narrowed. There was one thing every character was looking for.

Milk. In the hardware store. They came there to find it. But it wasn't there, of course. So where would you find it?

Gamache got up and walked to the door.

'My store?' asked Monsieur Béliveau. 'You think he hid the plans in my store?'

'Where else do you find milk?' asked Beauvoir, walking to the window. Looking out, he saw Gamache standing at the bistro door, also looking toward Monsieur Béliveau's general store.

But then Gamache turned away.

Jean-Guy followed the Chief's gaze. Past Monsieur Béliveau's store, past the village green, past the three tall pines, past Clara's place to Jane's home. At Jane Neal's now-empty house, Gamache's gaze paused.

Ruth's best friend. Instead of recommending Jane for the artwork, she'd tossed Al Lepage into the pit.

'Ruth,' Jean-Guy asked. 'After you spoke to Fleming, did you go over to your friend Jane's place? Did you talk to her about this?'

Gamache turned from Jane's home and looked directly across the village green, to Ruth's place.

He saw movement in the window. Jean-Guy.

Ruth had wanted to see Beauvoir, urgently, but didn't want anyone else to know why. That's why she sent the message about Lysol.

Ruth.

Who'd saved herself by betraying someone else. Ruth. Who'd been forced to face a terrible truth. She was a coward.

She'd have turned in the Jews hiding in her attic.

She'd have named names to McCarthy.

She'd have pointed out heretics to the Inquisition, to avoid the flames and save herself.

And she'd almost certainly have looked at the crosses on a distant hill and whispered 'Gethsemane' into a Roman ear.

And then she'd have sat down and wept.

'No, I didn't go to Jane's,' said Ruth. 'I was too ashamed. I needed to be by myself.'

'So you stayed here?' Jean-Guy asked. 'You drew the curtains and locked the door and stayed in your home.'

'At first.'

'And then?'

'My God,' said Monsieur Béliveau to Ruth. 'He must've seen.'

'Seen what?' Jean-Guy demanded.

*

445

Gamache's eyes moved on, swiftly now. Up the hill. Past the old schoolhouse.

And then his gaze stopped. And Armand Gamache started walking. Then running.

'The church,' said Beauvoir. 'You went to St Thomas's. That's what Fleming saw.'

He ran out of Ruth's home. Gamache was already at the bottom of the wide wooden stairs. He took them two at a time. Beauvoir got there just as Gamache yanked open the large door to the small church.

'Where do you find milk?' Gamache asked, turning around only briefly to speak to Beauvoir.

'A church,' said Jean-Guy. 'The milk in the play isn't literal.'

'It's a metaphor. For kindness and healing.'

Gamache was scanning the rows of wooden pews, the simple altar, the unadorned walls. More a chapel than a church.

'And forgiveness,' said Beauvoir. 'You don't find it in a hardware store, but you might find it here. Ruth came to St Thomas's after betraying Al Lepage. To pray for forgiveness. Looking for milk.'

'John Fleming was a churchgoing man. Enjoying his relationship with a God he mocked and taunted,' said Gamache. 'He either followed her or had come here himself, for a moment of gloating, knowing what he'd done to her.'

They heard movement behind them as Ruth and Monsieur Béliveau arrived.

'Where did you sit?' Gamache asked her.

'Over there,' she pointed. 'By the boys.'

'The boys', the soldiers of the Great War, who lived

forever in the stained-glass window. They marched through mud and chaos. This was no civilian monument to the glories of war. They were young and they were far from home and they were afraid.

But one young man had turned so that he was looking directly at the congregation. And on his face, alongside the terror, was something else.

Forgiveness.

Beneath the window were written the names of the dead from Three Pines. The boys who would never return to the old railway station, to the parents who waited.

And under their names the words 'They Were Our Sons.'

Ruth had sat in the light pouring through their bodies. And wept.

And when she left? Someone came out of the shadows.

Gamache dropped to his knees and pushed the pew to one side. Beauvoir joined him and together they started prying up the wide wooden floorboards.

And there, in a long metal tube, they found what they were looking for. The plans for Armageddon hidden in the chapel of St Thomas. The doubter.

Gamache looked at his watch. It was six o'clock.

CHAPTER 41

—

'Good evening, I'm Susan Bonner and this is the *World at Six*.'

Adam Cohen could barely hear the words for the pounding in his ears.

'Our top story tonight, an astonishing find in Québec's Eastern Townships.'

He checked his device. All electronics were blocked inside the penitentiary, but there was a code the guards used and Cohen had programmed it in. His device showed five bars. And no messages.

Closing his eyes for just a moment, Adam Cohen gathered himself and then got out of the car and walked, resolutely, toward the small door in the thick wall.

'Our top story tonight, an astonishing find in Québec's Eastern Townships.'

'*Merde,*' said Isabelle Lacoste. The broadcast streamed over her laptop in the Incident Room.

It was six o'clock, and it was worse than they thought. The CBC did not yet know the exact location of Gerald Bull's Supergun, but they'd narrowed it down to this region.

The story unfolded. One journalist had a report on Gerald Bull's unlikely life and mysterious death. Another told the story of Project Babylon, and Saddam Hussein, and the coming together of two madmen.

Three, Lacoste knew. Three madmen.

'I heard you coming,' said Fleming in his soft, flawed voice. He studied the young man in front of him. 'You used to be a guard here, didn't you?'

But Adam Cohen heeded Gamache's warning, not to tell Fleming anything. Not to engage the man.

'Does he need a change of clothes?' one of the five guards who'd accompanied Cohen asked.

'No,' said Cohen. 'We won't be gone for long. He'll be back by midnight.'

'Before I turn into a pumpkin?' asked Fleming as they put the cuffs and restraints on him. 'Or something.'

'You sure you want to do this?' asked another guard. The one who'd been Cohen's friend when he'd worked at the SHU. The one Adam Cohen had gone to with the authorization. Because he knew this man would trust him.

And he had. He'd accepted without question the letter from the Sûreté authorizing Cohen to take Fleming.

Fleming was watching this exchange, his reptile eyes sliding from one man to the other, sensing, perhaps, a betrayal in progress.

Jean-Guy skidded to a stop. He'd turned the corner and was sprinting across the bridge to the Incident Room to tell Lacoste to call off Cohen.

'Where're you going?' he called after Gamache, who'd missed the turn and was running, plans in hand, toward the bistro.

'We have to make sure these are the plans.' Gamache held them up but didn't stop running.

'They say Project Babylon, *patron*. What else could they be?'

'Highwater, that's what. More misdirection.'

Beauvoir looked at the old railway station behind him, then at Gamache in front of him.

'Shit,' said Jean-Guy, and raced to catch up with Gamache.

In the bistro, Armand hurried over to Professor Rosenblatt, who'd moved to the sofa by the fire.

'You found them?' the elderly scientist said, standing up.

'We hope so.'

Gamache opened the tube and tipped the scroll out. He sat down and unrolled it onto the blanket box. Rosenblatt joined him, bending over the paper.

'Is it them?' asked Beauvoir.

Rosenblatt didn't answer. He made humming sounds, his finger tracing the lines of the schematic.

Come on, come on, thought Beauvoir. Behind them, the clock on the mantel said six minutes past six. Somewhere in the background he could hear the Radio Canada news. The French service also had the story of Gerald Bull and Project Babylon.

Olivier and Gabri must be in the kitchen, Beauvoir thought. Listening. Along with the rest of the world.

'Are these the plans?' he demanded.

Adam Cohen walked beside his friend down the long corridor. He felt sick and wondered if it was the flu, or the overpowering stink of disinfectant, or the memories conjured by that smell. Of eighteen long months in this hellhole, guarding these psychopaths.

Was it the thought of what he was about to do that was

450

turning his stomach? Or was it more simple than all that? Less heroic. Was it just garden-variety fear, rooted and blossoming into terror?

Behind Cohen, with two heavily armed guards in front and two guards beside him, John Fleming was shuffling, his chains clinking. And mixed with that sound was humming. An old hymn.

By the waters of Babylon . . .

Agent Cohen walked on, his eyes riveted on the bright red exit sign. His hand in his pocket, clutching the device. Willing it to leap to life with a message.

Professor Rosenblatt studied one page, then the next, and the next. Looking at the schematics, pausing now and then to consider, then moving on.

'I see how they solved the trajectory problem, just here,' he said, pointing at a diagram.

'Are they genuine?' demanded Gamache, his own patience worn thin and finally worn through.

Rosenblatt straightened up and nodded. 'I believe so.'

'I'm sorry to interrupt,' said a woman's voice, and they turned to see Mary Fraser and Sean Delorme at the door. 'We saw you come over from the church. Is that what I think it is?'

Gamache rolled the plans back up.

'Yes.'

Mary Fraser looked genuinely relieved. Then she held out her hand.

For an instant Gamache thought it was a peace offering. Shaking hands to signal a truce. Perhaps even congratulations for doing what she could not.

Then he saw her face and realized the hand wasn't offering, it was demanding.

Gamache handed the scroll to Beauvoir, then walked wordlessly past Mary Fraser to the telephone on the bar. He glanced at his watch.

Twenty minutes past six.

He was halfway through dialing Lacoste at the Incident Room when he heard a tiny, familiar click.

He froze, then slowly turned and saw Sean Delorme holding a gun.

In his peripheral vision he saw Jean-Guy with his hands up in hasty surrender. He'd taken a few steps away from Gamache.

'It's best that you hang up the phone.'

Gamache did and turned to Mary Fraser. 'Not CSIS?'

'You really don't understand our world, do you? And this is not the time for explanations.'

She still looked like Mary Poppins, right down to the oversized handbag and the spoonful-of-sugar expression.

'You took that picture,' said Gamache. 'Of Gerald Bull and Dr Couture. And John Fleming. You were the fourth person in Brussels.'

He'd stepped to within feet of them but she didn't seem concerned. She knew he was unarmed. She had nothing to fear from Armand Gamache.

She nodded. 'You've worked a lot out, Monsieur Gamache. I was young, of course. And now I'm making up for those mistakes. The plans, please.'

Beauvoir lowered the hand holding the scroll.

'No, you can't,' said Professor Rosenblatt, stepping forward. Delorme and Fraser glanced over to him, and in the moment it took to turn back, Beauvoir had swung his arm behind him and was holding the plans for Project Babylon over the fire.

Delorme raised the gun and took aim, but Gamache stepped between him and his son-in-law, spreading his arms out. '*Non.*'

The act was so unexpected, the sequence of events so rapid, that Delorme hesitated.

'You'll have to kill us all,' said Gamache. 'Are you prepared to do that?'

'If you're prepared to die, we're prepared to do it,' said Mary Fraser. 'The few for the many, remember?'

'You have a warped idea of the greater good,' snapped Beauvoir. 'For your information, this is what it looks like.'

He dropped the plans in the fireplace just as Professor Rosenblatt stepped in front of Gamache. Behind him, Armand heard a whoooosh as the design for Project Babylon went up in flames.

'Shit,' shouted Delorme, and shoving the professor aside, he scrambled toward the fireplace, but Gamache and Beauvoir grabbed him, knocking the gun from his hand.

It was over in a matter of moments, the time it took for the plans to be fully consumed by the fire. Beauvoir held on to Delorme while Gamache's eyes swept the room.

Mary Fraser had taken a few steps forward but stopped when she saw it was too late. Now her eyes were on Professor Rosenblatt, who'd stooped and picked up the gun.

Gamache turned to him too, and there was a pause. As long as a breath, it seemed to last forever, as the elderly scientist held the weapon and looked at them. And they looked at him.

And then he handed the gun to Gamache.

'Well, it's over,' said Gabri, walking into the bistro from the kitchen. 'Almost the whole newscast on the goddamned gun.'

He stopped and Olivier, directly behind him, bumped into him and was about to say something when he saw what was happening.

Mary Fraser looked at them, then she turned to Gamache. Her face was pale and she trembled with rage. 'You have no idea what you've just done.'

She looked from him to Beauvoir and finally to the elderly scientist.

'Gabri's right,' said Beauvoir. 'It's over.'

He released Delorme, shoving him toward Mary Fraser.

'You're a fool,' said Mary Fraser. 'It's not over. It's barely begun.'

'Aren't you going to stop them?' asked Rosenblatt as the CSIS agents made for the door.

'Let them go,' said Gamache, walking swiftly to the bar and the telephone. 'There's something more important right now.'

He dialed Lacoste.

John Fleming felt the full sun on his face for the first time in decades, without the shadow of bars and barbed wire and guard towers.

It was getting late, later than the young agent knew, thought Fleming as he followed him to the unmarked car.

Fleming had known this day would come. He knew he'd be free again, one day. He'd felt it in his bones. He'd waited patiently for it. Planned for it. And now he was about to execute that plan.

He watched the young man's back and heard the tall grasses sway in the meadow and smelled the distant pine forest in the cool evening air. His senses, dormant for years, were sharper, more powerful than ever.

He could even smell the musky fear soaked into Adam

Cohen's uniform. Fleming drank all this in as he slouched toward the car.

Fraser and Delorme were barely out the door when Gamache heard Lacoste pick up the phone. Without waiting for hello, he spoke.

'We found the plans. Call Cohen. Stop him.'

In the Incident Room, Lacoste hung up and hit the speed dial. And listened to the first ring. The second.

'Wait,' said Cohen when they reached the car and the guard was about to transfer the prisoner into the backseat.

He brought out his device.

Still nothing.

Cohen replaced it in his pocket and nodded to his friend.

Lacoste tried again, this time punching in the numbers herself, carefully.

Cohen's phone rang. And rang.

After the fifth ring, she hung up. It hadn't even switched over to voice mail.

Then she tried texting. It bounced back.

'Well?' asked Gamache, as he, Beauvoir and shortly after them an out-of-breath Professor Rosenblatt arrived in the Incident Room.

'Nothing.'

'What do you mean, nothing?' Beauvoir demanded.

'He's not answering,' she said. 'Not to the phone and the text bounced back.'

'What could that mean?' Beauvoir asked, but Gamache did not. He knew what it could mean.

*

John Fleming was locked into the backseat of the secure vehicle, handcuffed to the metal plate, restraints around his arms and legs.

The guard tested them, tugging on them to make sure they were secure.

'He's all yours,' said Cohen's friend, handing him the keys. 'You'll have to sign for him.'

He gave Cohen his own device and indicated where he needed to sign.

Cohen did. 'That's new.'

'I guess we got them after you left. Dedicated devices and network. Can't be hacked.'

In the backseat Fleming smiled. You can guard against anything, except, of course, a betrayal.

'*Merci*,' said Cohen, shaking the guard's hand. 'I'll be back in a few hours.'

'No rush.'

'Something's blocking the transmission,' said Professor Rosenblatt.

'What does that mean?' asked Gamache.

'It means your young agent might not even realize he's not getting messages. All the bars would light up, everything would look normal, and is, but the messages wouldn't be registering.'

'How do we get around it?' Lacoste asked.

'You can't. It's not a software issue,' said Rosenblatt. 'It's the hardware. He'd have to have one of their devices.'

'Call the SHU,' said Gamache. 'Get him back.'

Cohen put the car in gear, but kept his foot on the brake.

His device was sitting in the cupholder.

'Let's go,' said Fleming. 'What're you waiting for?'

Picking up his device, Cohen decided to call Chief Inspector Lacoste, to confirm. He punched her contact number and saw *Dialing* on the screen.

And then the message *Unable to Connect.*

Of course, he thought. She's in Three Pines. There's no cell phone service.

'Come on,' said Fleming. 'You're wasting time. Your boss won't like that.'

Cohen put his phone down and the car rolled forward. And stopped.

'Now what?'

Cohen picked up his device and called the landline in the Incident Room.

Dialing. Dialing.

Unable to Connect.

That was strange.

'Time's a-wasting,' said Fleming. 'Every moment counts. You know that.'

But his soft, flawed voice held an edge of anxiety.

Agent Cohen looked in the rearview mirror at the glowing eyes and eager, hungry face. Then he looked down at his device. All five bars were lit up. The network was connected. And yet there were no messages. None at all. From anyone, in over forty-five minutes.

And then he remembered his friend's new device.

With hands that trembled so badly he almost dropped the phone, he punched into the utilities mode, took out the penitentiary code, put in his own, and the device started lighting up.

It vibrated, the red light flashed. And it started ringing.

In the backseat, John Fleming saw this and started pulling, yanking, on the chains binding him to the vehicle.

*

The operator put Lacoste through to the guard room. The phone rang, and was picked up, just as her line indicated an incoming.

She hung up and clicked over and for a moment all she heard, loud enough so that Gamache, Beauvoir and even Professor Rosenblatt, sitting at the next desk, heard . . .

A shriek.

Gamache's face went white and his eyes widened, as the ungodly noise filled the Incident Room.

'Chief?'

They heard the young voice, straining to be heard over the scream.

'Is that you?' Cohen yelled.

'Where are you?' Lacoste shouted.

'I can't hear you. I have Fleming.'

'Take him back,' yelled Lacoste. 'We have the plans. Take him back.'

All they heard now was the shriek. And then it descended into a growl.

Some rough beast.

'Adam?' Gamache leaned into the phone, shouting, 'Can you hear me?'

And then . . .

'I hear you, Monsieur Gamache,' shouted Adam Cohen. 'He's going back.'

CHAPTER 42

—

'What'll happen to the Supergun?' Reine-Marie asked. 'Now that the plans are gone.'

They were gathered in the bistro, the Gamaches, Lacoste, Jean-Guy, Clara, Myrna, Brian, Ruth and Monsieur Béliveau. Professor Rosenblatt was sitting in a comfortable armchair, nursing a large cognac.

Olivier had locked the door, apologizing to his other patrons, '*Désolé*, but this is a private gathering.'

The sun had long ago set, the night had drawn in. They sat around the fireplace, their faces lit by the glow.

'It'll be taken apart, and taken away,' said Chief Inspector Lacoste.

'To be reassembled somewhere else?' Monsieur Béliveau asked.

'Maybe,' said Gamache. 'But with the plans gone, well, they'll have quite a time of it. And unfortunately the firing mechanism seems to be missing again.'

Beauvoir and Lacoste looked at him, then looked away.

'The firing mechanism's missing?' asked Brian. 'Where'd it go?'

'I have no idea,' said Armand with a smile.

'Mary Fraser and Sean Delorme,' said Myrna. 'They aren't CSIS?'

'I don't know who they are,' said Lacoste.

'Well, I'm sure they won't get far,' said Clara.

'What do you mean?' asked Lacoste.

'Well, you're going after them, aren't you?'

'For what?'

Clara looked dumbfounded. 'Well, for threatening to kill the professor and Armand and Jean-Guy, for starters.'

'Delorme pulled a gun on us, yes,' said Armand. 'But stood down. No one was hurt. Beyond that they did nothing wrong.'

'Isn't that enough?' asked Gabri.

'We have to choose our battles,' said Beauvoir. 'And if there's a trial, we'd have to explain about Bull and the plans—'

'And why you burned them,' said Gamache. He knew why Beauvoir had dropped them in the fire. It was a father's instinct. Jean-Guy would rather die than have his child born into a world that contained Gerald Bull's monstrosity.

'It's a dangerous game you're playing, letting them go,' said Professor Rosenblatt.

'It's a dangerous world,' said Armand. 'Even nine-year-old boys know that.'

'But, but—' Clara sputtered.

'But they killed Antoinette,' said Brian. 'And Laurent. They must have. They all but admitted it by threatening to kill you too, for those goddamned plans.'

He waved toward the fireplace, where the plans were no longer even ash. Project Babylon had disappeared into the atmosphere.

'But how did Mary Fraser and Delorme know Laurent

had found the gun?' Gabri asked. 'They weren't here. Someone must've told them.'

'That's true,' said Brian. 'They were in Ottawa. Someone here must've called and told them about Laurent. That must be why it was a day between when Laurent found the gun and when he was killed. They had to drive down and find the boy.'

'Yes, that was our thinking,' said Lacoste.

'Was?' asked Reine-Marie.

'The murders got all complicated by the gun itself,' said Lacoste. 'And when Antoinette was killed and we found out about her uncle's connection to Gerald Bull and Project Babylon, the case took on a whole other aspect. But I was trained that, at its heart, murder is always human and often simple.'

She looked at Gamache, who nodded acknowledgment.

'While you were reading the play this afternoon, I was going back over the case. It started here, as you said, when Laurent came running in.'

She pointed to the door, and they saw again the boy, covered in dirt and pieces of bark and lichen. He was shouting about his find, opening his skinny arms wide, straining to capture the enormity of his find.

A huge gun. In the woods. With a monster on it.

Had it been any other child, had it been an adult, they might have listened.

But it was Laurent Lepage. A boy who slew dragons and rode Pegasus, and fought back invading armies to protect the village.

And did it again the next day. A new day, a new adventure, a new story of great danger and ever greater heroics.

It had been funny, when he was six. By seven it was

461

tiresome. By eight it was annoying. By nine it was too much. But it was in his nature, as his father said, and Laurent would not be stopped.

'No one believed him,' said Lacoste. 'Or so it seemed. But there was one person here that afternoon who did believe him. Who knew it could be true. He followed him the next day, knowing Laurent would probably return to the gun, which he did. Partly to see the thing again, but also because in his excitement Laurent had left one of his father's cassette tapes behind. This person killed Laurent and took his body to the side of the road, making it look like an accident.'

Once again, she looked over at Gamache.

'We didn't believe the boy,' she said. 'We thought his death was an accident. We were wrong.'

'I didn't believe him either. His death didn't seem like an accident, but finally it was something human and simple that confirmed it. Something you two asked about.' He looked at Gabri and Olivier, listening intently.

'His stick,' said Olivier.

'*Oui*. Whoever killed the boy didn't know him well. Didn't realize he carried that stick with him everywhere. It would be by his body.'

Even more than 'death', even more than 'murder', the word 'body' shook Armand. He paused to regain his composure.

'But the stick wasn't with him,' said Reine-Marie, jumping in to help her husband.

'So who killed Antoinette?' asked Brian. 'Was it the same person?'

'Well, that brings us to Project Babylon,' said Lacoste.

'Whoever killed Antoinette obviously knew that her uncle was Guillaume Couture,' said Jean-Guy Beauvoir, taking up the story. 'And knew he worked with Gerald Bull.

He might not have known Dr Couture was the architect of Project Babylon, but probably suspected. It had long been rumored that Gerald Bull was more salesman than scientist. When no plans were found in his Brussels apartment or anywhere associated with Dr Bull, most intelligence organizations and arms dealers gave up. They figured Project Babylon was a bust and its creator was both delusional and dead. But there were some people who suspected that Gerald Bull was telling the truth. Maybe even more than suspected. Maybe they knew because they were in the area when it was being built. And so when Laurent found the gun, this person believed him. And knew if the plans for Project Babylon were anywhere, they'd be in Guillaume Couture's old home.'

As Beauvoir spoke, first Myrna, then Reine-Marie and finally the rest began to glance over to the only one who fit the description. Who was in Three Pines when the massive weapon was being constructed. And who was in the bistro when, thirty years later, Laurent found it.

Monsieur Béliveau.

The grocer sat perfectly contained, apparently oblivious to the looks, to the facts that were beginning to pile up around him.

'The other possibility is that it was someone from the outside,' Armand Gamache continued. 'Someone who didn't necessarily know Gerald Bull but knew about Project Babylon. It was, after all, a kind of open secret, with more and more information seeping out after Bull's death. Project Babylon and its murdered creator became a curiosity, a sort of cautionary tale. But for some, as Professor Rosenblatt said, it was more than that. It became an obsession. Suppose Gerald Bull was finally telling the truth? The plans would be worth hundreds of millions of dollars. And finally, after years of patiently looking, of keeping their ears open for any nugget of information, they heard something significant. A little boy had found a great big gun. In the woods. Not far from Guillaume Couture's home.'

'Are you suggesting someone had been looking for Project Babylon for thirty years?' asked Clara.

Isabelle Lacoste leaned forward, and everyone in the circle did too. Listening intently, drawn into the story.

'What would people do for power? For wealth?' she asked. 'People spent their lives panning for gold, believing they'd find the mother lode. Some people spend all their spare time tinkering in the basement, trying to perfect an invention. Some sit day and night in front of one-armed bandits, thinking any moment they'll hit the jackpot. People spend their lives writing a book, or looking to cure cancer.'

She looked over at Gamache and Beauvoir.

'We have colleagues who've spent all their spare time trying to crack a decades-old case. Rational people do become obsessed. And Project Babylon has every element necessary to grab and hold someone. Power and wealth beyond imagining. Is that worth years of work? Decades? Maybe not to you, or me. But to some, yes. The payoff is life-changing.'

'And all you need to do is be willing to take a few lives along the way,' said Beauvoir.

Eyes that had been glancing over to Monsieur Béliveau now shifted. To the one person in the room who had admitted to spending years researching Gerald Bull. Had even known the man. And known Guillaume Couture. Probably realized Couture was the architect of Project Babylon, and might even have known Antoinette was his niece.

And who lived nearby.

Michael Rosenblatt looked at them, smart enough to recognize what those glances meant. Smart enough to recognize that the facts were building a wall around him.

'But he stepped in front of Armand,' said Reine-Marie, taking her husband's hand. 'To protect him. He would never have done that if he'd killed Laurent and Antoinette.'

'*Merci, madame,*' said the elderly professor.

But while he said nothing, Armand wondered if that was true. He was glad Delorme hadn't fired, but he should have. As soon as those plans hit the flames, Sean Delorme should have shot.

But hadn't.

'So who killed Laurent and Antoinette?' Reine-Marie asked. 'Do you know?'

'I'm waiting for more information,' said Lacoste. 'We have our suspicions.'

'And so do I,' said Ruth. 'I suspect you still have no idea.'

'We'll find out who did it,' Lacoste assured Brian. 'Believe me. It's just a matter of time.'

Brian got to his feet, weary and disheartened. 'I think it was the CSIS agents, and you let them go. I'm going back to the B and B. I need time alone.'

Professor Rosenblatt got up. 'I'll walk with you, if you don't mind. If I'm allowed.'

Lacoste nodded.

'I did not kill Antoinette Lemaitre,' said Professor Rosenblatt, looking at them all, pausing at each face. 'And I did not kill that child.'

Armand walked Brian and Professor Rosenblatt to the door.

'You're coming with us?' asked Brian.

'*Non*,' said Gamache. 'We'll be here for a couple hours yet, waiting for Agent Cohen.'

Brian turned back into the bistro, and for the briefest moment his face held an expression Jean-Guy recognized. Another exhausted man washed up on shore.

And then Brian left, walking ahead of Rosenblatt, who remained on the *terrasse* talking to Armand. Through the window, the villagers could see the two men, their heads together, Armand's hand on Rosenblatt's arm.

'He's thanking him,' said Myrna. 'For stepping in front of the gun.'

'You think?' said Ruth.

And then Professor Rosenblatt left, walking alone toward the lights of the B and B.

'Did you give him a head start?' asked Ruth when Armand returned to his seat.

'What do you mean?'

'He saved your life. He saved both of yours.' She looked from Gamache to Beauvoir and back again. 'And now maybe you're giving him a chance to get away.'

'Do you think we'd let a murderer go?' asked Lacoste.

'Well, you let the CSIS agents go, or whatever they were,' said Ruth. 'Seems to be the new Sûreté policy.'

'If I helped a murderer escape, I'd have to live with that, wouldn't I?' Armand held the old poet's sharp eyes.

'I wonder if you could,' she said, getting to her feet. 'It's late and I'm tired.'

She looked at Monsieur Béliveau and put out her hand. 'Would you walk me home?'

It was a public declaration of friendship and trust. And perhaps lunacy. He was still a suspect.

'Of course,' said the grocer.

He looked at Isabelle Lacoste, who hesitated, then nodded.

Placing Ruth's hand around his arm, Monsieur Béliveau escorted Ruth from the bistro.

Armand watched them cross the village green until they disappeared behind the three tall pines.

A few minutes later, in the darkness of the village, a darker figure appeared. It was fleeting, and could have been missed, had Gamache not been looking for it.

'*Excusez-moi*,' he said, getting to his feet, nodding to Lacoste and Beauvoir, who'd also seen it. 'Please stay here,' he said to Reine-Marie, then shifted his eyes to Clara, Myrna, Olivier and Gabri.

'Why?' asked Gabri, getting up. And then he sat down heavily when he saw the expressions on their faces.

CHAPTER 43

———

Running, running, stumbling. Running.

Arm up against the wiry branches whipping his face. It was dark and he didn't see the root. He fell, hands splayed, into the moss and mud. His gun dropped and bounced and rolled from sight. Eyes wide, frantic now, he swept his hands through the dead and decaying leaves.

He could hear the footsteps behind him. Boots on the ground. Pounding. He could almost feel the earth heaving as they got closer, closer, while he, on all fours, plowed the leaves aside.

'Come on, come on,' he pleaded.

And then his scraped and filthy hands clasped the grip of the gun and he was up and running. Bent over. Gasping for breath.

He could lose them in the dark. He knew these woods better than most. Better than them.

His hand dropped to the pocket of his torn and muddy jacket. His fingers, knuckles scraped and bleeding, felt inside. And there it was. Safe.

But he was not. His pursuers were gaining on him, closing on him. He didn't seem able to lose them.

He stopped. Turned. Pulled out the gun. Leveled it at the two men and one woman chasing him. And when they were close, too close to miss, he pulled the trigger.

Armand and Isabelle and Jean-Guy had left the bistro, and walked swiftly, quietly, across the village green, keeping to the shadows of the pines, until they arrived at the Gamaches' home.

Jean-Guy stood on tiptoes and looked into the study window, then crouched down again.

'He's not there,' he whispered.

'Has he found it?' Lacoste asked.

'One way to find out,' said Gamache. He motioned to Beauvoir to go around back while he and Lacoste, bent over, ran along his verandah to the front door.

Isabelle Lacoste drew her gun and opened the door slowly, carefully. Then stepped inside. Scanning the room. It was empty. She moved swiftly to the study while Gamache went down the hall to one of the bedrooms.

Lacoste opened the desk drawer in the study, then closed it and left, meeting Gamache in the living room.

'Beauvoir's gun's missing from his bedroom,' he said.

'The firing mechanism for the Supergun is also missing.' She waved toward the study.

The verandah door opened and Jean-Guy called in, 'He's in the woods. I can hear him.'

They ran out the door, a few paces behind Jean-Guy, who was racing between the trees. He forced himself to slow down now and then to listen. To make sure they were still on the right track. It was pitch-dark but a man running through the autumn forest, through the dead and withered leaves, made a lot of noise. And that's what they followed.

It was a headlong pursuit. It was no use trying to hide the fact they were after him. It was a race now, through the dark woods. After the man who'd murdered Laurent Lepage. The man who'd murdered Antoinette Lemaitre.

The man who, with the stolen firing mechanism, would murder millions.

Up ahead the running stopped. But they did not. They kept going, straight into the raised gun.

He had them in his sights. He waited until he couldn't miss, and then pulled the trigger.

But nothing happened. He pulled it again. But by then it was too late, they were on him, Isabelle Lacoste tackling him, and Beauvoir piling on.

Armand Gamache, a few paces behind the younger agents, pulled out his device and turned on the flashlight app. And there, in the beam, was their murderer. The man who'd searched, like a pirate for treasure, like a leech for someone else's blood, for decades. And when he'd finally found Project Babylon, all it brought was death.

In the beam of light was Brian Fitzpatrick.

CHAPTER 44

A dam Cohen had arrived back and now sat in the bistro by the fire, picking the label off his beer. He'd been offered a stiff cognac, and had taken a sip because Gamache had one and it looked so good. But while it looked like maple syrup, it tasted like turpentine.

They had the bistro to themselves. It was late and Olivier and Gabri had cleaned up and left, handing the key to Gamache with the request that they lock up when they were done.

Now it was just the Sûreté officers, helping themselves to the chips and mixed nuts and the drinks.

Jean-Guy tossed a birch log onto the fire and the embers exploded then drifted up the chimney. They stared, mesmerized.

'But why didn't the gun fire?' Adam Cohen asked. 'Brian was pointing it right at you.'

'Seems the firing mechanism was missing from that too,' said Lacoste. 'We knew he didn't have a gun, and we suspected he'd look for one in the Gamaches' home, so Inspector Beauvoir deliberately left his behind, in his nightstand.'

'Why not just take out the bullets?'

'He might've checked,' said Beauvoir. 'But no one thinks to check the firing pin.'

'We learned that trick from Guillaume Couture,' said Isabelle Lacoste. 'He took the firing mechanism out of the Supergun for the same reason. So that no one else could use it.'

'He had a conscience after all,' said Gamache. 'But it took the murder of Gerald Bull for him to come to his senses and see that this was not just a job, not some challenge or a problem to be solved as elegantly as possible. What he'd created would kill hundreds of thousands of people.'

'The plans were missing,' said Jean-Guy. 'He might've thought Bull destroyed them himself, or he might've even suspected that Fleming had stolen them.'

'If he did suspect, he probably didn't want to confront the man,' said Isabelle.

'Why not?' asked Cohen.

'Would you?' she asked.

The young agent shook his head. He still looked pale and shaken from his encounter with John Fleming.

'All Dr Couture could do to disable Big Babylon was take out the firing mechanism,' said Lacoste. 'He must've taken it home and made it look like two separate pieces. He told his niece about it, but Antoinette didn't pay much attention until Laurent found the gun, and then was killed.'

'But what about Brian?' said Cohen. 'How did he know about Dr Couture and Project Babylon and Antoinette?'

'He told us they'd been together for ten years,' said Beauvoir. 'That meant they met in 2005. What else happened that year?'

'Guillaume Couture died,' said Lacoste. 'Antoinette moved into his home, and the obit appeared in the McGill

Alumni News. Brian Fitzpatrick was an alumnus. He admits now he recognized Gerald Bull in the photo.'

'But how did he even know about Gerald Bull?' asked Cohen. 'He's not a physicist.'

'No, but he was an opportunist,' said Lacoste. 'He'd become fascinated by the story of Dr Bull. In the interrogation tonight, Brian admitted he found out about Gerald Bull and Project Babylon while researching the area for a surveying course. Baby Babylon was mentioned in some obscure publications, and on digging deeper he found vague references to another possible missile launcher Bull had planned. Bigger, more powerful.'

'Worth a shit-load of money,' said Beauvoir.

'What started as a lark, a kind of hobby to find out more about Gerald Bull and this secret testing ground, turned into an obsession,' said Lacoste.

'And when he saw the obit,' said Beauvoir, 'and realized Dr Couture must've not only worked with Bull, but been close enough to have been with him in Brussels, that's when Brian decided to come down and make the acquaintance of Couture's only living relative.'

'Antoinette,' said Cohen. 'Ten years ago.'

'He's told us everything now,' said Lacoste. 'With the plans gone and the gun found there's nothing left for him.'

'But how did you know it was Brian Fitzpatrick who'd killed Laurent and Antoinette?' asked Cohen.

'It was, finally, very simple,' said Isabelle Lacoste. 'As I went back over the file, over the statements and evidence, and the sequence of events, a few things became clear. The killer had to have been in the bistro that day when Laurent came in. He had to have heard the story of the gun and believed it. That narrowed the suspects down considerably.

It also had to be someone who didn't know the boy well. Who left the stick behind. And it had to have been someone who knew that Antoinette would be alone that night. Who fit? A few people.'

'But only one person knew that Brian would be away in Montréal all night,' said Beauvoir. 'And that was Brian. He was also in the bistro when Laurent came roaring in.'

'Most of what we knew about Antoinette, and especially the night of her death, we heard from Brian,' said Lacoste. 'And most of it was a lie. Including that she was expecting guests. But what he didn't know was that she'd begged off of Clara's party and was taking her uncle's things to the theater instead. To get them as far away from her as possible.'

'And that was another clue,' said Beauvoir. 'The fact Antoinette did it when Brian was away instead of asking for his help.'

'You think she suspected him?' asked Cohen.

'I'm not sure, but it's possible. What is clear is that Brian started and even fueled the controversy surrounding the Fleming play. He was the one who told us Fleming wrote it. And he continued to support her in producing it, when everyone else backed away.'

'He wanted the controversy and the distraction,' said Beauvoir.

'A killer hides in chaos,' said Cohen, and the homicide investigators smiled.

'I was hampered by a misconception,' Lacoste admitted. 'I was sure the killer had to have been connected to Gerald Bull. Had to have been involved with Project Babylon either as a scientist or as another arms dealer or one of the intelligence agents. But that would put the person well into their fifties. It didn't occur to me the killer could be someone younger, who'd become obsessed with finding the gun. But once I set all that aside and just looked at the facts, all the confusion cleared away.'

'Brian says he didn't mean to kill Antoinette,' said Beauvoir. 'He says she came home and found him searching. In the argument she fell and hit her head.'

'Do you believe him?' asked Cohen.

'It might be true,' said Lacoste. 'But I think he'd have killed her anyway. He'd have had to. For the same reason he killed Laurent. To keep her quiet.'

'He'd been quietly searching the home for years,' said Beauvoir. 'That's how he found the Fleming play. And he took a job surveying the area. That gave him an excuse to look for the gun. He admits he even came within yards of it, but missed it because of the camouflaging.'

'He'd all but given up, when Laurent showed up in the bistro,' said Lacoste.

'Did you suspect him, sir?' Cohen asked Gamache, who'd been sitting quietly, listening.

'Not for a long time. I thought it was strange, though, that everyone else was upset by the Fleming play, except Brian. He said he was just being loyal to Antoinette, but it was more than that. He really didn't care. For him it was just a tool, a kind of stink bomb he tossed into the case. As it turns out, of course, he should have paid more attention to the play. The very thing he was searching for, had killed for, was in the one thing he dismissed. Fleming's play. *She Sat Down and Wept*.'

'I take it John Fleming was not pleased about being taken back to the SHU,' said Beauvoir, but on seeing the look on Agent Cohen's face, he immediately regretted his near-jovial tone.

'It was awful.' Even Cohen's lips were white and Jean-Guy wondered if the young man might wake up with white hair the next morning. 'I've never believed in the death penalty, but as long as John Fleming's alive I'm going to be afraid.'

'Did he threaten you?' asked Gamache.

'No, but ...'

Young Agent Cohen turned even paler.

'... I made a mistake, sir.'

'It's all right,' said Gamache.

'You don't understand,' said Adam.

'But I do, and it's done now. Please don't worry.'

They looked at each other and the younger man nodded.

'So Brian admits it all?' said Cohen, leaving the subject of Fleming.

'Hard to deny it, when we found him with the firing mechanism he stole from my desk,' said Gamache.

'That was dangerous, wasn't it?' said Cohen. 'Suppose he'd gotten away?'

'It wasn't the real one,' said Lacoste. 'That's safe under lock and key. We needed to flush him out. We didn't have enough evidence against him. He had to incriminate himself.'

'So you let him think you'd stolen the firing mechanism,' said Cohen to Gamache, who nodded.

Young Agent Cohen took a swig of his beer, then reached for the chips, putting some in his mouth before he realized they were not potato but apple chips.

He looked at Chief Inspector Lacoste, and Inspector Beauvoir. His bosses. And he looked at Monsieur Gamache. And he looked at the strong beamed ceiling and thick plank floors and solid fieldstone hearths of the bistro. He looked out the window, but saw only their own reflection.

And he finally felt safe.

CHAPTER 45

$\sim$

Isabelle Lacoste and Adam Cohen walked up the steps to the B and B. The porch light had been left on by Gabri and the door was, of course, unlocked.

'You said you made a mistake with Fleming,' Isabelle asked. 'What was it?'

Adam Cohen gnawed his lip and watched Gamache and Inspector Beauvoir walking, heads down and together, toward the light at the Gamache home. But then the two men paused, veered, and took a turn around the village green.

'I said his name,' said Cohen.

It took Isabelle Lacoste a moment to realize what Cohen meant, and then she too looked at the two men, strolling around the edges of the village green.

Adam Cohen, in his excitement, had called out over the phone. He'd said his name. Monsieur Gamache. And John Fleming, in the backseat, would have heard.

'I wanted to ask you about Professor Rosenblatt,' said Jean-Guy. 'What did you say to him tonight, out on the *terrasse*? Did you thank him?'

'*Non*. I warned him.'

'About what? He stepped in front of the gun. He saved your life and probably mine, and allowed the plans to burn. Kept them out of the hands of those CSIS agents or whatever they are.'

'I wonder if that's true.'

'What do you mean?'

'I mean that I don't think Professor Rosenblatt does much that is unconsidered. I think he knew the moment to get those plans had passed. And when he stepped in front of the gun, he knew that while Delorme might shoot us, he wouldn't shoot him.'

Gamache remembered that moment with complete clarity.

When Michael Rosenblatt had stepped in front of him, with the gun pointed at his chest, Gamache had had the overwhelming impression that Rosenblatt was in no danger.

In that split second, as the plans burned, Delorme should have shot. But didn't. To kill Gamache and Beauvoir, for plans that were almost certainly gone, would trigger an international manhunt. And so Professor Rosenblatt had done the only thing possible. He'd stepped in front of the gun, not to save Gamache or Beauvoir, but to salvage whatever he could of the situation.

'You think Rosenblatt's one of them? A CSIS agent, or something?'

'Or something,' said Gamache.

He did not believe Michael Rosenblatt was himself a killer, though he thought the man might be capable of it. But he did think Rosenblatt knew Mary Fraser and Sean Delorme much better than he pretended.

After all, who called them to Three Pines? Who told them about finding Project Babylon?

Gamache had suggested as much to the retired scientist when they'd parted on the *terrasse*. And warned him he'd be watching.

'You still think I'm mixed up in this?' Rosenblatt had asked.

'I think you know far more than you're telling.'

Rosenblatt had studied him closely. 'We're on the same side, Armand. You must believe me.'

'Do you swear it?' Gamache had asked. 'On your grand-son's life?'

Professor Rosenblatt had smiled and Gamache heard a small grunt of acknowledgment. 'I do.'

But then all amusement disappeared. 'You need to know,' said Rosenblatt, 'the clock hasn't stopped. It has simply been reset.'

Armand Gamache had watched him walk away, believing he was looking at the taproot. From which Mary Fraser and Sean Delorme and John Fleming had sprung.

Jean-Guy and Armand strolled in silence around the village green, through the cold, crisp fresh autumn evening.

'Professor Rosenblatt might not have been in any danger when he stepped in front of the gun, but you were, *patron*.' Beauvoir stopped and turned to face his father-in-law. 'Thank you.'

'Not everyone would have burned those plans, *mon vieux*. It was one of the most magnificent things I've ever seen. And I'm a man who's seen the Manneken Pis.'

A laugh escaped Beauvoir, and then a smaller, deeper sound before he muffled it.

'You're a brave man in a brave country, Jean-Guy. A man so remarkable needs to pass that courage on to his children.'

They walked in silence, by choice for Gamache, by necessity for Jean-Guy, who couldn't yet speak.

'*Merci*,' he finally said. Then fell silent again.

As they passed the B and B, Armand saw a shadow in a window. An elderly man, preparing for bed. Where he would dream, perhaps, of children and grandchildren and friends. A warm hearth, a good book, quiet conversation. A life that might have been.

The next morning a dark police van drove up to the Canadian side of the US border crossing at Richford.

A man and a woman in the uniform of the Judge Advocate General's office in the States stood just on the other side of the barrier, military police at their side.

Waiting.

The van stopped twenty meters short, its engine running. The army officers looked at each other and shifted from foot to foot. Antsy.

The van door slid open and a large, burly man with wild gray hair stepped out. Then he turned and reached out his hand to help an elderly woman from the vehicle. And, after her, a tall elderly man.

They walked on either side of Al Lepage. Their pace measured, their faces solemn. Returning the man. Finishing the deed.

The bar lifted, but just before he crossed, Ruth stopped him.

'I'm sorry,' she said. 'I sent John Fleming to you.'

'I know.'

'No, you don't know. He terrified me and I wanted to get rid of him. I gave him you to save myself.'

Al Lepage considered Ruth Zardo.

'I could have sent him away too. That's the difference between us. You saw evil and wanted nothing to do with it. But I invited him in.'

Al looked at the officers waiting for him. Then turned to the man and woman who had saved him once. He shook Monsieur Béliveau's hand, then looked at Ruth.

'May I?' he asked, and when she nodded, he kissed her on one cheek. 'I have no right to ask this, but please look after Evelyn. She knew none of this.'

Then he stepped across the border and became Frederick Lawson once again.

Before taking Al Lepage across the border that morning, Ruth had something she needed to do.

She picked up Rosa and walked over to Clara's cottage. Letting herself in, she found Clara where she knew she'd be. Ruth sat on the sprung and lumpy sofa that smelled of banana peels and apple cores and watched Clara at the easel, staring at Peter's portrait.

'Who hurt you once, so far beyond repair?' said Ruth.

'The line from your poem,' said Clara, turning on the stool to look at Ruth.

'I was asking you, Clara. Who hurt you once?' Ruth gestured to the easel. 'What're you waiting for?'

'Waiting?' asked Clara. 'Nothing.'

'Then why're you stuck? Like the characters in that goddamned play. Are you waiting for someone, something to save you? Waiting for Peter to tell you it's okay to get on without him? You're looking for milk in the wrong place.'

'I just want to paint,' said Clara. 'I don't want to be saved, I don't want to be forgiven. I don't even want milk. I just want to paint.'

Ruth struggled out of the sofa. 'I did.'

'You did what?' asked Clara.

'The answer to that question. All those years when I couldn't write, I blamed John Fleming. But I was wrong.'

Clara watched Ruth and Rosa waddle away. She had no idea what the crazy old woman was talking about. But sitting in front of the canvas, it slowly sank in.

Who could do such damage? Who knew where the weaknesses, the fault lines lay? Who could cause all that internal bleeding?

Clara turned back to the portrait of Peter.

'I'm sorry,' she said, looking into his faded face. 'Forgive me.'

She placed it carefully against a wall, and put up a fresh canvas.

She knew now why she was blocked. She was trying to do the wrong painting. Trying to make amends by turning painting into penance.

Clara picked up her brush and contemplated the empty canvas. She would do a portrait of the person who had hurt her once, beyond repair.

With one bold stroke after another she painted. Capturing the rage, the sorrow, the doubt, the fear, the guilt, the joy, the love, and finally, the forgiveness.

It would be her most intimate, most difficult painting yet.

It would be a self-portrait.

Evelyn Lepage sat in her kitchen contemplating the gas oven. Trying to get up the strength to turn it on. But all the bones of her body had finally dissolved. And she couldn't move. Not to save her life, and not to take it.

Out the window she saw a car pull up. Two elderly people got out.

'We've come to take you home, Evie,' came the elderly woman's thin voice from the other side of the door. It was almost unrecognizable for its gentleness. 'If you don't mind living with a broken-down old poet and her duck.'

Jean-Guy held the phone to his ear and looked out the window of the Gamaches' study, to the quiet village. Then he turned from the window to the papers, neatly stacked, on his father-in-law's desk.

All the offers. The answer to 'What next?' was in there.

And then the phone was answered.

'*Oui, allô?*' came Annie's cheerful voice.

'Armand,' said Reine-Marie, as they finished the breakfast dishes. 'Are you ever going to tell me what John Fleming did?'

Armand put the dish down and dried his hands on the towel.

'What John Fleming did is in the past. It's over, gone.'

She studied him closely. 'Is it?'

'*Oui.* But if, after this phone call, you still want to know about Fleming, I'll tell you.'

Reine-Marie turned around and saw Jean-Guy in the doorway holding out the phone. She took it, perplexed. And listened.

As the two men watched, the lines of her face re-formed, and her eyes filled with wonder. And all thought of John Fleming, of the Supergun, of the Whore of Babylon vanished, overwhelmed by a far greater force.

Reine-Marie looked at Jean-Guy, who was overcome with emotion. Then she turned to Armand, who was smiling, his eyes glistening. Then Reine-Marie sat down at the old pine table, and wept.

AUTHOR'S NOTE

Gerald Bull was a real man, a scientist, Canadian, an arms designer. I first came across his remarkable story in the mid-1990s when I worked as the host of a current affairs radio program for the CBC. My producer at the time, Allan Johnson, mentioned this man who'd built a massive gun called Baby Babylon right on the border with the United States, in Québec's Eastern Townships. It was, he said, the largest effin (Allan is a great journalist with a vast vocabulary) missile launcher in the world. And it was pointed into the United States.

It was believed that Gerald Bull was building this missile launcher, called Project Babylon, for Saddam Hussein, as the Iraqi dictator edged toward a regional war.

According to reports, Baby Babylon was built but did not work. It was a failure. But Gerald Bull was not put off, and there were rumors in the arms community that Project Babylon was actually two missile launchers, not one. There was a brother to Baby Babylon, called Big Babylon. This was a missile launcher so massive it would make the first one look puny. And all the problems of Baby Babylon had been solved.

Big Babylon would work. It would fire a missile into low Earth orbit. The West was not happy. A weapon of that sort could not fall into the hands of an unstable dictator.

In early 1990, Gerald Bull was murdered in Brussels. Five bullets to the head – though, true to his life, even the manner of his death is mysterious. His killers were never found, though they were rumored to be Mossad, the Israeli enforcers.

Dr Bull's life, his work, his death, was a sort of open secret at the time, though not well known outside a certain circle. With time, more and more information has come out.

Where we live, in Québec's Eastern Townships, many people remember the man, and many worked on the huge missile launcher. Indeed, my assistant Lise's husband, Del, drove us to the site of Baby Babylon, still fenced and chained.

Such was the power of the man that people hereabouts are not anxious to talk about him or his gun even now.

Discover the world of
LOUISE PENNY

CONNECT WITH LOUISE:

www.louisepenny.com

www.facebook.com/louisepennyauthor

The next case for
Chief Inspector Gamache

Former Chief Inspector Gamache has been hunting killers
his entire career and as the new commander of the Sûreté
Academy, he is given the chance to combat the corruption
and brutality that has been rife throughout the force.
But when a former colleague and professor of the Sûreté
Academy is found murdered, with a mysterious map of
Three Pines in his possession, Gamache has an even
tougher task ahead of him.

When suspicion turns to Gamache himself, and his possible
involvement in the crime, the frantic search for answers
takes the investigation to the village of Three Pines, where a
series of shattering secrets are poised to be revealed ...